Other Books & Stories by Lynn Bohart

NOVELS

Mass Murder

Murder In The Past Tense

Grave Doubts

Inn Keeping With Murder

A Candidate For Murder

SHORT STORY BOOKS

Your Worst Nightmare

Something Wicked

A HISTORY OF MURDER
An Old Maids of Mercer Island Mystery

By
Lynn Bohart

Cover Art: Mia Yoshihara-Bradshaw

Copyright © 2016 by Lynn Bohart

All rights reserved. This book or any portion thereof may not be reproduced in any manner whatsoever without the express written permission of the publisher, with the exception of brief quotations for the use of reviews or promotional articles approved by the author.

Published by Little Dog Press

ACKNOWLEDGEMENTS

I rely on a number of people to help me bring these books to you. They are friends and colleagues I trust to give me honest feedback. The writing group I belong to reads the books two chapters at a time over a period of 8 – 10 months, helping me to clarify the story and the characters, while also eliminating things that just don't work. My thanks once more to Tim McDaniel, Michael Manzer, Gary Larson, Irma Fritz, Jenae Cartwright and Brian Beckley. I also rely on a group of "beta" readers who then read the book from cover-to-cover. These include Karen Gilb, Bill Dolan, Valerie O'Halloran and my daughter, Jaynee Bohart. They not only catch mistakes, but help with flow, clarification and inconsistencies. I would be lost without my friend and colleague, Liz Stewart, who not only serves as my editor, but this time helped me with some of the research. She is the director of the Renton History Museum and has a Ph.D. in American History. My deepest thanks go to Renton Fire Chief Mark Peterson, who gave me advice on the barn fire (and some leverage), Bob McBeth for some information on the judicial system, and my daughter for help with some clarification on forms of mental illness.

Thanks to my friend, Mia Bradshaw, my cover designer. Mia is a wonderful craftsperson and shows/sells her work in Seattle. Please check out her website at www.miayoshihara.com.

Disclaimer: This book is a work of fiction and while many of the businesses, locations, and organizations referenced in the book are real, they are used in a way that is purely fictional. I also took some liberty with locations on both Mercer and Camano Islands to fit the storyline.

Dedicated to the many people who suffer from various forms of mental illness. May they find the support and peace they deserve.

CHAPTER ONE

I've begun to think that murder follows me around. No, really.

When I announced to my friends in December that I wanted our book club to help solve the murder of our close friend, Martha Denton, I had no idea I was opening a portal of some kind. But after closing Martha's case and shutting down a human trafficking ring, we were immediately drawn into the murder investigation of Trudy Bascom. She had been the assistant campaign manager to my nemesis and a woman I hated, Dana Finkle. By the time that case wrapped up, we'd not only helped to solve Trudy's murder, but saved Dana from being buried alive in a damp grave.

Now spring had rolled around, and I was ready for some warm weather and a rest.

All I got was the warm weather.

Spring in the Northwest is typically cursed with days, if not weeks, of rainy and dreary weather. The constant overcast skies can make people cranky, even depressed. When the sun finally does emerge, people do too, like butterflies from their cocoons.

By the first week in June, Seattle had enjoyed an unusual string of 70 degree days with cloudless skies. The weather was so inspiring, I found myself humming the opening song from *The Sound of Music* wherever I went, annoying my friends and co-workers because I can't really carry a tune.

I own the St. Claire Inn on Mercer Island in Seattle's Lake Washington area and had decided to go to Blake's Garden Center one day to replace several rose bushes left on life support after a harsh winter. Our gardens are a point of pride, so I was about to put my two miniature long-haired dachshunds, Minnie and Mickey, back in my apartment when I was interrupted.

"Mrs. Applegate," a male voice said. "I think you need to see something."

It was Mr. Piper, the owner of a construction company we'd hired to do some repairs in the attic above the bakery. The below freezing temperatures and massive amounts of rain between December and February had done some damage. April, my business partner, had noticed a couple of leaks above her commercial ovens.

"What is it, Mr. Piper? I was on my way out."

"Like I said, you need to see something. In the attic."

He was a handsome man in his fifties, with a shock of white hair and a broad smile. Right now his weathered face was pinched with concern, making my spirits drop. Imaginary dollar signs began to swirl around his head.

"Alright, let's go. I'll follow you."

We left through the back door to the kitchen and crossed the drive to the old barn, left over from the early nineteenth century when a grand hotel had stood on the property. The 5,000 square foot building sat on a slip of land that extended into Lake Washington, giving it a tranquil and nostalgic feeling. The back half of the building was surrounded by trees, stumps, and a few large boulders on slopes that dropped off into the water.

The bakery took up the front third of the building, while the back end was used to store and refinish antiques we sold inside the inn. We'd created a welcoming front entrance to the bakery.

Leading up to the door was a gravel path flanked by two flower gardens. On either side of a bank of windows were sets of refinished barn doors that were original to the building, but no longer functional. Distressed brick had been added to the bottom third of the front façade, and two window boxes hung just below the display windows filled with red geraniums. Block letters spelled out, "St. Claire Sweet Spot."

Mr. Piper led me into the furniture warehouse through the side door and turned left to climb the old wooden staircase. The dogs ran up ahead of me, their little feet clicking on the stairs, their tails flying, as I inhaled the sweet smell of wood and turpentine in their wake. I followed them to the landing that extended the width of the building and met up with the hayloft on the far side.

We stepped through the door into a large room that spanned the front third of the building, directly over the bakery. Two dormer windows looked out onto the back of the inn, the large deck and the surrounding grounds. The attic floor was covered in a threadbare carpet, and the walls were finished in faded redwood paneling.

We actually had two attics on the property: the one in the barn and a second one in the main building. While the barn attic had some old furniture and boxes of junk in it, it was used mostly to store holiday decorations and party supplies. The attic over at the inn was filled with furniture and boxes from past residents that we'd just never gone through.

But there was an important difference between the two attics; we believed the attic above the bakery was haunted. That's because most people who had ever gone up there got a headache, a bad feeling, or just the sudden urge to leave.

That's not to say we were averse to ghosts; we were actually pretty proud of our resident spirits. The inn itself was haunted by Elizabeth St. Claire, wife of the original owner, and at least one of her children, along with their dog, Max. While the ghosts in the main house were friendly and even playful, something more sinister seemed to live in the barn.

As I entered the room above the bakery, I noticed that Mr. Piper was moving toward the far end, where the dogs were bouncing around the feet of his assistant, Barry, asking for attention. Mr. Piper moved up next to the wall that had needed repair.

"Over here," he said, gesturing to me.

They had cleared a path through the stacks of boxes, so I made my way to where he was standing. Again, I noticed his grim expression.

"What is it? Is there more damage than you first anticipated?"

"No, Ma'am. It's this."

He stepped aside, revealing the exposed wall studs and a door that had been hidden behind a section of drywall. It was secured with a weathered, heavy padlock.

"For heaven's sakes," I said in surprise. "I wonder what's inside."

"I didn't want to open it until I got instructions from you," Mr. Piper said. "We'll have to remove these boards in order to gain access." He gestured to the two-by-fours that had been installed in front of the door to hold the drywall in place. "I didn't know if you'd want me to do that."

I paused for a moment, wondering if there was any reason I shouldn't give permission to remove the framework. But I couldn't think of one, and my curiosity was piqued.

"Go ahead. Remove it. I'd like to know where that door leads. And then, I'd like to know why someone would hide a door up here."

CHAPTER TWO

With my trip to the garden center postponed, I took the dogs back to my apartment before returning to the bakery. There, I waited with April until Mr. Piper gained access to the door.

Besides being my business partner, April had been my best friend since we both attended the University of Washington. When my ex-husband, Graham, asked for a divorce and gave me the inn as a consolation prize, April was the first one I called. Not to whimper about my failed marriage, but to ask her to go into business with me.

Since I'd graduated with a degree in business, I always thought that one day I'd own a bookstore or gift shop. But April had graduated with a degree in culinary arts, so we combined our talents and launched the bed and breakfast. I still owned the property outright, but she became our chief cook and baker, while I handled the antique sales and administration, and together we ran the inn.

She was busy making her signature orange scones for the next morning's breakfast when I popped in. The tantalizing aroma of citrus and sugar immediately made my mouth water. I perched on a stool at the end of her work counter and told her what Mr. Piper had found upstairs.

Her dark eyes grew round at the news. "A hidden door? That's kind of exciting."

April had skin the color of walnuts and apple cheek bones that would make Judi Dench jealous. For years, she'd worn her hair in braided corn rows, but since her husband had died in December, she'd changed to a more relaxed and soft style, which I thought suited her.

I considered April's comment. "It could just be an old empty closet." I feigned enough ennui to raise her eyebrows.

April was no fool. She knew how enthusiastic I could get whenever I found something unusual on one of my antique hunts. I often came home with an item so alien that I was forced to go to the internet to look it up. At other times, I came home with some odd thing that I just couldn't refuse.

On one such occasion I came home with Ahab, our talking parrot. He'd been part of an estate sale where I'd suddenly found myself bidding against a young punk-rocker who thought it would be funny to teach him a lot of blood-sucking lyrics from the artist, Marilyn Manson. I may be in my sixties, but I knew who Marilyn Manson was and couldn't doom the poor bird to such a dismal future.

But April wasn't buying my indifference about the hidden room.

"Oh give it a rest, Julia. You're dying to know what's behind that door. Maybe we'll find some old treasures," she said with optimism, cutting the scone dough into quarters. "And we can each retire in style."

"Oh, hell, I don't want to retire," I responded. "Do you? What the heck would we do?"

She laughed lightly, and her black eyes danced. "Probably just open another business."

"You could promote your new cookbook," I said with encouragement, thinking about the project she'd started during the investigation into Martha's murder. José, our maintenance man, was a graphic arts student and had designed the cover. April was just about done adding recipes, and our friend Rudy, a book club member and former journalist, had offered to edit it. We hoped to publish it in time for the holidays.

She smiled humbly. "Selling it here at the inn will be just fine."

"Well, the door upstairs had a padlock on it, as if someone had hidden something. With my luck, we'll find a dead body inside."

April chuckled again. "Don't be so pessimistic. Besides, you seem to thrive on solving mysteries. That is, when you're not almost getting yourself killed."

"Hey, I'm enjoying our book club getting back to reading," I said with a shrug. "Although Blair picked some historical romance. I'm about half way through. It's kind of boring. I mean, where's the intrigue? The danger? The twists and turns?"

"I take it you haven't seen David much the last few days."

My heart skipped a beat at the sudden change in subject. David was my new boyfriend and a detective with the Mercer Island Police. We'd met when Martha was killed the year before. He'd been one of the investigators.

I reached out and scooped a blob of dough from the bowl. "He and Sean are all tied up in that serial killer case. You know the one where they've found the remains of three different girls throughout the area? Now a fourth one has washed up here on the island."

She shook her head in dismay. "I heard about that. I hope they find the bastard."

"I guess Sean is now part of this big regional investigation task force, leaving David in charge here on the island. So he doesn't have time for much else."

Detective Sean Abrams was the lead detective in the Mercer Island Police Department and David's boss. Sean was also currently dating my daughter, Angela. It was weird by anyone's standards to be so closely tied to the man your daughter was dating.

"Is David still planning on retiring soon?" April asked.

"End of the year. He'll turn sixty-five in August. Although I kind of like him having a day job."

April glanced over her glasses at me. "You don't think you'll want him around all the time?"

"No, it's not that. But he's a detective. I like that. I like the idea of him out protecting the public."

April began placing the triangular shaped lumps of dough onto a cookie sheet. "He could always become a private investigator. Maybe you could join him. The Franks and Applegate Detective Agency," she said, using a flour-dusted hand to make a flourishing gesture in the air.

"Very funny," I replied, licking dough off my finger.

Mr. Piper appeared at the back doorway to the bakery. "We're ready for you, Mrs. Applegate."

I turned to April. "Care to join me?"

"Sure. Let's go find what we find," she said, placing a clean towel over the dough.

We followed Mr. Piper into the warehouse. As he angled for the stairs, I called out, "Hold on." I ran over to a small office at the back of the warehouse and grabbed a flashlight out of a drawer. I returned and asked April, "Any predictions?"

She smiled and shook her head, moving out in front of me. "No. You rely too much on my ability to foretell the future."

April had a sixth sense, but it wasn't something she liked to talk about. We followed Mr. Piper up the stairs in silence.

As we approached the landing, I said, "Are you going to be able to handle being up here?"

"I won't like it," she replied. "There's a bad feeling up here that I choose to avoid. But for this, I'll brave it. Even my curiosity sometimes gets the better of me."

A minute later, we stood in front of the hidden door. I glanced at April. Her dark features were pinched, as if a headache encroached.

"You okay?"

"Yeah, let's just get this over with."

I turned and nodded to Mr. Piper, who reached out and used bolt cutters to remove the padlock. It fell to the floor with a thud, swirling up a cloud of dust. Mr. Piper turned the old glass door knob. The door stuck in place for a moment, making him lean into it. It finally gave way, ready to release its secrets.

Stale air wafted over us as we peered into a darkened interior. The light in the attic barely shone beyond the doorframe. Since there was no light switch, I flicked on the flashlight.

At first, all I saw was a dusty floor, covered by a tattered, braided throw rug. As I moved the light around, it flashed across an old rocking chair, a small, wooden chest pushed up against the wall, some books strewn across the floor, a dirty cot in one corner, and finally, a crib.

"Oh, dear," I whispered upon seeing the crib.

I stepped across the threshold, feeling short of breath from the overpowering stench of rat droppings and urine. The space wasn't much larger than a walk-in closet, and the air was dank and oppressive. One wall was blackened with candle smoke, and cobwebs hung from the angled ceiling.

The way the room was laid out made my heart bleed. The crib, which sat next to the rocking chair, was made out of oak and had the distressed stencil of a teddy bear at each end. I glanced inside. Rats had made nests out of the mattress, so it was chewed up and stained with urine. The smell made me gag.

Most of a large, braided rug, which covered the central part of the floor, had been shredded, but one corner of it had been charred by fire. A stack of dusty cloth diapers still sat in a box, also chewed up and stained. And several baby toys, including a baby's bottle and binky were strewn across the floor. At one time the cot had been made up for someone to sleep there. But now the blanket, sheets, and pillow were in the same state as everything else.

The rocking chair was draped with a tattered, crocheted shawl. A book of children's poems lay on the seat. A heavy brass candlestick holding a thick, half burned candle sat on an up-turned milk box next to the rocker. Next to the candlestick was a book, opened and turned upside down. It looked as if someone had been reading it and then was interrupted.

I moved over and glanced down. The book was an old Nancy Drew mystery, *The Secret of the Old Clock*. I fingered the cover, remembering reading this very book when I was a little girl and thinking of the full collection of Nancy Drew books I had in my apartment.

"What is this?" Mr. Piper asked from over my shoulder. "Do you think someone just stored this stuff in here?"

"No," I replied. "Look over in the corner."

I flashed the light to where there was a stack of old, dirty dishes. "I think someone may have lived up here."

"She died here," April murmured from where she stood behind Mr. Piper.

I spun around to find my friend with her hands clasped to her temples. "April, are you okay?"

Mr. Piper stepped aside.

"She died here," April said again, her dark features laced with pain.

April's legs gave out, and she nearly crashed to the floor. Thankfully, Mr. Piper grabbed her elbow just in time.

"Let me get her downstairs," he said. "Barry, give me a hand."

Barry stepped over and took April's other arm. The two of them helped April out of the room, while I remained behind. I took a minimal breath to help reduce the stench and studied things more closely.

The atmosphere inside the room was more than oppressive. It felt as if someone had placed an anvil on my chest. And it was difficult to breathe through the pervasive, rank smell. I felt I could almost taste rat droppings.

There were no windows to let in light or air, and no light bulb or electricity. As I moved around, my foot rolled over something, throwing me up against the crib. I regained my balance and glanced down to where another half-burned candle lay on the floor. I waved the flashlight beam back and forth across the room, but there was no second candle holder.

That's when I heard the faint sound of whispering.

I whipped around, forcing the light to bounce erratically across the walls.

Nothing. No one.

I was alone, so I waited and listened.

The whispering continued. There seemed to be two voices. One made a clucking sound. The other voice was saying something, but I couldn't make out the words.

Then it stopped.

Footsteps brought me back to attention with a jolt. Mr. Piper was back.

"Is she okay?" I asked.

"Yes, Ma'am," he said from the doorway. "She said to tell you she was going to go lie down. Have you found anything else?"

"No," I said, my voice shaking a bit.

"What do you want us to do with all the stuff in here?" he asked, gesturing to the crib and rocker.

"Do you have to move it right away?"

He shrugged. "The floor in this area has been badly compromised," he said, gesturing to where the wood had buckled and splintered beneath our feet. "There's been quite a bit of water damage. Between that and the rodents, we should replace it. Besides, it looks like the access to get under the roofline is up there." He pointed to the ceiling where there was a recessed door. "We'll have to check under the roof for damage. However, I just got an emergency call from the other side of the island. I'll finish up here today, but I'll have to take care of that job tomorrow and probably the next day."

"Okay," I said. "Let's leave everything where it is for now."

He nodded. "Sounds good."

I stopped him as he began to turn away. "Mr. Piper, were you and Barry talking downstairs just a few minutes ago? Right below here? I heard voices."

He shook his head. "No. We got your partner outside, but by then she was feeling a little better and insisted that she could make it to the guest house on her own. So Barry went out to the truck to get our big shop vac to clean out all this rat mess. And I came back up here. I did take the phone call when I was on the landing though. Maybe that's what you heard."

"Maybe," I said skeptically. "Thanks. I'll go check on April."

I left the attic, ignoring the small chill that rippled down my back.

You'd think that after all the ghostly encounters I'd had over the years I'd be immune to them. But, in fact, each and every time was much like the first. My heart raced. I got chills. And my breathing would speed up. These were natural responses. After all, we're talking about contact with the other side.

So as I descended the stairs, I felt the adrenalin still pulsing through my veins. What were those whispers? They seemed different than anything I'd encountered before, which made me think they weren't from our resident ghosts, Elizabeth, or her daughter, Chloe.

So who was it? And why was there such a bad feeling up in that attic?

CHAPTER THREE

I emerged into the fresh air and took a deep breath, hoping to wash away the rat smell. I walked over to the guest house, which sat on the far side of the property, next to the garage. I climbed the porch steps and tapped on the door. There was a weak, "Come in," and I stepped inside. April was reclined on the sofa in the front room, an ice pack on her forehead.

"Wow, that looks bad," I said, crossing to the sofa. "Can I get you anything?"

"No," she said, looking at me through half-open eyes. "It's starting to fade."

"A headache?"

"Yeah. A bad one. It felt like electrical jolts shooting through my brain."

"Ouch! I'm sorry." I sat down on the arm of the sofa and reached out to grab a throw, putting it over her legs. "Well, you stay here. I'll finish the scones."

She smiled. "Thanks. They're ready for the oven. Three hundred fifty degrees for 15 minutes."

"Okay. But what happened? You said someone died up there. Who died?"

She shook her head. "I don't know. I only heard those words."

"Do you know if it was a man or a woman talking?"

"It was just a whisper in my head. And then the pain got so bad I couldn't see."

I sat back, thinking. "Something's weird up there. When Mr. Piper was gone, I heard whispering, too. It sounded like two different voices, but not as if they were talking to each other. It was more like one voice was, I don't know, just babbling. And the other voice was saying something, but I couldn't make out what it was."

April pulled the ice pack off of her forehead. "I heard that, too."

"I wonder if the babbling could have been a baby," I said, shifting my gaze to the window above the kitchen sink. "I mean it looked as if someone kept a baby up there. But why would they? There's no window in that room and no electricity or plumbing. It had to be cold in the winter and hot during the summer. Why would anyone keep a baby up there?"

April sat up, wincing at the pain in her head. She swung her legs around so she could lean against the back of the sofa. "You would if you wanted to hide for some reason."

"Hide? You mean like from the law?"

She shrugged and rubbed one temple. "I don't know. There are probably lots of reasons someone might need to hide. Maybe they were in the country illegally. Maybe it was a woman running away from an abusive marriage."

"Maybe it was a criminal," I added.

"Right. Maybe they were hiding from the law."

"Damn! Another mystery."

"But one we're not likely to solve," she said. "Too much time has gone by."

"Hmmm," I murmured.

She glanced at me. "What are you thinking?"

"Nothing. It's all just so curious." I stood up. "Like I said, I'll finish the scones. Don't forget we have that art class tonight."

"I think I'll pass. You and the rest of the *old maids* will have to go on without me."

April was referring to a concept our book club had adopted after our friend, Ellen Fairchild, had driven her Lexus off a cliff the year before. Moments before she died in the hospital, she warned the rest of us not to become old maids. What she'd meant was not to give up on life, to keep trying new things.

To honor her, we'd embarked on a series of adventures that each of us had wanted to do since childhood. Blair took us karaoke singing. Rudy enrolled us in horseback riding lessons, and we went skydiving with Doe. Right around the time it was my turn to suggest something, Martha Denton, my neighbor and member of the book club, was killed. As an avid mystery reader, I decided to solve her murder.

But Martha died before ever having the chance to suggest her own adventure. She'd often talked about taking an art class, so we'd signed up for an art class in her memory. It started that night.

"I hope this is what she would have wanted," I said, thinking about Martha. "She never got to tell us what she really would have chosen."

April smiled indulgently. "I'm sure she'd love what you're doing."

"Sure you don't want to go?"

"No. I'm going to rest and then see if I feel well enough to clean the oven over there."

"Sheesh," I said. "Take it easy. The oven will always be there. By the way, Mr. Piper got called to another job for the next few days, so I told him to leave everything where it was in the attic. But he said they'll have to replace the entire floor in that little room."

"Oh, great. More money," April lamented. She slapped the ice pack back to her head. "That's enough to give me another headache."

I left April and went back to the bakery. It took me almost an hour to finish four batches of scones for the next day's breakfast. I was coming through the rear kitchen door of the inn with a bakery box of them when I heard the front door jingle. I slid the bakery box onto the counter and almost bumped into my friend Blair, a member of the book club, as she came through the swinging door off the breakfast room.

"Whoa! Sorry," I said after we almost collided. "What time is it?"

"Not quite noon," she replied. "I came by to see if you wanted to have lunch. Mr. Billings is out of town and that new Mexican restaurant just opened downtown."

Mr. Billings was Blair's husband, even though their last name was Wentworth. That's another story for another time.

I'm only 5' 2", so Blair towered over me at 5' 8". She normally wore three-inch heels, which made it worse, but was dressed more casually today, wearing tight jeans, a muslin top, and sandals.

"I can't leave right now," I said. "April isn't feeling well. But I have some leftover chicken chili and cornbread in my apartment. Would that do?"

"I love chicken chili," she said with a smile. "Do you have cheese and sour cream?"

"Of course. Besides, I have something to tell you. Let's go."

Blair reminded me of what Marilyn Monroe might have looked like if she'd lived to be sixty-three. Her figure still made most men salivate, and she purposely accentuated it with tight pants and revealing tops. Add to that the blond hair and blue eyes, and voilà – Marilyn Monroe.

We passed my daytime manager, Crystal, who was busy folding clean towels at the reception desk.

"We'll be in my apartment," I told her. "April is taking a break. She's in the guest house, so call me first if you need anything." Crystal nodded and continued with her work.

I let us into the apartment where we were greeted with an immediate barrage of high-pitched barking.

"Hello, wieners," Blair said, leaning down to pet the dogs dancing around her feet.

Fortunately, all my friends loved the dogs, or at least tolerated them. That was a good thing, since I adored them. They looked like a coordinated set: Mickey was black with red accents, while Minnie was just a burnished, copper red. But right now they were climbing up Blair's leg.

"Okay you two, get down," I admonished them, leaning over to whisk them away from her ankles.

"No problem." She followed me to the kitchen and sat on a barstool on the opposite side of the counter, while I heated up lunch. "Hey, I saw where they found a body washed up on shore down by the bridge. It made me wonder how Angela's relationship is going with Detective Abrams."

I turned to her with a scowl. "A dead body made you think of my daughter's romantic relationship?"

She shrugged. "Actually, it just made me think of that hunk of a boyfriend of hers."

My daughter was an assistant prosecuting attorney for King County. We'd all met Detective Abrams during our first murder investigation, only to find out that Angela already knew him. She'd worked a case with him when he worked for the Seattle PD. They'd shared one intimate date and then broken it off. During the course of Martha's murder investigation however, they'd rekindled their relationship.

I went to the refrigerator and pulled out the container of chili. "You know his name is Sean, don't you?"

"Yes, but his official title makes him so much sexier," she said with a smile. "Along with those broad shoulders and that Army Ranger tattoo."

Blair's relationship with most men – okay, all men – was like a hummingbird to nectar. She responded to the opposite sex the same way I responded to chocolate.

"I find him a bit intimidating," I said. "In fact, I've seen him smile just a few times. I'm not sure what the two of them talk about."

Blair grinned. "My bet is they don't…talk that much, I mean."

"That's my daughter you're making jokes about, you know."

"She's an adult," Blair said with a shrug.

"Well, I don't think Angela knows what she wants yet. So I wouldn't be surprised if this doesn't last."

I spooned some chili into a bowl, placed it into the microwave and turned it on. Then I went back for the cheese and sour cream.

"Are you saying that because you *hope* it won't last, or because you suspect Angela will move on?"

I stopped and thought for a moment. "Both, I suppose." I went back to cooking. "I'm not sure Sean is the long-term relationship kind of guy. He seems so distant."

"Well, at least he'll keep her life interesting," Blair said.

A chuckle erupted from my throat. "I'm not sure that's a problem. She *does* work for the prosecuting attorney, you know."

"True. There is that. So what did you want to tell me?"

I perked up. "Oh, we found a secret room."

"What do you mean a secret room? Where?"

"Above the bakery. We had some water damage out there. We hired Mr. Piper to do the repairs, and in tearing out the drywall he found this little room hidden behind a locked door."

Blair had sky blue eyes that would change color, depending on what she wore. Right now, they looked like two glacial pools, opened wide to reflect the color of her blouse. "Really? How mysterious. What was in it?"

"That's what's so weird. There was an old crib, a rocking chair, a bed, some books and an old chest."

"So, just storage?"

"No. It was all set out as if someone had been using the room as a bedroom or a nursery."

The microwave beeped, and I pulled out the chili and began spooning it into bowls. Blair slipped off her stool and came around the counter to get napkins and silverware.

"Why would anyone create a nursery up there? Do you know if anyone ever lived over in the barn?" she asked.

"Not that I know of. While there is one overhead bulb in the attic, there's no electricity to this little room. But what's even weirder is the door to the room was locked with a padlock, and then the door had been covered over."

Blair turned to me as she set the table, her perfectly penciled brows clenched. "What do you mean?"

"The door to the room was hidden behind some drywall."

Blair paused, staring at me across the table. "No kidding? Okay, that's even more mysterious."

We had just sat down and begun to eat when my cell phone rang. It was Rudy, another member of our book club.

"Julia, I'm at the Crate & Barrel in Bellevue," she said. "They have that big chafing dish you were looking for. Do you want me to pick it up? I can give it to you when we meet tonight for the art class."

"Yeah, thanks, Rudy."

"Hey Rudy!" Blair yelled into the phone. "We have another mystery to solve. Better get over here."

CHAPTER FOUR

While Blair normally dressed for sex appeal, Rudy often looked like she'd just walked off the golf course. She came over after lunch in Bermuda shorts, a cotton shirt and a pair of Adidas.

"Did you golf today?" I asked her.

"No. Elliott and I were shopping. His ninety-year old mother's birthday is coming up."

Elliott was Rudy's ex, and Blair and I glanced at each other.

"Are you two getting back together?" Blair asked.

Rudy threw us an exasperated look. "No. But I love Nana, and she probably doesn't have too much time left."

"Right. And you had lunch with him last week just to discuss the shopping trip," Blair said with a roll of her eyes.

Rudy exhaled with annoyance. "I may not have the buddy-buddy relationship with Elliott that you do with *all* of your many exes, but we're on good terms. Anyway, so, what's the big mystery?"

I smiled. "Follow me."

The three of us traipsed across the back drive and entered the bakery. April's afternoon assistant, Lynette, was busy filling the display case with a new batch of brownies. As we came in, two women passed us on the way out, one balancing a bakery box in her hands. Lynette looked up when the three of us entered.

"Don't tell me, it's the newly formed Old Maids Detective Agency," she said with a smile.

"You've been talking to April," I said. "Where is she?"

"She ran to the store for a few things."

"The Old Maid's Detective Agency," Blair repeated. "That's not a bad idea. After all, we've helped solve two murders so far."

"Don't encourage her," Rudy said to Lynette. "It's like pouring gas on a fire."

Rudy had been a career journalist with a pit bull attitude that had helped her get some tough stories. But that personality put her in direct opposition to Blair's more carefree approach to life, and they often sparred with each other.

"Where's the fourth member of your team?" Lynette asked.

"Doe is flying back from San Diego today from a garbage conference," Rudy said, picking up a cookie crumb from a sample tray.

Our friend Doe Kovinsky and her husband had built a major trash and recycling business in the Seattle area. Now that her husband was gone, Doe ran it as the company's CEO.

"I wonder what they talk about at a garbage conference," Blair pondered. "How to keep from smelling like rotting fish when you come home at night?"

"No, probably more like finding ways to pick up and dump trash faster," Rudy said. "Today it's all about productivity."

"How boring," Blair said with a flippant wave of her hand. "All I care is that they pick it up when they're supposed to. C'mon, let's go look at this room."

We climbed the stairs to the attic. Mr. Piper was just slipping a hammer into his tool belt as we entered the room, while Barry clicked off the shop vac, leaving the air filled with dust.

The disgusting smell had dissipated somewhat, but I opened one of the attic windows anyway. As a fresh breeze blew in, I sucked in a breath of clean air and turned away from the window. My foot caught under an old chest of drawers, hurling me forward. Mr. Piper was just crossing behind me, and I flew into his arms, throwing him backwards onto an old mattress. I landed right on top of him.

We lay face to face, frozen in shock. His ribs poked me in my left breast. When I felt something protruding into my groin, I gasped and quickly scrambled to my feet, feeling my face flush.

He rolled to the side and got up, adjusting his tool belt.

I realized it was only the hammer and not his…uh, other tool, which had poked me, and I swallowed a sigh of relief. But Blair let out a strangled giggle as she tried to cover her mouth with her hand.

"I'm so sorry," I said to him, dusting off my jeans and keeping my eyes focused on the floor. "My foot caught on something."

"Uh...no problem. Are you okay?"

He reached out to touch my shoulder, but I flinched away. "Yes, fine. So, you're off to that other job?"

"Yes. I'll give you a call when we're done."

I glanced at him and then quickly away. "Thanks so much, Mr. Piper. We'll see you in a couple of days."

He nodded, and then he and Barry gathered up their things and left.

As soon as they were out of earshot, both Rudy and Blair erupted in laughter.

"I wouldn't mention that to David," Blair said through her giggles. "He might...you know, get the wrong idea."

"Right," Rudy said with a snicker. "If that hammer had been what you must have thought it was, it would have been the biggest hard..."

"I get it!" I snapped, interrupting her. "Let's move on."

They shared a final amused look, took deep breaths and allowed their laughter to fade.

"Okay," Rudy said, "let's see this room."

Mr. Piper had brought up work lights, so we flicked those on, and I directed one of the lights to shine into the room. Rudy and Blair stepped inside.

"How weird," Blair said. "So you don't think this room was used just for storage?"

"It doesn't look that way to me," I said, coming in behind her. "I mean, look how it's set up. The cot is even still made up like a bed."

The three of us stood side-by-side, staring at the small cot.

"And the door was locked?" Rudy asked.

"Yeah, with a padlock."

"Hmmm," she murmured.

"What?" I asked.

"Well, I was just wondering if the lock was used to lock someone in, or was added later to just lock the door when the room wasn't in use anymore."

I stared at her. "Lock someone in? As in someone might have been here involuntarily?"

She shrugged. "Maybe."

Thankfully, Mr. Piper had removed the crib's mattress. But Blair still wrinkled her nose.

"It reeks in here," she said.

"Rats made a nest out of the mattress and peed everywhere." I bent over and pulled the small chest away from the wall. "I wonder what's in here."

The old chest had a domed top and was made from dark, worm-eaten wood. Only a hole remained where the old key lock used to be. Rudy came up behind me as I lifted the lid. We both stared into the interior, coughing at the stagnant air that emerged.

"Huckleberry Finn," Rudy said, crouching down next to me. She reached in and lifted out the old book.

"And a baby's blanket," I said.

I pushed that aside and found a small, pewter necklace with a pendant made out of two oval pieces of glass surrounded by a pewter braid trim.

"Look at this," I said. The pendant contained a dried yellow flower inside. "I think it's a marigold."

Something brushed past my ear, and my hand flew to my neck as I spun around.

"What?" Blair said, watching me.

"I thought one of you touched me." A shiver ran down my spine at the memory. I glanced down again at the necklace. "I…uh, felt something when I said this was a marigold." My hand went to my ear again at the lingering sensation. I dropped the necklace back into the chest.

"There's an inscription inside this book," Rudy said, interrupting my train of thought.

I turned to her. "What is it?"

"'To my darling Rose. Love, Father.' That's all," she said with a grunt. "Not very helpful. What'd you say, Julia?" Rudy asked, turning to me.

"I didn't say anything."

Rudy furrowed her brows. "I swear I just heard you say something."

"Wait a minute," Blair said, raising her hand. "Listen."

We all stopped. The faint sound of whispering made us look at each other in alarm.

"Oh my God," Blair said, her eyes growing round with apprehension. "Can you tell what they're saying?"

We all got quiet again, but the whispering faded away.

"Darn it," I exclaimed. "But you heard it? Right?"

"Yes," Rudy said. "I've still got goose bumps. That was creepy."

"I wonder if Mr. Piper heard it, too," Blair said.

"I doubt it. They were making so much noise up here; they probably wouldn't have noticed it. But it seems to be gone now," I said. "Let's take the box downstairs. I need to get out of here. This place gives me the creeps."

We took the chest to the inn and put it on some paper towels on the counter.

"Anyone want some iced tea?" I asked.

"Yes," Blair replied. "Thanks."

"Me, too," Rudy said.

I washed my hands and went to the refrigerator where we kept a big beaker filled with iced tea. The girls sat down in front of the paned window that overlooked the back deck and the lake beyond.

"It's got to be 75 degrees out, and yet I'm still chilled," Blair said. She rubbed her hands along her arms as if to warm herself up.

"I know. April got such a bad headache up there earlier she had to go lie down."

"What do you know about the barn?" Rudy asked me.

"Not much," I replied. "Just that it's original to the property. And no one has ever liked going upstairs. There's a bad feeling in that attic." I pulled out the small bowl filled with packets of sweetener. "I can't help but wonder why someone locked that room," I said, putting the sweetener on the table and going to a bowl filled with fruit. I grabbed a lemon and began to cut it into slices. "I'm telling you, I think someone lived up there. Did you notice the empty cereal boxes? You know, the kind we used to have as kids."

"You mean the small ones you'd open by slitting it down the middle?" Rudy asked, getting up to grab three tumbler glasses out of the cupboard.

"Yeah. The labels had been chewed off, but that's what they were."

"So why would someone live in a closed space like that? And do we think the padlock means that someone was locked in?" Blair pondered out loud.

"Well, you've seen those scary movies where they lock someone up who is mad. I wonder if that was it," Rudy said.

I grimaced as I set spoons and a plate with sliced lemon on the table. "Wait a minute, an insane person with a baby? Okay, that's *really* a creepy thought."

"Isn't the history of the inn pretty sketchy?" Rudy asked, pushing a glass toward Blair. "I mean, I remember you saying that when you did some research, several people had bought the place and then suddenly left."

I nodded. "Yeah, it seemed like at least a couple of families moved in and then almost as quickly moved out."

"Because of the ghosts," Blair said.

I brought a bowl of mixed nuts to the table. "Probably. I think there have been sightings here almost from the beginning. It's weird, though; I've never felt threatened by the ghosts here." I brought the beaker of iced tea and some ice to the table.

"But a lot of people aren't like you," Rudy said, filling her glass. "Can't you imagine someone being freaked out by seeing Elizabeth for the first time?"

"Of course. I was," I said, pouring my own tea. "Maybe I'm just used to her now."

As soon as I said this, a drawer across the room slid open. We all turned to look.

"Speaking of..." Rudy said.

We often had to put up with cupboard doors that opened and closed on their own, or cups and saucers that moved. Chloe, who was ten years old when she died, liked to play tricks on people she didn't like, often putting me in an awkward position.

"The whole idea of ghosts still freaks me out a little," Blair said. "The thought that after you die you could be stuck in the same place for eternity is really sad."

"I'll have to admit, I'd want to move on," I said. "But there's definitely something about that attic in the carriage barn. April gets a headache every time she goes up there, and like I said, no one wants to stay up there very long. I've been waiting to hear if Mr. Piper and his assistant experience anything."

"But Mr. Piper hasn't complained?" Rudy wondered.

I shrugged. "Not yet."

"Maybe someone was murdered up there," Blair speculated.

Rudy gave her a scowl. "We don't need another murder mystery."

I arched my eyebrows. "We already have a mystery. Why did someone hide that room? But do you think we could ever solve it? We don't have much to go on."

"If someone was kept up there against their will, I doubt anyone will admit to it," Blair said, grabbing a handful of nuts.

"But we could make this one of our projects," Rudy suggested. "You've said several times that you'd like to have a book that traces the history of the inn, and God knows I like to write. So why don't we write one?"

My eyes lit up. "I love that idea."

Rudy was not only a great writer, but also an avid reader and book collector. The thought that she would help meant that it would be professionally done.

"We could work with the historical society and get old pictures from when the house was originally built. They might even have information on most of the families that have lived here since then," Rudy said.

"But don't you think we'd have to go all the way back to when the barn was built?" I asked. "After all, the barn predates the inn."

"Good point," Rudy said.

I turned to Blair. "You up for this?"

"Absolutely. Instead of reading a book for the book club this time around, we'll write one!"

"Does that mean we can stop reading that romance you suggested this month?" I asked.

Blair gave me a look of reproach.

"Can't blame a girl for trying," I said with a smile.

CHAPTER FIVE

The three of us met up later that night at the Mercer Island Senior Center to begin a four-week art class in honor of Martha. Richard Welping, a 50-something hunk who was somewhat of a local celebrity for his nude sculptures, taught the class. His sculptures were scattered around the globe in places as far away as Dubai and as close as Mercer Island City Hall.

The sculpture in City Hall was tame enough that even I could look at it without blushing, but a long-standing war that had simmered for decades between the prim and proper do-gooders in town and the more culturally liberal had almost derailed it. The do-gooders fought to keep it out of such a public place because they thought it inappropriate. The liberals had won, albeit barely. After all, it was the sculpture of a father and his half-dressed wife suckling her new babe. Only one of her breasts was exposed, the other one covered up by the baby.

And yet, the sculpture had been moved three times in an effort to strike a balance between relegating it to complete obscurity next to the third floor bathroom (the do-gooders' preferred choice), and finding a location where it would both honor the artist and reduce its exposure (no pun intended). The compromise was the alcove on the ground floor outside the Human Relations Department. How the do-gooders had missed the irony of *that* choice, I'll never know.

Richard Welping lived on the island and volunteered his time to teach one class a year at our senior center. He was single and built like a long-distance runner, with long gray hair pulled back in a ponytail. I felt sure it was his full lips and bedroom eyes that secured him the starring role in the dreams of most of the older women in Washington State, and maybe some of the younger ones as well. So naturally, I suspected the class would be filled with a bunch of 70-something women drooling over his every word, and not because they'd lost their false teeth.

The three of us arrived a few minutes early to join a small group of people in a room with metal shelves along one wall stacked with a variety of art supplies. The linoleum floor was stained with paint and embedded with glitter. Wooden easels were stacked in one corner, while five pottery wheels took up the other corner. In the center of the room were six long tables.

We'd been instructed to bring ten pounds of clay for the class. We each took a seat at one of the tables and saved a seat next to Rudy for Doe, who scooted in a few minutes before class started. She was still dressed in her signature black pants suit and silk blouse. As she dropped her large, black satchel on the floor, I leaned over to say, "You didn't have time to go home and change?"

"No. I came straight from the airport," she said, shaking her head. "So if my stomach growls, it's because I didn't have dinner."

I rummaged around in the bottom of my purse and brought forth a squished mini-Milky Way Bar. "Here," I said, reaching across Rudy to hand it to her.

Doe glanced at the mangled candy bar in my hand as if I'd just offered her a can of dog food. "I'm good," she said.

I retracted my hand, but not before Rudy snatched the small treat and ripped it open. "Thanks. I only had time for a breakfast bar."

My mouth dropped open ready to respond, but Rudy popped it into her mouth before I could say a word. A quick intake of breath made me turn to Blair.

"I don't believe it," she said, pointing to the front of the room.

I followed her gaze and was surprised to see one of the most outspoken do-gooders sit down in the front row next to his wife.

"What is Milton Snyder doing here?" I asked.

"That's what I'd like to know," Blair said. "I hope he's not here to disrupt the class."

Blair had been the one to select the class, I suspect because it gave her an opportunity to engage in her favorite sport – flirting. In this case, with Richard Welping. And she had four weeks in which to sharpen her skills. I was sure she thought having Milton Snyder there would only serve to sour the atmosphere.

"Maybe he's just dropping his wife off," Rudy suggested.

"No. Look. He's planted himself at a table, and he's got a bag of clay in front of him. Why would he join this class? He hates Richard Welping," Blair said.

"I don't think he hates Welping," Rudy countered. "He just hates his artwork."

"What's the difference?" Blair argued. "At least when you're sitting in his art class?"

"I bet it was Mabel's idea," I said. "She's a peacemaker by design. She must have talked him into taking the class so he'd have a better understanding of Welping's art. After all, Milton did lose his battle with the City."

"Maybe he's here to spy on Welping," Blair said.

Doe leaned forward to look at Blair with a startled expression. "Why? We're not going to be sculpting nudes, are we?"

"No," she responded. "This is just a general pottery class. The most suggestive thing we'll probably do is sculpt a flower opening to the sun." Her pretty face was twisted in a scowl. "So why is Snyder here?"

While Mabel Snyder reminded me of a butterfly, all flighty and breathy, her husband made me think of a tree stump. I admit that I have a tendency to judge certain people by their looks. It's not something I'm proud of, but it's something I can't seem to control. I'm visually oriented. And Milton Snyder's large, bald head and thick neck made me think of a tree stump. His stubborn personality only helped to reinforce the image.

"Maybe Julia is right," Doe said. "Maybe it's just a way for him to have a better appreciation of the artist's talent."

"I doubt it," Blair said. "Snyder is the most sanctimonious man I've ever met. He actually handed me his sweater at the Summer Celebration last year. A breeze had come up and he thought I might be cold." She gave us a 'get my point' look and her blue eyes glinted with anger as she returned her gaze to Snyder.

Since Blair's normal summer wardrobe consisted of tight pants and a form-fitting tank top that was two sizes too small, I was pretty sure Milton had offered the sweater because of her natural bodily response to a sudden cool breeze; he surely wasn't the kind to care about anyone's personal comfort. But our speculation about why

Milton Snyder was in the class was cut short at the sound of a familiar voice.

"Juuulia!"

Doe cringed. I turned in surprise as Goldie Singleton, my next door neighbor, waddled through the door. She scuttled across the room with Aria Stottlemeyer, the postmistress, looming right behind her. Any enthusiasm I'd had for the class quickly evaporated.

"Goldie, what are you doing here?" I asked, hoping she was in the building for a different class.

"I'm takin' Welping's art class," she said. "I have a few blank spots downstairs to fill," she said with a snort of laughter.

In truth, Goldie's home was filled from stem to stern with a mishmash of art and collectibles from around the world. If there was a blank shelf or wall anywhere in the house, I'd never seen it.

"Why are you gals here?" Aria asked, with her pointy nose in the air.

Aria was as tall as Goldie was short and had the face of my mother when she was constipated. She was extremely competitive, and I could already hear her snide comments about my future sculpted flower opening to the sun.

"Uh...we wanted to take an art class in honor of Martha," I said. "It's something she always wanted to do, but didn't have the chance before she died."

"That's just what you'd expect from the Mercer Island Heroes," Goldie said to Aria with appreciation. "But you should have your medallions on so that people know who you are."

She gestured around the room, and I noticed that several people were watching us. Goldie never missed an opportunity to remind us that we had earned the first-ever Mercer Island Hero Award from the mayor back in December, after we'd saved a young woman from a human-trafficking ring. In fact, it was the case in which Martha had died. But Goldie seemed much more enamored with the honor than we were, as illustrated by Doe, who withered under her suggestion. Even Rudy's thin lips turned into a frown.

"Uh...no, we don't like to call attention to that sort of thing."

"They're shy," Aria said, bumping Goldie's shoulder.

"Not shy," Goldie countered. "Humble. Heroes are always humble. Isn't that right, Julia?"

Tap. Tap. Tap.

We all looked up to find that our resident artist was ready to begin.

"Oh…oh, we'd better get a seat," Goldie said. "See you guys later."

The two women hurried off. I gave a sigh of relief. Doe opened her mouth to say something, but I cut her off. "I know. I know. Between the Snyders and Goldie, this art class could turn out to be a disaster. But we're here to honor Martha."

"May I have everyone's attention?" Welping said from the front of the room.

He was dressed in Khaki cargo pants and a loose-fitting muslin shirt. I heard a couple of twitters across the room and glanced up to see a few women smiling stupidly at him.

"This is meant to be a pottery sampler class," Welping said. "For the first two weeks, half the class will practice at the potter's wheel, while the other half practices hand sculpting. The second two weeks, we'll switch. So, why don't you each go to the wall and grab an apron before we get started? Then grab a box with your pottery tools at the front of the room."

There was an immediate shuffling of chairs and feet as everyone got up and headed for the far wall. And yet, Doe remained where she was.

"Aren't you going to get an apron?" I asked her.

Doe was one of the most perfect people I knew. She required order in her life. Her house was immaculate. Her car always looked like she'd just had it detailed. She was an extremely picky eater. And the one time when I'd seen her gardening, although she was kneeling in the dirt, she looked right out of a *Home and Garden* magazine. I often thought she'd been demagnetized in some way so that dirt just didn't stick to her.

That made watching her difficult, as she stared at the wall of stained aprons and struggled with the idea of having to wear one that had been worn by dozens of other people. It was like watching someone else eat bugs.

But she was a trouper and stood up to follow me to the rack of aprons. She grabbed the cleanest one she could find and carefully draped it over her head. She was about to tie it in a loose knot in the back, when Goldie came up behind her.

"Let me get that for you, Doe," Goldie said, grabbing the tie strings out of her hands. She cinched it tight, making Doe stiffen as if she'd been electrocuted. "You don't want to get anything on that nice outfit." Goldie tied the strings in a bow and marched off.

Doe remained frozen in place. Rudy leaned into her and said, "Just breathe, Doe. It will all be over in a couple of hours."

"Easy for you to say," Doe said with a curled lip.

For the next fifteen minutes, we listened to Welping discuss clay as a medium and how the various little tools we had in our boxes were to be used. I glanced down, thinking they looked like things a cave man might have used. There was a sponge, a couple of flat wooden spatula-type things, and several wooden utensils with metal prongs that looked right out of a dentist's office.

First Welping had us cut off a chunk of clay and knead it like bread dough to warm it up and remove air bubbles. Then he announced that those who would start on the potter's wheel would make a bowl that night, while the sculpting half would sculpt, yes, a flower. He'd set up a large porcelain rose in the front of the room as a model, lit by an overhead light. I saw Milton Snyder huff to himself, and I wondered again why he was there.

Welping read off the names of who would go to the pottery wheels first. Rudy and I were among that group. We picked up our clay and tool boxes and made our way to the back of the room, while the other half of the class got started with the rose.

While Welping demonstrated how to use the potter's wheel, I had a growing sense of unease. This had disaster written all over it, at least for me. What was it about a clump of wet clay, a spinning wheel, and me that Blair thought was a good idea when she registered us for this class?

A half hour later, however, I was feeling more relaxed. Using a potter's wheel is messy and clumsy at first, but working with the clay felt as organic as if I were out digging in the dirt. I enjoyed it.

I tried and failed twice to get a decent bowl going, but a misplaced finger or thumb sent the entire piece off center. It would then spin awkwardly, looking very much like a flat tire. At one point, Welping stepped in to help.

"Here," he said. "Let's start over."

He used the potter's wire to swipe my lump of clay off the wheel at the base. Then he rolled it into a ball and slapped it down again. "Now, be stingy with the water. Like this…" He leaned over as the clay spun and deftly stuck his thumb into the middle of it to open it up, while he held the sides of the clay with his other hand. "See?" he said when he was done.

By that time, the musky scent of his aftershave had me feeling heady, so I could only nod. He smiled and turned away. I heard a smug little laugh and looked over to where Rudy was giving me a smirk.

I continued working on the bowl, drawing it up and out as the wheel turned. This time, I concentrated on balancing the pressure between the hand I had inside the bowl and my fingers on the outside of the bowl. It was working.

After a few minutes, I stopped to take a rest. The bowl was now about six inches wide and four inches tall. I'd have to cut it down. But I'd finally gotten the hang of it, and looked with pride at my construction.

I snuck a peek at Rudy, who was hunched over her wheel, focused like a laser. Her shoulders were tensed and her teeth clenched; she was doing battle with the clay rather than caressing and smoothing it. I smiled to myself. We were all so different in how we approached things.

Because I wanted to shorten mine, I grabbed what looked like an ice pick and then got the wheel going again at a good pace. This was a critical moment. I had to be careful. If I didn't hold the sharp tool steady, the top edge of my bowl would be crooked and ruin the entire look.

I kept my foot on the pedal and leaned in. Using the fingers of my left hand, I put pressure inside the bowl near the top rim and then stuck the pick into the clay to slice off about two inches. Since I was so focused on the bowl, I forgot what my foot was doing and pressed down even further. The wheel sped up.

And then it happened!

Frankly, they should warn you when you take a pottery class that there's a point at which an object will actually take flight when released from a high speed turn. Whatever that calculation is, I was quick to reach it and watched the top two inches of my wet, floppy clay go airborne in a matter of seconds.

There is a saying that before disaster strikes, people often see their life flash before their eyes. Well, it's not true. Rudy didn't have time to see *anything* before the clay smacked her right in the left side of her face.

Everyone stopped and stared. Rudy paused and cast me a threatening look, before using the back of her hand to wipe off the mess that now lathered her skin. With a flick of her wrist, she flung the sloppy clay onto the floor and then glanced down at her blouse and apron, which were now covered in splotches of wet, gray clay.

"Time for a break," Welping announced from the front of the room.

After apologizing profusely and helping Rudy to clean herself up, we joined Doe and Blair again at the table.

"What happened to you?" Blair asked upon seeing Rudy. "It looks like the potter's wheel threw up on you."

A chunk of Rudy's hair was clumped together with clay. She had big wet spots all over her apron and blouse, and across one cheek was a red welt where the strip of clay had slapped her. And yet she was a picture of restraint. All she said was, "Let's just say I was helping Julia with her bowl."

Blair and Doe looked at me and began to laugh.

Damn!

"So how did you guys do?" I asked, hoping to change the subject.

Doe had something in front of her that looked more like a cauliflower than a rose, but Blair's was almost perfect. *Was there anything she wasn't good at?*

"Yours is beautiful," I said to her.

"She's right. Nice job, Mrs. Wentworth."

It was Welping. *He knew her name?*

Blair smiled demurely. "Thank you so much, Richard. I just copied yours. You're so expressive with your hands."

Oh, god!

She fluttered her eyelashes and leaned toward him, allowing him to stare longingly at her cleavage.

"You can't manufacture talent," he said. "I think you have a good eye."

She leaned into him a bit more. I thought she might fall off the chair, so as he wandered away, I reached out and grabbed the sleeve of her blouse.

"Careful. Don't want to find yourself on the floor."

She giggled. "At least not alone," she said, watching him walk away. "Boy, he has dreamy eyes."

"Those aren't his eyes you're looking at," Rudy quipped.

Since it was a break, a couple of the women grabbed their purses and left the room. Others got up and just milled around. We huddled up and took the opportunity to fill Doe in on finding the hidden room in the attic and Rudy's idea to write a book. She agreed, and we began to brainstorm how to proceed. After a few minutes, I excused myself to use the ladies' room, but when I returned, someone tapped me on the shoulder. I turned to find Milton Snyder staring down at me.

"The Snyders have lived on the island since the turn of the century, you know," he said.

Doe and Rudy wheeled around to listen in.

"Um…okay," I replied.

"I overheard you talking. What you said about finding that secret room," he said. "My great grandfather was the first Baptist minister on the island. You should come talk to me. I could tell you a lot about your property."

I glanced over at Rudy, who gave me an almost imperceptible shake of her head.

"Um…well, we'll see," I said to him. "We're just throwing some ideas around. But thanks."

I turned away, hoping to end the conversation.

"Mrs. Applegate," he said sternly.

I turned back to face him. "What is it?"

"You shouldn't ignore me. You know, a young woman was murdered in that barn."

CHAPTER SIX

Despite the red flag raised by Milton Snyder, the four of us avoided him at the end of class and decided that we would find the information we needed some other way. In fact, as we parted, we decided to meet the next night to begin planning our approach.

I got to bed early, because one family had booked the entire inn from Tuesday through Friday to hold a reunion. They were all due to arrive the following day.

The first member of the Welch family rang the bell at the front desk at nine o'clock the next morning. Since there were five children and a baby between eight adults, Crystal and I were kept busy pulling out rolling cots, a crib, and making sure each room had ample towels and amenities.

Most of the group was ensconced in their rooms by noon. Shortly after, a taxi rolled up to the front porch. An elderly couple emerged. I met them at the front door to help them inside. They were Ruby and Harvey Welch, the matriarch and patriarch of the family.

"Welcome to the St. Claire Inn," I said with a smile.

"I hope my daughter and sons have arrived," the elder Mrs. Welch replied, ignoring my greeting.

I paused at the rudeness, but replied, "Yes. I believe everyone is here now. Do you need help with your bags?"

The taxi driver was in the process of unloading two big suitcases from the back of the car. Mrs. Welch didn't even glance behind her before saying, "That's what we pay the driver for. Harvey, do you need to use the bathroom?"

The elder Mr. Welch had to be in his late seventies or early eighties. He was stooped and balding and walked with a cane. He glanced at his wife.

"No, Ruby. And stop asking me in front of other people."

She twisted her thin lips into a scowl. "Fine." She turned to me. "We'll check in now."

"Uh…of course. Why don't you step over here to the counter?"

I moved behind the reception desk and turned the book around to allow her to sign in. She took the book and used a skinny index finger to run down the sign-in sheet to verify which of her family members had arrived.

"I see my sons have arrived. What room are Rebecca and the kids in?" she demanded. "I don't want to be too close to the baby."

"I…uh, put them in the suite, number 6. You and your husband will be in number 4."

She heaved a deep sigh, as if she would have to tolerate the inconvenience of just a single room between them.

"I suppose that will be fine. We'd like to go to our room now."

"Just sign here," I said, pointing to the book. "And I'll get your key."

I returned to the office and took the appropriate key off the wall. When I handed it to her, I said, "Please let me know if you need anything else. Your room is right at the top of the stairs," I said, pointing above my head. "We have a small service elevator down that hallway, if you'd care to use it."

The suite door opened above us and two young boys ran out, clomping down the stairs, slapping each other and laughing.

"Robbie! Stewart!" the elder Mrs. Welch snapped.

The two boys slid to a halt at the bottom of the stairs, a look of fear etched into their young features.

"Hello, Grandma," they said like two little robots.

A woman with long, dark hair appeared on the staircase behind them. "Boys, go outside and play. But stay close," she said.

The boys disappeared into the breakfast room without another word and out the back door.

"Hello, Mother," the woman said, coming down the stairs.

"Hello, Rebecca. Did Robert come with you?"

"No. He had to work."

"Of course he did. Our first family reunion in ten years, and he's tied to his desk."

Rebecca's fine features tensed. "This is a busy time of year for him, Mother; you know that. He couldn't help it."

"And you have no influence over him, I take it. Or more likely, you just didn't say anything."

"That's not fair," Rebecca said. She glanced at me.

"If you'll excuse me," I said. "I have to help in the kitchen." I quickly took my leave and joined April, who was checking inventory in the pantry. "Boy, I have the feeling this is going to be the week from hell," I said to her.

"Why?"

"Mr. and Mrs. Welch, Sr. just arrived. Did you ever see the movie *Mommy Dearest*?"

April grimaced. "You're kidding?"

" No. The elder Mrs. Welch doesn't look anything like Joan Crawford, but I bet she'd be a shoo-in for the role if they did a remake."

÷

That afternoon, as I helped April clean up the afternoon snack tray, I filled her in on the book we planned to do.

"I love the idea," she said. "Mind if I join you for the meeting?"

"Of course not. This will be a group effort."

"You said Milton Snyder told you that a young woman was murdered here. Did he say anything else?"

"No. And I didn't ask."

"So you're not going to interview him?"

"Not if I can help it. His wife, Mabel, isn't so bad. But he's…"

"What?"

I took a deep breath. "He's not a nice man."

April lifted her eyebrows in surprise. "What does that mean? He's mean-spirited? He tells dirty jokes? He…"

"He's a bigot," I said. "Narrow-minded. A religious zealot. Discriminatory. He's not a…"

"Nice man," she said, finishing my thought. "I get it."

"Right. I have trouble being in the same room with him. So interviewing him is out of the question."

"Okay. Maybe I should interview him."

My head snapped up in surprise. She only laughed.

"Hey. You said he's a bigot. Maybe being interviewed by a black woman would rattle his cage."

"Actually, that's something I'd pay to see."

"So, what time do we meet tonight?"

"Seven-thirty," I said.

"Do I need to bring anything?"

"God, no. I'm making sugar-free brownies."

She nodded and we finished up. Afterwards, I took the dogs for a short walk around the block, and then stirred up a batch of sugar-free brownies since Blair was a diabetic.

The sun was setting by the time everyone arrived. We met in the main kitchen. Doe came straight from work with a Subway salad in hand. She was still dressed in her work clothes, but quickly stripped off her suit jacket and grabbed a glass of wine.

"Well, at least this mystery doesn't involve anyone getting murdered," she said, taking the lid off of her salad bowl.

"Uh…didn't you hear what Milton Snyder said last night?" Blair said.

"Yes," Doe said. "But who listens to him? Anyway, for once I'd like to forego chasing killers and almost getting ourselves killed in the process."

"A locked room is enough mystery for me anyway," I said. "And I think this book idea is wonderful."

"And if the book turns out well, you could sell it here and at the museum," Doe continued.

"I like that idea," April said.

I had brought a couple of small pads of paper and pencils to the table and began to write. "So how do we start?"

"It would make sense to start at the historical society," Doe said. "I think you might even get Kris to agree to partner with you."

Kris Sargent was Executive Director of the Mercer Island Museum, where Doe was a board member.

"This might be a dumb idea," Blair said, "but I'm assuming that you'll include information about the ghosts, right?" Everyone nodded and murmured their agreement. "Well, then maybe the museum would consider staging an exhibit about ghosts after we're done with the book, featuring the inn as the centerpiece."

Blair glanced at Rudy with a slight raise to her eyebrows. She was waiting for Rudy's customary snide response. But this time, Blair was rewarded.

"I think that's a great idea," Rudy said. "And I bet it would be a popular exhibit."

"Especially with the kids," Doe agreed.

Blair beamed at the approval.

"Maybe you and I could go meet with Kris," I said to Doe. "What's your schedule look like this week?"

"I have some time tomorrow afternoon," she said, taking a bite of her salad.

"Good. When we first moved here, I developed a tentative timeline for the property. But there are holes in it. I think that's the first thing to do – fill in who lived here and when."

"Right, then we can begin to research if any of those people or their descendants are still around," Rudy said. "If so, we could call and ask for an interview."

"And don't forget neighbors," April said. "For instance, Goldie and Ben have lived next door forever. They must know a lot about this property."

"Good point," I said, writing that down. "I'll go over and talk to them."

"And any other people who have lived here a long time," Doe said. "It's amazing what people in a neighborhood whisper about. If there was something funny going on over here, I bet other people either knew about it or at least suspected something."

"I could start searching newspapers from back then to find out about the island itself," Rudy said. "It would be nice to put it all in context to the time period."

"What a great idea," I exclaimed. "It could follow some of the historical changes on the island – political and cultural."

"But also, once we have the names of whoever lived here, I can check on whether their kids showed up in articles about sports or theater," Rudy continued. "Maybe dignitaries visited. The old society pages might have even talked about trips people took. In the old days, people were interested in things like that."

"Since we don't really know what we're looking for in the way of that hidden room, I guess for right now we're looking for everything," I said.

"I think if we're writing a book about the property, we'll have to consider anything and everything," April said. "Then we can pick out the highlights."

"We'll need photos, too," Rudy said.

"Hopefully, the museum will have some," Doe said. "But if we can find living family members, they might have photos as well."

"So, the first thing to do is to confirm the names of the families who lived here and *when* they lived here. From there, we can figure out who might still be around and see if we can talk with them." I looked around at four nodding heads.

"Voter rolls would help with that," Rudy said. "I can check those."

"Plus, Island Realty has been here a long time," Blair added. "I bet Ginger would have information about the property."

Ginger Graves was the current owner of Island Realty and had taken over from her mother. Since she was near our age, she would have access to a lot of island history

"Good point, Blair," Doe said. "You're pretty close with her, aren't you?"

"Yeah, she's in my Pilates class. I could talk to her," Blair said.

"What can I do?" Doe asked.

"You and I will take the museum," I said to her. I turned to April. "Any chance you could go through some of those boxes in the attic upstairs? That's all mostly stuff left over from past owners. I'm sure there are some things up there that might help."

"Absolutely," she said with a nod. "You know there's a bunch of old furniture up there that may have been original to the house."

"That's right," I replied. "It wouldn't hurt to go through everything we have, just in case. Maybe it's even time to bring some of that stuff down and refurbish it."

April rolled her eyes. "Looks like I'll have to get José to help me."

"What do you think about a display of some of the original furniture when we do the book launch?" I asked her.

"I like it," she replied with a lift to her eyebrows. "But does that mean we'll also sell some of the furniture?"

I smiled. "Yes. I suppose it's time to get rid of some of that stuff. I'm not attached to any of it." I fingered the little necklace I'd brought to the table from the box. "I think we should also try to find out who might have made this necklace."

"But carefully," April interjected.

"Why do you say that?" Doe asked.

April turned solemn eyes her way. "Because when I was in the attic, I heard someone say they died up there."

"And Milton did say someone was murdered," I reminded her.

"Sounds like a mystery to be solved," Blair said.

"We are *not* investigating a murder," Doe insisted. "There are murders everywhere, every day of every year. We don't have to be the ones to solve them. Let's just research the history of the inn." She looked around the table, encouraging us to agree.

"Doe's right," I said with a sigh. "We have plenty of work ahead of us. I don't really want to add a murder to the list."

I felt my nose grow, and the surprised looks confirmed that my friends didn't believe me. But Doe seemed satisfied, and so we dropped it.

We ended the evening discussing our assignments in further detail, and I went to my apartment later thinking about what Milton Snyder had said at the art class. Add to that what April had heard in the attic, namely that someone had died up there, and I went to bed dreaming of mysteries of a more sinister nature than just a locked room.

CHAPTER SEVEN

I eased into the next morning by taking a cup of coffee and a bowl of oatmeal onto my deck. It was just 6:00 a.m., and I found both the crisp morning air and the trickling sound of a small rock pond next to the deck refreshing.

As usual, the dogs bounded into the yard. Minnie ran frantically around the perimeter of the fence several times, as if to burn off pent-up energy; something she did every day. A few minutes later, both dogs had stretched out in the sun, while I sat at my small table eating breakfast and making notes about how we might organize the book.

After breakfast, I joined April in the kitchen and helped her set out food for the guests. The breakfast room was filled with thirteen people and a baby. Since there were three generations of the same family, you'd think breakfast chatter would be at an all-time high. Instead, the room was nearly silent.

I glanced over at the kids' table and was surprised to see them all staring sullenly at their plates. I suspected the Wicked Witch of the West had nothing on the elder Mrs. Welch. After all, even Ahab, our talking African gray parrot, was quiet.

And then all of a sudden, he wasn't.

"C'mon, make my day," he squawked when he saw me. That elicited sudden laughter from the kids.

"Children!" the elder Mrs. Welch snapped. "Don't encourage him. And don't you dare touch him. Birds carry disease, you know."

Really? What an old biddy, I thought.

I held my tongue and joined Crystal, our daytime manager, at the front desk.

"They're here all week, right?" I said under my breath.

She smiled. "Yes. And I've already fielded complaints about the water pressure, the lack of children's books in the library, and the fact that we only sell brownies and fudge behind the counter here. Nothing healthy. Oh, and she doesn't like the fact that you let the dogs run loose."

By 'her' I assumed she meant the elder Mrs. Welch.

"God," I said with an exhale. "This is going to be a long week."

"You think Elizabeth will make an appearance?"

Elizabeth St. Claire had died in the same fire that had killed her son and young daughter, Chloe many years before. She made rare appearances around the inn, but often expressed herself by slamming cupboards or drawers. Chloe, on the other hand, liked to play tricks on unsuspecting guests she didn't like. Often it was children. But occasionally, adults were her target.

"I'm more worried that Chloe will take a liking to Mrs. Welch," I said. "So be prepared. I'll try to keep the dogs in my apartment."

I took Mickey and Minnie to my apartment and then joined April fifteen minutes later upstairs in the attic. Unlike the barn attic, the attic in the house didn't trigger any oppressive feelings, even though there were rumors of a young girl who had jumped to her death back in the 1980s from the faux balcony that hung off the side of the building. Her image had been seen several times gazing out the upstairs window, as if looking for a long lost love.

"What do you think?" I said, glancing around the room.

We stood at the door, surveying the hodge-podge of stuff in front of us. There were old upholstered chairs, a glass-topped wooden desk, two old fans, a large chest of drawers, a Cinderella mirror, boxes and boxes of junk, and a large armoire in the corner.

"I say we do a brief inventory first. Then at least we'll know what we have," April replied.

"Sounds good," I said. "Let me get a pad of paper."

I went back downstairs and grabbed a pad and pencil from the office behind the reception desk. I was halfway back down the hallway when a voice stopped me.

"Is there a lifeguard on duty here?"

I turned to find the elder Mrs. Welch.

"Um…no. I'm afraid we don't have a lifeguard. There's a sign," I said, gesturing toward the back deck. "Swim at your own risk."

"Do you really think that would hold up in court?" she said, her leathery features twitching with skepticism. "My grandchildren would like to swim. How can they if there isn't a lifeguard? And there's no sand. What kind of beach is this if there's no sand?"

I stepped toward her. "I'm sorry, Mrs. Welch. But it says very clearly in our brochure and on the website that there is no lifeguard."

"My daughter made these reservations," she said with a huff.

She turned on her heel and left, presumably to chew out her daughter. I returned to the attic.

I spent the rest of the morning helping April organize and inventory everything. We labeled things by the family they had belonged to, if we could determine that; otherwise, they went into a general pile.

We took a break for lunch, and then I joined Crystal at the front desk to discuss a supply run to the store. The elder Mrs. Welch appeared again, making my muscles tighten.

"I thought my daughter would have told you about our food restrictions. But it seems even that has been left up to me."

Mrs. Welch, Sr. was a thin, angular woman with sharp edges everywhere. Even though her daughter Rebecca had made the reservations, I had a sneaking suspicion the family reunion had been her mother's idea.

"My husband is allergic to onions," she told me in a restrained voice. "So let's be sure we don't have anything for breakfast that includes onions, and frankly, cheese gives him gas. So let's avoid that. My son's wife is lactose intolerant, and I can't have anything with gluten."

"Uh, well, okay," I said. "Good to know. I…uh, I suppose we can make scrambled eggs with water, and fry up some bacon and sausage."

"Oh, and my niece is a vegan," she said.

"Of course she is," I said, forgetting to filter my sarcasm. "We'll just make a giant fruit salad each morning that everyone can enjoy."

"I don't appreciate mockery," she said quietly and walked away.

April was out in the bakery, finishing up a couple of cinnamon swirl coffee cakes when I stormed in a few minutes later.

"What's the matter? Is Dana Finkle back in town?" she asked, noticing the angry look on my face.

Dana Finkle had been the one person who could make my blood boil. That is, until we saved her life, and she moved out of town. But the elder Mrs. Welch had taken her place.

"It's Mrs. Welch, Sr. isn't it?" April said.

"That woman!" I almost shouted.

Lynette was filling a tray with fig bars and looked up.

"Okay, calm down," April said. "What happened?"

I told April about the list of food restrictions.

April laughed. "Well, Julia, this is *our* bed and breakfast. They didn't inform us of all of this when they made the reservations. And it's very clear in our promotional materials that we provide a variety of breakfast items each day for our guests. So that's what I plan to do. I'll make sure there's something for everyone. And if they don't like it, they're more than welcome to eat downtown."

April's common sense short-circuited my anger.

"I…uh…okay. But let's label everything, just so everyone knows what they're eating. I'd like to minimize my interaction with that old biddy, if I can. And I'd hate to think of what might happen if her husband should eat your scrambled eggs and cheese by mistake. According to her, I'd have to break out the air freshener."

÷

It was mid-afternoon when Doe's big black Mercedes came down the drive. I climbed in and joined her in a ride to the museum, happy to get away from the Welch family.

Kris Sargent, the director, was in her early forties, with short black hair, big round eyes and a ready smile. She had a sharp mind and had done wonders at the museum, which was nothing more than an old Victorian house that someone had willed to the historical society.

"So, you're writing a book about the inn. That's a terrific idea," she said from behind an antique writing desk. "How can I help?"

"We're wondering how to find information on the property," I said.

"Oh, that's easy," she said. "First of all, as part of the New Deal back in the 30s, the Works Progress Administration employed people to go out and document every piece of property in King County. It was a way of giving people jobs back then."

"Really?" Doe said, taking notes. "I didn't realize that."

"Yeah, they would sketch a floorplan, take photographs, and document all structures on the property."

"So, there should be a record of both the inn and the barn?" I asked. I felt a chill of excitement at the thought that we might find some concrete information about the hidden room.

"Yes, if the barn existed then."

"I was told it was built at the same time the original hotel was built. The hotel burned down, but the barn didn't," I said.

"Then it should be part of the record."

"What about changes to the structures themselves?" Doe asked.

Kris sat back. "The tax assessors' reports should note any permits obtained for major renovations or additional construction. They'll also show any demolitions."

"Are those available to the public?" Doe asked.

She nodded. "Oh, yes. You can look up anyone who owned the property and then also go to the paper to see if you can find any additional stories. Like when the fire destroyed the St. Claire home, there were probably stories about who bought the property and how they renovated it. There was also a weekly paper back in the 1920s. It was called the *Island Chatter*."

"Do you have any information here?" Doe asked.

"Sure. A couple of the families, including the Bremertons who built the original hotel, left some furniture and personal possessions behind that were donated to the museum. And John St. Claire moved out without taking anything. Over the years, many of the pieces were sold off, but some of the nicer pieces were kept, plus most of their personal possessions."

A lump formed in my throat to think that personal things that had once belonged to Elizabeth and Chloe were still here on the island. I wondered if they knew that.

"What about the ghosts?" Doe asked.

Kris smiled. "Well, we don't have anything that would prove the ghosts exist, but we have letters and diaries from some of the residents which might include stories *about* the ghosts. Actually, you'll have an entire treasure trove of things to research."

"We're also interested in any unusual stories about the property," I said, thinking we'd have to get to the gossip if we were going to find information about the hidden room.

Kris chuckled. "Well, there are lots of those. As a bona fide haunted location, there's an abundance of odd stories."

"I don't mean just about the ghosts," I said. "But also the families. My guess is that some of them had their own quirks and eccentricities."

I didn't want to push it and waited for her response. She seemed to consider my comment a moment.

"The person you ought to talk to is Lavelle Bennett. She's ninety-six now, I think, and lives at the Mercer Assisted Living Center. But she has all her faculties. Anyway, since she's lived her entire life on the island, and her mother before that, she'd be the best place to start."

"I've met Lavelle," Doe said. "A couple of times. Remember, we had that reception for her when she turned ninety?"

"Yes. She was a long-time volunteer here," Kris said to me. "I'm keeping my fingers crossed that she'll be around to celebrate her centennial. Why don't I ask my assistant to begin pulling some files on the property, while you take a shot at interviewing Lavelle? We can make our conference room available pretty much any time it's not being used and the museum is open."

"That sounds perfect," Doe said.

We all stood up and began moving towards the door.

"Should we call ahead to make an appointment with Lavelle?" I asked.

"I doubt it. Last time I was there, she was craving visitors. I imagine she'll be thrilled you've come to pay a call."

We left the museum and went directly to the Mercer Assisted Living Center, which sat near Luther Burbank Park, overlooking the water. It was a cream colored, three-story building, with a pleasant Southwestern style interior. We stepped up to a long counter to engage a young man. His name tag read "Ronald."

"We're here to see Lavelle Bennett," Doe said.

It was late afternoon, so we hoped to catch Lavelle before dinner. Ronald nodded and punched something into a computer. He looked up at us.

"She's in the solarium right now," he said. "I'll need you to sign in and take visitor badges."

We signed the register and filled in our names on sticky name badges. When we'd finished, he leaned forward and pointed down a hallway. "Just take this hallway past the restrooms. There will be a sign."

We thanked him and made our way to the back of the building where a big, open room encased by windows on three walls overlooked a patio and a large patch of lawn. The lawn sloped steeply toward the water, dropping off into the lake. There were perhaps fifteen people in the room, sitting and playing cards, reading, or just gazing outside.

Doe glanced around. "I don't see her. Oh, wait a minute. There she is," she said pointing outside.

I followed her gaze and saw a woman with puffy white hair sitting outside in a wheelchair next to a glass-topped table. I followed Doe onto the patio, which extended across the back of the building just in front of the large picture windows of the solarium. There were several residents parked out there, either at tables or in wheelchairs. A two-foot, flagstone wall separated the patio from the well-manicured lawn.

As we approached Lavelle, I decided to let Doe take the lead in introducing us. We moved in between a few of the residents and stepped around in front of Lavelle, whose eyes were closed as she dozed in the afternoon sun. Doe reached out to touch her forearm.

"Lavelle?" Doe said quietly. The woman didn't respond, so Doe touched her arm again. "Lavelle? Are you awake?"

Her eyes popped open, and she let out a screech that scared the beejeezus out of me, making me jump backwards. I slammed into a wheelchair behind me.

The chair lurched forward, and I turned just in time to see it heading for the short wall. Someone had forgotten to lock the wheels. The elderly woman in the chair let out an unearthly scream as she careened toward a nursing aide standing in front of the wall.

Hearing the scream, the aide began to turn just before the wheelchair slammed into her, throwing her over the wall. The wheelchair came to an abrupt halt, but the poor nursing aide did a front somersault and began rolling down the hill, picking up momentum as she went.

Time seemed to stop, as everyone watched in horror. As she approached the short drop off into the lake, I ran to the wall, not really knowing what I could do. At the last minute, she dug her toes into the grass and came to a jarring halt, inches from the ledge. In truth, the drop off was just a foot or two, so she probably wouldn't have been hurt, but still... she lay prone on the grass, feet and arms splayed, breathing hard.

Everyone on the patio turned to stare at me.

"I'm so sorry," I said, reaching out to pull the old woman's chair back.

A burly male attendant stepped in and grabbed it.

"I'll take care of her," he said. "Perhaps you could sit down somewhere before you kill someone."

I thrust out my chin. "It was just an accident," I said, watching the woman who I'd turned into a human bowling ball pull herself up off the grass. She might have been in her fifties and didn't look amused. As she hefted herself back up the slope, I felt a hand on my elbow.

"Julia, let's come back over here," Doe said. She pulled me over to where Lavelle Bennett sat.

"It was an accident," I repeated in my defense.

Doe just nodded. "I understand. Let's sit down."

We took seats at the table next to Lavelle, who was fully awake by this time and staring at me in surprise.

"You should play for the Seahawks," she said with a smile.

I tried to smile back, but came up short. My propensity for mishaps of this kind was legendary amongst my friends and a constant source of entertainment.

"I'm really sorry," I said to Lavelle. "I was just startled, that's all."

"That's okay," she said with a dismissive wave of her hand. "We don't get much entertainment around here, so this will be all the talk at dinner tonight and probably the rest of the week."

The woman who had taken the tumble struggled back over the wall to the patio. Her formerly starched white uniform was covered in patches of grass green and dirt brown. She leaned in to whisper something to the male attendant, and then gave me a hateful glance before disappearing inside.

Meanwhile, Lavelle said, "Don't worry about her. We call her Nurse Ratched. You just became our hero." She glanced over at Doe. "You're Doe Kovinsky. From the museum board."

"Yes," Doe said with a warm smile. "I was wondering if we could talk to you for a moment."

You could tell that Lavelle Bennet had been a strong woman during her life. She still had good bone structure, with wide-set eyes and a square jaw. And, while her skin sagged in soft folds around her eyes and chin, her eyes glinted with life.

"And you're Mrs. Applegate, aren't you?"

I smiled. "That's right. My name is Julia."

"I've read about you in the newspaper. It's so nice to have visitors," she said in a breathy voice. "My daughter lives in Stanwood and only gets down on the weekends."

"We were hoping you could help us. Julia owns the St. Claire Inn, and we're writing a book about its history. We were wondering if you recalled any interesting stories about the place," Doe said.

"We're working with Kris Sargent, down at the museum," I said. "But while she's pulling some things together for us, she suggested we come speak to you."

Her eyes lit up. "I do know some stories about that place," she said with a wry smile. "And it's not all about the ghosts, you know."

My heart rate sped up a notch. "That's exactly what we're hoping for. We know the property has a rich history. So we want to know everything." I pulled out a small tape recorder. "Do you mind if we record you?"

She swished a hand in front of her face again. "Of course not. Where should we begin?"

"As far back as you can remember, I suppose."

She straightened up in the chair and took a deep breath. "We lived in a small home about half a mile from the original hotel, up on SE 24th. I was born in 1923, just after the hotel burned down," she said. "But my mother used to talk about how grand it was to have such a fancy hotel on the island. Lots of dignitaries and famous people would ferry over from Seattle to stay there. They played croquet out on the lawn during the summer and had lavish parties with fireworks over the lake. The locals would sit up on the hillside and watch. That was before all those homes were there, of course. I guess even a state senator held his daughter's wedding at the hotel. It was a big deal because they had to bring everything over from the mainland. The island was pretty rural back then, so there weren't a lot of services over here."

"And the horse barn was used for horses and carriages?" I asked.

"Oh yes. While there were a few cars in Seattle, there weren't many on the island, yet. Our roads weren't very good, and it was difficult to get them over here or serviced if they broke down. I remember Mr. Bremerton had one, though. But he didn't let anyone else drive it. He paid to have the road from the ferry to the hotel plowed every year, so he could drive it back and forth to pick up important guests. But horse and carriage was still the main means of transportation over here."

Lavelle went on to talk a lot about the Bremertons, who owned the hotel. Her mother had been a teacher in those days, and so knew a lot about the goings-on there through the Bremerton children. But things didn't get interesting until Lavelle moved on to 1930, when Gramley Miller rebuilt the hotel after the fire and turned it into a brothel.

"That was a big deal on the island, let me tell you," she said with her eyebrows raised. "No one wanted a brothel over here. It was exactly the opposite of what the hotel had given us. Instead of lavish parties with upscale dignitaries, there were all sorts of low-life people coming over on the ferry. That was back during Prohibition, you know. But we were so isolated, the owners got away with having alcohol. And even if the law showed up, the rumor was that Miller had places to hide the booze. Anyway, drunks started appearing on people's property and in the downtown area. And our police force was so small, they had trouble handling it."

"Were there any stories about trouble at the brothel?" I asked, trying to be careful not to alert her to where I was going.

"Oh yes," she said. "I was eleven when one of the girls was murdered there."

"Murdered?" I said.

"What happened?" Doe asked.

"I guess one of the men strangled her because she wouldn't do what he wanted her to do. Of course, back then, my mother tried to whitewash what really happened. But the kids all knew what was going on over there. Then there was the guy found floating in the lake."

"What happened to him?" I asked

"No one knew. As I recall, they ruled it an accident. He'd been drinking, so they thought he might have fallen in the lake and drowned. But I know my mother thought he'd also been murdered because he had a cracked skull."

"Boy, I had no idea," I said. "I wonder if we'll be able to corroborate any of that. Do you remember when it was?"

"We had a little weekly newspaper back then," she said. "I forget what it was called."

"Kris said it was the *Island Chatter*," I said.

"Oh, that's right," she said. "It didn't have a very big circulation, but I bet Kris has copies in the museum. You might be able to find a story or two. There's lots of history to your property," she said to me. "My dad told me years later that there was even a room upstairs in the barn where they'd lock up the drunks until they sobered up."

A light bulb burst to life in my head. "Really?"

"Yeah. I guess it was a makeshift jail. Makes sense," she said with a shrug. "There was a jail downtown, but it was small and getting people down there would have been a problem. So if someone was too drunk or causing trouble, my mom said they'd lock them up in the barn overnight. Anyway, after the brothel burned down, the property stood empty for quite a while. We kids would go over and play in the barn. There was never a good feeling upstairs in that attic though, so we just played down where they kept the horses."

"That bad feeling is still there," I told her. "No one likes to go up there."

"Well, there's no telling what Miller did to the girls over there. He was a mean son-of-a-bitch," she said with distaste. "He'd shoot people's dogs or livestock if they strayed onto his property, and rumor had it that he forced the women to work there. I guess a lot of them were young and poor and weren't there willingly."

"So he might have kept women as prisoners?" I asked, horrified.

"That could've just been a rumor, of course, but I wouldn't have put it past him. His wife was gone, but he had a son my age. His name was Joshua. I hated that kid. He was as mean as his dad. He'd try to feel up all the girls, and I remember once he cut the head off a squirrel and put it in someone's desk, just because the kid wouldn't hand over his lunch to him the day before. Believe me, no one was sorry when the place burned down and they moved away."

"Do you think someone could have set the fire on purpose?" Doe asked.

"Funny you should ask. The fire happened just after Prohibition ended. Other bars were opening up in Seattle, and the business here on the island dropped off. Rumor had it that Miller set the fire himself so he could collect the insurance."

She gave us a 'know what I mean?' wink just as the dinner bell rang.

CHAPTER EIGHT

We offered to wheel Lavelle to the dining room, which was just down the hall. As we rolled her in, we were greeted with a polite applause from a table of women by the door.

"Told you," Lavelle said over her shoulder. "You're a celebrity."

Doe deposited Lavelle at a table in the middle of the room. "Thanks, Lavelle. I hope we can visit you again soon."

"Absolutely," she replied, taking Doe's hand. "I have a lot more I could tell you."

Doe patted her shoulder. As we turned to leave, Lavelle's dinner companions giggled, throwing glances at me. I assumed it was in reference to Nurse Ratched's near death experience on the lawn outside. I hurried out, avoiding any more eye contact.

"The Hero of Mercer Island strikes again," Doe said under her breath as we walked toward the front counter.

"Very funny," I spat back. "But the Mayor gave us those awards because we saved a young woman from a sex trafficking ring and helped bring a murderer to justice, not because we were taking out aides at a nursing home."

"This isn't a nursing home," Doe chided me as we turned in our name badges and signed out.

"I know that. That's not the point. I just don't want people thinking I knocked that woman down the hill on purpose."

Doe put a hand on my shoulder. "No one ever thinks you do these things on purpose, Julia. We know it's just…circumstance."

"And that I'm a klutz."

"No. You're not a klutz. Things just seem to happen to you."

"Things that don't happen to other people," I said churlishly.

I turned for the front door and pushed through to the walkway.

"We all bear our burdens, Julia," Doe continued as we headed toward the car. "I'm obsessed with work to the exclusion of hobbies, or frankly, even men. Rudy is cynical to the point I think it blurs her vision at times. And Blair…well, Blair is just Blair."

I laughed. "No need to explain that one."

We got to Doe's Mercedes, and I stopped at the curb. Another car was just pulling into the space next to it.

"Personally, I find your…klutziness…as you call it, one of the most endearing things about you," Doe said from the other side of the car. "Really. I do."

"Thanks. I appreciate that," I said, stepping off the curb and up to the car door.

I grabbed the straps of my purse and swung the bag around to loop it over my shoulder, but my timing was off. I slammed it right into the face of the man getting out of the car next to us. He rebounded against his car door with a cry of surprise, his hand to the side of his face.

I glanced quickly at Doe. She cocked her head to one side with a smile and got into the car, while I turned to make my apologies and render aid.

÷

Doe left me at the inn, and I was just about to make dinner when I got a call from David. Since Sean, his boss, was serving on the task force investigating the serial killings, David was holding down the fort on Mercer Island. He sounded tired and frustrated and asked if he could take a break and stop by. He offered to bring Italian food, so I offered to set a table on the back patio.

The Welches were out for dinner in Seattle and things were quiet. April had retired to the guest house early. Our night manager was on duty at the front desk until 10:00 p.m., when I would take over and be on call until morning.

I set a round glass table by the patio door for dinner and had the sunken fire pit crackling just for ambience. The evening was warm and clear, and Lake Washington was a picture of white clouds and sail boats. Our large, earthen pots were strategically placed around the deck, filled with an assortment of flowering annuals to add color, and several birdfeeders served as fast food joints for the birds and squirrels in the area. The view could have been a page right out of a travel magazine.

David arrived in a long-sleeved shirt, tie and crisp dark slacks. His broad shoulders were slumped, and those brown eyes that I counted on to cheer me up seemed bleary. He carried a brown paper bag filled with aluminum trays of eggplant parmesan, noodles, and garlic bread. He placed the trays on the table and then straightened up and stretched.

"You look exhausted," I said.

I popped open a Coke and handed it over to him and then began to serve up the food. He slumped into one of the cushioned deck chairs and loosened his tie.

"It's been brutal," he said. "You know, I worked as a cop in Baltimore before we moved here. I even worked two serial murder cases back then. And yet, I've never seen anything like this. These deaths are clearly related, and yet there is not a shred of evidence to go on." He took a long drink and then reached out and grabbed my hand and drew me to him. "Sorry, I didn't properly say hello."

I leaned down to share a moment of bliss as our lips touched. "Not to worry," I said when I re-emerged. "I'm just glad you could get away for a few moments. Where's Sean now?"

"He went back to Seattle. He and Angela went out to grab a bite."

"And then everyone's back at it, I guess," I said.

He took another long drink and then sighed. "Yeah. Sean spends most of his time with the task force over there, while I handle stuff here. He was here this afternoon because we ID'd the body that washed up under the bridge."

I was about to scoop some eggplant parmesan onto his plate. "And?"

"It will be in the paper tomorrow. She's from the island. So now it really does bring the case home."

I finished serving and dropped into a chair. "Who is she?"

"A girl named Melody Reamer. Seventeen. Been missing since just before Christmas. So she's obviously the most recent victim. Now we're trying to recreate her life before she disappeared." He sighed again before picking up his fork.

"And she'd been murdered in the same way as those other girls you found?"

"Yes." David stopped talking and just stared at his plate.

Three other bodies had been found over the course of two months; two of the bodies appeared to have been in the ground several years. All were young women in their late teens, with long blond hair. The reason a serial killer was suspected was that each of them had been killed by using a garrote. David said the medical examiner had determined this because the bones at the base of each throat had been thinly sliced with something like a wire under pressure. In one case, the wire had cut almost two inches into the neck bones.

"Do you have any idea why these bodies are suddenly showing up?" I asked, cutting off a piece of eggplant.

He looked up and rotated his neck to release tension. "We conferred with a geologist, and he thinks it's because of the harsh winter we had. The bodies had been buried in shallow graves or on hills. Rain washed away the topsoil or the hillsides gave way."

"What about the one that washed up on shore here?"

He paused a moment, as if reliving seeing Melody Reamer for the first time. "She'd been weighted down with something tied around her ankles. But she must have gotten caught in some rocks, and the ropes were cut loose. She just floated to the surface." He rubbed his eyes, as if that might dispel the image.

I reached out and placed my hand on his forearm. "I'm sorry, David. This must be a really tough case."

"Yeah," he said, sitting back. "You know, my wife, Jolene, always wanted a daughter. It was something that just wasn't meant to be though, and something that always bothered her. I mean, don't get me wrong, I love my son. But I knew there was a hole in Jolene's heart for the girl she never had." He stared out at the lake for a moment. "We talked about adopting, but she just wasn't interested. She went to her grave carrying that sadness. So, I think about these girls and what it must be like for their parents. It was hard enough to watch my wife go through life without ever having had the chance to have a daughter. Imagine what it must be like to lose one?"

His haunted expression cut me to the core. I thought of Angela and how I would survive if anything ever happened to her, and all of a sudden I didn't have an appetite.

I pushed my plate away. "It would be a pain that would be with you forever."

There was a long moment of silence between us. The sound of a motor boat coming close to shore brought us out of our reverie.

"Well, we have a mystery of our own," I said with false enthusiasm.

He turned tired eyes my way. "What's that?"

I filled him in on the secret room and the idea to write a book. He looked mildly interested and seemed to force his mind away from the gruesome details of the investigation. He reached out and put his hand over mine.

"I like this idea, Julia," he said. "You're creative. In fact, all of you are. And Rudy could do the writing. Just don't get in trouble again. I won't be available to help you out for a while."

I smiled. "I won't. This is more of a mystery of manners. We're just very curious as to why someone would have had a locked room up in the attic and then cover it up with drywall. Doesn't it seem odd to you?"

He shrugged. "Yes. But you never know what secrets are worth keeping secret."

"Meaning?"

"Meaning…you never know what someone will do to *keep* their secret. Just be careful."

CHAPTER NINE

After David left, I called Goldie and asked if I could come over. Although her incessant talking and urge to carry a shotgun drove Doe nuts, I usually enjoyed her quirky personality.

She and Ben lived in a large, ramshackle home that sat just north of the inn. I often walked over the back way, through a short grove of trees along the water. But tonight, I went out the front door to the street and down their driveway, passing a myriad of colorful gnomes on the way. Goldie had hundreds of them inside and out, some peeking out from behind a leaf or bush, some arranged into family groups.

A large gnome guarded the front door. Its big, pointy red hat looked slightly lethal under the fading evening light, and its leering grin gave me a little chill. It was hard not to imagine that he had strange, devious thoughts. And yet a light-spirited melody jingled when I rang the doorbell. I shared the porch with the creepy gnome until the distorted shape of a small woman appeared through the cut glass sidelight.

"Hey, Julia," Goldie said opening the door. "Come on in."

I stepped across the threshold into what I thought of as Goldie's alternate universe. Her home was filled with an eclectic collection of souvenirs, artwork and furniture from their travels around the world. As I glanced at the dark hardwood floors and dark wood paneling, mosaic carpet runners and a mix of framed prints and paintings, I wondered where in the world Goldie would put a piece of her own artwork, since every nook and cranny was filled. A cloisonné vase from Tibet. A framed original poster from the movie *Chinatown*. An ottoman made to look like an elephant's foot. A collection of Murano glass jars from Italy. A pewter teapot from Poland. Everywhere you looked, there was something to catch and hold your interest.

"Sorry to bother you guys so late," I said, shifting my gaze away from a snow globe from the Black Forest. "But I wanted to tell you about a project we've decided to undertake."

While I only stood 5'2", Goldie was even shorter than me, although heavier in the hips. She and Ben were holdovers from the seventies. In fact, Goldie still dressed like a college student. But Ben had served in the military and had earned the nickname "The General" from people in the neighborhood for the way he strode the streets with his walking stick. He was close to six-feet tall, with a barrel chest, broad shoulders and a booming voice. And he walked and talked as if he were commanding, or at least reviewing, the troops.

"You and the girls have a project? Wow, that sounds interesting. Go on into the living room. I just brewed some coffee," Goldie said, bustling into the kitchen.

I stepped down into the sunken living room, with its thick, plush carpet and large river stone fireplace. Ben was sitting in a high-backed leather chair, reading under a Tiffany lamp.

"It's good to see you, Julia," he said, closing his book and standing up. I caught a glimpse of the title as he set the book down. It was General Stanley McChrystal's, *Team of Teams*. Ben gestured to a chair opposite his. "Have a seat. What can we do for you?"

"I wanted to tell you guys about a project and get your input."

"I saw the Piper Construction truck over there the other day. I hope you're not renovating the inn. It seems perfect the way it is," he said. He reached over and grabbed a match to relight his pipe.

"No, we're not renovating. We just have to fix the roof on the carriage barn. With all the rain we had last winter, we found some leaks. This is something different."

"Different how?" Goldie said, coming in with a tray of mugs filled with steaming liquid. She set the tray down on a large, Moroccan coffee table inlaid with abalone. She gave me a mug and then took one to her husband. "What's up?"

I leaned forward and added sugar and cream to my coffee and then sat back in my chair, cradling the mug between my hands. "The girls and I have decided to do something different with our book club this summer. Instead of reading a book, we're going to write one."

Goldie's gray eyes flew open and her impish face came alight. "Are you gonna write a mystery? Cuz, boy, you could come up with some good ones after all the mysteries you guys have solved."

I smiled to myself. "No, it won't have anything to do with a murder mystery. Although it does involve a mystery of sorts."

"What's that, Julia?" Ben asked, chewing on his pipe.

I shifted uncomfortably, wondering how much I should tell them, remembering David's warning. "Mr. Piper had to remove a wall up in the barn's attic and he found a tiny, hidden room. There were some…uh…toys and furniture in it, as if someone had used it as storage, but of course we wondered why it had been covered up."

"Oooh, oooh," Goldie uttered. "Maybe someone was living up there."

"We thought of that, but there isn't any electricity or plumbing. Anyway, when we found it, we thought there must be a lot of interesting stories about the property, all the way back to when the hotel was there. So we've decided to write a book. Maybe in the process, we'll uncover the story about the hidden room."

"Oooh," Goldie cooed again. "You could call it *The History of the St. Claire Inn.*"

I paused. "Um…yes, that would be a good title."

"Seems like you should pay a visit to the museum," Ben said thoughtfully. "I bet they have boxes of stuff."

"Doe and I were down there today. But I was hoping that maybe you might have some stories to tell. You've lived here long enough to see at least a couple of families go through there."

"Oh, more than that," Ben said, rolling his eyes. "We've seen some strange things all through this neighborhood, haven't we Goldie?"

Goldie was like a self-contained energy source. She had quick, frenetic movements and always seemed to be in motion. Just then, she was sitting at the end of the sofa almost bouncing up and down like a child.

"Sure have, Ben. Like that couple on the corner who were into S & M."

Ben scowled. "I doubt that's the kind of story Julia's interested in."

"Well, we've been here since the Pattisons, and they moved out in…something like 1975."

"Seventy-six," Ben corrected her.

"Oh, yeah. We built our home in 1974."

"They were an odd pair," Ben mumbled. "Always touching each other."

A laugh bubbled up in my throat. "Really? *Touching* each other?"

"Yeah," Goldie said with a chortle. "They had two little girls, you know? The girls always held hands. And every time we saw the parents, one of them had a hand on the other. In fact," Goldie said excitedly, "I remember Mrs. Pattison liked to smooth out Mr. Pattison's shirts. Just smoothing," Goldie said, demonstrating in thin air. "All the time…smoothing."

"And Mr. Pattison liked to tap his fingers on his wife's shoulder. I never could quite understand that. Was he reminding her of something? Or just making sure she was still there?" Ben said with a smile.

"They were weird, let me tell you," Goldie added.

I pulled a small notepad from my pocket. "Do you mind if I take notes. This is great stuff."

Goldie's eyes opened with enthusiasm. "Oh, there's more," she said. "The Kettle sisters were my favorite. The property stood vacant for years after the Pattisons left, you know, probably because of the ghosts. But the Kettle sisters finally came along and bought it. They were twins. Tall. Skinny. And *really* old."

"Now, Goldie," Ben admonished her.

"I don't mean anything by that. After all, I'm old as dirt," she said with a laugh, followed by a snort. "But they musta been in their seventies when they bought that big property. Just the two of 'em. And then all of a sudden they started holding séances."

That got my attention. "I never heard about that."

"Oh, I musta mentioned it to you once or twice," Goldie said with a wave of her hand. "Didn't I ever mention the Kettle parties?"

"Well, yes, but I didn't realize they were séances. So the sisters knew about the ghosts."

Ben chuckled. "There were all sorts of rumors about the ghosts, Julia. If people didn't know about them when they moved in, they found out quickly enough. And we're pretty sure that's why most people moved out so quickly. But the Kettle sisters were different. They *wanted* to communicate with the ghosts. They had some phony-baloney psychic named Miss LaFontaine who would show up in long, colorful robes."

"Did she wear a turban?" I asked, holding back a chuckle.

"No, but she had everything else, including big, gaudy jewelry. In fact, she wore a pendant with an eye in the middle of it." Ben shook his head in disdain.

"She even had a crystal ball," Goldie added, almost clapping her hands in delight.

"You're kidding." This was better than I'd imagined.

Ben smiled. "We got invited to one of the parties, and the only thing that happened was a scarf that Miss LaFontaine was wearing kept falling to the floor."

"It was funny," Goldie snickered. "She kept wrapping it back around her neck, and then it would fall to the floor a few minutes later. She'd look around to see if someone was yanking it off and playing a joke on her."

"Oh, *someone* was playing a joke on her, all right," I said. "I bet that was Chloe. She loves to do stuff like that."

Goldie's eyes grew wide. "So you think the ghosts were there?"

"The ghosts are always there," I confirmed. "It's just that they pick and choose when they'll make themselves known. Remember that Chloe was just ten years-old when she died. She loves to play tricks on people."

"Well, if that scarf trick was Chloe, it's the only supernatural thing that ever happened at one of those parties that I'm aware of," Ben said.

"That must've been a disappointment," I lamented.

"Yes, but the sisters musta seen the ghosts at other times," Goldie added. "I heard a scream or two from over there during the summer. Curdled your blood, I tell you. I'm not sure how you do it, Julia. We were in the living room when Elizabeth showed up at that party you had back in February. That was as spooky as it gets."

"You'd never seen her before?"

They both shook their heads.

"I've been over there when odd things have happened," Goldie said. "When a cupboard closed by itself or a cup moved."

"Me too," Ben said with a nod. "But I always explained it away. As a military man, I don't usually give in to flighty things like believing in ghosts," he said, looking at me over the rim of his glasses. "So I've been a skeptic all these years. But there was no ignoring that night your friend disappeared."

He was referring to the night we'd invited Jason Spears to do a little ghost hunting at the inn. He'd written a book called, *The Most Haunted Hotels in the Northwest*, in which the inn was featured. It was the same night that Dana Finkle had been abducted and almost killed. Elizabeth had appeared in order to alert us that Dana was gone.

"Elizabeth has helped out on numerous occasions. But I doubt she would like to be used for entertainment," I said, bringing the discussion back to the Kettle sisters. "Where did the Kettle sisters hold the séances?"

"Up in the attic," Goldie said.

My heart rate sped up. "The attic? In the barn?"

"No. Upstairs in the main house," she replied. "But I heard they held one out in the old horse barn, but even Miss LaFontaine wouldn't stay up there. She said she kept hearing voices and then she got a bad headache and had to be taken back to the house."

I wondered if Miss LaFontaine had more psychic talent than they realized, since that was exactly what had happened to April.

"Their niece died shortly after that," Goldie said, "And the sisters moved to Queen Anne Hill to take care of her daughter."

I was furiously taking notes. "Any idea what the niece's name was?"

"Sure," Goldie said. "She married the son of Anthony Ferrar."

"The big railroad guy?"

"Yep," she said. "Their grandniece, the one they helped raise, later landed Randall Rolston, the banker. I think she still lives in the family home on Queen Anne. But you know, that barn of yours is a funny place," Goldie mused. "Vicky Pattison told me that one night when they were out barbequing, they saw a light up in the attic. She said it flickered and moved around like someone walking back and forth with a candle. But when they went up to check, no one was there."

"We've never seen anything like that. How did most people use the carriage barn, anyway?" I asked, hoping to identify a reason for the hidden room.

Goldie shrugged. "I think just as a garage or for storage. Although the Crenshaws tried raising and selling rabbits. They bought the property from the Formosas."

"And John Crenshaw used to restore old cars out there," Ben said. He arched his brows as he tapped out the old tobacco from his pipe. "But he had a temper, I'll tell you."

"What do you mean?" I asked.

Ben shared a cautious look with his wife. "Crenshaw's wife was quite a good-looking woman, and he had four daughters. I saw him run off a young kid more than once who was trying to woo one of the daughters. We also heard that his wife had an affair or two. In fact, Crenshaw was arrested once for hitting his wife."

Goldie leaned forward in her seat again. "Yeah, and then one of the daughters had a baby," she said, as if she was telling a state secret.

"A baby?" I said, perking up.

"Yeah, it was Ruthie, the oldest one," Goldie said. "She was real pretty, but kind of out-of-control, if you know what I mean."

"What happened to the baby?"

She shrugged her rounded shoulders. "Don't know. One minute she was going to keep it, and the next minute the baby was gone."

"I figured they gave it up for adoption," Ben said. "They never talked about it much. In fact, while the girl was pregnant, they just took her out of school and kept her home until the baby was born."

My mind was racing, wondering if Ruthie Crenshaw had kept the baby in the little hidden room for some reason.

"Do you know why they moved away?" I asked.

Ben leaned back in his chair and crossed his long legs at the ankles. "John Crenshaw owned a trucking company. He was around big burly men all day, and yet he was scared to death of living in that house."

"The ghosts again," I said.

"He never mentioned them, but he often talked about how oppressive it was over there and how the barn had an evil presence. He said his wife and daughters were frightened to live there. We have it on good authority that they even called out an exorcist to try to rid the barn of the evil presence."

"You're kidding," I said..

"That barn has been there a very long time," Ben said. "Something bad could have happened out there. If I had to put money on who owned the property when something bad did happen, I'd vote for the brothel."

"We met Lavelle Bennet today," I said. "She talked about the brothel. Do you know her?"

"Sure. She used to live up by Mercerdale Park. She's got to be *really* old, though," Goldie said.

"Yes," I said, with a smile. "I'd bet she's even older than dirt."

Goldie chuckled and then snorted again. "Good one, Julia. What did she have to say?"

"She told us about two possible murders there. She also suggested that the guy who owned the brothel forced the women into prostitution and then burned the place down once Prohibition ended."

"You know, Jack Pattinson said something once about a possible murder over there," Ben said, leaning back and sucking on his pipe. "He'd heard from the realtor that there had been some trouble on the property. You know, Julia, a number of these families have lived on the island for generations. I'd bet with some real digging, you'll get some great stories."

"Well, Milton Snyder mentioned a murder to me the other night at the art class," I said.

"That old fart?" Goldie said. "I wouldn't listen to him."

"Now, Goldie, his family has lived here for decades."

"Yeah, but I think he'd say anything to get attention."

"I don't plan on interviewing him," I told her. "I don't like him any more than you do. But we have a lot of research to do. A lot of families lived there."

"Like the Formosas?" Goldie said. "I always thought they were hiding something."

"Why do you say that?" I asked.

"We saw them just a couple of times, but they were a mixed family, like us," Ben said, gesturing to Goldie. Goldie was white. Ben was African-American. "Mr. Formosa was Asian, but his wife was white. I think Mr. Formosa may have worked for the government. There were often big black cars that came and went from over there."

"And men in dark suits hanging around outside," Goldie said. "They lived there less than two years."

"Yep," Ben said. "Moved out right after we heard gun shots."

"Gun shots?"

"Yeah. And this time, it wasn't me," Goldie said with a twinkle in her eye.

Goldie had a reputation in the neighborhood for shooting off her father's shotgun. She'd even put a hole in my ceiling one night in February when an intruder had me in a chokehold.

"Who got shot?" I asked.

"We were told no one," Ben said. "The police came out and said a gun went off accidentally."

"But you said gun *shots*, as in multiple shots," I reminded him.

He glanced at his wife. "Yep, that's what I said. We heard at least two shots."

"So a gun went off accidentally, twice?"

He merely raised an eyebrow. "That's how they explained it."

Ben was a bit of a conspiracy theorist, so I wondered if this story was true, or if he was embellishing it.

÷

I left Ben and Goldie around 8:00 p.m., my mind reeling with all this new information. There had been a whole bunch of weird things connected to the St. Claire Inn. I huddled up in my living room with the dogs and sorted through my notes, including the notes I'd taken several years earlier.

What I knew for sure was that the Bremertons had originally built a hotel on the property in the early 1900s. That's also the same time the carriage barn was built. The hotel existed for some twenty years, until a fire destroyed most of it. It was rebuilt and then a man named Gramley Miller bought it and used it as a brothel.

Whether by accident or on purpose once again, fire destroyed the building in 1935, and the property remained unclaimed until John St. Claire bought it in 1945. He demolished what was left of the brothel and built his home. Fire would kill his wife and two of his children in 1962, prompting him to take his remaining child and leave the island. After that a string of owners would live there until Graham and I bought it in 2003.

As I sat and thought about the barn and its long history, it dawned on me that despite the fact that the crib and rocker we'd found in the attic were from the late twentieth century, the hidden room may have been built when the barn was built. Who knows what the owners of the old hotel may have used it for? We already knew the brothel had used it as a makeshift drunk tank, so back then it wasn't hidden.

For some reason, at some point in time, someone had put up a false wall to hide the room and its contents and then added a padlock. Why?

The mystery deepened.

CHAPTER TEN

I awoke the next day filled with a renewed sense of enthusiasm for the book. I had no illusions that it would appeal to anyone but people who lived on the island and possibly some of the guests that stayed at the inn, but the inn's story was beginning to sound more colorful than I had originally imagined.

We had decided to go to the museum as a group to do some research, so all four of us rode in Doe's big Mercedes down to the old Victorian home/museum. On the way, Rudy filled us in on some research she'd already done on her own.

"I was able to access the tax records," she said from the back seat. "And I put together a timeline."

She produced copies of a list she'd made, showing the property timeline, along with a few notes on some of the families.

1906 – 1920	Bremertons built the hotel and the carriage barn. The hotel burned in 1920.
1920 – 1929	Property vacant. Gramley Miller bought in late 1929 and built brothel.
1929 – 1935	Brothel opened mid-year 1930. Burned in 1935.
1935 – 1944	Property vacant.
1945 – 1963	John & Elizabeth St. Claire built home. Partially burned in 1963.
1963 – 1967	Property vacant.
1968 – 1970	Robert & Holly Foster bought in 1967/remodel and move in w/children.

1970 – 1973	Property vacant.
1973 – 1976	Oliver and Nancy Pattison – renovated upstairs.
1976 – 1979	Property vacant.
1979 – 1983	Pettie & Pearl Kettle bought and renovated kitchen.
1983 – 1984	Leased by Puget Sound Security (Robert & Vera Formosa).
1984 – 1989	Property vacant.
1989 – 1996	Peter & Rouanne Crenshaw – added guest house
1997 – 2002	Property vacant.
2003 – Present	Graham & Julia Applegate, now the St. Claire Inn.

"I got copies of building and renovation plans and permits, too," Rudy said. "That's how I was able to see when the building had been renovated. For instance, it sounded like the hotel was quite a bit larger than what the inn is now and more dramatic in its style. I'm hoping the museum will have some pictures. But fire destroyed most of that building. So when Gramley Miller bought it for the brothel, he had to tear it down and start from scratch. The brothel ended up much smaller in comparison and not nearly as ornate."

"You don't need scroll work on the front porch for that kind of business," Blair said cynically. "All you need are a couple of beds."

"Well, speaking of the brothel," I said, "Doe and I learned a lot from Lavelle Bennet down at the assisted living center yesterday."

I filled them in on what Lavelle had told us, including the story about the death of one of the prostitutes, the drunk found floating in the lake, and that Gramley Miller may have used the attic in the barn as a jail. Thankfully, Doe was concentrating on driving and didn't mention anything about my almost killing one of the employees.

We met Kris Sargent in her office, where she passed out cotton gloves and instructed us on how to handle the materials to avoid damage. She traded our pens for pencils, and then she took us to the conference room, which had been the original dining room of the old home. Set at one end of the table were two file boxes, a shoebox, and several fat manila envelopes.

"This is the paperwork and photos we have on the property," she said. "There are also some furniture, clothing and household items in storage if you're interested. The only family we don't have anything on are the Formosas."

"How'd you get all this stuff?" Rudy asked.

She shrugged. "Many times people donate things that have been in the family a long time. But in the case of your property, Mrs. Applegate, most of the families left in a hurry," she said with a lift to her eyebrows.

"The ghosts?" I asked.

"That and the fires. We also consider it a historical property because of the hotel having been there, so we ask the realtors to let families know we'd be interested in anything they might find after they've moved in. You'd be surprised what people find tucked away behind posts or even plastered into walls. Plus, we've added to the collections, especially with old newspaper articles and photos." She moved towards the door. "Just let me know if you need anything else."

I thanked her, and she left us to get started. I moved to the end of the long table and pulled the boxes over.

"We'll have to be careful to keep the families separate," I said, sorting through the big envelopes. "Here, Blair, why don't you take the Bremertons." I slid the archival box toward her. "Rudy, why don't you take the Pattisons." I slid two envelopes in her direction.

"Did Goldie or Ben have anything to say about them?" she asked.

"Just that they were always touching each other," I said with a rueful smile. "Even the kids."

She raised an eyebrow. "Well, that should be interesting."

"Doe and I can start on the big boxes. When all is said and done, I'm hoping we can get some real working facts and photos."

Everyone donned the gloves, and we got down to work. We took notes on family names, births, deaths, weddings, photographs and interesting tidbits. It was a long and arduous process. Several times, one of us was up making a Xerox copy of something we thought we might want to include in the book or holding up a photograph for the rest of us to see.

After almost two hours, Doe spoke up. "Here's something interesting. Ruthie Crenshaw, daughter of Peter and Rouanne, had a baby out of wedlock."

"Goldie mentioned that," I said, putting down a folder on the Kettle sisters. "But how did you find that out?"

"It's in this diary," Doe said, holding up a small blue book, frayed around the edges. "Let me read this to you. *'Today was a tough day. I found out for sure that I'm pregnant. I know that it's Bob's baby, but I'm afraid he's not going to want it.'*" Doe flipped ahead a few pages and continued to read. "'*Bob told me I ought to get rid of the baby. He doesn't want it. I cried so hard. I thought he loved me.*'" Doe flipped forward several more pages. "Here's where it gets really good," Doe said. "'*We brought little Brianna home today. She's so beautiful. I never thought I could love something so much. I just wish my mom and dad weren't so angry. They still want me to give her up for adoption. But until then, they have set up a nursery in the attic upstairs.*" She flipped back and forth through a few more pages. "That's the last entry in the diary."

"The attic?" I asked.

"Yeah, that's what it says," Doe replied, glancing back at the page. "Do you think that's the hidden room?"

"Wait," Rudy said. "Wouldn't that be the wrong attic? She says upstairs. That makes me think it's the attic in the inn."

"True," I agreed. "But maybe not. Maybe she just didn't make a distinction."

"But why set up a nursery in the attic in the barn?" Blair argued. "You wouldn't put a baby to sleep out there and then go back to the house."

"That's the point, I guess," I said. "We can't figure out why anyone would keep a baby up there. Goldie and Ben did say that the family took Ruthie out of school while she was pregnant, and then they thought they put the baby up for adoption. Let's make note of the information, but I don't think we ought to use it in the book."

"At least not without Ruthie Crenshaw's permission," Rudy said. "According to my timeline, they were there in the early 90s. So she could be very much alive somewhere. We ought to try and find her."

"I agree," I said, making a note on a yellow notepad by my side. "In fact, we're probably going to have to get permission to use a lot of this information," I said, nodding at the stacks of pictures and notes on the table.

"Good point," Doe said. "We'll have to have a chat with Kris about that."

I opened a second box and pulled out a handful of paper. I shuffled through the top layer and then stopped. "Well, surprise, surprise. Judge Wendell Foster lived there at one time."

Everyone stopped and looked up from what they were doing.

"You've got to be kidding," Doe said. "That old coot?"

"Wait a minute," Rudy said, pulling out her property timeline. "Is Robert his first name?"

76

"Uh...just a second. I have a newspaper clipping from April, 1968." I flipped through a stack of paper. "Yeah, here it is. It announces that Judge Robert Wendell Foster and family had finished renovating the St. Claire property and moved in. It even has a picture, although it's not very good."

"That explains it," Rudy said. "I found the Foster name in the tax records, but there he was listed as Robert. I'm kind of surprised it's not more well-known that the judge lived on the island."

"Maybe no one wants to acknowledge it," Blair said.

Judge Wendell Foster was a living legend in the area, but not in a good way. He was the modern-day version of the Wild West's hanging judge. His reputation was that of a strict, if not brutal, justice who handed down the toughest sentences and was overly cruel in his verbal judgements. He was known to terrorize prosecuting and defense attorneys alike. Graham had had to prosecute several cases in Foster's court and always came home looking beleaguered and defeated, heading straight for the liquor cabinet.

"Maybe Elizabeth scared him off," Blair said. "I remember a law suit filed against him by one of his female law clerks, who said he was a misogynistic pig. I doubt he'd like the ghost of a woman wandering through his home uninvited."

"I remember that lawsuit," Doe said. "He liked to belittle women and put them in their place. Let's face it, as a ghost, Elizabeth would have been in control," Doe said. "After all, he couldn't very well send her to jail."

Everyone chuckled.

"Or commit her to a life sentence," Blair said.

"No, since she's already serving one," I said.

I had not only grown accustomed to the ghosts at the St. Claire Inn, I felt protective of them. I often thought about Elizabeth stuck for eternity, roaming the halls wondering where she was. It made me sad.

"Is Judge Foster even still alive?" Rudy asked.

"I think so," Doe replied. "At least I've never heard that he died. He's not on the bench anymore, though."

"No," Rudy said with a sigh. "He retired from the State Supreme Court eight or ten years ago, I think. He's got to be in his nineties by now."

"Well, he's certainly one I wouldn't want to write about without his permission," I said.

I was sorting through things in the cardboard box when I found an article in *Newsweek* about Judge Foster. The date was 1971. I sat down to read it and learned that he and his wife, Holly, had three children. The oldest was a daughter, named Rose. The middle child was a son named Mansfield. And then they had a younger daughter named Emily. I related this to the group.

"I think his son is also a judge," Rudy said.

"Jeez, two in one family," Blair said. "I wonder if he's as awful as his dad."

"Foster's wife's name was Holly," I said, glancing up at Doe.

"So?" Doe asked.

"You might want to see this." I passed her the old magazine.

Doe glanced down and her dark eyes grew large. "She looks just like me."

Blair leaned over to study the photo. "Ewww, she does. That's creepy."

Holly Foster was tall and slender, like Doe, with the same thick salt and pepper-colored hair, high cheek bones and dark eyes. The likeness was eerie. Doe passed the photo to Rudy.

"Whoa," Rudy said. "You have a doppelgänger."

"I'm not sure I like that," Doe said.

"Here's something else," I said, holding up a newspaper clipping from the *The Island News*. "It's an article reporting that Rose Foster, the oldest daughter, was found dead, floating in the lake. It says here that it was a tragic accident. She was only sixteen."

"I don't remember that," Rudy said. She made a note on the pad of paper next to her. "Isn't *The Island News* the old weekly around here?"

I nodded. "Yeah. I guess back when the Bremertons built the hotel, they had something called *The Island Chatter*. Then it became *The Island News*."

"And now it's the *Mercer Island Reporter*," Rudy said. "I'm going to check into that more."

"What's in this box?" Doe asked, pulling a small wooden box toward her that we hadn't yet opened. She flipped up the lid. "Ugh," she grunted, waving her hand in front of her face. "It smells like smoke."

"Well, there have been three fires on the property," Rudy said.

Doe began to shuffle through the contents of the smaller box. "This stuff looks *really* old. In fact, I think it might be from the brothel."

"No kidding," I said, moving around to look over her shoulder.

"Yeah, look at this," she said holding up a faded yellow garter. "And this," she said, holding up an old, dented flask.

"Why don't you look through that book?" I said, pointing to a small journal. "It might tell us something."

Doe picked up the charred book and then sat back. We each went back to the artifacts in front of us.

"This is another diary," Doe said after a few minutes. "The corners of several pages are burnt, but you can read most of it. It belonged to a woman named Lollie Gates. According to the inside page, she's from the Point Grey area in British Columbia." She looked around at us. "I think she was one of the prostitutes."

"What does it say?" Blair asked.

"She talks about how sad she is. She misses her mother and sister and feels completely alone," she said. "And she describes the dirty men who paw at her every night. It's disgusting," Doe said with a shake of her head. "She sounds young."

"May I?" I asked, reaching for the book.

She passed it over. I opened it and felt a slight breeze whisper past my ear. I swiped my hand against my neck, before flipping pages. I stopped to allow my eyes to skim a page dated June 10, 1935. The handwriting was small and delicate.

"*Today was so bad,*" I read out loud. "*Mr. Miller forced me to be with three different men. I can't say no, or he'll beat me. But I hate it so much. They grab me and make me do dirty things. I cry, because I know I will never see my family again. But they just laugh and make fun of me. And then just when I finally have time to myself, Mr. Miller comes for me.*"

I dropped my hands. "God, how sickening. So Miller *was* forcing women to prostitute for him. I wonder how old Lollie was."

"Go to the last page," Doe directed me.

I flipped to the back of the journal.

"Read it to us," Rudy said.

"It's dated August 13, 1935 and starts with, '*Today is my birthday. I'm twenty today, but no one cares. And I don't feel well. My tummy is upset. Mr. Miller said I have to work anyway. It should be my time of the month, but I've missed it again. Now I have no excuse not to work.*'" I stopped and looked up at my friends. "She was pregnant!"

Doe nodded. "Looks that way. But keep reading."

I glanced down again. "She talks about wanting her mother," I said, skimming another couple of pages. "She wishes her mom was there because she'd know how to make her feel better. She hopes her little sister, Anna, won't befriend strange men like she did." I glanced up. "So, she was abducted?"

"That's what I thought," Doe said. "And then if you read to the end, something bad seems to happen."

I looked down and began to read out loud again. "*I told Mr. Miller I had to lie down. I feel really sick, and I can't eat. It just comes back up. I can't work anymore today. I told Mr. Miller, but he said if I didn't, I'd pay with my life. He threatens me a lot. But I just can't do this anymore. So what if they kill me? I'm dead inside already. Oh God, I have to hide this. Someone is coming.*"

"It just stops," I said. I flipped a page, and then another. There were no more entries. "That's it. That's the last entry. August 23rd," I said, closing the book.

"So someone came for her," Blair said quietly. "And then what?"

"We'll probably never know," Rudy said. "Maybe he threw her out because she was pregnant."

"I hope that's all that happened," I said with an edge to my voice. I placed the book on the table. "This makes me think of Rosa." The girls all nodded, remembering the young woman we had saved from a sex trafficking ring back in December. "But with no friends and being pregnant in the middle of the Depression, this girl would have been really desperate. It makes Rosa's freedom even more meaningful."

I left the book where it was and turned my attention back to the box I'd been working in, pulling out some photos from the original hotel. I shuffled through them, stopping to contemplate a picture of Mr. Bremerton.

"Wait a minute!" Blair exclaimed, making us all look up again.

She had Lollie Gates' small diary in her hands, and her face was turned toward me, her eyes round with alarm.

"What?" I asked.

"The entries didn't end where you said they did. There's more." She glanced back down at the page and suddenly sucked in a breath.

"But that's not all…this ink is fresh." She held up her index finger to show me a dark smudge at the tip.

"Hunh?" I hurried around to her side of the table to look over her shoulder. "What do you mean?"

Blair held the little book open. "Here's the last entry you read," she said, pointing to the passage about someone coming up the stairs.

Then she flipped the page. I inhaled in surprise. Written in the same careful penmanship were two short sentences. And in several places the ink glistened under the overhead light. I reached in and grabbed the book, my heart racing.

"That was NOT there. I'm positive." I read the two sentences silently and felt lightheaded.

"C'mon, Julia. Read it out loud," Doe said from across the table.

I gulped. "It says, '*I died here…and now I live in the dark.*" I looked up at my friends, feeling my mouth go dry.

"Didn't April say she heard someone say something like that up in the attic?" Blair asked, her sprayed on tan looking decidedly pale.

"Yes," I replied. A chill had snaked its way down my back, leaving me feeling jittery. I let my gaze drift back to the book. And then I dropped it as if it was on fire.

"What?" Rudy said, jumping up. "What is it?"

I fought for breath as I pointed to the book. "The…the writing…" I stuttered. "The writing…just disappeared."

Rudy grabbed the book and flipped to the back. She shuffled pages back and forth, looking for the writing. She shook her head. "It's gone."

Both Doe and Blair got up and hurried around to look over Rudy's shoulder. I sat back down, my body humming. But three sets of gasps had me out of my chair again.

"What now?"

Rudy put the book on the table and pushed it forward so that we could all see. We watched in fascination as letters begun to form again in that same careful script. The two sentences that emerged made my heart feel too big for my chest.

"*I died here,*" the words said again. Followed by, "*I was murdered.*"

And then the words faded and were gone.

CHAPTER ELEVEN

We quit after that. Frankly, we were spooked. We replaced things in their containers and returned to Kris' office where she gave us a large envelope for the copies we'd made. We never mentioned the mysterious writing.

On the way back to the inn, we were quiet. The ghostly writing had unnerved us. But when we got to the inn, we agreed to take assignments. I volunteered to talk to Angela about the judge and to find out whether he was still around. Rudy would research old newspapers to find out more about the brothel. Doe would use her various board connections to try to ID community roles for some of the people in question. And Blair would talk with Ginger Graves, the realtor.

After everyone left, I called my daughter.

"You want to know about Judge Foster?" Angela asked. "Why?"

I explained about the hidden room and the book we were writing. Since Angela worked in the prosecuting attorney's office in Seattle, I thought she might have a lead on the judge.

"We've been doing some research down at the museum," I told her, getting a chill again at the memory of the automatic writing. "And it turns out the judge and his family lived here for a couple of years in the late sixties."

"Really? Well, I don't know much about him. He'd retired by the time I started practicing. But his reputation still lingers in the halls of justice around here, believe me."

"What do you mean?"

"For one thing, the current prosecuting attorney clerked for him at one point. You'd think he might be an admirer of Judge Foster. But there used to be a painting of the old judge down the hallway from the prosecuting attorney's office, and he had it removed before he moved in."

"Ouch!"

"No kidding. My understanding is that no one wanted it, so they finally hung it in one of the lower courts."

"So, Foster wasn't well-liked even amongst his peers?"

"I guess not. And he's also been the fodder for some well-worn jokes that have circulated around the courthouse for years. Believe me when I say that no one is sorry he retired."

"But you don't know anything about his family life?"

"No. He'd already moved on to Olympia and the Supreme Court by the time I entered law school. But the rumors continued after he went to Olympia. Some people think he took bribes under the table, and that's how he was able to buy a big piece of property up on Camano Island. Others say he often cheated on his wife. Others snicker about his sexual proclivities."

"You're kidding."

"No. I know one guy who says he swears he saw the judge leaving a gay bar many years back, and another guy who said he knows someone who participated in a swinger's club with him. But I suppose if you want to know more about Judge Foster, you ought to talk to Dad. After all, he actually had to argue cases in front of him."

My husband and I had separated amicably and maintained a friendly relationship over the years. But that didn't mean I enjoyed calling him. Mainly because most often I had to go through his thirty-three year old, pencil-thin wife, Kitty, who had the vocabulary of a second grader and relied on garbled clichés to make a point.

"Okay, thanks, sweetheart," I said without enthusiasm.

After dinner, I called the governor's mansion in Olympia. When I called after hours, Graham wanted me to call the landline, which meant I almost always got Kitty. I think he enjoyed forcing me to engage with his new wife.

"Hi, Kitty. It's Julia," I said when she answered. "I hope you're enjoying this warm weather."

"Oh, hi Julia," she said with a lazy drawl. "Yes, thank God the rain has stopped. I hate the spring. It plays haddock with my allergies."

Count to three.

I held my breath for a moment longer, hoping I wouldn't laugh out loud.

"Um…mine, too," I said with a shake of my head. "Well…I know it's late, but I was wondering if there's any chance I can speak to Graham."

She sighed. "Sure. I'll get him."

I heard her high heels clickity-clack away from the phone and clenched my teeth in frustration at the thought that I'd been replaced by a cross between Dolly Parton and one of Lily Tomlin's TV characters. As I contemplated the successor to my throne, a voice said, "Julia, how are you?"

That deep melodic sound could still start my engine. But this time, I drew a mental picture of David, erasing anything I might still feel for Graham.

"I'm good, Graham. How are you?" I replied, taking a deep breath.

"Good, if you think sitting in a suffocating room for four hours this afternoon arguing over the education budget is a fun way to spend your time."

"Oh," I murmured, stifling a laugh. "Sorry. I guess being governor isn't just shaking hands and going to cocktail parties."

"Hardly. But what can I do for you? Everything okay at the inn?"

"Yes. In fact, we're booked solid until Halloween. I just wanted to ask you something. The girls and I are writing a history of the inn, and I wanted to know what you could tell me about Judge Wendell Foster. For instance, is he even still alive?"

"As far as I know. But why?"

"He lived here for a couple of years back in the late sixties."

"No wonder I never felt comfortable there."

"Wait a minute! You always said you loved the inn."

"I loved what we did with the place. But I never felt comfortable there. There's a weird feeling there, Julia, and you know it."

"The ghosts, you mean?"

"You know I don't talk about ghosts," he said quickly.

I chuckled. "Oh, that's right. It wouldn't look good."

"No, it's not that," he said. "It's just that…well, not everyone is as open-minded as you are."

"Graham, whether you like it or not, you *saw* Elizabeth that time on the stairs. You were as fascinated by her as I was. You can't deny it."

"Maybe," he said. "But if anyone asks, I can't say with confidence that I wasn't hallucinating. By the way, what does your new *boy*friend think of the ghosts?"

There it was.

"So you know about David."

"I'm the governor. People tell me things."

"Well then I'm sure you know that David is a cop. And yet he's open-minded enough to accept the possibility of ghosts." I wasn't sure I'd just portrayed David accurately, but hell if I was going to tell Graham. "Anyway, forget it. I didn't call to talk about ghosts. Just tell me what you know about Wendell Foster. Angie said there were lots of stories about him - possible bribes, womanizing, stuff like that."

"You're not going to put that in your book, are you?"

"No. Of course not. But I'm trying to find out who he was and what life must have been like for his family on the island. What do you know about him?"

"Not much. He had a legendary temper. There were a lot of rumors about him, like Angela said. But nothing anyone could prove," he added. "You didn't tangle with Judge Foster or he'd exact his revenge on you. But I know that the death of his daughter nearly derailed him."

"I read about his daughter's death. What do you mean by 'derailed?'?"

"He was a bastard on the bench, but always in complete control. And yet when Rose died, he started acting…I don't know…strange. He'd mumble to himself, get off track…even talk gibberish. He finally had to take a leave of absence."

"I suppose the death of a child might cause anyone to lose it," I said.

"Yeah, but I bumped into him once in the hallway and told him how sorry I was to hear about Rose. He turned away and mumbled, '*Damn my children.*' I have no idea what that meant."

I heaved a big sigh. "Still not anything I could use in the book. Is there something positive I could say about him?"

Graham chuckled. "He *was* a brilliant legal mind, there's no doubt about that. Young law clerks and attorneys alike would hang around his court just to see what they could learn from him."

"I could use that," I said with enthusiasm.

"Listen," Graham said. "If you want to know more about Judge Foster, you ought to talk to Charlotte Rowe. She was his secretary for years. She's retired now, but I think she lives on Queen Anne Hill. Do you want me to see if I can find her address?"

"Would you? That would be great."

"Okay, I'll text you. I'll even give her a call to introduce you if you want to go talk to her. Hey, since I have you, I've got a favor."

"What?" I asked cautiously.

"It's nothing big, really. It's just that it's Kitty's birthday next week. I was never very good at birthday presents…"

"You're kidding, right?" I interrupted him. "I still *treasure* that humidifier you bought me for our tenth anniversary."

"Funny," he replied. "Anyway, I was wondering if you had any ideas. You know Kitty well enough. I always buy her jewelry, because, you know, that's safe, and she likes it. But I wanted to do something more meaningful this year. What do you think would be something she could use, but would mean something long-term?"

I hesitated a moment and then replied, "How about a nice dictionary?"

CHAPTER TWELVE

Blair and I decided to drive over to Queen Anne Hill the following afternoon. Charlotte Rowe was a tiny woman in her late sixties, with frizzy, thinning gray hair. She greeted us at the door of her small but elegant Craftsman-style home, dressed impeccably in crisp slacks, a print blouse and short jacket. She wore a string of pearls at her neckline. I guess once you've served as a prim and proper assistant to a man like Judge Foster, it's a habit that's hard to break.

"Please, come in," she said, with a slight Southern accent. "It's so very nice to have visitors."

We stood in the broad entrance to her home, facing an oak staircase that led to the second floor. Oriental carpet runners covered hardwood floors, while framed floral prints graced the walls.

"I notice a slight accent," I said. "Kentucky?"

"Yes," she said. "You have a good ear."

"I had a friend in college from Kentucky. It's a very refined accent, I think."

Her face beamed with pride. "My thoughts exaaaactly."

She led us into an elegant living room, with a large picture window overlooking the wide porch.

"Your husband said you had some questions about Judge Foster." She gestured to the antique sofa under the window. Blair and I sat down.

"Ex-husband," I corrected her.

"Of course. You can imagine I was surprised to get a call from the governor," she said with a chuckle.

"Yes, sorry about that," I said, a little chagrined. "But he offered to be my front man."

"Oh, no worries. I crossed paths with your…ex-husband many times over the years. He was always very polite to me." She sat in a chair facing us and turned to Blair. "And Mrs. Wentworth, what does your husband do?"

I cringed slightly at the assumption that Blair did nothing. But then, of course, she didn't. And she seemed unfazed by the question.

"My husband owns Wentworth Import Motors," she said with a sweet smile.

"Oh, my," Mrs. Rowe cooed. "My husband had a vintage Mustang that he just loved. Do you like fast cars, Mrs. Wentworth?"

Does the Pope like to pray?

Blair grinned. "I do. And men like their toys. Cars, electronics, barbecues," she said, laughing.

Mrs. Rowe joined in with a chuckle. "Oh, yes. Rupert liked all of those things."

"What did your husband do, Mrs. Rowe?" Blair asked.

"Oh, please, call me Charlotte. He owned a string of hardware stores throughout the area. He was a man's man, if you know what I mean."

"How did he feel about you working for Judge Foster?" I asked boldly.

You would have thought I'd asked if she liked eating flies. Her face froze, and she swallowed, as if the fly just wouldn't go down.

"I'm sorry, I've been very rude. I've made some lemonade. Let me get us something to drink."

She rose and disappeared down the hallway. I glanced at Blair.

"Well, that tanked the conversation," she said.

"Yeah, I wonder if she was telegraphing what her husband thought about Foster, or what *she* thought."

Blair's eyes grew wide. "You don't think she had an affair with him, do you? Didn't Angela say there were rumors?"

"Shhh," I warned her. "You don't want her to hear us. But who knows. She worked for him for so long. I guess anything is possible."

"But she's probably not going to know too much about Mercer Island," Blair whispered. "She'd have been too young to have worked for him when the Fosters lived there."

"Yes, but over the course of thirty years, he might have said something. Plus, she may have met members of the family."

"Here we go," a chipper voice said. Charlotte returned, carrying a tray with three glasses of lemonade. She put the tray on a glass coffee table. "Please, help yourselves."

She took a glass, while I handed one to Blair and took one for myself.

"Now, where were we?" she said. She seemed to have regained her composure. "You were asking about Judge Foster." She took a sip and swallowed before continuing. "I want to be sure I don't betray any confidences, you understand. But I'm sure you've heard that he was a difficult man. Cantankerous. Bull-headed. Bad-tempered. All the things his critics said about him were true. Lawyers hated to be in his court, but then so did the criminals," she said with a brief smile. "And my husband, well, my husband hated him. But I must tell you that Judge Foster was brilliant. One of the finest minds I've ever known." Her eyes glinted slightly as she walked us down memory lane.

"Do you know much about his family?" I asked. "We know he had a wife and at least three children."

I had decided in advance how to suggest that there might be more than the three children. A cloud seemed to draw across her face.

"I don't think he was much of a family man, if you know what I mean. I don't remember him ever leaving early to go to a soccer game or award ceremony for his children. I think his wife did all of that. He was married to the job, like a lot of men. And he was very, very good at it."

"But there *was* tragedy," I prompted her.

"Oh, yes," she said, taking a long drink. "Losing his daughter, Rose, was, I think, the most tragic event in his life. That was before I came to work for him, of course, but I caught him on more than one occasion just sitting in his office and staring at her picture. She was a lovely girl. Long blond hair and deep brown eyes. She had his coloring, you know. Holly had almost black hair and eyes like midnight. Emily and Mansfield took after her." She paused a moment. "For as long as I knew him, he had only two pictures in his office. One of his wife and one of his daughter, Rose."

Blair and I snatched curious glances at each other. "No pictures of Emily or Mansfield?" Blair asked.

"No. And he never talked about them. It was as if they didn't exist," she said quietly.

"Did you ever meet his wife?" I asked her.

She brightened up. "Oh yes, on several occasions. She was an elegant woman. Tall. Statuesque. And gracious almost to a fault." She smiled to herself and released a small chuckle. "In fact, she was the exact opposite of the judge. I often wondered what attracted her to him. But opposites attract, or so they say."

"Rose's death must have been hard on her, too," I said.

"Oh, yes. She was a beautiful woman, and yet you could see the pain in her face."

"How did Rose die? We saw a newspaper article that mentioned she was found in the lake," I said.

Charlotte took a deep breath and leaned forward conspiratorially, as if she didn't want the neighbors to hear. "Well, I only know this because I sat with Mrs. Foster at a reception once, when she'd had a little too much to drink. Although Rose's death was reported as an accident, Mrs. Foster implied that she suspected that poor Rose might have been murdered."

I felt myself blanch. "Murdered? Why wasn't that picked up by the press?"

She shrugged. "I don't know. She said that the judge would never allow anyone to talk about it. But Mrs. Foster said that it looked like something had been wrapped around Rose's neck. But of course, she was found in the shallows of the lake."

"But wouldn't there have been an investigation?" I asked.

"I'm sure there was. But maybe that was the power the judge had over law enforcement and the media back then. He was an intensely private man. I doubt he would have allowed anyone to speculate, at least until something else was discovered, and I guess it never was. No evidence was found that would point to murder. Twenty years later, though, and Mrs. Foster still hadn't gotten over it."

"I don't know how you ever would get over that," I lamented.

"I agree," she said. "But, from what I'd heard, when Rose's body was found, they actually thought she might have been a victim of the Green River Killer. That was all the talk then, you know."

"Do you know why they suspected the Green River Killer?"

"No. Other than the timing. But her death was ruled an accident. I honestly don't know if they ruled out murder, or if the judge's influence just made them stop investigating. But since most of the media was focused on the Green River killings, the reason for Rose's death was buried along with her. As I said, Judge Foster was a very private man."

"I'm just surprised he wouldn't want to do everything he could to find the killer, if in fact it was murder," I said.

"His law partner told me that the judge did hire a private investigator, but after just a few weeks, the judge fired him. So, perhaps it really was an accident. I think Rose's death crushed him, though. It crushed them all. Emily, the second daughter, was admitted to a mental institution not long after that. She's schizophrenic, I think. And the son was sent off to boarding school."

"What about their son, Mansfield?" Blair asked. "Isn't he a judge himself now?"

"Yes," she said with a nod. "He's a district court judge down in Kent. Mansfield Foster. Now there's a piece of work."

I lifted my eyebrows. "Why do you say that?"

She swallowed a sip of her lemonade. "I shouldn't gossip. But if Judge Foster was demanding, distant and controlling, Mansfield is known as a real bully. I've stayed in touch with a number of people in the court system since I retired, and he's left a trail of secretaries, law clerks and legal assistants behind as he's moved up the ranks. No one can stand to work for him."

"Does his sister, Emily, still live in the area?" Blair asked.

"As far as I know she still takes care of her father on their estate on Camano Island."

"Takes care of him?" I asked. "He's still alive?"

She shrugged. "Yes, but he's in his nineties now," she responded. "When I was there several years ago, he was in a wheelchair, and Emily served as his primary caregiver. She functions pretty well on medication. And, as I recall, she works part-time as a librarian up there."

"Do you keep in touch with the judge?" I asked.

She sighed. "No. We were never very close, even though I worked for him all those years. But I visited that once, just to say hello. Emily had turned the sun porch into a downstairs bedroom for her dad so that she could handle him more easily in the wheelchair, even though the house has a small elevator. He was very frail. He'd been a heavy smoker his entire life and had emphysema, oxygen tank and all. Frankly, I'm surprised he's still alive. But I haven't kept in touch since then, and I haven't heard that he died. I think the paper would report that."

"You wouldn't happen to have a phone number, would you?" I wondered.

"I can do better than that," Charlotte said. "I'll give Emily a call if you'd like."

CHAPTER THIRTEEN

I returned to the inn to find the entire Welch family in residence. The parents were enjoying bottled daiquiris on the deck, while the matriarch and patriarch were ensconced in the living room at the game table, playing Scrabble. It was another sunny afternoon, so the kids had taken over our small play area in the back, and were chasing each other around the swing set, laughing and screaming. As I passed the breakfast room, looking for April, Ahab called out, "Look what you've done. I'm melting…melting."

"Not gonna work, Ahab," I said to him. "You're not the Wicked Witch of the West, and the kids aren't leaving anytime soon."

"She's dead. You killed her. You killed her!"

I shook my head with a smile and went to find Crystal in my office. She was finishing up a reservation.

"Where's April?" I asked.

"She's upstairs in the attic," she replied.

"Everything okay?"

She rolled her eyes. "I suppose. But Mrs. Welch, Sr. complained that we don't have a backgammon game. Apparently, that's her favorite. And she's not fond of the little vignette you created by the front door."

"Seriously? What's wrong with birds?"

I used a little side area just inside the front door to create displays of some of the antiques we sold. Over time I'd created shipboard displays, early American displays, ghost displays, even a mafia display. Currently, I had a display of antique birdhouses, framed bird prints, two antique bird cages, a couple of bird feeders, and a small bubbling pond lined with a scattering of ceramic birds. To me it just screamed summer.

"She thinks it's tacky for a bed and breakfast to push antiques for sale right at the front door."

"Well, who made her Queen of the Ball?" I harped.

Crystal just gave me a shrug. "Maybe before she leaves you could fashion an entire display of old biddies out there," she said with a smile.

I erupted in a laugh. "I have a bunch of etchings of the Salem witch trials. How 'bout that?" We both laughed and then I caught myself, glancing over my shoulder. "Careful. We don't want them to hear us. They'll be gone by this weekend."

"Longest week of my life," Crystal lamented.

"Well, our job is to make their stay as memorable as possible."

"Then where's Elizabeth when you need her?" Crystal said with a wicked grin.

Ding!

We both jumped. Someone had slammed the bell at the front desk. It was the elder Mrs. Welch.

I stepped out to the desk. "What can I do for you, Mrs. Welch?"

Her pinched features were crowded down the center of her face, making me search for a place to focus my eyes.

"There's a movie on On Demand tonight that the family wants to watch together. We'd like to move one of the TVs down to the living room."

"I'm sorry, but we don't have cable connection down here," I said.

I thought her beady little eyes would have impaled me with spears if they could have.

"You've got to be kidding!"

"Uh…no, I'm sorry. But we have a TV in each of the rooms."

"But how can a large group watch something together?"

"Well, this is a bed and breakfast, not a movie theater. But you're welcome to gather in the suite upstairs and watch it there."

She threw her narrow shoulders back, turned on her heels and left. "They won't let us do it," she complained for all to hear as she returned to the living room.

I sighed loudly and turned back to Crystal. "I'll be up in the attic. But if anyone asks, I melted down with the Wicked Witch of the West."

"You mean the Wicked Welch of the West," Crystal said, grinning again.

"Don't you dare insult my favorite movie," I warned her with a raised index finger.

I climbed the stairs to the second landing and traversed the hallway to the back stairs that led to the attic, where I found April sitting on the floor surrounded by boxes and loose papers.

"How are you doing?" I said.

"This is a *job*," she said, looking up and wiping her brow.

I stepped over and glanced down to the mess around her. "Which box is this?"

"The one with stuff from the Crenshaws and Pattisons. I'm trying to organize it." She looked around. "But I found more stuff in that little closet. A box of Halloween costumes that must have belonged to one of the families with kids, three boxes of Christmas decorations, a box of office supplies, some vintage dolls, a box of hair dye..."

"Hair dye?"

She chuckled. "Yeah. Who knows?"

"Anything that we can use for the book?"

"Yes," she said. She struggled to her feet and stepped over a pile of papers, heading for a battered old chest of drawers. "I found this stuck all the way in the back of the bottom drawer." She lifted up an envelope from the top of the chest and handed it over to me. "It's a letter to Lollie Gates - the prostitute you told me about."

The small envelope was stained and wrinkled, and contained note-sized paper. I pulled it out and read.

Dear Lollie: We hired a private investigator, Mr. George Bourbonaise, to find you. We know that Mr. Miller had you abducted, so we instructed Mr. Bourbonaise to deliver this letter directly into your hands. Please don't let anyone know you have it. We believe it could put you in danger, so Mr. Bourbonaise has been instructed not to interfere right now. He is just to deliver the letter and leave. We know where you are and are organizing a way to bring you home safely very soon. We are heart sick at losing you for so long. Don't give up hope. We love you and can't wait to have you home again. Mother

"They were going to rescue her," I said with a defeated tone. "And look," I said, reaching out to touch a spot where a drop of water had blurred the ink. "I bet this water smudge is a tear drop." I shook my head sadly. "Oh, Lollie, what happened to you?"

A sudden breeze blew past us, making us both whirl around.

"She's here," April said, looking up. "The instant I found the note, I heard a voice say her name in my head."

My back flinched as a shiver traversed my spine, and I looked around the small room, wondering if she might materialize. When she didn't, I said, "So this chest of drawers must have come from the barn attic."

April nodded. "And even though others have probably used it since then, no one ever found the letter. It was jammed into a crevice in the back of the drawer. Whether she did that, or it just happened over years of use, I don't know."

"How did *you* find it?"

She smiled knowingly. "With a little help. I was looking through this hutch next to it," she said, gesturing to an early American kitchen hutch. "I heard something. When I turned around, that bottom drawer had slid all the way open."

I lifted my eyebrows in surprise. "So, Lollie opened the drawer for you."

April shrugged. "Either her or one of our other resident ghosts."

"Regardless," I said, as I glanced down at the piece of paper in my hands. "This is important and something we could actually use in the book without asking anyone's permission." I looked up at April again. "This could be a bombshell. I wish we could find Lollie's family."

"Put Rudy on it," April said with a sly smile. "Let's face it; if anyone can find a needle in a haystack, it's her."

"Good idea."

"By the way, I found one more thing you'll want to see," April said.

She weaved her way through some furniture to a box in the corner and reached in to grab something. She turned to me, and I gasped.

She had rolled out a vintage *Wizard of Oz* movie poster.

"Oh my God," I said, rushing forward to get a closer look. "I think that's an original. I knew I should have come up here years ago to clean this room out." I reached out and touched it with reverence.

"Here, you take it." April rolled it up again and handed it respectfully to me. "I have no doubt you'll know what to do with it."

"Are you kidding? I'll drop it off this afternoon to have it framed. I can't wait. I know just where I'll put it. Thank you, April."

I gave her a hug and left her shaking her head and chuckling as I went back downstairs to my apartment. I gave Rudy a call and explained about the letter from Lollie's mother.

"And we think Lollie came from Vancouver, B.C., right?" Rudy said.

"Yes. I think her diary said the Point Grey area. And her sister's name was Anna. I'm not sure where Point Grey is."

"I'll find it and then drive up there in the next day or so and see what I can find out."

"How would you even know where to start once you get there?" I asked.

"We have two last names – Gates and Bourbonaise. I'll start with the local papers to see if Lollie Gates was ever reported missing. And then go to the Royal Canadian Mounted Police. If the family is still around, I'll find them. Give me a few days, though," she said.

"Wow, you're in the groove, aren't you?"

I heard her chuckle. "Yep, this is what I used to do, Julia. I'll let you know if I find anything. What will you and the princess be doing?"

"Blair and I are going up to Camano Island tomorrow to talk to Emily Foster and maybe the judge himself," I replied.

"Is Emily the girl who went to a mental institution?"

"That's the one," I said more lightly than I felt. "Although she won't be a girl anymore."

"Doesn't matter," Rudy said. "Just remind Blair to be on her best behavior."

"Why?"

"Because you don't want to tick someone like that off."

CHAPTER FOURTEEN

The Puget Sound is peppered with off-shore islands, which makes living the island dream a reality for many people. Camano Island sits off the coast about 70-minutes north of Mercer Island. Thanks to a phone call from Charlotte Rowe, Emily Foster had agreed to see us, albeit reluctantly.

We hit the road in Blair's Porsche, feeling excited at the prospect that we might learn something of value about Judge Foster. Maybe even have the opportunity to meet him. Of all the people who had lived on the property, he was the most well-known and the one most likely to grab people's interest in the book.

"For the first time, I know a little of what Rudy used to feel like when she was on a story," I said, as we sped north on Interstate 5. "You should have heard her yesterday when I told her about that letter we found in the attic."

"Who'd have thought there would be so much intrigue to your property?" Blair said.

"I suppose that's true of a lot of places that have been around this long. After all, babies are born, people marry, people die, they commit suicide…"

"They kill each other," Blair said with a sideways glance at me.

"That too, I guess. Why is it that we seem to keep falling into the middle of a murder situation?"

"That's easy," she said. "You're a magnet."

"Moi?"

"Yes. It's like you have little bug antennae on your head that reach out and find someone who wants to kill someone else," she said, using her right hand to serve as makeshift antennae.

"Not true at all," I said with a lift to my chin. "You guys are as much to blame on this one as I am. After all, it was Rudy who suggested the book."

"But let's not forget where the hidden room was found. *Your* property," Blair said.

"Touché. Speaking of the book, I wish Doe didn't have to work so much. She's missing out on all the fun."

"That woman is all work and no play, as they say," Blair said.

"She just said something like that to me recently, and how she doesn't have hobbies or other interests like I do. Did you know she bought a gun?"

"Yeah, she told me," Blair said. "That's not so weird. I know several women who have guns, and they know how to use them."

"Doe told me she bought it for protection since she lives alone. I think the murder investigations we've been involved with have spooked her."

"You can't blame her," Blair said. "It reminds you that the world isn't always such a nice place."

"Yes, but now she's taken a firearms class and has been going to the shooting range just for fun."

"Good for her," Blair said with appreciation. "I've always thought I'd like to learn to shoot."

I glanced over at Blair and contemplated her with a gun.

Blair lacked the natural danger sensors most other people are born with. In fact, back in December, she led two killers on a dangerous, high-speed chase without a second thought, actually driving through the showroom windows of her husband's auto dealership in order to leave them behind. And in February, when we ID'd the guy who broke into the inn and stole Ahab, she barged into his apartment on a whim and engaged him in battle with a golf umbrella. The thought of Blair with a gun brought a funny feeling to my stomach.

"I think you should stick to cars," I said. "Cars can be your thing, and guns can be Doe's."

She snuck a peek at me and those blue eyes twinkled. "You're sooooo transparent."

I shrugged. "I just appreciate being alive."

We continued to chat until we reached exit 212, which took us through the small City of Stanwood to the Camano Gateway Bridge; the only way on or off the island. Then we breezed through the downtown area and into the countryside.

My GPS guided us across the northern tip of the island on winding roads to the west coast, where we turned onto Marianna Road and followed a barbed wire fence for almost a half mile until we found a metal gate, surrounded by a claustrophobic forest of trees and undergrowth. A small brass plaque set into a brick framework to the gate bore the Foster name. Blair pushed the button on an intercom box that looked ready to fall off its pole and waited. A static noise arose, and then a voice said," Yes?"

"Ms. Foster, I'm Julia Applegate," I called out, leaning across Blair. "Ms. Rowe called you."

"Oh, yes. You're writing a book."

"Yes. About the St. Claire Inn."

"Um…okay. Come in."

There was an electronic click, and the gate began to open slowly inwards. We pulled onto a narrow gravel road that wound its way through a tunnel of overhanging trees. To the right and left was a tangle of bushes and vines.

"Wow," Blair said, glancing out the window. "Talk about privacy. It's like living in the middle of a forest. I'd hate to get lost in there."

The road continued for a quarter mile and opened up into a circular gravel drive in front of a sagging, squared-off Victorian-style building, complete with a widow's walk and peeling blue/gray paint.

"Jeez," I exclaimed, peering through the front window of the car. "What a monstrosity."

Blair turned off the engine. We both paused a moment, staring at the dilapidated mansion with its dark, navy blue trim.

"It must have been worth some money at one time," Blair said. "But not now."

"I would have thought the judge would have done pretty well for himself over the years."

"But who knows where all the money went," Blair said. "This place can't be cheap to keep up. Let's go see what we can find out from his daughter and then get out of here. I already don't like it."

As I stepped out of the car, a movement on the second floor caught my attention. I glanced up to see a curtain at one of the front windows drop back into place.

"Someone was watching us," I said, nodding toward the upstairs window.

Blair followed my gaze. "This place gives me the creeps."

We crossed the gravel drive and climbed the rickety stairs to the front door, passing several old ceramic pots housing long-dead plants. I raised the knocker and knocked twice. We waited for just a minute before a lock clicked. The door opened an inch or two. An eyeball appeared at the crack.

"You're Mrs. Applegate?" a voice asked.

I tried to focus on the eyeball. "Yes. This is my friend, Blair Wentworth. We just need a few minutes of your time."

The eyeball blinked. And then the door opened further. A woman in her late fifties or early sixties appeared. She was dressed in a baggy denim jumper and a dark blue, long-sleeved blouse. She had intense brown eyes and long, dark frizzy hair flecked with gray that looked like it was at war with itself. She wore it clipped back at the sides, I presumed as a way to control it, but tufts of it stuck out in places, making it appear as if she'd just walked through a wind storm.

"Please, come in," she said. She took a gulp of air, as if she were out of breath. "We don't get many visitors anymore."

Not a surprise, I thought, glancing around.

We followed her into a sitting room that was decorated in early shabby, but not-so chic. The room was dark and the air stale, with an overlay of something sour. I felt my throat constrict.

"Please sit down," she said, gesturing to a worn and lumpy sofa.

Blair stared at the sofa as if she was afraid it might swallow her up. I lowered myself onto one end of it, prompting her to do the same. But she sat as far forward as she could, probably to make as little contact with the stained upholstery as possible. Emily Foster sat in a chair facing us. As I glanced around the room, I spied a cobweb spun between the curtains that hung haphazardly on one window.

"So what would the ex-wife of the governor want with me?"

I was startled at the reference, but then thought that Charlotte Rowe must have mentioned my pedigree when she called.

"I…uh, well, our book club is doing some research on the history of the bed and breakfast I own," I said. "We hope it will make a good book."

"And then you'll sell the book?"

Emily had very round eyes that didn't seem to blink. She stared at me curiously, like a small child might stare at a science project. Her head was tilted to one side.

"We might sell it. We haven't decided. But we've created a timeline from back when there was a hotel on the property in the early 1900s."

She sat quietly, continuing to watch me through a long, awkward silence. At one point, she seemed to lose focus, as if she'd had another thought. Then her eyes refocused on me again. When she didn't say anything, I added, "And we came across the fact that your family lived there at one time."

There was another long silence. She sat so motionless that I wondered if someone had pulled her plug. And she still hadn't blinked. It was unnerving.

"You did live there, didn't you?" Blair asked her finally.

Her head swiveled toward Blair, and she seemed to actually notice Blair for the first time. She took in the blond hair and shapely figure, and the corners of her mouth turned down.

"Yes, of course," she replied tersely. She returned her gaze to me. "But I was very young. You may want to speak with my brother, Mansfield."

"We'll do that," I said. "But we'd love to get your perspective."

"What do you want to know?"

"For instance, do you have fond memories of living there?" I asked.

"No."

That took me back. I glanced at Blair. This wasn't going as well as I'd hoped. Emily exuded a peculiar energy and seemed to vacillate between tolerance and mild hostility.

"Really? Why not?" I asked.

"It was very isolated. My father was gone a lot."

"I see. That would have been tough. Especially for a young girl. But you must have had friends," I said, thinking everyone had friends.

"No," she replied. "My father didn't like strangers hanging around."

"But certainly your mother had friends. Maybe your parents entertained? After all, your father was quite well-known, even back then."

Her brows clenched. "No. I don't remember any parties. We just lived there."

"You must have had birthday parties," I said. "Do any of those stand out?"

"No."

I felt a kinship to dentists. Pulling teeth had to be easier than this.

"Well, what about you and your siblings? You must have had games that you played."

She paused and began to use one hand to pull an errant strand of hair behind her ear, while a frown turned down the corners of her mouth. "I don't like games. I don't want to talk about games."

"Uh, okay. Did you go out in the barn much?"

She stiffened, as if starch had suddenly hardened in her veins.

"The barn is still there?" she said with a single blink.

"Yes," I replied. "When my husband and I bought the property in 2003, we renovated the ground floor of the barn. The front of it is now a retail bakery. We use the back to store and refinish antiques we sell at the inn."

"So you've remodeled it," she said, her eyes glinting.

"Just the ground floor."

"I see."

She began to twist her fingers together, and once again her head tilted to one side. This time, it appeared as if she was listening to someone for a moment. Then she was back.

"What else?" she asked.

"Um...so, as a kid, you must have at least played out in the barn," I said again.

I stopped speaking and glanced at Blair, who was being unusually quiet. Her pretty face was a mask as she studied Emily.

"Sometimes," she said. "Mansfield liked to play games out there." She used her right hand to pull her hair behind her ear again. I noticed that her fingernails were bitten down to the quick.

"It might be interesting to know what kind of games for the book."

Her head snapped up. "No. They weren't nice games. I told you, I don't like games. He would lock me in a room until I could answer his stupid riddles."

Her entire body had begun to vibrate, and I realized I needed to dial things back. "I'm sorry. Of course, we wouldn't mention that." I wondered if the room her big brother locked her up in was the one in the attic.

"Games. Games. Games," she said. "Mansfield loves his stupid games. But I don't. I don't like to play his stupid games." She snuck a glance at Blair and her lips drew into a sneer.

"We don't have to talk about Mansfield's games," I said. *God, this woman was infuriating.* Was she hiding something or just as dense as a lump of clay?

"We've heard someone died out there," Blair said quietly. I flinched, but Emily froze and seemed to hold her breath, her gaze still resting on me. "Back when it was a brothel," Blair added. "We were told one of the prostitutes was killed out there."

Emily released a quiet sigh and seemed to relax. She let her gaze drop and said, "I didn't know that. That's too bad."

"Too be honest, we think it's haunted," I said. "Had you ever heard that?"

She seemed to consider the question about ghosts a moment and then took a deep breath. "Yes. The neighbor kids talked about it. And I used to hear whispering in the attic."

Finally! A break.

"We've heard whispering, too," I said.

She glanced up. "Is it that woman who was killed? Is she the one who whispers?"

"We don't know. But anyone who goes up into the barn attic gets a weird feeling. And several of us have heard the whispering."

A brief smile played across her lips. "Would you like something to drink?" She stood up and left the room before we could reply.

"What the…?" I said, watching her disappear.

Blair jumped up and began perusing books thrown into a bookcase in the corner. I came up behind her. "Okay, she's actually spooky."

"I agree. But look at some of these books." Blair's finger was running along some titles. "*Abnormal psychology. The Tragic Brain. What's Normal or Abnormal? Family Deviations.* What *is* all of this?"

"I don't know, but I'm sending my clothes to the cleaners as soon as I get home," I said, taking a whiff of my blouse. "I'm not sure I'll ever get the smell out."

We heard a door close and footsteps. I hurried back to my seat, but Blair stayed where she was. A moment later, Emily appeared with two glasses of ice water. She handed one off to me and kept the other one for herself, taking a long drink. The affront to Blair was obvious and very curious. Emily took her seat again, casting a glance toward Blair and the books right behind her.

"What else can I tell you, Julia? May I call you Julia?" she asked, returning her gaze to me.

"Yes, of course. Um…what was life like back then on Mercer Island?" I asked, taking a sip of water. It tasted like iron, and I put it on the dusty coffee table in front of me.

She put her own glass on a side table and folded her hands in her lap. "Quiet. My father was gone most of the time, as I said. He was a very busy man."

"And you were around thirteen when you lived there?"

"Yes. Thirteen and half. And I think we were there only two years or so."

"And your father is still alive. Is that right?"

"Yes, he lives here with me," she said. It made me think of the curtain on the second floor. "He's in his nineties now and confined to a wheelchair. I take care of him."

"I saw the curtain move in an upstairs window before. Was that your father? Does he like to look out the window?"

She blinked several times and tucked a clump of hair behind one ear before she replied. "Yes, that must've been him. He likes to watch for who comes and goes."

"I see. And you work at the library here on Camano Island?" I asked.

"No…no, not anymore. I look after my father full-time now."

"Your father had quite an illustrious career," Blair said. "A district court judge and then he went to the state Supreme Court."

She turned to Blair with a friendlier expression. "Yes. He's a brilliant man. Everyone says so."

"And your mother, did she work?" Blair asked, returning to the sofa.

"Of course not," she said with a dismissive chuckle. "My father would never have allowed that. My mother's job was to take care of my brother and me."

"And your sister, Rose," I said.

Her eyes shifted to me. "Yes. Of course."

"We read some of the old *Mercer Island News* articles from back then. I guess Rose was quite the debutante," Blair said.

Emily flinched as if a muscle had cramped in her face. She didn't even look at Blair when she said, "Yes. Rose was quite beautiful. Everyone said so." Then, she snuck a glance in Blair's direction, and her expression darkened again.

Blair's looks had opened a lot of doors for her during her lifetime. But on occasion, her looks, and her sense of confidence about her looks, could be intimidating. Right then, I felt that Emily Foster was silently screaming for relief.

"Rose was three years older than you, is that right?" I asked. "You must have been close."

There was a long pause as Emily stared into her lap. "No. Rose was very popular. She made friends easily. I'm quieter."

Right now I couldn't imagine *anyone* being close to this woman.

"Still, it must have been hard. She was so young," I said. "Just sixteen."

"My mother took it very badly," she said.

"And your father?" I asked.

"My father..." she started to say, flinging her hand to the side. By mistake, she swept the water glass to the floor. "Oh, blast," she wailed.

She jumped up and disappeared again. I retrieved the glass, putting it back on the grimy side table. Emily returned with an old kitchen towel and fell to her knees. She began to rub the carpet the way you would to remove a deep stain.

"It was just water," I said to her. "It will dry."

It was as if she hadn't heard me. She continued to rub the carpet furiously, making me think of Lady Macbeth and, "Out, out damn spot." Finally, she sat back on her knees breathing hard.

"Father wouldn't like it that I spilled. He might punish me."

With that, she stood up and threw the towel onto the side table and sat down again. I returned to the sofa, feeling that perhaps this had been a bad idea. I heard Rudy's warning in my head and was beginning to wonder if Emily should still be institutionalized.

"What else can I tell you?" she asked. "It's almost time for my father's medication."

"I was just wondering why your family moved away after only two years," I said. "Was it Rose's death?"

Her expression became guarded. "You'd have to ask my father that. I don't really know."

My heart rate sped up. "May we speak to your father?"

"No," she snapped, as if realizing she'd put herself in a trap. "No. He doesn't take visitors anymore."

She had become agitated again. "Oh, don't worry. That's no problem. We're enjoying talking with you. You said your sister was very popular. Did she have a boyfriend?"

Emily seemed to stop breathing again. She stared hard at me before answering. "Rose had a lot of boys following her around."

"Did *you* have any boyfriends?"

"Of course not. I was too young."

"Of course. Sorry. And you didn't have any other friends?" I asked.

"There was a little girl at the house. But she wasn't my friend."

My heart nearly leapt from my chest. "A little girl?"

"Yes. She lived there. In the walls. I don't know what her name was, but she would steal things from my room and leave them other places. And then I would get in trouble for it."

My heart raced. *Was she talking about Chloe?*

"How do you know this little girl stole things?" I asked.

"Because I saw her." She seemed to regard me for a moment as if gauging whether I'd believe her or not. "She was always in her nightgown."

"Did anyone else see her?" I asked.

There was a long pause, while she shifted in her seat. "I probably need to go," she said, standing up. "I have to give my father his medication."

"Oh…uh, of course," I said with disappointment. "Thank you so much for your time."

We got up and followed her into the foyer. She opened the door, letting in a cool and refreshing breeze. As Blair stepped past her, she asked, "Did a member of your family suffer from mental illness?"

Emily flinched as if someone had slapped her. "Why do you ask that?"

"I just noticed the books in your bookcase."

"Oh, those. Those are mine," she said stiffly. "I attended the university at one point and thought I might like to be a psychiatrist."

Blair just nodded. "Well, thank you again."

CHAPTER FIFTEEN

We were both silent as Blair turned the car around and retreated up the road, as if fearful that Emily Foster might be able to hear anything we said. But once we'd cleared the gate, I blurted out, "Oh, my, God, I thought we were in the middle of a horror movie back there. That woman isn't just weirder than weird, she's nuts."

Blair didn't respond. She turned right at the end of the drive and kept driving.

"I'm not sure I'll be able to sleep tonight," I continued my rant. "I'll probably just keep seeing that living room in my dreams. God, it looked like it came right out of the *Addams Family*." I expected a chuckle, but was rewarded with silence. I turned to Blair. "What's up? Why are you so quiet?"

Her eyes seemed locked on the road ahead, and her fingers were clasped tightly around the steering wheel. "I'm just tired," she mumbled.

Blair was rarely tired. She was one of the few people I knew that seemed infused with an inexhaustible supply of energy.

"C'mon, Blair. What's wrong?"

. She took a deep sigh, tapped one finger on the steering wheel and then pulled the car to the side of the road. A tear glistened at the corner of her eye, and she whisked it away before saying, "Emily is clearly mentally ill, but I don't think we should call her nuts."

"I…uh, okay. You're probably right."

"I know I've made fun of goofy people before, and sometimes it hasn't been too kind. But this is different. She's been diagnosed and hospitalized. She really is mentally ill."

"Okay. I get it. But what's going on? You seem upset."

She took a deep breath and stared at the surrounding countryside, as if grappling with something. Finally, she said, "I've never told you about my brother."

"I didn't even know you had a brother."

She turned to me with a pained look in her eyes. "He died when he was 26. He was also mentally ill."

The air in the car seemed to go still. I just stared at Blair for a long moment. "I'm so sorry, Blair. I...boy, I had no idea."

There was a long pause between us. She turned to look out the window at an open field.

"It's not your fault. I've never talked about it to anyone. Stuart was four years younger than me. He was diagnosed with bipolar disease when he was fifteen. At first, we thought he was just moody. One minute he'd be bouncing around the room, and the next he'd be closed up in his room for days. Eventually we couldn't ignore it, and my parents took him to a psychiatrist." She stopped and just stared outside.

"That must have been awful," I said, hoping to sound supportive.

"It was. He would get so depressed sometimes, that we feared he would hurt himself. Then one day, my mother saw cuts on his arms. My parents got him into counseling, but it didn't help. Eventually, he got into drugs. He got arrested a couple of times. My parents put him into rehab. He left after only a week and was picked up on the street in one of his manic states, running around naked. He was admitted to a psych unit for six weeks. When he came out, he did really well for about three months until he went off his medication. He said he didn't like the side effects. It was a roller coaster. One minute we had the old Stuart back, and a couple of days later he'd be talking to himself in the corner or standing on a bridge downtown, thinking about jumping off."

"I'm so sorry. What happened?"

Her lungs expanded with another deep breath. She let it out slowly. "I went off to college, met Ramos and got married, while my parents struggled to keep it together. It took some time, but they got Stuart into a good program that seemed to work. He was living in a halfway house. He even had a girlfriend. But then she dumped him."

She turned to me with tears in her eyes. "That was the last straw. You have to understand, that for as much pain as Stuart caused my family, it was twice as bad for him." I inwardly flinched, knowing where this was going. "One day, he found his way onto a freeway overpass."

She stopped talking and sat limply in her seat, tears streaming down her face. I exhaled, realizing that I'd been holding my breath. I reached out and took her hand.

"Why didn't you ever say anything?"

"It just never came up," she said, pulling a tissue out of her purse and dabbing at her eyes. "And if it had, I would've avoided it."

I sat back and allowed my head to flop against the headrest. "God, I'm so sorry, Blair. What an idiot I am. Is that why you were so quiet in there?"

"Yes. Because as nutty as Emily Foster is, and believe me, she *is* nutty," she said, with a glance my way, "we don't know the demons she's struggling against. And although weird, she seems to be functioning okay."

"Agreed," I said in defeat. "I apologize."

She shook her head. "It's okay. I know you didn't mean anything by it." Blair shifted those blue eyes my way, the remaining tears glistening across her cheek. "But I was quiet because I was also watching her. I was trying to understand her."

"And?"

"I think she was hearing voices. Did you see how she would tilt her head to one side?"

"So, she hears voices *and* saw Chloe at one time. I mean, hearing voices is different than seeing and hearing ghosts, right?"

Blair gave me a sympathetic smile. "Yes. You're not crazy just because you see the ghosts, Julia. Besides, we've *all* seen them."

"I'm not sure if that makes me feel better or worse," I responded.

"Yes, but remember that Chloe was playing tricks on Emily," Blair said, changing the subject. "And, Chloe only does that when she doesn't like someone."

"Right. But who would like Emily?" I said. Blair turned to give me a chastising look. "Sorry," I said, raising my hand in apology. "So Chloe didn't like Emily. What does that mean? Too bad we can't talk to Chloe. We could probably learn a lot from her. Because let's face it, other than confirming Emily's…illness, we didn't learn much from her today."

"Oh, I don't know," Blair said thoughtfully. "It could be we just don't see it yet."

My phone jingled, interrupting us. It was Rudy, and I put her on speaker phone.

"Hey, Rudy, what's up?"

"Where are you?" she asked.

"We're just leaving Emily Foster's place."

"Well, I've been researching Lollie Gates, and I talked to my old boss, Rush Dooley. He used to be the editor at the *Seattle Times*. Anyway, I told him what we were doing, and he already *knew* about the hidden room."

"You're kidding. How?"

"One of his reporters found out about it years ago when he was doing a story on Gramley Miller's brothel. He was trying to corroborate rumors about the sex trafficking and underage girls."

"Did they ever run the story?" Blair asked.

"No. There wasn't enough corroboration, so Rush killed it. Anyway, Rush told me that Gramley Miller's grandson, *Frank* Miller, owns a bar down in Puyallup called the Hardliner Pub. I'm headed to Canada tomorrow to check into Lollie Gates family, but thought maybe you and Blair would want to drive down and see what you can find out.

I glanced over at Blair. "I'm in," she said. "What should we ask?"

"I'd play it cool. I certainly wouldn't say anything about Lollie's diary or the letter April found from her mother. But maybe there were stories about the brothel passed down through the family," Rudy said. "Maybe he even has old photos from back then. I'd just tread lightly. I did a little research on him, and he has a record for assault and battery. He's not an easy guy to get along with, so to speak. So I wouldn't go in there suggesting that his grandfather was trafficking in women."

"Okay," Blair said. She turned to me. "You good with that?"

I nodded. "Okay, we'll take a trip down there tomorrow," I said. "How's the rest of your research going?"

"I made a bunch of phone calls this afternoon to newspapers in Canada. I have a solid lead on Lollie's family. I think they still live in the Vancouver area. And I'm hoping to find out something on that detective – Bourbonaise."

"Sounds like you have your work cut out for you," I said.

"Yeah, and with a little luck, I'll come back with some solid information. So what happened with Emily Foster?"

"Besides the fact that Julia wants to burn her clothes?" Blair said.

"We didn't learn that much," I said.

"Okay, well good luck with Frank Miller."

÷

After Blair dropped me off, she left to do some errands. I checked in with Crystal and was about to go find April when I glanced through the breakfast room windows. Mr. Piper's van was parked next to the bakery. He was back on the job, and I felt a sense of relief at getting the work done. I walked over to the barn and climbed the stairs to check in with him.

I entered the room, but before I could even say hello, he blurted, "Mrs. Applegate, I'm so glad you're back. I'm afraid we found something you need to see."

"Not again," I said with a light chuckle.

He didn't share my smile. Instead, he glanced at Barry, who was standing at the end of the room with the shop vac in his hand. Barry's face was drawn and pale, making my adrenalin kick in.

"What is it this time?"

"We finally made it up under the rafters," Mr. Piper said. "And we…well, we found this."

He gestured to his feet. I glanced down to where an old, faded pink diaper bag sat on the floor. It had been torn and chewed by rats, and had streaks of something dark down the inner sides.

"I don't get it. It's a diaper bag."

"You need to look inside," he urged me. The edge to his voice gave me pause.

"Okaaay," I replied.

I crouched down and pulled it open, thinking I'd find some antique porcelain dolls or something. Once again my nose was assaulted with the smell of rat urine. I peered inside, but it took a few seconds for my eyes to make out the contents. When they did, I inhaled sharply.

"You okay?" Mr. Piper asked.

"Oh, my God," I exclaimed, struggling to stand again. Mr. Piper reached out a hand to help me up. "Where…where did this come from?" I asked, gasping for air.

"Under the roof," he said, pointing to the small latched door in the ceiling of the room I had begun to think of as the nursery. "I found this along the side of the building, tucked behind a support beam. I thought it was just trash and almost left it, but grabbed it at the last minute. I…I could tell from the weight that something was in it, so I brought it in here to check. That's when…" He shook his head, took a breath and stopped speaking, unable to continue.

I glanced back down at the object at my feet, a chill crawling up my spine. From inside the bag, the hollow eye sockets of a small, misshapen skull peered back at me.

"It's a baby," I said quietly. "The bones of a baby."

CHAPTER SIXTEEN

David told me to leave everything where it was until he could extricate himself from a burglary case. Meanwhile, I called April, and she joined us in the attic, even though I feared her headache might return. I watched her as she crouched down to take a look into the diaper bag. Instead of tensing, her facial muscles seemed relaxed.

"How do you feel?" I asked her.

"Fine," she said. "But how sad." She shook her head and then put a hand to her right ear and leaned into it.

"What?" I asked, watching her.

She paused and then stood up. "I heard something."

Mr. Piper eyed her curiously. He had dismissed Barry for the day, but stood guard with us as we waited for David.

"I don't know," April said. "Whispering again. I only caught a snippet, but it sounded this time like the name *Mary*."

"We heard some whispering up here, too," Mr. Piper said. "I just thought it was…uh, just a breeze or something."

The sound of tires on gravel made me glance out the dormer window. David's big SUV had pulled up, and he emerged from the driver's side. A patrol officer climbed out from the passenger side, a camera slung over his shoulder. I met them at the top of the stairs and led them to where Mr. Piper and April waited.

"This is Mr. Piper," I said to David. "He found the diaper bag."

"Detective Franks," David, said extending his hand. The two shook hands, and then David donned rubber gloves. "Where'd you find it?"

"I went up under the roof to look for leaks. I found it behind a support beam."

"And you didn't know what it was?"

"No. I just picked it up out of curiosity. But when I brought it down and looked inside…" he said, stopping. He took a deep breath.

"That's okay," David said. "You did the right thing by letting us know."

He shifted his attention to the diaper bag and crouched down to take a look inside. He reached behind him and gestured to the patrol officer, who handed him the camera. David snapped a photo before moving anything. As he shifted things around to look inside, he snapped more photos. He took a long moment to study the skull, and then stood up.

"I think I'd like to have you show me where you found this," he said.

"We'll wait downstairs," I said.

David followed Mr. Piper into the hidden room and up a folding ladder. They climbed through the small door that led under the roof and disappeared from sight. As the rafters rumbled with their footsteps, we left the patrol officer to stand guard over the diaper bag and returned downstairs.

April had a small round table in the corner of her office at the back of the bakery's kitchen. We each took a chair and sat down.

"Did you get a headache?" I asked her.

She turned dark eyes my way and raised two fingers to her temple. "No. In fact, it's like the oppressive feeling up there is gone."

"What about the voice you heard?"

"It was just a whisper again and very hard to understand." She was drumming the fingers of her right hand on the table, thinking. "But something tells me this is an important find, Julia. I think someone wanted us to find that diaper bag. Maybe that's why there's been such an oppressive feeling up there for so long."

"That's an interesting theory. But, God, who would stuff the body of a baby in a diaper bag? The inhumanity of that is just mind-boggling."

"I don't know," April said. "This whole thing is getting weird."

"No kidding. First the locked door. Then the hidden room. The automatic writing in Lollie Gates' diary. The letter from Lollie's mother, and now this."

"Speaking of Lollie Gates," April said, glancing over at me. "You said that her last diary entry made it sound like she was pregnant. Maybe she had a baby up there. Maybe it was stillborn and she tried to hide it. Or maybe this is the baby that was kept in the hidden room for some reason."

"But why?" I said in frustration. "No one hides babies, do they?"

"Again, it could all have to do with that brothel. If Gramley Miller kept women up there against their will, he wouldn't think twice about keeping a baby up there," she said.

She had a watercooler in the corner and got up to fill a small paper cup with the crystal clear liquid.

I shook my head. "No. Think about it. The furniture up there isn't from as far back as 1935. Maybe the seventies or eighties. Same with the diaper bag. I don't think this baby was from the brothel."

"So one of the more recent families? After John St. Claire left."

"Yeah, and come to think of it, we haven't been looking at the St. Claires at all," I said. "I wonder if they play into this."

"Don't you think you would have heard from Elizabeth if they did?" April asked.

"Not if she was the culprit," I replied cold-heartedly.

The door to April's office slammed shut, making us both jump.

"I think that's your answer," April said, gesturing to the door with the cup.

I shrugged. "Sorry, Elizabeth," I called out. I got up and reopened the door and then sat back down.

"So, what do we do now?" April asked, coming back to the table.

"Probably nothing," I replied. "The police will have to investigate."

"I guess it has to be murder, right?" April said. "I mean, why would anyone stuff the body of a baby in a diaper bag and hide it unless it was murder?"

"Yeah, and poor David is so busy with this serial killer. I don't know how he's going to find the time to launch an investigation into this."

"I won't," a voice said as he rounded the corner and stepped up to the door frame. "This is a cold case, so it will have to wait."

"But, David, it's a baby," I pleaded.

He filled the doorway, while the patrolman stood behind him, holding the diaper bag.

"I understand, Julia. But these bones have been there a long time, and I just don't have time or the manpower. I'll talk to the forensics guys and see if they think there's any reason to even come out. I doubt they will. Too much time has passed. And I'll deliver the remains to the medical examiner. But don't hold your breath. It could be weeks before she gets to it."

"But you *do* think it was murder," April said, hardly tempering the hope in her voice that she was wrong.

"Most likely," he said. "The skull is cracked. Someone hit this baby with a blunt instrument."

"Oh, God," I moaned, slumping back in my chair. "But wouldn't that move it up the priority ladder?"

He leveled a solemn look my way. "I'll get to it as soon as I can, I promise. But this baby has waited years to be discovered. It can wait a few more days."

"You wouldn't say that if it was your baby," I said.

CHAPTER SEVENTEEN

I called the girls after dinner to report on our discovery of the baby's remains. Afterwards, I spent the evening wondering how the baby died, replaying our strange interview with Emily Foster, and pondering the potential murders when the property was a brothel. It was true; the rocks turned over as a result of our research for the book had revealed some pretty weird stuff, and the history of the inn was taking us down a dark path.

The next morning I awoke bleary-eyed and a little depressed as a result. But since I had a job to do, I pushed my depression aside and spent the morning paying bills and returning calls that resulted in several more reservations. The elder Mrs. Welch stopped by to inform me that someone had knocked at her door twice during the night, but when she answered it there was no one there. Unless it was one of her grandchildren, I suspected Chloe had finally decided that the elder Mrs. Welch required a lesson in manners. I told her that I would check into it and then, of course, didn't.

Blair arrived at 11:00, and we called the Hardliner Pub in Puyallup to see if they would be open on a Sunday, and if Frank Miller would be there.

"Frank isn't here right now," the woman on the phone said. "He'll be back for the lunch crowd."

"Okay, great," I said. "We'll come down for lunch. Thanks."

I let Crystal and April know where I was going, and then Blair and I headed south to Puyallup in my Pathfinder. Forty minutes later, we pulled up in front of a dive bar off Hwy 167.

The building was less than inviting. It was square, with a flat roof and in need of a coat of paint and a good gardener to trim the short hedges that flanked the entrance. Only three cars were parked out front, and from the looks of the outside, I wasn't expecting much in the way of ambience inside. I wasn't proven wrong.

The pub was small and dark inside, with a long, chipped bar that ran along the back wall. Square tables were scattered throughout the center of the room, draped with worn and greasy-looking, checkered vinyl tablecloths. A single tired pool table sat off to one side of the room, while the other side was rimmed by faded red leather booths.

I quickly slid into a booth near the door, feeling out-of-place and wiping something sticky off my shoe. Three bikers, complete with Harley Davidson leather jackets, sat at the bar guzzling beer, while a couple of guys in jeans played pool. That was it. So much for the lunch crowd.

We waited until a young waitress appeared and dropped stained paper menus before us. As she leaned forward to put two foggy glasses of water down, her peasant blouse flopped open, revealing both breasts sans bra, complete with the tattoo of a pink tongue extended and ready to lick her nipple.

"I'll be back in a minute," she said and disappeared.

Blair turned to me. "How do you propose we do this?"

I stared after the waitress for a moment, my mind blurred as I tried to erase the image from my mind.

"Uh…what? Oh, let's just ask for Miller," I replied. "We're not bill collectors or the police. We just want a few minutes of his time."

Blair glanced down at the menu, rubbing two fingers together as if she'd picked up something greasy off the table. "Do you really want to eat here?"

"God, no. Let's just order iced teas. How bad could that be?"

Blair nodded toward the clouded water glasses. I followed her gaze. "Good point. I'm going for a Pepsi."

The waitress returned, and we ordered our drinks. "Is Mr. Miller here?" I asked, as she turned to leave.

"Sure. He's in his office. Are you the gal who called earlier?"

"Yes. Any chance we could talk to him?"

"We're researching a book," Blair said.

Her eyebrows arched. "Are you kidding? Frank loves the spotlight. I'll let him know."

When she'd left, I said, "She probably thinks you meant that we were writing a book about the bar."

"I hope so," Blair responded. "Otherwise, I was afraid he'd blow us off. He could probably care less about property his grandfather owned a million years ago."

"Good point," I agreed.

A minute later the girl returned with our drinks. "Frank will be out in a minute. Did you want any food?"

"Um…I don't think so," I said, pushing the menu toward her.

"Good call," she murmured, picking up the menus and disappearing again.

I had downed half my Pepsi by the time a big man with a barrel chest and crew cut appeared from a side hallway. His head looked like a revolving bowling ball with facial features, as his beady eyes scanned the room. When his gaze landed on us, he lumbered over.

."I'm Frank Miller," he said.

It sounded as if a bull frog lived in his throat.

"I'm Julia Applegate, and this is my friend Blair Wentworth."

He nodded. "What's this about? Carey said you were writing a book or something."

"Yes," Blair said, leaning forward. "We were hoping we could talk to you for a few minutes."

Blair had worn black stretch pants, a print blouse cut down to her navel, and her signature three-inch heels. Miller's eyes sought out her cleavage, and a small smile flickered across his thin lips. This was a normal ploy of Blair's, but Miller's reaction turned my stomach. This guy just oozed smarm.

"Sure. I'll talk to you," he said in a syrupy-sweet way. "Why don't you come to my office?"

I had the distinct feeling he meant Blair only, but he turned on his heel and led us past the pool table and to the end of the side hallway. We followed him into an office that smelled like a blend of human sweat, cigarette smoke and hamburger grease, which almost triggered my gag reflex.

"Have a seat," he said. He gestured to two straight-backed, wooden chairs that sat across from a battered old desk. He fell into a rolling chair, which creaked and rattled under his enormous weight.

He scooted forward, resting his meaty forearms on the desk. "Now, what can I do for you ladies?"

I saw how he watched Blair slide into her chair and made an immediate decision to let her do the talking.

"We live on Mercer Island," Blair said as she tilted forward with one elbow on the arm of her chair. "Julia owns the St. Claire Inn there."

His eyes shifted momentarily in my direction with a brief look of recognition. "The St. Claire Inn," he said.

"Yes," I replied. "Do you know it?"

"Um…no." He turned back to Blair. "So why are you writing a book about a bar in Puyallup?"

"Oh, we're not," Blair said with a demure smile. "We're writing a book about the property Julia's inn sits on. Your grandfather, Gramley Miller, once owned a…well, a business there."

His eyes narrowed, and the muscles tightened around his mouth. He sat back. "Why all the sudden interest in my grandfather?"

Blair paused. "I'm not sure what you mean."

"Like I told that other guy, I don't know anything about my grandfather's business."

Blair glanced at me and then back at him. "What other guy?"

"Some kid. He came here asking about my grandfather and that old whorehouse. Said he was writing an article."

"Well, we have no idea who he is," I said. "We're researching the *history* of the St. Claire Inn and the property it sits on, and your grandfather happens to be part of that history."

"Well, I don't know anything," he said gruffly. He pushed back his chair as if to stand.

"I'm sure you know more than you think," Blair said quickly, sitting back and crossing one leg over the other. She dangled her bare ankle in full view of Miller's gaze. "Your grandfather must have told stories that have been passed down in the family."

He followed Blair's movements and seemed to make a decision. Reluctantly, he relaxed back into his chair. "Sure, there are stories. I never knew him, though. He died before I was born. What kind of things are you looking for?"

"What life was like," I said, attempting to sound casual. "The island was pretty isolated back then."

"It was the middle of Prohibition," Blair added. "And yet I bet the brothel business was booming."

A smile curled up the corners of his mouth. "Yeah, from what I heard, business on the island was pretty damned good."

The note from Lollie's mother flashed through my mind and the anguish she felt at having lost her daughter to prostitution. I tightened my fingers around the arms of my chair to prevent me from saying something I might regret.

"How did they get away with serving booze there, anyway?" Blair asked.

His beady eyes twinkled. "There's always a way to hide something you're not supposed to have," he said. "My uncle said that my grandfather built the floor a couple of feet off the ground with a trap door behind the bar."

"So they kept the booze below the floor," Blair said. "Brilliant."

He gave a nonchalant shrug. "That's the story. But obviously he was peddling more than booze, so Granddad also had a big trunk with a false bottom in it that he used to transport his…uh…*other* product," he said with a chuckle. "Old Gramley knew how to get away with things. I wish I'd known him."

I felt a sour taste in my mouth at the image of young girls being folded into a trunk so that Gramley Miller could abduct them and transport them to the brothel. And his grandson talked about it like it was a joke. My grip on the armrests grew tighter.

"You admire him," I said through clenched teeth.

His eyes shifted my way. "He did what he had to do to make a living. You have a problem with that?"

"I have a problem with someone who abuses women."

Oops!

His eyes narrowed, almost getting lost in folds of flesh. "Those women knew what they were getting into."

"What happened to your grandmother?" Blair interjected quickly, changing the subject. "It must have been hard for her, living on the island back then."

He glared at me a moment longer and then shifted his attention back to Blair. "She didn't stay there long. Originally, Granddad's plan was to rebuild the hotel that burned down. But Prohibition kicked in, and he decided he could do better out there with a brothel – away from prying eyes as it were."

"So she left him?" Blair asked. "We thought she died."

"No, she packed up and left, taking my mother with her. My mother was only six at the time. They moved to Leavenworth."

"I understood Gramley had a son...Joshua," I said, remembering Lavelle's comments about the bully who took his revenge out on other kids.

"Yeah, that's my uncle. My grandmother left him behind."

The contempt for his grandmother was palpable.

"Is your uncle still around?" Blair asked.

He shifted those beady eyes to Blair. "No. He died a few years ago. But he raised me."

"*He* raised you?" I asked. "Not your mother?"

"No. I moved out when I was thirteen and moved in with my uncle."

"What did your uncle have to say about living on the island?" Blair asked.

I knew she was trying to keep the conversation neutral, but it was difficult. Miller had clearly inherited the nasty genes in the family.

"He had no complaints," Miller said.

"It must have been hard for a young boy to grow up out there without his mother," Blair said.

"Why? She was a pain in the ass. It was better that she left."

"Seriously?" I blurted. "You're talking about your grandmother."

Blair reached out and placed her hand over mine, effectively shutting me up. "Wasn't the brothel ever raided?" she asked. "I mean it must've been pretty well known that there was alcohol out there."

He shrugged his massive shoulders again. "I suppose. But old Gramley paid the police to leave him alone. They were even given a little on the side, if you know what I mean."

He chuckled, and I felt myself seething inside again. I opened my mouth to say something, but Blair cut me off. "We found a small room out in the old carriage barn," Blair said. "Up in the attic. Someone told us it was used as a jail for men who got out of hand. Did you hear anything about that?"

"Yeah. I did hear about that. They were out in the middle of nowhere, so they had to take care of a lot of things themselves."

"That's what I thought," Blair said. "They had to be self-sufficient. Was there even a doctor on the island back then?"

"Hell if I know," he said.

He had begun to tap his stubby fingers on the desk, and I had the distinct impression that he was getting tired of us. But I had an idea where Blair might be going with the comment about a doctor, and I tensed up even more at the prospect.

Blair sat back and threw an arm out in a casual gesture. "Well, those girls must've had, you know, occasional medical problems."

"Women," he corrected her. "Not girls."

"Sorry," Blair said. "But I bet some of them got pregnant. Any stories about that?"

The room grew very quiet as the three of us stared at each other. Count to five.

"I don't know how they handled that," he said in a low monotone.

"Too bad," she replied. "That would make an interesting section in the book. You know rural medicine back in the 1930s and all. Especially since we were also told there were a couple of deaths on the property. We heard that one of the johns was found floating in the lake, and one of the working girls died there. Did your uncle or grandmother ever mention anything about that? We'd love to corroborate those stories."

Blair amazed me. The tension in the room had grown so thick it was difficult to breathe, and yet she looked cool as a cucumber. She even leaned forward now in her chair, inviting Miller's gaze. But his expression was cold and flat.

He stood up. "You'll have to excuse me a moment."

And with that he left the room.

"Whoo," I said, standing up and wandering over to a bookcase, trying to walk off the tension that had begun to cramp the muscles in my extremities. "He's a little bit scary," I said, shaking out my hands and arms.

"What are you doing? He's going to be back in a minute," Blair scolded me.

"Yes, and then it's time to go," I said, turning to her. "I don't think this is a guy we want to dally with."

"Don't you want to find out about Lollie?"

"Yes, but he's not going to tell us. And I'd like to keep my head attached to my neck."

"He won't do anything to us," she scoffed.

I was pacing back and forth in front of a floor-to-ceiling bookcase filled with a jumble of books, empty beer bottles, tin boxes, and small trinkets. I stopped to admire a Berliner gramophone and then fingered a beautiful wooden jewelry box, inlaid with ivory flowers on the lid. It had to be a good seventy-five years old.

My friends will tell you that there are three things that 'speak' to me in life: chocolate, *Wizard of Oz* memorabilia, and rare antiques. I opened the lid of the jewelry box to peek inside, when a picture of Frank Miller and a much younger woman caught my attention on the shelf behind it. The woman had bleached blond hair and breasts the size of Blair's.

"This must be his wife," I said, closing the jewelry box and picking up the picture. I turned to show it to Blair.

The woman was gussied up in a slinky black dress and flashy jewelry and looked happy as a clam. On the other hand, Miller stood next to her looking uncomfortable stuffed into a tuxedo that was clearly too small for him.

"Put that back," a gruff voice commanded.

I looked up to find Miller advancing on me. I backed up a step, as he reached out and grabbed the photo from my hand. "I think I've told you all I'm going to. Time for you to go." He dropped the photo back onto the shelf, face down.

He'd lost his phony friendliness and was visibly angry. Blair looked over at me with alarm.

"Sorry," I said. "I wasn't snooping."

"Like I said," he growled, grabbing my shoulder and turning me toward the door. "Time to go."

Blair got up. "We're going," she said, forcefully stepping in between me and Miller.

He could have swatted Blair aside like a fly, and yet he didn't. Her boldness seemed to surprise him.

"Thank you for your time," she said with a brief smile.

She turned and moved me to the door, while Miller went back behind his desk and picked up his cell phone. Blair stepped into the hallway, but I stopped and poked my head back into the room.

"Let me know if you ever want to sell that gramophone."

Blair grabbed my wrist. "Julia, let's go," she ordered, yanking me from the room as the door shut behind me.

Just then, my phone began to play "*Rock Around the Clock*." Blair and I just stared at each other.

"Answer it," she said impatiently.

My mother had died almost a year and a half earlier, and yet had taken to calling me on my cellphone when she sensed I was in danger. I'm not kidding about that; she's dead and yet she occasionally called me. I never said my life was normal.

I reached into my purse and pulled out my phone and swiped it on. "Hello."

"Watch out!" my mother said. "You're about to walk into a storm."

"Mom, the weather is fine. It's seventy degrees out."

Blair sighed and turned toward the end of the hallway. We began to walk slowly that way.

"That's not what I mean. There's trouble right around the corner."

And then she was gone. I shook the phone, but – nothing. This happened all the time. One minute she was there, the next minute gone.

"What did she want?" Blair stopped to ask.

"She said we're heading into trouble."

Blair's graceful brows furrowed.

We were about to emerge into the main room, but paused to survey the situation. The guys in jeans had been replaced at the pool table by a couple of big, ugly guys with beer bellies and scraggly beards. One was checking his phone, before they both stopped and glanced up at us. I looked at the bartender, but he quickly turned his back. This made me glance around with a nervous twitch in my stomach. Although the bikers were still at the bar, and the guys in jeans watched us from a booth, the energy in the room had changed. And the waitress was nowhere in sight.

"I think we need to be careful," I said quietly to Blair.

I followed a step behind her as we moved into the room. Blair was just circling the pool table toward the door when a pool stick appeared to block her way. She stopped short, and I bumped into her back.

"Where you going, ladies?" one of the big, ugly guys asked, swinging around to stand in front of us.

Blair glanced down at the pool stick and then lifted her chin to look the guy in the eyes. "We're leaving," she said, allowing the strap from her Dooney & Burke bag to slide off her shoulder.

Uh, oh!

"So soon? I thought we'd have a little fun first." He leaned into Blair, flashing a grotesque smile, which showed a prominent gold canine tooth. The sour odor of his breath wafted past her shoulder, nearly knocking me over.

Blair silently pushed her purse back to me. I took the bag and instinctively stepped back, hoping against hope she wouldn't engage with this guy. She had a history of doing that kind of thing, but this time it seemed lethal.

"You're a fine lookin' woman," Gold Tooth said, allowing his eyes to undress her. "Why don't we take a ride in my pickup out there?"

"Sorry, but we have some place to be," Blair said with a steady voice.

She tried to sidestep him, but he blocked her again.

"Really? Then why are you here stickin' your nose into places you don't belong?"

"I don't know what you mean," she responded.

"Don't you?" He reached out and ran his index finger down her chest and into her cleavage. "Oh, I think you do, little lady."

He began to slide his fingers under her blouse, and Blair reacted.

In one quick movement, she brought her fist up to give him a sharp uppercut to the chin. His jaw snapped shut, catching his tongue. Blood spurted out and down his chin. He howled, and Blair used the moment to snatch the pool cue out of his hands.

She stepped back and held it up as a weapon.

"We're done here," she announced. "My friend and I are leaving."

Gold Tooth wiped blood off his chin. "You bitch. I'll put you in your place."

He made a move to grab her, but then heaven interceded.

The hanging light over the pool table exploded, sending shards of glass in all directions. Everyone in the room jumped, and we ducked. Gold Tooth flinched back, brushing glass fragments off his shirt.

Then the strip lights above the bar began to pop in quick succession, one after the other. There were gasps from around the room as the light bulbs burst. The bartender ducked behind the bar, while the bikers quickly backed off their bar stools.

Hurray, Mom!

In the past, she'd manipulated cell phones and overhead lights. This particular light show gave us enough time to scoot around Gold Tooth and make it halfway to the door.

"Hold it!" Gold Tooth snarled. He rushed up behind us and whirled Blair around. "What kind of game are you playing?"

"Back off," she warned, holding up the pool cure again. "We just want to leave."

Gold Tooth nodded to his friend, who stepped up even with him. The second thug smiled mean-spiritedly.

"Let's not be rude, ladies," he slurred through a missing front tooth.

And then things seemed to go from bad to worse.

The three bikers began to move slowly up behind them, as if to join the effort. Horrified, I realized we were about to face five men, none of whom looked very friendly.

I glanced to the hallway where Frank Miller stood watching us with a smile. I reached for my cell phone, wondering how fast I could dial 911. But before I could, something happened that would have made me laugh under different circumstances.

Two of the bikers reached out and tapped the big, ugly guys on the shoulders. They turned around, and suddenly fists flew.

The third biker jumped in between the fight and us and pushed us toward the door.

"Get outta' here," he snapped.

We didn't need any more encouragement.

"Thank you," I whispered, as one of the bikers threw Missing Tooth guy over a table.

The third biker merely smiled and then turned to join the fight.

Blair dropped the pool stick and we rushed out the door.

We ran into the parking lot to my car. Blair pushed me toward the passenger side and right into the bumper of a small, banged up red pickup that hadn't been there when we arrived.

"I'll drive," she said.

No need to convince me. I climbed into the passenger side and handed over the keys. She fired up the engine and backed out of the parking space, just as a chair came crashing through the window and landed on the hood of the red pickup.

"I hope that's Gold Tooth's pickup," I said, as we pulled away. "He deserves it."

CHAPTER EIGHTEEN

We'd only gone around the corner, when all of a sudden Blair yanked the wheel to the right and pulled over to the side of the road.

"What the hell was that?" she yelled, slamming her fist against the steering wheel.

She pulled her hands back, and I saw that her hands were shaking. For all her confidence in the middle of the situation, clearly her adrenalin had kicked in, just as it had with me. I could still feel it thrumming through my veins.

"I don't know," I said, my voice quivering. "Whatever it was, it was scary. And I think we were set up by Miller."

She glanced over at me. "What do you mean?"

"I noticed him just before the fight broke out. He was standing in the hallway with a smirk on his face. He was enjoying it."

Blair heaved a deep sigh. "Well, he's pissed me off." She put the car in gear and pulled back onto the road.

"Yeah, but there's nothing more we can do," I said. "It's obvious he doesn't want to talk about the brothel or the deaths there."

"But why would he get so upset about you looking at that picture?" she asked. "Other than he looked as ugly as ever in it."

"I have no idea. And frankly, I'm not sure I want to find out."

The ringtone on my phone began to play *Rockin' Around the Clock* again. I grabbed it and clicked it on. "Mom?"

"You okay?" she asked in her raspy voice. "I told you that you were headed for a storm."

"Right. Well I wish in the future you could be a little bit more specific."

"Can't. I can only work off of the energy I feel. Sorry."

I glanced sideways at Blair, who was navigating traffic to get onto the freeway. I never quite knew what my friends thought about my dead mother calling me on my cell phone. It was strange by anyone's standards, and still even made me a little squeamish. On the other hand, wouldn't most people want to talk with their parents again once they were gone?

"Well, thanks for your help. We barely got out of there alive."

"Anytime, Button. What in the world did you get yourself into this time?"

There was crackling on the phone. "We have a bad connection," I said.

"Really?" she said. "I must've forgotten to pay my bill." She snorted with laughter.

"Funny, Mom." There was more crackling. "You still there?"

"Yeah. So what happened?" she asked.

"We're researching the history of the…"

A hissing noise erupted and then the line went dead. I shook the phone. I clicked it on and off and back on. Still nothing. So I put it away.

Blair glanced my way. "It still gives me the creeps to think that your dead mother just casually calls you on your cell phone, you know?"

"Well, she doesn't…really. She only calls when I'm in some kind of danger. And usually, it's just to warn me. We never get to talk much. But there was some sort of interference this time, and the line went…" I sucked up some air and purposely didn't finish the sentence.

"Dead. The line went dead. Just say it," Blair said.

I rolled my eyes. "I know. I know. My life is weird. Now if we could only figure out what the deal is with Frank Miller, who killed that baby, what happened to Lollie, and why there is a hidden room in my barn, maybe my life would go back to normal."

"Until the next body shows up," Blair said, glancing sideways at me. "Remember? You're the murder magnet. Don't forget your bug antenna," she said, using her hand to pretend she had antennae again.

"Well, I wish that bug antenna had helped to warn us about Miller and his boys."

"Yeah, that wasn't how I thought we'd be spending the afternoon," she said, dropping the mirth.

"No," I agreed. "Seemed like an extreme way to get rid of us. But where do you get your chutzpah, Blair? Sometimes you amaze me."

She paused and then leaned her left elbow on the arm rest as she drove. "Stuart."

"Your brother? What do you mean?"

"His illness controlled him. It controlled all of us. And I felt helpless. We all did. So when I left home, I vowed to never let that happen to me. I would always be in complete control."

"But he had a disease," I said.

"I know. I didn't say my reaction was rational. I took a series of self-defense classes, always dumped my boyfriends before they dumped me, and then got married."

"To Ramos, right?"

"Yeah. He was exciting, successful and had money. I dropped out of school and hit the racing circuit with him. My mother was furious. But it was on my own terms."

"Do you mind if I ask a personal question?" Blair had been married four times and each one of her ex-husbands would still come to her aid at the drop of a hat. But she rarely talked about her past marriages. "Did you initiate each divorce? You don't have to tell me if you don't want to."

"That's okay. Yes, I did. That's not to say that any of them wouldn't have dumped me at some point. But I could tell when the relationship was going sideways, and I opted out first." She shifted those blue eyes my way again. "I told you…I want to be in control." She turned back to the road. "I know I seem like a dumb blond, but…"

I burst into laughter. "Oh, Blair, there's not a one of us who thinks that. Give us some credit. I'm just glad you know how to use a pool stick."

She snuck a glance at me. "Husband number two," she said with a sly smile.

÷

I spent the evening with April on the back porch of the guest house. She barbecued chicken, while I filled her in on what had happened that afternoon at the bar. She didn't have much to offer, other than some real admiration for Blair.

"That woman has balls," she said.

"April!" I exclaimed.

"Well, she does," she said with a chuckle. "But where does she get it? Maybe you and I ought to join her Pilates class. Perhaps it's just a front for a mixed martial arts class or something."

"Well, she sure isn't lacking in confidence," I said. "I'm not sure what would have happened, though, if my mother hadn't popped those lights."

"I'm curious about why Miller would take a chance like that in the first place," April said, as she turned the chicken on the grill.

"What do you mean?"

"Threatening two older women in public," she responded. "You could have reported them."

"I'm not so sure about that. We have no proof that Miller instigated it. And in order to report it, we would have had to stick around until the police arrived. Not something I was willing to do."

"Which is what Miller was probably counting on," April said.

"I'm just glad we got out of there. Sometimes I think you have to just cut your losses."

"Hmmm," she murmured, using a spatula to pull the chicken breasts off the grill. "I still go back to why. What's Miller hiding or trying to protect? It's not like he's going to get arrested for something his grandfather did. Nor does it sound like he's worried about his reputation."

"No. Apparently not. In fact, Rudy did some research on him and I guess he's been arrested before," I said, placing plates and silverware on the table. "I shudder when I think of him standing there with that smirk on his face. What if someone had gotten hurt? What was he thinking?"

"But that's just it. A guy like that doesn't think," April said. "But more than that, I think he's hiding something."

CHAPTER NINETEEN

A week had passed since finding the hidden door. A week filled with amazing and heart-sickening discoveries. What had started out as a fun research project had very quickly disintegrated into multiple murder scenarios. It made me wonder where this would finally end.

I spent most of the morning doing bookwork. As I toiled away, Doe called.

"Hey, how's the garbage business?" I said.

She chuckled. "It stinks. How often are we going to run that joke?"

"Until I get tired of it," I said, laughing. "Besides, I need something to lighten my mood."

"Yeah, finding that baby had to be tough. Plus, I talked to Blair. She told me about what happened at the bar in Puyallup. How are you?"

"Okay, I guess."

"Well, I'm reporting in on *my* assignment. Even though I've been stuck in the office, I called several of my board buddies and reviewed the list of people who lived on that property with them. Other than Judge Foster, no one recognized any names."

"So none of the other people who lived here ran in Seattle circles," I said.

"Guess not."

"Okay, thanks."

We hung up and I finished my bookwork before joining April upstairs to finish sorting through boxes and furniture in the attic. We marked things we wanted José to move to the barn for refinishing and stacked things for the trash or the Goodwill in a corner. We finished with a box of pictures, cards, and letters we could use in the book.

Late that afternoon, David called to invite me to dinner.

"Any chance you could meet me down here at the station for a quick bite?" he asked. "I'll only have about a half hour, but I'd much rather spend it with you than the other guys in the squad room."

"Sure. I have my art class again, so how about I grab some takeout from that Mandarin place on 24th and bring it to you a little before six? Door-to-door service."

"Sounds perfect. See you then."

I hung up, smiling to myself. This was still a new relationship. I didn't yet have the deep level of confidence I might have after a year or so of dating, which meant I was afraid little things like serial killers might derail my budding romance.

I picked up some Kung Pao Chicken and fried rice and headed over to the police station. I texted David from the parking lot, and he met me at the front door. The two of us wound our way down a hallway to a small conference room and spread the food and plates out on the table.

"This smells great," he said, spooning some of the rice onto a paper plate. "I didn't have lunch." He served up some rice and chicken for me and then sat back to begin eating.

Although he looked a little frazzled around the edges and had circles under his eyes, his sexy gray hair and brown eyes still made my heart skip a beat.

"Any progress on your case?" I asked.

He was practically wolfing down his dinner. He paused a moment to chew and swallow before answering.

"The burglary that was just reported or the serial killer?"

"The serial killer," I responded.

"The FBI profilers are in Seattle now. According to them, we should expect that the four bodies we've found are just the tip of the iceberg."

I was about to take a bite and stopped to stare at him. "That's depressing."

"No kidding. But we're making some headway. They've found dental records for two of the girls."

"So you're able to identify them?"

"Yes, but I can't tell you who they are yet. The families have to be informed first."

"That's okay. So, Sean is still over in Seattle?"

He nodded. "Yeah. Since Melody Reamer is the most recent victim and she's from here, they're hoping her death will be able to tell them something concrete. But we're so short-staffed here that I'm barely keeping my head above water. Pete Meredith broke his ankle in some Iron Man competition, and Joe Talbot caught bronchitis from his daughter. We only have five detectives in our department."

"So that leaves you," I said.

He rolled his eyes. "Me and Gary Pepper. And we've had two robberies and a rape down at Luther Burbank Park."

"Not to mention the baby," I said.

"Exactly," he mumbled. "By the way, the ME said she'd get to the baby as soon as she could." He reached out to grab my hand. "But how are you? How's your history book coming along?"

I loved that about David. He always seemed as interested in what I was doing as he was in his work. Not something Graham had been so good about.

"We've put together a timeline of all the people who lived on the property, and we've done a couple of interviews. Did you know that Judge Wendell Foster lived there with his family for a couple of years?"

His eyebrows arched. "No kidding? That old bastard?"

"Did you know him?"

"No," he said, shaking his head. "Even though I've had to appear in court many times, it was never in front of him, thank God. But I've heard stories." He chuckled. "Thank goodness Foster retired before Sean came along. I can't imagine *that* going too well."

"No," I said, smiling. "I wonder how he's holding up under all of this stress."

"Sean? He thrives on this stuff. Remember, he used to work in the Seattle PD, so he knows all of those guys. I just wish I had more information to feed him. But we don't have much to go on, other than the fact that Melody Reamer met a friend for dinner over in Ballard on December 23rd. According to her friend, they finished dinner around 8:45 and said goodbye. Melody's car was found six days later up in Kirkland."

"And yet her body washed up on Mercer Island," I murmured "I heard on the news that the police are asking for help."

"Right. She was probably dumped into the lake somewhere in Kirkland."

"Did you ever find her cell phone?"

"No. So we don't know if someone called or texted her after her dinner in Ballard and asked her to meet them in Kirkland. But we've interviewed just about everyone she knows, and no one can think of why she would even *go* to Kirkland."

"I wonder if she met up with someone at the restaurant and drove them home or something," I said.

"We thought of that. The friend she had dinner with left the restaurant first, so we don't know what happened after that. But Melody's car had a full tank of gas when it was found. We checked her debit card record and found where she got the gas, so Sean was out there today, talking to them and trying to get a copy of the security video. We're hoping the video might show if there was someone in the car with her." He took the final bite of Kung Pao Chicken and washed it down with the last of his Coke, while I toyed with my dinner.

"Too much death," I muttered.

"Sorry. This isn't a topic for dinner. Let's change the subject. Did you find out anything more about that hidden room?"

I didn't want to admit that I was including *all* the deaths we'd run across in our investigation in my statement, so I just said, "Yeah, a few things. That little room was apparently used to lock up drunks back when the brothel was there. But we're also pretty sure that Gramley Miller, the brothel owner, abducted under-aged girls and forced them into prostitution. He may have kept them up in the attic."

David's eyes grew wide. "Wow. How'd you find that out?"

"A diary at the museum," I said. I didn't mention the automatic writing. David was new to this ghost business, and although he had an open mind, I wasn't quite sure how he felt about it. After all, he was a cop. "We also found a letter up in our attic that was written to one of the prostitutes named Lollie Gates. The letter was from her mother. She was planning to rescue her daughter."

"What happened to the girl?"

"Technically, we don't know." I paused, thinking of the voice that had said, "*I died here.*" "But she says in her diary that Gramley Miller, the brothel owner, threatened to kill her if she didn't perform, and then her diary entries just abruptly end. And it appears she was pregnant."

"Pregnant? Wow," he said, folding his empty paper plate and tossing it into a nearby trash can.

"We did find out that at least one out-of-wedlock baby was born to a young girl who lived on the property, though."

"That's interesting," he said. "You don't think it was the baby we just found, do you?"

"No. The girl we're thinking of lived there in the early nineties. In fact, we're trying to find her. She's probably still alive. But I still want to know why a baby might have been hidden away in that room up there."

"It could have belonged to one of the prostitutes," he said.

"We thought of that. But the furniture and the diaper bag says to me that the baby we found wasn't from the brothel. That crib was definitely from the 1970s or 80s. So was the diaper bag."

David smiled. "You'd make a good detective."

"Don't forget, old furniture is my business," I said with a smile.

He sighed and sat back, holding the Coke can in his hand. "What else did you learn?"

"Ben and Goldie had some great stories to tell. The Kettle sisters, who lived there just before Graham and I bought it, used to hold séances."

David's eyebrows lifted in surprise this time. "Oooh, spooky," he said with a grin.

"I know. Funny, huh? And when the Formosa family was there, lots of government-looking guys in dark suits and dark cars would drive up."

David started chuckling. "I think I'd much rather be working on your mystery than mine."

The door opened and a young, dark-haired man poked his head in to speak to David.

"Sean's on the phone. They've found another body."

CHAPTER TWENTY

That cut our date short, so I arrived at the Senior Center early for our art class. I can't say I was looking forward to going back. I envisioned another sloppy clay disaster, but a promise is a promise, even if it's to a dead person. And I'd made a promise to Martha. Besides, she might be watching.

As luck would have it, Goldie was there, too.

"Oooh, Julia, I have news," she blurted out, hurrying across the floor. I looked for Aria Stottlemeyer, but Goldie was alone.

"What is it?"

"Aria can't be here tonight, but I had lunch with her today. I told her about the book you're writin'. And guess what? Her great-grandfather used to run the ferry between Seattle and Mercer Island."

I didn't respond for a moment, assuming there was more to the story. Finally, I said, "I'm not sure that will help us."

"Oh, yeah, it will," she said with enthusiasm. "Because his son, Aria's grandfather, wrote his memoir." Goldie's eyes twinkled with excitement.

"I'm still in the dark here, Goldie. How does that help us?"

Goldie released a loud "huff" in frustration. "Don't you get it? Aria said she edited the book for her grandfather, and there's a story in there about the brothel and how some guy came looking for a young prostitute."

Now my antennae went up.

"Really? Anything more?"

"Yeah, she said she remembers a paragraph on Gramley Miller and what a bastard he was and how people on the island suspected he was trafficking in women, but no one had proof. I guess her great-grandfather even said he thought he heard a girl call for help when Miller was coming back from a trip."

"Call for help? From where?"

"He said the voice was coming from a trunk." Goldie's normally jovial expression had turned grim.

"We've heard about the trunk," I told her with a solemn sigh. "That's how he transported women. You okay?"

She had dropped her chin. "I guess so. Just hard to believe how rotten some people can be."

"Do you think there's a chance I can see the memoir?"

"Sure. Sure. Aria said she'd get it from her mother and drop it off to you. But I guess her great-grandfather heard all sorts of things from people riding the boat. Anyway, I thought you'd want to know."

"Yes, that's great. Thanks, Goldie." I glanced up and noticed Doe in the hallway. She poked her head into the room, saw Goldie and immediately disappeared. "Excuse me, Goldie. I need to use the ladies' room before class starts," I said.

"Oh, sure. I'll save you guys seats."

I hurried into the hallway and saw Doe sneak into the restroom. I followed and found her pretending to fix her hair, which was never out of place.

"You can't hide in here forever," I said.

"I realize that," she said. "But this is a two-hour class. I'd just like to limit my exposure."

"Well, Goldie just told me that Aria's great-grandfather used to run the ferry between Seattle and Mercer Island. He used to tell a story about a guy who came to the island looking for one of the prostitutes."

Her big, dark eyes got bigger. "You think he was talking about George Bourbonaise?"

"I hope to find out. Aria's great-grandfather wrote a memoir, and she is going to drop it off to me."

"Okay, I'll give Goldie a break," she said. "She's trying to help. I'll give her that."

"Just like she did with Dana's case," I reminded her.

"You mean by shooting a hole in your ceiling?"

I heaved a sigh. "Yes. My ceiling will never be the same. But she may have saved my life and she has a good heart."

"Yes, she does," Doe agreed. "So I'll grin and bear it."

"Good. Cuz Aria isn't here tonight, and I think Goldie is sitting with us."

As we left the restroom, I noticed that Doe was dressed in pressed blue jeans and a crisp, cotton blouse; it was her idea of the 'grubby' look. I spied the strings of a blue plaid apron folded up in her purse and smiled to myself. She'd come prepared.

We returned to the room, which had filled up considerably. Blair had arrived and was at the front of the room chatting with Mr. Welping. Rudy was in Canada doing some research, probably the safest place for her, given my propensity for accidents.

I took my seat and Doe leaned over. "By the way, have you recovered from yesterday?"

"You mean from our meeting with Frank Miller?"

"More like 'encounter' from what I heard," she said.

I started to respond, but something grazed my elbow. I turned to find Mabel Snyder fluttering by my side.

"Hi, Julia," she said in her breathy voice. "Can I talk to you for a second?"

"Um, sure."

She seemed to want privacy, so I got up and we stepped a few feet away.

"I hope you know that Milton is really a generous soul," she said, glancing around to make sure her husband couldn't hear. He was sitting at the other side of the room, arms folded across his chest.

"Uh…I'm not sure what you mean,"

She glanced past me at the girls. Doe was on her cell phone, but Blair had come back and sat boldly watching us.

"I know that a lot of people think…um…that he's closed-minded and even mean-spirited. But look, he's here, you know," she said, gesturing to her husband. "I convinced him that Mr. Welping was really a fine artist and that his work wasn't all about the…uh…you know, naked bodies he sculpts," she said, lowering her voice to a whisper.

Her hands flitted by her sides, as if they had a mind of their own.

"I'm glad he's giving it a try," I said. "But why are you telling me all of this?"

"Because you have a lot of influence."

"So you want Julia to help improve Milton's public image?" Blair said, stepping forward and interrupting us.

"He just wants what's best for the community," she said in a pleading voice. "His family has lived here forever. He loves this island."

"We do, too," Blair said. "And we don't want to keep it locked in the Victorian period."

"Blair," I said, putting a hand up to ward her off. "What is it that you want me to do, Mabel?"

She began to wring her hands. I glanced down. There were two large bruises on her forearms where someone had grabbed her.

"What have you been doing?" I asked, nodding toward her wrists. "Did you have an accident?"

She quickly pulled the sleeve of her blouse down to cover the bruises. "No. I just…uh, I was working in the yard, she said, glancing once again toward her husband, "Just keep an open mind about Milton. He's not such a bad guy. And he told me about the book. He has some good information about your property; you really should talk to him." She spun on her heel and was gone.

"You're not going to talk to him, are you?" Blair asked.

"Not if I can help it," I said, as I watched the little woman approach her husband. Her hands were now balled into tight fists. She sat down, and he turned with a scowl. He said something to her that made her flinch.

"Looks like trouble in paradise," Blair said, watching them.

"More than just trouble, I think."

Tap. Tap. Tap.

Mr. Welping was at the front of the room. There was a lot of shuffling feet as people took their places. The three of us sat down, just as Goldie scooted in and sat next to me.

That night, the potter's wheel group was assigned the task of throwing a cup and then adding a handle, while the sculpting group would build the mask of an animal of their choice: cat, dog, or bird. Welping spent some time discussing the mask and then the cup and handle. We donned our aprons, gathered up our materials, and headed off to our respective places.

By the break, I had a reasonable-looking mug and had made it without incident. I returned to the table where Doe and Blair stood chatting. Before I could engage them, however, I heard a cough and turned to find a heavyset woman standing next to me.

"Excuse me, Mrs. Applegate?" she said. "I heard about the book you're writing."

Did everyone know about what we were doing?

"Yes?"

"I might know something about your property," she replied. She wore glasses and kept pushing them up her nose. "My family used to live across the street from the St. Claire home. I remember when the Formosas used to live there."

Blair and Doe came up behind me to listen in.

"We haven't learned much about the Formosas," I said.

"They were very strange," the woman said. "By the way, I'm Verity Small," she said, holding out her hand. "It's so nice to meet you."

I shook her hand. "These are my friends, Blair Wentworth and Doe Kovinsky," I said, turning to include Blair and Doe.

Verity said, "I brought you this." She held out a manila folder for me.

The folder was filled with copies of newspaper articles. I scanned the headlines, and then crinkled my brow. "I don't understand. What does the trial of Colton Halfmore have to do with my property?"

"You don't remember that trial?" she asked with a disappointed downturn to her mouth. "It was in all the papers. It went on for months."

"I remember it," Doe said, coming up to my side. "He was the CEO of some big industrial chemical company that was dumping waste over by Alki Beach. There were several deaths associated with the case. In fact, one person who was scheduled to testify against him was shot to death, as I recall."

"I remember that," I said. "But what does he have to do with us?"

"Look here," she said. She pointed to a section in the first article that spoke about a man named John Yang. "Yang was Halfmore's chief financial officer. He testified against Halfmore and helped to put him in prison. My family always thought that John Yang was Mr. Formosa."

Lightbulbs sprang to life in my head. "So the St. Claire property was what? A safe house?"

"That's what we thought," she replied.

"That would explain some things," Doe said.

"Yeah, like the guys hanging around in dark suits," Blair said.

Verity's eyes brightened. "Yes, the men who hung around tried to keep out of sight, but of course we lived right across the street and would see them all the time."

"Did you ever see the Formosas?" Blair asked.

"Only twice. But big, dark cars would come and go. And we never saw the Formosas leave the property. Until May nineteenth of that year."

"Why do you remember the date?" I asked.

She pulled out a second newspaper article and handed it to me. "Because it was only a week later that John Yang testified against his boss."

"But we heard there were shots fired on the property, and that's when they left," Blair said.

She nodded. "Yes, that's true. No one's ever been able to tell us what that was all about. But the family moved out immediately after that."

My mind was racing, trying to connect the dots. "So you think someone compromised the safe house, and the police, or the FBI, or whoever, moved the Formosas to another safe house?"

She nodded enthusiastically. "Yes. Then he testified and the family disappeared. We think they were in the witness protection program."

"Whoa," I exclaimed. "That's a pretty dramatic story. That would be great for our book. I just wish there were some proof."

"But there is," Verity said, her eyes alight with enthusiasm. "If you read the stories in here," she said, indicating the folder, "you'll read about Mrs. Yang. She was blind and had a guide dog. A golden retriever named Cory. Well, guess what?"

We waited in anticipation, until Blair said impatiently, "What?"

"When I was out gardening one day, a golden retriever came into our yard. He was the friendliest dog. Anyway, then one of the men we'd seen patrolling the grounds showed up to take him back. And he said, 'C'mon, Cory, let's get you back to the house.'" She rocked back on her heels and beamed with pride.

"No kidding," I said. "Well, thank you, Verity. May I keep these?" I asked, referring to the folder.

"Of course. And feel free to use my name if you use the story."

I thanked her again, and she returned to her table, while Doe and Blair and I huddled up.

"Well, that's a bombshell," Doe said. "Do you think we ought to use it?"

I shrugged, glancing down at the articles in the folder. "I don't see why not."

"Makes me think maybe we ought to talk to Milton Snyder, too," Doe said. She nodded to where he was sitting again with his arms folded across his chest.

"Is he even making a mask?" Blair asked. "I didn't see him sculpt anything last week."

"Doesn't look like it," I replied. "I'm more inclined to think that it was Mabel who wanted to take the class, and he's here as her guardian."

"Or bodyguard. But against what?" Doe asked. "It's not like Richard Welping is going to make a pass at her."

Blair was studying Snyder, her eyes narrowed in thought. "No. He wants to make sure Welping doesn't have us sculpt anything suggestive. I bet if he even showed a picture of one of his nude sculptures, Snyder would be on his feet complaining."

"What a bore," I said. "Who'd want to go through life that way?"

"Well, it doesn't change the fact that he may know something important about your property, Julia. Something we could use in the book," Doe said. "Look, I'll go talk to him. I haven't contributed much to this enterprise yet, so it's the least I can do. Let's see what he has to say."

"You're a brave woman," I said.

She gave a dismissive wave. "Oh, no worries. Remember, I'm the queen of garbage. If he gives me any grief, some of his neighbor's trash might suddenly start showing up on his lawn."

CHAPTER TWENTY-ONE

I heard on the news the next morning that animals had unearthed the remains of a young woman off a trail outside of Everett. Jewelry found with her body had already helped to identify her. She was a young high school student who had disappeared in 2008.

Too many young girls had died with no way to find the killer. Add to that our own discovery of the destitute young Lollie Gates and the baby, and it all left me feeling dispirited. As I helped April with breakfast, I filled her in on the news about Aria Stottlemeyer's memoir and the Formosas. Then the discussion turned to the serial killings.

"Boy, after the Green River Killer and Ted Bundy, I'd hoped we were done with serial killers in the Pacific Northwest for a while," she said.

"Yeah, I've avoided reading about the case in the newspaper. But David and I have talked about it."

She began to whisk some eggs. "Do you think the press will pick up the story about the baby?"

I shrugged. "Eventually, I suppose. Once police start investigating."

"I guess the first challenge will be to find out who he or she is. Or was," she said, correcting herself.

"Yeah," I said, cutting up melon for the fruit salad. "You said you thought her name was Mary."

"I heard the name 'Mary.' But I'm not sure it was in reference to the baby. It sounded like there was more to the word, but I just couldn't grasp it."

"Like what? Mari...time? Marry me? Merry month of May?"

"No," she said, stopping to think a moment. "More like mari...mari*gold*," she said, turning to me.

"Marigold? *The* marigold?" I said. "The one we found in that box from the hidden room."

"It could have been that."

I turned and hurried across the kitchen to where the old box still sat on the counter. I opened the lid and lifted out the necklace with the marigold pressed into the pendant. I returned to where April stood.

"What do you think?" I said, handing it to her.

She put the bowl of whisked eggs onto the counter and took the necklace, placing the glass pendant in between her thumb and index finger. All of a sudden, one of the cupboards above our heads opened and closed twice in quick succession. We looked at each other in surprise.

"Was that Elizabeth? Or Chloe?" April asked.

"More like Elizabeth. Unless Chloe is climbing on the counters now," I replied. "But I wonder why?"

The cupboard did it again, making us both jump. April opened her fingers and glanced down at the necklace. "I have an idea. Elizabeth, is the baby's name, Marigold?"

Short pause. And then...tap...tap.

"Oh my gosh," I said. "Thank you, Elizabeth."

"But now what?" April asked. "We know her name, but it's not like you can tell David. I mean how could we explain how we got it?"

"Agreed," I said. "But what if we could learn more? Her last name, for instance. Maybe Elizabeth can tell us more."

A sudden rush of air blew through the kitchen, forcing the back door open and closed with a bang. We both stood staring at it.

"I guess not," I said with disappointment. "Maybe she's still mad at me for suspecting her."

"You think?" April said.

÷

After breakfast, I ran to the art store and picked up my newly framed *Wizard of Oz* poster. I had scheduled the morning to clean my apartment, and so once I was done, I hung the print in the corner of my living room. It was offset by a shelf that held a collection of *Wizard of Oz* snow globes. Then I stood back to admire it, as the dogs danced around my feet.

"What do you think?" I asked them.

Minnie looked up at me and barked, bouncing up and down. Mickey began to spin in a tight circle. Something he did whenever he got excited or thought I was going to give him a treat. I just laughed.

"You two," I said. I leaned down and gave them each a pet. "No treats right now. I have to go back to work."

The *Wizard of Oz* always made me happy, so by the time noon rolled around, my spirits had lifted considerably. After lunch, I decided to spend some time at the front of the inn, weeding and fertilizing my roses. The sun was out, and there was a light breeze. I donned my wide-brimmed straw hat and floral gloves and took the dogs with me outside. As I pulled weeds and turned the earth humming to myself, my cell phone rang. It was Blair.

"Hey, Julia, any chance you'd like another guest for a couple of days?"

"Why? What's up?"

"We have pests. And by pests, I mean carpenter ants. They're in the walls. We have to fumigate to get rid of them, so the pest control guys want to come out tomorrow and put a tent over the entire house. Mr. Billings is in Houston, but I'll have to move out."

I smiled. "Maybe you have ghosts and just don't know it."

"No. These aren't the kind of pests that walk *through* walls. They're the kind that live *in* the walls. It's creepier than having Elizabeth here."

"Well, c'mon over. You can stay in the apartment with me."

"Thanks. The pest control guys will be here first thing in the morning. I have some errands to run, so why don't I plan on being there right after lunch?"

"Hey, why don't I call Mansfield Foster and see if we could get an appointment for tomorrow afternoon?"

"Okay. It will be like trading one disgusting pest for another. I'll see you tomorrow."

I hung up and was about to resume my gardening when a voice stopped me.

"Your flowers are beautiful, Julia."

The dogs barked once and then threw themselves at the feet of my new neighbor, Caroline Keefer. She had crossed the street and come up to the rose garden with her daughter, Amelia. She and her husband had bought Ellen Fairchild's home after Ellen had driven her new Lexus off a cliff back in December.

"Thank you," I said, standing up. "We lost so many roses after that harsh winter, I had to plant new ones," I said, stretching my back. "How are you settling in? I noticed you had some workmen over there. Are you doing some remodeling?"

Caroline was around five foot nine, with short, curly black hair. Her husband worked for Boeing, and Caroline had worked for Microsoft before she had Amelia. Now, she worked as a programmer from home. Caroline leaned down to pet the dogs. They were licking Amelia's ankles and making her giggle

"We're retiling the downstairs bathroom. Jack doesn't want to do too much yet. He thinks we need to live there awhile before we'll really know what changes we want to make."

"And I get the feeling you know what you want already."

She smiled at me, showing a perfect set of whitened teeth. "I like to cook. I'm actually kind of a foodie. So there are some changes I'd like to make in the kitchen. And I'm definitely going to start an herb garden."

"April has talked about putting in an herb garden. You two should get together." I looked down at Amelia, who was ignoring the dogs now and pulling at her mother's hand. She faced the inn's front porch and seemed to be staring at something.

Amelia was four years old and a Down's Syndrome child. Although mildly challenged, she had an impressive vocabulary and a bright, engaging smile. Today she looked adorable in a bright pink jumper with matching sandals and a headband to accent her own dark curls.

"Do you like to cook, Amelia?" I asked her.

She turned and squinted up at me. "Mummy lets me bake cookies," she said, her scrunched little face alight with enthusiasm.

"I bet you bake good cookies, too," I said. "April makes really good cookies. You should come over one afternoon when she puts them out for guests."

Amelia turned back to the front porch. "Okay. Can I play with Chloe?"

I bit off a sharp intake of breath. While I often saw Elizabeth's ghost, I had only seen brief glimpses of Chloe, her daughter. Instead, Chloe usually made herself known by playing tricks on people. Now, twice in two days someone had admitted to seeing her: Emily Foster and Amelia.

"She's been talking about Chloe ever since we all sat on your deck a couple of weeks ago," Caroline said. "She says Chloe lives at the inn. In the walls," she emphasized in a whisper.

Caroline gave me an apologetic nod, as if we should just humor her daughter. I watched Amelia a moment and then turned to her mother.

"Are you busy right now?"

"Uh...no. Why?"

"Why don't we go sit on the back deck again?" I glanced at my watch. "It's almost three o'clock. April will be putting the cookies out soon." I looked down at Amelia. "Would you like that, Amelia?"

She turned her face up to mine again, her small, slanted eyes squinting into the sun. "Uh huh. But can I play with Chloe?"

"Of course, honey." I turned to her mother, whose wide-set eyes were clenched with curiosity. "Then I can tell you all about Chloe."

The three of us traipsed inside. I told Caroline that I'd meet them on the deck and turned for the kitchen. Ahab called out behind me, "What have you learned, Dorothy?"

I chuckled to myself, but ignored him and pushed open the swinging door. April was there, filling a tray with peanut butter cookies and brownies.

"I heard voices," she said.

"Yes. It's Caroline and Amelia from across the street. I invited them over for lemonade and cookies."

April smiled. "I think Amelia is adorable."

"Yes, and guess what? She said she wants to play with Chloe."

April turned to me wide-eyed.

"Have you told her about Chloe?"

"No. That's the point." I went to the sink to wash my hands. "She seems to think she can see her." A slight shiver ran down my back at the thought.

April stopped gathering cookies. "I suppose that's not unheard of. You see Elizabeth. Amelia is a special little girl. Perhaps Chloe purposely lets herself be seen by her."

"At least she hasn't played any tricks on her," I replied. "Caroline said Amelia talks about Chloe a lot. So I thought maybe it was time to explain."

"Good luck with that," April said with a brief smile.

I dried my hands and then found a small plate and filled it with several cookies. I grabbed a pitcher of lemonade and three glasses and put everything on a tray and took it out to the deck. Amelia was already sitting on the steps leading to the side yard, laughing and talking excitedly to thin air. Her mother looked up at me with concern.

"I've never seen her do this before," she said. "I'm beginning to wonder if she has an imaginary friend."

I put the tray on one of the patio tables and sat down. "Her friend isn't imaginary, at least not in the traditional sense. Perhaps I should explain."

For the next few minutes, I related the history of the inn and the ghosts. Since Caroline was a computer nerd, and her husband Jack was an engineer, I presumed they were linear thinkers and not the sort to believe in ghosts. So I was prepared for a negative reaction.

Instead, Caroline listened, glancing over every once in a while at her daughter. When I was finished, she said, "So you think Amelia might actually *see* Chloe, the little girl who died here?"

I shrugged. "It appears that way. I didn't think too much about it before. But if you think back to when you were here before, Amelia was on the swings and kept yelling, 'Higher! Higher!' as if someone was pushing her."

Caroline's eyes popped open. "Oh, dear, that just gave me the chills. Yes, I do remember that. But Amelia is such a creative little girl, I just thought…well, I don't know what I thought. But why can't I see Chloe?"

"There's the rub. I don't know. I've never fully seen Chloe myself. And I've never seen Fielding, her brother, although I think he's here somewhere. As I said, I have seen Elizabeth many times. But I've just caught glimpses of Chloe. But maybe because of…because of Amelia's condition, maybe she's more sensitive."

Caroline slowly let out a sigh. "Well, this is something, isn't it?"

"Are you okay with it? I mean, not everyone is comfortable with the idea of ghosts."

"I'm not sure," she said with another sigh, glancing over to where Amelia was giggling to herself. "When I was a little girl, I thought I saw my grandfather after he died. I probably wasn't much older than Amelia is now. My mother chastised me and told me to stop telling lies. I argued with her, and so she punished me. I don't want to do that to Chloe."

"I think parents often discount things their kids say," I said. "It's natural, because children have such vivid imaginations."

"Yes. But I saw my grandfather twice more after that and never told my mother. I never told anyone. I felt too ashamed." She turned to Amelia again, and her expression softened. "She doesn't deserve that. Besides, Amelia doesn't have any friends. It's nice to see her so happy." Her voice shook a bit, and I poured her a glass of lemonade and handed it to her. "Thanks," she said. "You know, it's tough when you have a special needs child. People stare. They whisper. I worry about her, and what life will be like when she gets older." Caroline took a sip of lemonade, and I could see a tear glistening in the corner of her eye.

"I have a feeling Amelia will do just fine," I said, pouring myself some lemonade. "She seems quite bright, and she's very personable. Believe me, Chloe doesn't like everyone. She's notorious for playing tricks on people she *doesn't* like, especially children. I think she likes Amelia."

Caroline beamed a little at that. "Oh, my gosh. Amelia has a friend. A *dead* friend," she said with a chuckle, glancing back at her daughter. "But a friend." She paused and took a swipe at the corner of her eye with the heel of her hand. "I think I'm good with that."

"What will you tell your husband?"

"Well, that's a whole other matter," she said, turning to me. "I think we may have to ease into that one."

"Hold on," I said, getting up and going inside. When I came back out, I dropped a book on the table in front of her. "Leave this lying around, just to see what happens." It was Jason Spears' book, *The Most Haunted Hotels in the Northwest*. "The inn is featured in it."

"Well, that ought to start a conversation," she said with a smile, pulling the book towards her.

"No doubt," I replied, glancing over at Amelia again. "Wouldn't you just love to know what the two of them are talking about?"

As if she'd heard me, Amelia suddenly turned in our direction. "Mama, Chloe said there's a baby here. Can I see the baby?"

I felt the blood drain from my face.

"Um...I don't know." Caroline turned to me. "Do you know what she's talking about?"

I stared at Amelia, my heart rate on overdrive. "Amelia, what else does Chloe know about the baby?"

Amelia twisted away from us a moment and seemed to be listening to someone. A few seconds later, she jumped up and ran to her mother. "Mama, guess what? Chloe says the baby looks just like me!"

CHAPTER TWENTY-TWO

It took a few moments for me to recover from the shock, and then I had to explain to Caroline why I had tears in my eyes. Once more, she listened attentively. The fact that her daughter had just told us that the baby we'd found was a Down's Syndrome baby was the hardest part to relay. And I worried that my new neighbor would become a stranger.

"I've seen the police car over here a couple of times, but I know you're dating a detective. I didn't realize you'd found a body," she said, clearly flustered. Amelia had run off to the swings, and Caroline watched her. "I think I'm a little overwhelmed by all of this."

"I understand," I said. "It's a lot to take in. I hope it won't stop you from coming over. We are all very friendly over here, even the ghosts," I said with a little chuckle, hoping to keep the conversation light.

"I think I'd better get Amelia home," she said, standing up. "Thanks for the treats, Julia."

She called to her daughter and a minute later, they were gone. I noticed too late that she'd left behind the book about haunted hotels, and my heart sank.

With a sigh, I took the book back inside with me, passing a few members of the Welch family as they came in for snacks. I hurried into the kitchen to avoid getting caught, and told April what had happened.

"You can't blame Caroline, Julia. That was a lot to absorb in just a few minutes. But, wow!" she exclaimed. "So Marigold might have been a Down's Syndrome baby. That might explain why someone was hiding her."

"Yes, but how disgusting," I said.

"Let's face it, people with disabilities haven't been accepted into the mainstream for that long, Julia."

"I know. But to hide her away like that as if she were some sort of abomination. It makes her death even sadder."

I left April and went to my apartment to call the girls. I was wound up and had to blow off steam. I talked to each one of them for ten to fifteen minutes, so by the time I was done, I was done. I'd worked through my shock and anger and resumed my normal schedule. But I have to admit, my dreams that night were anything but restful. I had this intense feeling of compassion now for Marigold. I wanted to protect her.

And I wanted revenge.

÷

Blair arrived the next day with her overnight bag and moved into my guest room. The dogs were ecstatic to have a visitor and followed her around the bedroom as she settled in, their tails wagging, noses poking into everything.

"We're scheduled to see Judge Foster at two o'clock," I said, shooing Mickey away from Blair's purse. "Rudy gets back from Canada this afternoon. By the way, we're all going to meet here after dinner tonight to review things. Why don't you get settled and meet me out front. I need to finish up some things in the office before we go."

"Okay. I want to change first, anyway," Blair said, putting her cosmetic bag on the night stand.

Blair had on tight black jeans and a ruby-red tank top that had to be a size too small. Since this was standard Blair-wear, I wondered why she would change. But rather than ask, I just left for my office.

As I rounded the corner to the inn's entrance, I came upon the elder Mrs. Welch and her husband hovering over the reception desk, talking to Crystal. The ever-cranky Mrs. Welch appeared to be complaining about something, and my first impulse was to make an about-face and hurry back to my apartment. But Crystal's pale blue eyes met mine. Her expression flashed an SOS signal. I couldn't abandon her.

"What's on the agenda today for the Welch family?" I asked in an upbeat tone. "The Space Needle or Pike Place Market?"

Mrs. Welch spun in my direction, nearly knocking over her husband who had to reach for the counter to keep from falling.

"You haven't done a thing about whoever is pounding on our door at night," she snapped. "Poor Harvey here has a heart condition and needs his sleep."

"I take my hearing aid out at night," he mumbled. "I don't hear anything."

"Quiet, Harvey!"

"I think you said someone was knocking on your door, not pounding," I said. "And I've asked around, but no one here has any idea who's doing it. You're sure it's not a member of your family? Perhaps someone is sleepwalking or it's one of the grandkids."

She puffed up her scrawny chest. "You think one of my grandchildren is harassing us in the middle of the night?"

"I really don't know," I said. "It could also just be the building. You know…normal creaks and moans."

"Maybe it's the old pipes," Crystal offered with a hopeful glance at me.

I gave her an appreciative look. "Yes, I bet that's what it is. Just old pipes knocking."

Mrs. Welch glanced back and forth between the two of us, as if deciding on our veracity. Just then, Blair appeared behind me with the dogs prancing along at her feet.

"What's up?" she asked.

Mrs. Welch gave her the once over. "Old pipes," she said with a sneer.

I turned to Blair. "Mrs. Welch thinks someone is knocking at her door in the middle of the night."

Blair erupted in a light-hearted laugh. "Oh, that's just Chloe. She plays tricks on people she doesn't like."

I'm usually the one who mutters things out loud that should have been left unsaid. But Blair often functioned without a verbal filter of any kind, making me turn to her with a warning scowl.

"Chloe? Who's Chloe?" Mrs. Welch demanded.

"A ghost," Blair said nonchalantly, missing my signal. "The inn is haunted. Everyone knows that. I'm going to grab something to eat before we go," Blair said to me. And she disappeared around the corner into the main kitchen, oblivious of the awkward silence left behind.

"What in the world was she talking about?" Mrs. Welch said with clenched brows.

I sighed. "The inn seems to have a couple of resident spirits. Haven't you seen the book on the coffee table in the living room?"

I was referring to the book I had tried to loan to Caroline just the day before. I had several copies lying around.

Mrs. Welch's eyes narrowed into a suspicious squint. "What book?"

"*The Most Haunted Hotels in the Northwest*," I replied. "This Inn is featured in it. Chloe is one of our ghosts. She's a little girl."

"That explains it," Harvey suddenly perked up. "Little kids hate Ruby."

And with that, he shuffled away, leaving his wife speechless for once.

÷

Mansfield Foster had an office in Kent, some twenty miles south of Seattle. He operated out of the regional court there. I reviewed Rudy's notes about him as we drove. He was 62-years old, divorced, and had a reputation as a man not to cross or even criticize among his peers. He'd served as an assistant prosecuting attorney for eight years before becoming a highly-paid corporate attorney. He was 48 when he was appointed district court judge when the sitting judge died unexpectedly.

Blair and I arrived at the Parkridge Building about fifteen minutes before our appointed time. Blair had changed into a black pencil skirt and white tailored blouse, with a wide, black leather belt. She wore her hair down in loose curls and had on black, patent leather, 3-inch heels. She meant business.

We entered the building and approached a long, polished counter, where a woman sat staring at a computer screen.

"We're here to see Judge Foster," I told her.

She gave us a vacuous smile. "Of course. His office is on the third floor. Jenny will check you in."

I thanked her, and we took the elevator to the third floor, where Jenny did, in fact, check us in. We had to sign a sheet and take a visitor's badge. We were a few minutes early, so I anticipated a wait. What I didn't anticipate was a thirty minute wait. By the time Jenny finally chirped that the Judge would see us, I'd almost dozed off.

She showed us into a large office with a picture window that overlooked a greenbelt and walking path. The room was decorated in polished wood and leather and had all the command and presence you'd expect from a judge.

The man who came out from behind a huge walnut desk was approximately six feet tall, with broad shoulders and a trim waist. He wore his hair short, and like his sister, Emily, had intense, penetrating brown eyes that didn't blink. As he reached out a large hand to grasp mine, I felt uncomfortable under his stare.

"It's nice to see you again, Mrs. Applegate."

That took me by surprise. "I'm sorry. Have we met before?"

He smiled, which did nothing to soften his expression. "Many years ago. Back when your husband was the prosecuting attorney. I was corporate counsel at the time for Vextel. We met at a campaign event for Judge Hartley."

"I'm sorry. I attended so many events with Graham back then…"

"Of course," he said, releasing my hand. "I wouldn't expect you to remember me. I was nobody then."

That stung.

"I do apologize, Judge Foster. I don't have a good memory for many of the people I met at big events like that."

He gestured to two chairs on the opposite side of his desk, as he returned to his chair. "It's quite all right, Mrs. Applegate. I'm sure it was difficult to live in the shadow of your husband for all those years. Eventually, it probably became too much."

Really? Was he referring to my divorce? This guy could turn honey sour, I thought to myself.

"Actually, Julia has done quite well for herself since divorcing Graham," Blair spoke up. "I don't think she needed to be a Governor's wife to complete her."

He seemed to notice Blair for the first time, and his gaze skimmed her from head to toe. It was common for Blair to use her appearance as a way to manipulate men. But today she seemed different. She looked elegant sitting with her back straight and feet planted firmly on the floor. She met Mansfield Foster's gaze and barely blinked.

"I'm sorry. I didn't get your name," he said to her.

"Blair...Wentworth," she said, giving a slight emphasis to her last name. She sniffed the air. "And I recognize the Kilian Straight to Heaven cologne you're wearing. Very nice. Very expensive."

His eyes glinted, and he cocked his head to one side. "Your husband owns Wentworth Import Motors."

She smiled as if she had just swallowed good wine. "Yes. And if I'm not mistaken, he sold you the BMW M6 convertible parked out front," she said, crossing one shapely leg over another.

This time, his eyes followed her movements. "Yes, your husband has good taste in cars."

Blair merely smiled again. "He has good taste in everything."

I smiled inwardly. *Damn, she was good!*

The shadow of a smile flickered across his face, and then he turned his attention on me. "My assistant said you wanted to talk about a book you're writing on the St. Claire Inn. What can I help you with? I lived there for only a very short time when I was a teenager."

"We're just trying to paint a picture of what life was like back then. We've already spoken to your sister."

His eyes flared momentarily, and his right hand clenched around a pencil lying on the desk. Then his composure returned. "Emily," he said. "I see. Well if you've met Emily, you've been to the compound."

His sarcasm made me pause. "You mean the family home?"

He shrugged. "I suppose you could call it that. What did Emily have to say about Mercer Island?"

"She mentioned that it was lonely living on the island. Emily was only thirteen then. Is that right?"

He leaned back in his chair, as if none of this mattered to him. "Yes. I'm two years older than she is."

"What did you and your friends do after school and on weekends back then?" I asked, remembering what Emily had said about her brother locking her up.

"Our home wasn't a place where kids wanted to hang out. So I'd go over to my friend, Timmy's house. Soapbox racing was big, and he and I spent a lot of time building cars and taking them on the hills."

"Emily mentioned that you liked to play games," Blair said.

The air in the room went still. It was a long moment, as we all stared at each other and the sound of a lawn mower outside purred in the background.

Finally, "All kids play games, don't they?" He said to Blair, as if to challenge her. When she didn't respond, he said, "Emily played mostly with her dolls. She had names for them and pretended they were real. She pretends a lot of things are real. I assume you know that she's not well."

"Yes, we do," Blair replied. "I'm sorry about that."

It grew quiet again.

"What about your older sister, Rose?" I asked. "Did she have a lot of friends?"

He turned to me. "She had a boyfriend."

My senses came alert. "A boyfriend? Do you remember his name?" I pulled out my little notepad. "You don't mind me taking notes, do you?"

"As long as you're not going to testify against me in court," he said with a wry twist to his mouth. "Chris Stephens. That was the guy she hung around with most. His family might still be around. But if you want to talk to him, you're out of luck. He died our first year there."

I heard Blair suck in a quick breath. "What happened?"

He shifted his attention to Blair again. "I don't know much about it. I just remember my father telling Rose that Chris was dead. Then I heard my parents talking about it later. The police thought he'd been in a fight. He was beat up pretty badly. His body was found where Luther Burbank Park is now." A brief smile played across his lips.

"Your sister must have been crushed," Blair said.

The smile disappeared. "I'm sure she was. At least she did a lot of wailing and carrying on about it," he said without emotion. "But then my parents shipped me off to boarding school on the East Coast, so I don't know what happened after that. At least until my sister died the following year," he said, dropping his chin.

It was the first time he'd shown any emotion.

"We heard about that; it must have been very difficult for your family. How did she die?"

His chin came up and he gave me a haunted look. "I was told she fell into the lake and drowned. None of us had ever had swimming lessons, so who knows?" he said with a shrug. He paused a moment and seemed to reflect on something. "She was so damned upset about her boyfriend's death though, that..." He stopped, his hands balled into fists on his desk. His eyes narrowed, and he looked up. "I wouldn't want to see any speculation about how my sister died in your book," he said quickly.

"Of course not," I said. "We'll be very careful. But that's a lot of tragedy for one family to absorb in such a short time."

His eyes seemed to glaze over for a moment. "Yeah, well, when God closes a door, as they say..." He was tapping his index finger on the blotter of his desk.

"What do you mean?" Blair asked.

He snapped back to attention and straightened up. "What else can I tell you about the property?"

His desire to change the subject was obvious, so I followed his lead. "What was life like on the island in those days?"

He shrugged. "Our family didn't spend a lot of time together. My father wasn't home much. He'd often stay in Seattle overnight. Sometimes even on the weekends. So Rose would sneak out to be with Chrisss...," he said, drawing the boy's name out with obvious distaste, "while Emily was in the barn talking to her dolls. And as I said, I'd go to Timmy's house. The only time we spent much time together was during the holidays."

"So Emily spent a lot of time in the barn," I said carefully.

He paused a moment, watching me. "Her behavior wasn't a secret back then. Her teachers knew it. And the other kids knew it. It's one of the reasons friends didn't like to come over. Anyway, she used to say that a woman lived out in the barn." A cynical laugh erupted from his throat, and he shook his head. "Emily said a lot of weird stuff like that. But it got worse after I was sent away. Around the time Rose died, Emily was diagnosed with schizophrenia and hospitalized." He stopped suddenly and began to rise. "Look, I don't feel comfortable talking about any of this, and I certainly wouldn't want any of it in a book."

Blair jumped in. "If you'd like to see the section on your family before we publish it, we'd be happy to show it to you."

He relaxed back into his chair, but my senses were on alert. Emily had mentioned a *girl* who lived in the walls out in the barn, not a woman. Could she have been talking about Lollie?

"I'm curious," Blair spoke up. "I have a younger brother who used to spy on me. He was such a pain in the ass. Is that how you know Rose would sneak out to see her boyfriend?"

An evil smile slid across his face. "Yeah, little brothers," he said, as if they all had espionage in common. "I followed her and watched her and Chris a couple of times."

"You mean you watched them have sex?" Blair asked.

His eyes flared and his right hand balled into a fist. "Not something I want to discuss."

"It's funny when you think about how many teenagers had sex back then, and yet so few ever got pregnant."

Foster went still, and we all sat for a few seconds, staring at each other. April was right; Blair had balls. Finally, I decided to go from one awkward subject to another.

"So why did your family move after only two years? There have been lots of reports of paranormal activity at the inn. Did you experience any of that?"

He shifted those intense brown eyes to me, picked up the pencil and started tapping it rapidly on his desk. "First of all, I don't believe in ghosts. Let's get that straight up front."

"But did anything happen that you were aware of? Your sister said there was a woman living in the barn. I assume that wasn't true."

"No. There was no woman living in the barn," he said with irritation. "Emily has mental health issues, I already told you that." He paused, still tapping the pencil. Finally, it seemed like he made a decision, and the pencil stopped. "But my mother said she saw a woman in the parlor once, who just walked through a wall. And in addition to the woman in the barn, Emily said there was a dog she used to play with, a big black Lab. But of course, there was no dog, either. We didn't have any pets, and my father would have never allowed a dog on the property. You have to understand that my mother suffered from depression and, well, you already know about Emily. So there were no ghosts."

"You never saw anything?" I asked.

"No. Of course not."

"But we have," I said.

Count to three.

"You're serious?" he finally said.

"Yes. We've had paranormal investigators out to verify it." I paused for a second and then decided to take a chance. "We've even heard voices out in the barn. Up in the attic."

"In the attic?"

"Yes. Did you ever experience anything like that? As a kid, you must have spent time over in the barn."

Inside, I felt like I was hyperventilating, wondering if he knew about the baby in the diaper bag. But on the outside, I maintained a semblance of calm.

"Yeah, sure, we all played over there when we first moved to the island. We'd play hide and seek up under the rafters until my father made it off limits."

"Why was that?" I asked.

He shook his head and seemed to turn inward. "My dad was a strict disciplinarian and had all sorts of rules." His expression became guarded again. "Listen, I don't mean to be rude, but I really do have to get back to work. There's not much more to tell. I hope I've been helpful." He stood up and we stood with him.

"Yes, thank you very much, Judge," I said. "I'll let you know when we think we're ready to publish."

We moved towards the door, but I stopped. "By the way, you don't have any family photos from back then that we might include in the book, do you?"

He stopped with his hand on the door knob. "I'm afraid you'd have to go back to Emily for that. She'd have any of the family photo albums."

Great.

CHAPTER TWENTY-THREE

When Blair and I made it back to the inn, we found a young man at the front desk talking to Crystal.

"Oh, Julia," Crystal said when she saw me. "This man is here to see you."

The young man had short, blond hair, wide-set eyes and a gold ring in his left ear.

"What can I do for you?"

"Are you the owner?" he asked.

"Yes. I'm Julia Applegate."

"I understand you're writing a book about the inn."

I paused a moment, wondering how he would know about the book. "Yes. My friends and I are researching the history of the property. Why?"

"I was hoping to talk to you about it. I'm a reporter."

"I'm afraid we're not ready to promote it yet."

"I don't mean to promote the book," he was quick to say. "I meant to help research one of the stories."

That piqued my interest. "Why don't we sit over here," I said, gesturing toward the breakfast room.

"I'll be in the apartment." Blair took my key and then disappeared down the hall.

"My name's Jake Dooley," he said, reaching out a hand.

I shook the young man's hand, but his name sent my mind whirring. *Where had I heard that name before?* We moved to one of the tables, where he placed his shoulder bag on the floor.

"What is it you have in mind, Mr. Dooley?"

He rested his elbows on the table, and I noticed a set of tattoos on one arm.

"My grandfather used to be the editor at the *Seattle Times*. He's the one who told me you're working on a book."

I inhaled quickly. "Of course. Your grandfather is Rush Dooley."

He gave me a shy smile. "Yes. He mentioned that he talked with your friend, Rudy. She told him about the book. And she was particularly interested in an article that Peter Vance wanted to publish fifteen years ago about the brothel that used to be here. Pops also mentioned Frank Miller down in Puyallup, the grandson of the guy who owned the brothel back in the thirties."

I felt a nervous twitter inside. "I'm not sure we're going to include anything about Mr. Miller," I said, remembering the guy with the tennis racket-sized hands and his aggressive friends.

"I'd still like to know anything you might know. I've decided to do an investigative piece of my own."

"On the brothel or on the death of one of the girls?"

"Both," he said. "I have Peter Vance's notes and original draft, and I went down to see Miller a couple of days ago. But he wasn't very helpful."

"I see," I said with a smile, remembering what Frank Miller had said about someone else coming to interview him. "We spoke to Frank Miller, too. He wasn't very helpful to us, either. But even if he knows anything, he probably wouldn't want to talk about it. At least not about any deaths on the property. And not to a reporter."

"I think he knows much more than he lets on," he said. "Fifteen years ago, Vance had somehow found out about a guy named Jack LaRue. He worked for Gramley Miller in the brothel. According to his notes, LaRue's family told Vance that Jack was paid to bury one of the prostitutes. I asked Frank Miller about that and he was pretty brusque with me. I got the feeling he knew something, but didn't want it divulged."

I shrugged. "Can you blame him? You're talking about his grandfather. Is Vance still around? Maybe you could ask him where he got the information."

"No. He was killed in a car accident up in Bellingham quite a while ago."

"Well, if Frank Miller isn't interested in talking, how will you investigate it?"

"I was hoping you could help."

I chuckled. "Sorry. We only know about it because of what *your* grandfather knows."

"Yes, but you're out talking to people. You're liable to hear something," he said, hopefully.

I thought about Lollie and everything we'd learned about her, but it didn't feel right to mention any of that to a reporter.

"Well, we haven't learned anything, yet."

He sat back with a disappointed look. "Vance's notes also led me to Frank's sister. Her name is Mary Haley, and she lives in Leavenworth. I'm going up to speak to her tomorrow."

"You've done some good research. Do you know who Vance's anonymous source was?

"My Dad thinks it was Gramley's ex-wife, Miller's grandmother. Apparently she lived here on the property for a short time and then left Miller and moved east of the mountains with her daughter. Listen, Pops doesn't know I'm going after the story. I'm in the graduate program at the UW in Communications."

I dipped my chin and smiled. "So you're not working for the paper…yet."

"No. But I thought this would be the perfect opportunity to show them what I can do. I don't want to float in on my Pops' coattails."

"This could be dangerous, you know," I told him.

He laughed. "For something that happened in the last century? I doubt it."

I arched my brows. "You'd be surprised what lengths people will go to protect their reputations." I thought about Frank Miller and the evil thugs he'd sent after us. "I'd just be careful if I were you."

CHAPTER TWENTY-FOUR

Blair and I spent the rest of the afternoon sorting through notes and putting information into the computer, careful to mark things as fact or just rumor. Clouds and a strong breeze rolled in as afternoon moved into evening, and a summer rain threatened. When Rudy swept in after dinner still dressed in her plaid Bermuda shorts and sleeveless blouse, she received a critical look from Blair.

"Is that what you wore to see people in Canada?" Blair said critically, giving her the once over.

Rudy glanced down at her shorts and tanned, weathered legs. "No. I had time for a quick round of golf this afternoon. So what?"

Blair shrugged. "So it's supposed to rain."

"This is Seattle. It's always supposed to rain," Rudy said with an exaggerated scowl. She leaned over to pet the dogs, who were begging for attention. "Besides, it's still in the low 70s, so not exactly coat and muffler weather."

A short knock got the dogs barking again, forcing Rudy to pause. A moment later, Doe stepped in holding up a bottle. "I brought wine."

Blair cheered, and I went to the cupboard for glasses. As I deposited the glasses on my small antique table, I said, "It just so happens that I have some oatmeal cookies left over from the snack tray." I returned to the kitchen and took the aluminum foil off of a plate on the counter.

"Jeez, Julia, you're always so good about feeding us. Next meeting is at my house, and I'll make the snack," Doe said.

"Done," I said. "But you know it's not a problem. We're an inn, after all. There's food around here all the time. And I have the hips to prove it."

Doe laughed. "I was just about to say that you look like you've lost a couple of pounds."

"Nothing like having a new man in your life to help you lose weight," Blair said with a lift to her brows. "All that extra exercise."

"Well, there hasn't been much of that lately," I responded forlornly. "David's been too busy at work."

"Speaking of police work," Rudy said. "Any more news on the baby?"

"No, not yet," I said. "The medical examiner has the remains, so we're just waiting to hear from her."

"Did you tell David about what Amelia said?" Doe asked.

"No," I said with a sigh. "Somehow using our ghosts as a source for police work doesn't seem like such a good idea. Did you learn anything in Canada?" I said, turning to Rudy.

"Yes, but let's get settled first," she said.

We each grabbed our drink of choice. Doe took a seat in my wingback chair under the new *Wizard of Oz* poster, while Blair and Rudy took the sofa. I dropped into my recliner and invited the dogs into my lap.

"Okay, let's have it," I said to Rudy.

She had just taken a bite of cookie and almost choked, realizing she had to talk. "Okay, here goes," she said, swallowing. "I tracked down Lollie Gates' niece. Remember she mentioned a sister named Anna in the diary? Anyway, Luanne is Anna's daughter and Lollie's niece -- and she still lives in the old family home just outside of Vancouver. According to her, back in the fall of 1934, Lollie met a man at the library where she worked. He asked her if she'd ever thought about becoming a teacher and said that he represented a small school district on one of the islands in Washington State that was looking for someone who could start immediately. He said it didn't pay much, but it was a nice family community. She was thrilled. It's what she'd always wanted to do. So he told her to pack a bag and meet him at the train station that night. They never heard from her again."

"That bastard," Blair murmured, snacking on a cracker.

"Eight months later, Lollie's parents hired George Bourbonaise to find her," Rudy continued. "But the man who took her had given a phony school name, and so Bourbonaise had to search every island in Puget Sound looking for it. He came to Mercer Island last. He asked around, but there was no hint of her until someone mentioned the brothel. So he came posing as a john."

"Oh, God, he didn't have sex with her, did he?" Blair asked, alarmed.

"No. I don't think he even made contact with her. His instructions were just to locate her. He had a picture of her, so once he ID'd her, he went back to Canada to make a report."

"But why not try to rescue her?" Blair asked.

"According to the niece, her family suspected she'd been abducted. When they lost touch with her, they started asking around. Two other girls from the surrounding area had disappeared under similar circumstances. One turned up dead in Seattle. They were afraid for Lollie's safety."

"And that's when they wrote the letter we found," I said.

"Right. They paid Bourbonaise extra to come back with the letter and deliver it, while they planned a rescue mission. But then Bourbonaise dropped out of sight. So then they weren't sure if he was lying about finding her or not. They thought maybe he'd just run off with the money."

"But they knew where she was," Blair said. "Or thought they did. Why not just come here themselves?"

"Remember, this was back in 1935. Communication wasn't so easy back then, or quick. No cell phones or social media. So, they waited almost a month after Bourbonaise went back to give her the letter. They didn't hear anything and couldn't contact him, so her father and uncle came down. But by that time, the brothel had burned down and the property was abandoned."

"And any trace of Lollie was gone," Doe surmised.

"Yes," Rudy said. "*Except* the father and uncle started asking around on the island. They found a Baptist minister who had taken in one of the other girls who had escaped the night of the fire."

"Oh my God," Doe exclaimed. "That was Milton Snyder's family." Doe turned to me. "I was going to tell you that I went to see him this afternoon. But go ahead, Rudy. You finish and then I'll tell you what he told me."

"Okay. The young prostitute that the minister took in said that Gramley Miller had come for Lollie one night and dragged her out of the attic. She heard Lollie scream a few minutes later. The next day Miller showed up to take away all of her belongings."

"Wow," Blair said with a heavy sigh. "So Gramley Miller murdered her."

"Looks that way," Rudy said.

"What about Bourbonaise?" Doe asked. "They never heard anything more about him?"

"Well, we know he went back and gave Lollie the note, but he was never heard from after that. I spent some time with both the local police and the *Vancouver Sun* up there. That's their biggest and oldest newspaper. Anyway, after the brothel burned, Jack LaRue, a guy who worked for Miller, returned to Canada and used to hang out at a little pub on the outskirts of town. The owner of the pub directed me to an old guy who lives in a nursing home now. He knew some stories about LaRue. He said that LaRue used to talk about how Miller paid him $200 to get rid of Lollie's body, and then threatened to kill him if he told anyone."

"Wasn't that a bit dangerous?" Doe asked. "Telling tales out of school, so-to-speak? Miller could have come after him."

"I guess he didn't have any proof that Miller had killed her, and it wasn't too long after that that Miller died anyway. Did you learn any more from Snyder?"

"Mostly the same stuff, but more on Bourbonaise. The name of the girl who stayed with Snyder's great-grandfather after the fire was Kristina Fields. She was also from Canada and eventually the Snyders took her back up there. Anyway, she told Grandpa Snyder that she was the one who initially talked to Bourbonaise. Bouronaise paid to take her to a room, but no, he didn't sleep with her; instead he pumped her for information on Lollie and gave her a little money for the trouble."

"Sounds like a decent guy," Blair said.

"Yes. And when they went back down to the bar, she pointed Lollie out to him."

"Do you think she ratted out Lollie to Miller?" Rudy asked.

"No. She was hoping to be rescued along with her. Bourbonaise returned, and he asked for Kristina again and gave her the letter. She's the one who gave it to Lollie."

"So I wonder how Miller found out about Bourbonaise," Blair said.

"Grandpa Snyder thinks it was none other than the guy who ran the ferry," Doe said.

"Aria Stottlemeyer's great-grandfather?" I exclaimed.

Doe nodded. "According to Grandpa Snyder, Old Stottlemeyer was a big drinker and a big talker. *And* he was paid by Gramley Miller to keep his ears open."

"He was on the take?" My mind was whirring. *What would Aria think?*

Doe just smiled. "Remember what Goldie said...that he used to hear a lot of talk on the ferry. Well, I guess he got paid to pass some of what he heard along to Miller. For instance, he had a fog-horn on the boat that he'd only blow if the cops were aboard. That would warn Miller to hide the booze and the girls."

I sat back and began to chuckle. "It's not funny, but I'm sure it's not what Aria thinks of her great-grandfather. Now I really want to get my hands on that memoir."

"So he must have told Miller that Bourbonaise was looking for Lollie," Rudy said.

"Right. And when Bouronaise came back the second time, Miller probably killed them both," Doe said.

Blair perked up. "So I wonder where LaRue buried Lollie."

Rudy shrugged. "All this old guy said was that LaRue once told him he buried her where she would feel close to home."

"I wonder what that meant," Blair said.

"Where is the family home?" I asked Rudy.

Rudy gave me a sympathetic smile. "Right on the water."

"She's still here," I said breathlessly. "That's why her spirit is still here."

Blair looked over at me. "You want to find her, don't you?"

"Don't you?"

"Yeah, but you're not going to start digging big holes in your property, are you?"

"No, of course not," I said, quietly pondering where I could start digging.

"But where?" Doe asked.

"I presume down by the water," Rudy said.

Everyone was quiet for a few moments, and then Blair perked up again. "Maybe Miller's grandson, Frank, knew about the murders and that's why he kicked us out of his office. Now I want to go back and find out what he knows."

"Wait a minute," Doe said. "I'm not sure I want to turn this into a murder investigation again. I thought we were just researching the inn for a book."

"You're right, Doe. In the beginning, we were just trying to discover the reason for the hidden room," I said. "But now I think we have to consider Lollie…"

"And the baby," Blair said.

Doe sighed in defeat. "Here we go again."

"So, tell me about the baby," Rudy said.

"We really don't know much more," I said.

"Well, it wasn't Lollie's baby," Rudy said. "She was probably pregnant, but killed *before* she had a baby. So it could have belonged to one of the other girls."

"But why would they kill it?" Blair argued.

"Are you kidding?" Rudy said. "Back then, if a baby was deformed in any way, there would have been tremendous pressure to get rid of it."

"I don't want to talk about that," I said.

Rudy shrugged her narrow shoulders. "Look, even if it hadn't been a Down's Syndrome baby, babies wouldn't have been good for business. Or maybe one of the other women was jealous. I doubt we'll ever know. What did you learn in Puyallup? You said Frank Miller kicked you out?"

"Only because Julia was going through his personal belongings," Blair said.

"What's that supposed to mean?" Rudy asked.

We explained about the confrontation at the bar in Puyallup.

"Whoa," Rudy exclaimed. "He sounds dangerous. Do you think he was hiding something?"

"Yes," we replied in unison.

"Then maybe Blair's right and you need to go back and see what you can find out," Rudy said.

"And raise a hornet's nest? No thanks," I said. "You should see this guy. He could kill a bull moose with his bare hands. Besides, Rush Dooley's grandson also talked to him and didn't learn anything, either."

"Jake?" Rudy asked.

"Yeah. He came to see me this afternoon. He told me not to tell his grandfather, but he's trying to pick up the story that Peter Vance was writing fifteen years ago about the death of one of the prostitutes. He's already been to see Miller and got the same reception we did. Well, not the confrontation with the thugs. But anyway, we learned a lot yesterday from a different source," I said, nodding toward Blair. "We met with Mansfield Foster, the judge's son."

"What a charmer," Blair said with scorn. "But he did confirm how Rose died and the death of her boyfriend. A guy he didn't seem to like very much."

I glanced down at my notes. "The boyfriend's name was Chris Stephens. His body was found over where Luther Burbank Park is now."

"An accident or a murder?" Doe asked.

"Mansfield said he'd been beaten up pretty badly," Blair responded.

"And Mansfield was shipped off to boarding school right about then," I added. "And of course, Rose died a year or so after that. He seemed to suggest her death could have been suicide because she was so despondent about the death of her boyfriend."

"Does anyone think the judge might have killed the boyfriend to get him out of his daughter's life?" Rudy asked.

"He *was* a control freak," Blair said. "And maybe a sex pervert."

"Okay," Doe said, putting her hand up. "We're going down a road we shouldn't go down."

"You're right," I said, chagrined. "In fact, I'm beginning to wonder if we should even do the book. We keep uncovering really unsavory things about people."

"Wait a minute," Rudy said, putting down her wine. "Let's not get cold feet now. We can always decide later whether we want to produce a book or not."

"But don't you think we're getting in too deep?" Doe said. "We're talking about people's personal lives here."

Rudy seemed to contemplate this for a minute. "Look, I've spent my entire life as an investigative reporter. This comes as second nature to me, whether it's someone's personal life or not. If there's a story, there's a story. That said I'm not interested in anyone's sex life. But if someone was murdered, that's always worth investigating."

The rest of us contemplated that for a moment.

"You're right," Doe relented. "As long as we keep things in perspective."

"Agreed," Rudy said. "Now, let's go over what we have."

CHAPTER TWENTY-FIVE

We spent the next hour and a half putting together an outline that included details about each family that had lived on the property. It included Ruthie Crenshaw's pregnancy, Lollie Gates and the brothel, the suspicious death of Judge Foster's daughter Rose, and much more. We finished, and Rudy and Doe left. Blair went to get ready for bed, while I sat in my chair, reviewing our work.

"What do you think?" Blair said a few minutes later from the hallway, dressed in a sleeveless, pink nightgown.

I glanced up, rubbing my eyes. "I'm not sure. I agree with Doe that we're getting in pretty deep."

"But?"

I sighed. "I agree with Rudy, too. I feel responsible for Lollie now. And the baby. I want to know what happened to them. I want some kind of closure."

"Well, it's still early. Why don't we organize the photos?"

We spent the next two hours organizing photos and chatting about the different storylines we'd run across. It was after midnight when I stood up and stretched.

"I need chocolate," I said, pulling my arms over my head. "You haven't had anything to eat in a while; can you have a cookie?"

She raised her head and looked at me through bleary blue eyes. "No. I'm good. I think I'll go to bed. I'll see you in the morning."

We left things on the table in organized stacks. Blair went to her bedroom, while I stepped out into the inn's main hallway, leaving the dogs behind.

The inn was quiet, except for the rhythmic ticking of the grandfather clock near the front door. As I passed the reception desk, I heard the faint sound of music from one of the upstairs bedrooms. I turned the corner into the breakfast room, which was lit with a small accent lamp, leaving most of the room in dark shadow. I moved quietly so as not to wake Ahab, whose cage was draped in the far corner.

I pushed open the kitchen door and let it swing closed behind me. I'd seen April bring in some of her mint chocolate chip brownies earlier that afternoon. We usually boxed them up and had them for sale behind the reception desk, along with her fudge. But I knew she'd leave a stash for me in an antique jar I kept in the corner.

I grabbed a glass of milk and put two brownies on a plate, thinking I'd have one in case I got hungry in the middle of the night. With both hands full, I used my right hip to swing the door open again and step through.

I ran right into Blair and threw up my hands, flinging both the plate and glass to the floor.

We both let out high-pitched screams, which woke Ahab. He started to squawk, "Help! Help!"

"Oh my God, Blair! You scared me to death," I said, bending over to catch my breath.

"You did pretty good yourself," she said, leaning against the breakfast counter to steady herself.

"I do believe in spooks. I do believe in spooks," Ahab squawked. In the background, the dogs had started to bark in my apartment.

"They're heeeeere," Ahab squawked loudly.

"Shhhh," I hushed Ahab.

"Are you two drunk?" a snarly voice said.

Blair and I whirled around to find four members of the Welch family standing in the shadows of the foyer, including the elder Mrs. Welch, her pinched features looking even more, well, pinched. I contemplated blaming the ghosts, but thought better of it and then just blurted out a lie I would come to regret.

"Drunk? No, of course not, we…uh…uh, just saw a…a…spider."

"Mouse," Blair said at the same time.

I paused, holding my breath, wondering how we would get out of this. Why hadn't I just admitted to bumping into Blair in the dark?

"Which was it?" the elder Mrs. Welch said with annoyance.

"A spider mouse," Blair replied before I could respond.

I pressed my lips together, holding back any comment.

"What's a spider mouse?" her daughter asked.

"They're creepy little…"

"Tiny mice," I interrupted Blair, bumping her hip with mine. "They're very small." I used my thumb and index finger to demonstrate.

"With lots of creepy legs," Blair added.

"No," I said with an eruptive laugh. "No. She's…um…just joking. They're just tiny little mice. Quite cute, actually. They come in sometimes because of, you know, all the food," I said, gesturing around the room. "We just set some traps, and…"

"Squash them," Blair announced.

I dropped my gaze, not really knowing how to save the moment. When I glanced up, the six of us stood awkwardly staring at each other. Finally, Mrs. Welch said, "You people are weird."

The group turned toward the stairs and returned to the second floor, mumbling to themselves. We watched them go, and then I turned to Blair.

"Spider mice? Really?"

Blair shrugged. "They could exist."

"Why are you out here, anyway?" I asked, leaning over to pick up the plate. "I thought you were going to bed?"

"I decided I was hungry and was hoping you still had some of those mixed nuts."

I sighed loudly. "C'mon." I picked up my squished brownies and threw them onto the plate and then grabbed my empty glass. I marched through the kitchen door again, to which Ahab remarked, "Going so soon?"

This time, I flipped on the light in the kitchen. My dead brownies went into the trash and the plate and glass into the sink.

"Give me a second," I said. I grabbed a wet towel and went back to wipe up the milk. When I returned, Blair had pulled out the can of nuts. I served up another brownie for me, and then the two of us sat at the table next to the window. I started to chuckle.

"What?" Blair said.

"That was too funny," I said, cutting off a piece of brownie with my fork. "You realize that the elder Mrs. Welch is a retired science teacher. I bet she's upstairs right now googling 'spider mice.'"

Blair started to laugh with me. "Then I'm sure you'll get a lecture from her tomorrow."

We were sitting at opposite ends of the table. Blair happened to glance out the window towards the barn. "What's that?"

"What?"

"There's a light up in the attic out in the barn," she said, leaning forward and pulling the curtain aside. "Do you think it's April?"

I got up and peered through the window. Sure enough, a light glowed in the upstairs window. It moved back and forth, as if someone were walking around with a candle or small lantern. A chill ran the length of my spine.

"No. Why would she be up there?"

"Maybe it's a ghost," Blair said, peering out the window.

"Goldie said something about one of the previous families seeing someone walking around the attic with a candle, but when they got there, the place was empty."

Blair got up. "C'mon."

"Whoa!" I responded. "Where are you going?"

"We need to find out who's out there."

"Wait! I've been attacked twice by intruders here. What if it's not a ghost?"

"Then we kick their butts," she said, heading for the door.

"Blair!" I glanced at her feet, which were encased in fuzzy pink slippers. "What are you going to do, smother them to death? Let's at least go get shoes. And then I want to call April, just in case it is her. And we're only going to see if the barn has been broken into. If it has, we're calling the police."

"Fine," she said with a scowl.

We went back to my apartment, and I called April. She was watching TV, but said she'd get her robe and meet us out back. We hurried to put on shoes. I grabbed a big flashlight and the key to the barn, and Blair grabbed the baseball bat I kept in the corner in case of intruders. Then we went out the back door of my apartment and circled around the north end of the inn.

We hurried to the front of the bakery and peered up to the two dormer windows of the attic. The light was still crossing back and forth, from one end of the room to the other, as if someone was just roaming around.

A footfall made us whip around.

"What?" April whispered, putting up her hands. "I said I'd meet you out here."

She was draped in a blue robe, but had on tennis shoes.

"Okay," I said in a quiet voice. "What do you think?" I asked her.

She studied the light for a moment. "I don't know. Could be an intruder. Have you checked the doors?"

"Not yet."

The three of us crept to the front door, our feet crunching on the gravel walkway. It was locked.

"Let's check the side door," I whispered.

We tip-toed as quietly as we could to the side door. It was also locked.

"What do you want to do?" April asked. "Do you think someone broke in and then locked the door behind them?"

I shrugged. "I don't know. I can't imagine why anyone would break in and then go to the attic."

"So you think it's a ghost," Blair said with a hint of enthusiasm.

"I don't know that, either. But since there is a history of this happening, I say we go look."

April looked cautious, but Blair lifted the baseball bat. "Let's go," she said.

I unlocked the door, and we slipped inside. The warehouse was dark, with only the moonlight coming through the one window along the south side of the building. Our stacks of antique furniture loomed above us like misshapen monsters in the dark. I flicked on the flashlight, and we began to climb the stairs.

We reached the landing without incident and stopped to listen. The door to the attic stood open.

"Most likely Mr. Piper left the door open," I whispered. "Do either of you hear anything?"

They both shook their heads.

"Okay, here we go."

I approached the open door with trepidation. This might be a ghost, but what if it wasn't? After all, I'd confronted an intruder recently who had stolen Ahab and almost killed me in the process. I stopped just outside the door and turned to my companions.

"Are you ready?" I whispered. They both nodded with grim expressions. I eyed the bat Blair held in a striking position. "Just don't hit me in the back of the head with that."

"Hmpf," she grunted.

I inched forward, the two of them right behind me. The light continued to flicker in the room, and then it went out. I stopped.

"The light went out," Blair whispered behind me.

"I can see that," I whispered back. "Hello," I called out. "Is someone there? We've called the police."

Nothing. I turned to Blair and April. April nodded. We kept going.

We stepped cautiously through the door and were greeted with the distinct odor of burning candle wax. I used the flashlight to find the source. The candle holder we'd found in the hidden room sat on top of an old chest of drawers, a lazy swirl of smoke rising from its wick. I stepped forward and picked it up. There was liquid paraffin in the well of the candle and the wick was still warm.

"Damn," I said, exhaling.

Blair moved over to the wall and flicked on the overhead bulb. The room was flooded with a dim, but otherwise welcoming, light.

"Let's look around," I said. I turned off the flashlight.

We wandered around the room, pushing boxes and furniture aside to make sure no one was hiding. We even stepped into the hidden room. The small door that led under the roofline was closed and nothing was amiss.

"So are we all in agreement?" Blair said. April and I turned to her. "Ghosts?"

"Yeah," I agreed. "But why? Why would a ghost show up here in the attic with a candle, when it's never done that before? At least not as long as we've lived here."

"Because there's still a story to be told, and now we're paying attention," April said.

"Do you hear the voices again?" I asked her.

"No," she said. Her eyes shifted, as if she were listening to something. "In fact, it's eerily quiet."

"C'mon," Blair said. "Let's go back. This place gives me the creeps."

We returned to the ground floor and locked the door before returning to the front of the building.

"I wonder if it has anything to do with the baby in the diaper bag," I said, glancing back up to the second floor.

"Why would it?" Blair asked. "We've already found it."

I shook my head. "I don't know. There's got to be a reason."

"Look!" April exclaimed, pointing to the upstairs window again.

The candle flicker was back. I whirled around and raced back inside. Before I could make it all the way into the room, however, the light went out again, leaving me breathless and frustrated in the doorway.

"So?" Blair asked, coming up behind me.

"It went out again."

I stepped into the room and flicked on the overhead light. "No one's here," I said, glancing around.

Then something I saw made me gasp.

"What is it?" April asked.

I pointed to where the candlestick had been moved to the other side of the room.

CHAPTER TWENTY-SIX

Dreams are like elusive butterflies. They flit from one scene to another with sometimes only a random connection or familiarity between them. And yet when you're in a particular dream, it seems to make perfect sense.

Once I fell asleep that night, I was treated to a parade of visual images: prostitutes selling themselves to men with big cigars; entire nurseries of babies struggling to get out of locked rooms; pregnant women running from sweaty men with big hands; and ghosts leaving candles to burn down the room they had been meant to illuminate.

So it was no surprise that I greeted the next day bleary-eyed and a little cranky. Blair had left early for her Pilates class and to run some errands, so I went to the kitchen to help April with breakfast. I was standing at the counter in the breakfast room rubbing my eyes, when old Mrs. Welch sidled up to me and whispered in a harsh voice.

"I hope you didn't mean that you saw a mouse *spider* last night, because mouse *spiders* are indigenous to Australia and extremely venomous."

Inwardly I cringed. *Dammit!* I knew she'd go look it up.
"Uh...no. It was just a little mouse, like I said. Not a spider."

"I certainly hope so. I wouldn't want to put the children in danger."

I turned to admonish her for such a careless remark, but her expression shut me down. I was sure that if she could have shot darts from her eyes, I would have been impaled like a pin-cushion.

"No, of course not," I said. "My mother always called them spider mice…because, uh, you know, they're so small. That's all. I learned it from her." I silently hoped my mother wasn't listening from the nether-world. If she was, I knew she would take it out on me the next time she called.

The elder Mrs. Welch pressed her thin lips into a straight line and stomped over to a table where her husband sat toying with an English muffin. "Well, I took care of *that,*" she said.

I exhaled in relief. Maybe that would be my only encounter with her that day. I couldn't help but glance through the back windows to the barn, thinking about the strange occurrence the night before. I wondered what our snooty guest would think of that. She was already getting woken up at night, presumably by one of the ghosts knocking on her door. Would that I could mobilize all of them to teach her a lesson.

The morning progressed normally. The Welches left after breakfast for some sightseeing. April had shrugged off the candle-wielding ghost from the night before and was working in the bakery as usual. On the other hand, I kept checking the dormer windows in the second story of the barn, as if I might see the candlelight again in broad daylight.

Rudy called just before lunch to tell me she'd located the Kettle sisters' niece, Grace Rolston, and had made an appointment to see her. We decided to drive to Queen Anne that afternoon. But first, Blair returned with news.

"I stopped by the senior center," she said, catching me in the kitchen of my apartment. "They hold their craft class today. A couple of their regulars have lived on the island forever, so I thought I'd give them a try. And I learned something interesting."

I looked up from the turkey sandwiches I was making. "What's that?"

"I found Ruthie Crenshaw," she announced. "The girl who had the baby out of wedlock."

"Really?" I said, putting the plates on the table. "Does she still live here?"

"Yes, down by the bridge. She's married to a doctor." Blair paused with an expectant look.

"You want to go see her," I said matter-of-factly.

"Don't you?"

"Yeah. But I can't. Rudy just called. She found the Kettle sisters' niece and we decided to go see her this afternoon. Why don't you go see Ruthie alone? You know the drill. We want pictures, any unusual stories, and if you can slip it in, what happened to her baby?"

"That's going to be awkward," Blair said.

"Not really. We're researching the property and the people who lived here at one time. I think it's pretty natural that we might have run across the fact that she was pregnant. Just keep it casual and if she's concerned, we won't use any of it in the book. We're just trying to fill in some blanks."

÷

Grace Ferrar Rolston, niece of Pettie and Pearl Kettle, lived in a big Victorian on Queen Anne Hill. It was painted a pale pink with a deep raspberry trim and had a broad front porch and steep steps leading up to the front door.

We were greeted by a slim, attractive woman in her early to mid-forties, dressed in jeans and a short-sleeved cotton blouse. She was tall like her grand-aunts, but had brown hair and hazel eyes.

"It's so nice to meet you," she said, leading us into a sitting room. "Can I get you anything to drink?"

"No, thank you," Rudy said. "We don't want to take up much of your time."

We were interrupted by some loud banging, which made us all turn toward the back of the house.

"I'm sorry about that. We're gutting our master bedroom upstairs and combining it with a second bedroom to enlarge it."

"Your home is lovely," I said, looking around at a plethora of quality and expensive antiques that filled the room.

"Thank you. I've lived here my entire life – well, except for the years I was away at college. My aunts moved in after my mother died. My father was gone a lot, so they really raised me."

"Is your father still alive?" Rudy asked as we followed her into a beautiful sitting room.

The antique furniture was exquisite and once again, I felt myself salivate.

"Yes, but he and his new wife live in Florida now," Grace said. "Please sit down," she said, gesturing to the sofa. "So, I understand you're writing a book about the St. Claire Inn. I visited my aunts a couple of times there, but of course I was very young, so I don't remember much."

"We were wondering if you had any photos from back then," I said. "We'd like to show how the building might have changed over the years."

"I do," she said, grabbing a photo album from the table next to her. "Since I knew you were coming, I found this old album in Aunt Pettie's cedar chest. It has some great pictures." She opened the book and turned it around for us. "For instance, here's a photo of Aunt Pettie and Miss LaFontaine."

She pointed to an old color photo of a tall, angular woman standing next to a heavyset woman in a blue flowered caftan.

"This is Miss LaFontaine," she said.

The woman in the photo had several thick chains dangling around her neck. When I noticed she was also wearing a large pendant with an eye in the middle of it, I nearly laughed out loud.

"She was a psychic they hired to hold séances out there," Mrs. Rolston said, sitting back. "You won't believe this, but my aunts both believed in ghosts. They claimed that they saw a woman dressed in a nightgown come down the stairs and walk through a wall."

"Really?" Rudy said with false surprise.

I shot her a warning glance.

"Oh, yes," Mrs. Rolston said. "They reported all sorts of unusual activity. They even said that they'd seen Harry Houdini there."

Well, that was news to me.

"Houdini?" Rudy said with suspicion.

"According to Aunt Pearl, they were in the parlor having tea one night and suddenly there was a man sitting in the chair next to the fire, shuffling a deck of cards."

"And they knew it was Harry Houdini?" Rudy asked.

"I guess so. They had pictures of him and said it looked just like him. I don't have it anymore, but I guess they found an old newspaper article with a photo of Houdini visiting the hotel. That was long before the St. Claires owned the property, of course."

"Did they ever see him again?" I asked. "I mean, Houdini?"

"Once. Or at least they thought it was him. Aunt Pettie said they saw someone out in the attic of the barn, walking around with a candle one night."

My heart clenched at the mention of the candle. I didn't for one moment think our visitor the night before had been Harry Houdini, but apparently the candle-carrying ghost had been doing this for a while.

Mrs. Rolston pulled the photo album back and flipped through a couple of pages. Meanwhile, I glanced at Rudy, who raised her eyebrows and gave me a brief smirk. She was enjoying this.

"Here's a picture of one of the séances," Mrs. Rolston said, turning the book towards us.

A group of six people were sitting around an octagonal table in what looked like the attic of the barn. Miss LaFontaine was at one end, facing the camera, her long, frizzy hair catching the light.

"Were any of the séances successful?" I asked, already knowing the answer.

"No," Mrs. Rolston admitted. "But I understand Miss LaFontaine became ill at this one. She had to excuse herself."

I remembered what Ben and Goldie had said about the psychic getting a migraine, just like April had. My gaze drifted back to the picture, and I focused on the details.

Suddenly, it felt like my heart was too big for my chest. I leaned in to peer more closely at the group of believers.

Behind Miss LaFontaine was the hazy image of a young girl I'd seen in pictures at the inn. She had on a calf-length nightgown, and long, dark hair with wide-set, dark eyes.

Chloe!

Mrs. Rolston and Rudy were talking about the séances and ignoring me. I picked up the book and drew it towards me, fascinated.

Chloe hadn't been in the picture moments before. I was sure of that. But I also felt sure that if I offered the picture to my companions, her image would disappear. She meant this moment for me alone.

I studied Chloe's image, realizing that her attention wasn't focused on Miss LaFontaine, but on someone else in the photo. She was pointing a finger at a familiar-looking young man standing behind one of the guests at the table.

As soon as I realized what she was doing, her image faded.

I inhaled sharply.

"What?" Rudy asked, turning to me.

I glanced up. "Huh? Oh, nothing." I turned to Mrs. Rolston. "Any chance we could take this picture and use it in our book? I'll make sure you get it back."

"Certainly," she said, reaching for the book and carefully removing the photo. She handed it to me. "You know, my aunts were heartbroken when they had to leave Mercer Island."

"We understood they came to take care of you," Rudy said.

"That's partly true," she said wistfully. "But they were also broke. They'd sunk everything they had into that property. That's one of the reasons they started having the séances. They hoped the séances would become popular. When they didn't, my aunts went further into debt. Finally, the one thing of value they still owned was stolen and they were forced to sell."

"What was that?" I asked, my body still humming from the ghostly encounter with Chloe.

"A unique diamond and pearl necklace their mother left them." She flipped pages again. "Here's a picture of it."

We both glanced down at the multi-tiered, diamond necklace draped around Aunt Pearl's neck. I stared at it in awe.

I'd seen that necklace recently -- draped around the neck of Frank Miller's wife!

"How was it stolen?" Rudy asked.

"They had a young man working there as caretaker, and they caught him going through the drawers in their bedroom one day. Of course, he lied and said he was just looking for something, so they fired him. It wasn't until he was gone that they realized the necklace was also gone."

"And they couldn't have him arrested?" I asked.

"They reported it to the police, but he disappeared. No one could find him. And shortly after that, they came to live here."

"Could we tell their story in the book?" I asked her, tearing my gaze away from the necklace. "The séances, Houdini, and the necklace?" She nodded, and I added, "Any chance we could also show this picture?"

She removed the second picture and handed it over. "I think my aunts would be very pleased." She stood up. "Now, I was wondering if you'd like to see the rest of the house. I googled the St. Claire Inn and noticed that you sell antiques. Nothing is for sale here, but we have quite a collection."

CHAPTER TWENTY-SEVEN

"Okay, what gives?" Rudy asked as soon as we were back in the car. "What was going on with that first picture you got Mrs. Rolston to give you? You clearly saw something you didn't want to discuss."

"It was Chloe. She was in that picture."

Rudy's face crinkled in confusion. "What? I didn't see her in that picture."

"I know. One minute she wasn't there, and the next minute she was. That's when I picked up the book. And guess what?" Rudy shot me a curious glance as she turned a corner. "She was pointing directly at a young man in the picture."

"Yeah, there was a guy standing in the background. So what?"

"I know that man." I reached into my purse and removed the picture. "This guy in the background is a young Frank Miller," I said, staring at the photo again.

"Frank Miller? You mean the guy from the bar in Puyallup? Gramley Miller's grandson?"

"That's the one. I'd recognize that bowling ball head of his anywhere. But I've also seen that necklace Mrs. Rolston showed us."

"Do tell," she said.

"He has a picture of him and his wife in his office. The necklace is draped around his wife's neck in the picture. And it was the moment he saw me holding the picture that he kicked us out."

Rudy inhaled in surprise. "*He* stole the necklace."

"He must have been the caretaker, so yeah, I'd bet my life on it."

187

÷

When we arrived back at the inn, we found Blair and April at the front desk.

"We have news," I blurted. "C'mon. Let's go in here."

We went into the breakfast room and sat down. We told them all about the Kettle sisters, the séances, the photos, the stolen necklace, and then Chloe and Frank Miller. I removed the two photos from my purse. Blair took them first.

"You're right. This is the same necklace from the picture in Miller's office," she said.

I'd counted on Blair's confirmation. She had a photographic memory, especially for things like expensive jewelry.

"And that's a young Frank Miller?" April asked, pointing to the picture of the séance.

Blair peered at the photo. "Oh, yeah. That's him. Beady eyes and all. I bet that's why he kicked us out of there so quickly. You were holding the picture of the necklace he stole, and we were there asking questions about the inn."

I sat back. "So, he worked here, and yet he tried to play dumb with us."

Blair sat back, too. "Now what?"

"I could tell David. Maybe they could arrest him for theft," I said.

"He could just say he found it at a garage sale," April said.

"Even with the photo of him at the séance?" Blair asked.

"Yeah," Rudy agreed. "That wouldn't be enough proof. And there's probably a statute of limitations on things like that, anyway."

"But Mrs. Rolston said he worked there, and they caught him going through their house, looking for stuff. He disappeared and the necklace disappeared," I said.

"Yes, but that's still not enough to arrest him," Rudy replied. "Besides, the sisters are gone now."

Blair sat back with a huff. "Bummer. Well, I have news, too. I visited with Ruthie Crenshaw."

That got everyone's attention.

"What did you learn?" Rudy asked.

"She did have a baby. But she gave it up for adoption, just like she'd implied in her diary. She'd like to have her diary back, by-the-way. But she did give us permission to tell her story. She and her daughter have re-connected, so it's no secret."

"Well, at least we have that," I said. "Jake's already been to see Frank Miller, and he found Miller's sister, Gramley Miller's granddaughter. He wanted to partner with us on the story, but I was honest in saying that we weren't sure where we were going with all of this."

"Did you tell him about Lolllie?" Blair asked.

"No. But I might if for some reason we don't do the book."

÷

Rudy and Blair left to do some shopping, while April and I went back to work. Around 4:00, I excused myself to catch a nap. I ended up sleeping for almost two hours. A soft knock at my door woke me. It was early evening, and April stood there holding a ceramic dish with freshly made macaroni and cheese.

"Oh God, that smells good," I said, stepping back to let her in. "But where's Blair?"

"She'd promised to have dinner with her sister-in-law. She'll be back later. So you're stuck with me."

"Never," I said with a smile.

April and I sat at my small kitchen table to share dinner.

"By the way, right after you laid down, that young man, Jake, called," April said. "He had an appointment this evening up in Leavenworth with Mary Haley, Gramley Miller's granddaughter, and was hoping you'd go with him. I wonder what he hopes to find out from her."

"She might be the keeper of old family photos and stories passed down from generation to generation. Actually, I wish I could've gone with him."

As we ate, I filled April in on our findings thus far, and then April took the dishes back to the main kitchen. I changed into my nightgown and settled into my recliner to catch up on a mystery I was reading.

It was after nine o'clock, and I was well into a rather twisted psychological thriller when there was another knock at my door. It was Crystal, who had agreed to work a little late to pick up some extra hours.

"That young reporter is here to see you," she said. "I told him you'd turned in for the night, but he says he has something important to tell you."

I sighed. "Okay. I'll meet him in the library. I'll be there in just a minute."

It took me a few minutes to get dressed again, and then I joined Jake in our library. He was standing at the floor-to-ceiling bookcase perusing the books.

"How was your trip to Leavenworth?" I asked.

He turned. "Good. I'm sorry to bother you."

"Not a problem. Please, sit down." I gestured to a leather sofa, while I took an upholstered chair nearby. "Crystal said you wanted to tell me something you learned."

"Yes. I saw Mary Haley today. She confirmed that Miller abducted young women and forced them into prostitution. That was the reason her mother left him. She said he often went to Canada and brought girls back."

I nodded. "We pretty much knew that. In fact, Frank Miller told us that his grandfather used to transport his 'product' in the false bottom of a big chest."

"That's what she said, too. But it gets worse. She says he murdered at least one of the girls, and maybe more."

"How would she know that? Her grandmother left Miller pretty early on, didn't she?"

"Yes. But remember, her grandmother left her son, Joshua, behind. He was very close to his dad, and his dad confided in him. Gramley died shortly after he left Mercer Island, and then Joshua was sent to live with his mother in Leavenworth. Mrs. Haley said her he didn't get along with his mother. Joshua was too much like his father. Mean. Dishonest. Even cruel. But he talked a lot."

"And he talked about what his father had done."

"Bragged was more like it. Miller made it look like the first girl he killed had fallen into the lake and drowned. The second girl he killed because she was pregnant and had talked to a private investigator."

"Lollie," I said sadly.

"What?"

I gave a deep sigh. "That would be a girl named Lollie Gates. We found a letter from her mother telling her they were coming to rescue her. The private investigator you mentioned had snuck it to her through another one of the girls. But Lollie never actually talked to him. Anyway, we also have her diary where she talks about not feeling well. The way she described it, we assumed she was pregnant."

"Well, Mrs. Haley says that there's an old wooden jewelry box with inlaid ivory flowers on the top that was left to her by her grandmother. It has a ledger and some letters in it that can prove what she says. But she doesn't know where it is. She thinks Frank stole it when he stayed with her for a week several years ago."

"Why are you telling me?"

"Because I'm hoping you'll help me get it back."

"Whoa," I said, holding up a hand. "My first encounter with Frank Miller wasn't anything I want to repeat."

I related the story about what had happened to me and Blair at the Hardliner Pub.

"So he's hiding something," Jake said. "He didn't threaten me in any way when I was there, but he pretty much stone-walled me and told me not to come back."

"And now that's exactly what you want to do."

He shifted uncomfortably in his seat. "Not necessarily through the front door."

My eyes opened wide. "You want to steal the box back."

"I don't even know that he has it," Jake said.

"Oh, he has it," I responded, remembering the jewelry box sitting on Miller's bookshelf. "It's in his office."

Jake looked like he'd just won the lottery. "So, let's get it!"

"And how do you propose we do that? He knows both of us."

"Like I said, we wouldn't go through the front door."

"So we'd break in and steal it? Not interested."

"Why not?" a voice said from the hallway.

We both looked up to see Blair standing there. She swept into the room and sat next to Jake on the couch.

"We've done riskier things than that," she said.

"How long have you been standing there?"

"A while," she said with a shrug. She turned to Jake. "I say we go in under the cover of darkness."

He turned to me with a conspiratorial look. He had an ally.
Damn!

"Look, I already called the bar and Miller will be gone this weekend," he said.

"How did you find that out?" I inquired.

"I said I was coming into town for the weekend and was hoping to get an interview. The woman who answered the phone said Miller was leaving town."

Blair turned to me with a look of glee on her face. "See?"

"No, Blair. I am not getting arrested for this."

"We won't get arrested. We can go to the bar to hang out. And then we'll go looking for the restroom, which I might add is down that same hallway," she said.

"And what if the office door is locked?"

"I can handle that," Jake said. We both looked at him in surprise. "Hey, I've learned a few things in college."

"How to pick locks?" I asked. "What happened to U.S. History and Algebra?"

He smiled. "Some things you learn don't show up on a midterm."

CHAPTER TWENTY-EIGHT

The question of whether and how to break into Frank Miller's office kept us busy for the rest of the evening. Jake volunteered to spend the next two nights casing the bar to gather information, and then we promised to confer with him on Sunday afternoon to make our final decision.

I climbed into bed knowing that if I didn't go along with the plan we'd cooked up, Blair would go without me. So I slept little that night, pondering all the things that could go wrong and how I might look in an orange jumpsuit.

The next day was Friday. The pest control guys were done, and Blair was scheduled to return home. Friday was also the day the Welches were scheduled to leave. So, after breakfast I was kept busy checking out members of the family and helping turn rooms. Mr. and Mrs. Welch were the last to go.

"I hope you enjoyed your stay," I said, as Mrs. Welch approached the desk.

I knew they hadn't, but felt obliged to ask. She ignored me while she searched her purse for her glasses. Harvey wandered over to my bird display and lowered himself into one of the antique chairs I had for sale.

"I can't imagine why your inn is rated so highly," she said, putting on her glasses. "You have very little in the way of entertainment, unless you consider your ghosts a form of entertainment. I assume that's who you'll say kept knocking on our door in the middle of the night, because it certainly wasn't any member of my family."

"I'm sorry," I said. "But, yes, I think it was Chloe. She's the little girl who died here, and she likes to play tricks on people. You aren't the first of her targets."

Mrs. Welch's face constricted as if she was passing gas. "That's ridiculous and you know it. There are no such things as ghosts."

The front door was closed, and yet a sudden gust of wind swirled around us. The small whirlwind circled Mrs. Welch for a moment, lifting her skirt, and then moved to the end of the counter, where it threw the myriad of local sightseeing brochures sitting in a rack into the air.

Harvey jumped up, and Mrs. Welch flinched back in alarm as the tiny tornado of wind approached her once again. As suddenly as it started, the tornado inside the room disappeared and the brochures fluttered to the floor.

Mrs. Welch clutched her chest and looked truly alarmed.

"Yeah, I didn't believe in ghosts at first, either," I said without sympathy.

She turned back to me with an icy look. "Please get our bill."

I stepped into our office to run a copy of their bill. "Here you go." I handed it over, thinking she would scrutinize every single charge. But she didn't. She folded it up and stuffed it into her purse just as the taxi flashed past the front windows.

"Would you like help out with your bags?"

"No. Let's go, Harvey," she commanded. But this time her voice lacked the authority it normally carried.

Harvey came to attention and stood up as the door opened. The driver confirmed his fare and grabbed their bags. Mrs. Welch stomped out without a word, but Mr. Welch stopped at the door and turned to me. He pointed a gnarly finger at the framed picture behind the reception desk. It was the Wicked Witch of the West flying over Oz, spelling out 'Dorothy' in pink smoke.

"I see that you admire the Wicked Witch of the West." He smiled ruefully and shook his head. "You wouldn't if you lived with her." He gave me a wink and then left.

÷

We spent the rest of the morning doing laundry, cleaning rooms and adding amenities to get ready for new guests.

Around noon, Doe called to say she had the afternoon off and wondered if I wanted to drive up to Camano Island to get the photo albums from Emily Foster. I called Emily, who readily agreed to a visit at 3:30 that afternoon.

We drove north in Doe's Mercedes, chatting about the book and some of the strange things that had happened so far. I said nothing about the potential theft of Frank Miller's jewelry box. I knew Doe would try to talk me out of it.

We took the Stanwood exit again, and I guided Doe to what Mansfield Foster had described as the family compound. The second time there, the reference made perfect sense.

The property covered at least twenty acres and had no close neighbors. It was fenced off from the rest of the world by barbed wire and butted up against the western cliffs of Camano Island. The only thing missing was a vicious guard dog.

Once again, we announced ourselves at the front gate, and Emily buzzed us in. As we stood waiting for her to answer the door, I couldn't help but glance up to the second floor window again. The curtain was partially open, and I thought I could see the shadow of something just behind the curtain. Was that the judge sitting in his wheelchair watching us again?

It was a few moments before Emily unlatched the heavy wooden door. Two dark eyes peered at us from the shadowed interior. When she noticed Doe, her eyes flared, and she swung the door wide.

"I thought you were coming alone," she murmured.

"I brought my friend, Doe Kovinsky. She's helping with the book."

Emily stared openly at Doe, as if she were seeing a ghost. And then I remembered how much Doe looked like Emily's mother.

"Welcome," she said stiffly. "Come in."

She stepped back and allowed us inside. She was wearing the same denim jumper, but with a dark green blouse. We followed her into the living room again, where she had already set out two glasses of lemonade. As I sat on the sofa, I noticed that she was still staring at Doe.

Doe looked up and caught her gaze. "Thank you for seeing us," she said.

That seemed to short-circuit Emily's brain, and she blinked. "Of course," she said, glancing away shyly. She turned to me. "I'm glad to see you again, Julia. You said you were hoping to see some photos."

"Yes. We visited with your brother. He said you had the family photo albums."

The moment I mentioned her brother, she seemed to tense up. "How *is* Mansfield?"

"Um…he's fine," I said. "I take it you don't see him often."

She gave a halting shake of her head. "Only when he wants something. He's very busy, you know. Just like my father was." Her gaze drifted over to Doe again. "Do you have children, Mrs. Kovinsky?"

This took Doe by surprise, and she glanced my way. "Uh…no, I don't. Were you and your brother close growing up?" she asked, probably hoping to change the subject.

"No. I wasn't close to either of my siblings."

"Your brother said the three of you used to play over in the old barn. I bet that was fun," I said, hoping to find out more about the attic.

Her head jerked in my direction. "Play?"

"Yes, he said you used to crawl under the rafters until your father made it off limits."

Her breathing sped up, and she took a couple of deep breaths. "Yes, yes, of course, we played over there. What else did he say?"

"He said you thought a woman was living over in the barn. You told us about the little girl who lived in the walls, but not about a woman."

I watched her closely, and every muscle in her body seemed to clench. "No. No." She shook her head, and one hand flew to her temple. "There was no woman. I…I was just pretending."

Her breathing had become ragged, and I realized that this was something that might have put her in the hospital so many years before. Something she'd probably worked very hard to forget.

"He also said something about being sent off to boarding school," I said quickly, hoping to redirect her thoughts. Her breathing began to return to normal.

"Yes. He didn't want to go, but my father insisted. It was right after Chris Stephens died. That was my sister's boyfriend." She sat up straight again, more relaxed. She turned to rest her gaze on Doe. "What does your husband do, Mrs. Kovinsky?"

Again, Doe threw a concerned look my way. "Uh…my husband died several years ago."

"I see. I'm sorry," Emily said. 'You look just like my mother, do you know that? Just like her. Would you like some lemonade?"

She offered one of the glasses to Doe, who seemed to have frozen in place. Doe finally took it. "Thank you. Do you have a picture of your mother?"

Emily sucked in a big breath and smiled broadly. "I'll get the photo album." She got up and hurried out of the room.

"Jeez, Julia. This woman is creepy," Doe whispered, putting the glass back down.

"I know," I said, getting up and wandering around the room.

The living room was probably decorated exactly as it had been when Holly Foster was alive. But if the rest of the house looked like this, Emily had never hired a housekeeper or moved into the 21st century.

I began perusing the bookcases as Blair had done on our first visit. When I found a couple of original *Oz* books on one shelf, I felt a thrill down to my toes. I pulled one off the shelf just as the sound of a door closing brought me to attention. Emily returned, holding a large padded photo album. She saw me at the bookcase.

"Do you like the *Wizard of Oz*?" she asked, noticing the book in my hand.

"It's my favorite movie, and I collect Oz memorabilia."

"Julia is somewhat of an expert on the *Wizard of Oz*," Doe said.

"Just the movie," I corrected her.

Emily dropped the photo album on the coffee table and hurried over next to me. "Really? I love the movie, too. Who's your favorite character, Julia?"

Oh, my God. I had something in common with Emily Foster.

"Uh…well, I guess the Wicked Witch of the West."

She gave a little laugh. "Oh, I'm so glad. I thought you would say Glinda. Everyone loves Glinda, but I think she's horrible. Don't you? She's so pretty and that voice drives me mad. I just want to…I just want to…" She brought her clenched fist up to her face for a moment and then let her hand drop. "I like the Cowardly Lion," she said, her eyes glinting. "I always wanted to be him."

"What do you mean?" I asked.

A hesitant smile flickered across her face. "Because he took charge of his life and was finally free." She paused and then returned to her chair. She pulled the chair forward so that she sat on the opposite side of the coffee table. "Let's look at photos," she said, abruptly changing the subject. She flipped open the album. "This book holds the pictures from when we lived on Mercer Island."

I sat down again next to Doe, while Emily flipped some pages and then turned it toward us.

"Here's a picture of my mother," Emily said, pointing to a black and white photo of a tall, elegant woman with short, wavy, dark hair. She turned her dark eyes on Doe once more, with an anticipatory stare.

Holly Foster did indeed look like a younger version of Doe. She had high cheekbones and wide-set eyes. Doe stared at the photo a moment, her face a blank slate. She was probably weighing whether or not to acknowledge the fact they looked like one another. I decided to do it for her.

"There *is* a resemblance," I said, trying to downplay the similarity. "Who is this next to her?" I hoped to shift attention away from Doe.

"That's my sister, Rose," Emily said. "She was very pretty. Everyone said so."

"Yes, she was," I agreed.

For the first time, I noticed that Rose and Emily didn't look very much alike. Rose was fair-skinned and blond, while Emily looked more like her mother.

"It's sad that Rose's boyfriend died so young. She must have been heartbroken," Doe said.

"Yes. She was. She blamed my father. He could get so mad sometimes." The flat of her hand reached involuntarily for her cheek.

"Did he hit you, Emily?" I asked.

She pulled her hand away from her face and slipped it under her thigh. "I was bad sometimes. Father had to discipline me."

"Did he discipline Chris Stephens, too?"

"Once," she said. "He didn't want that bastard kid hanging around Rose."

Doe and I exchanged glances as my heart rate sped up. *Bastard kid? Had the judge been involved with Chris Stephens' death?*

"It sounds like your father was very strict," I said, watching her closely.

"He just wanted to protect Rose. But it didn't do any good."

"Um…how did Chris die? Was he murdered?" I asked.

Her head snapped up, and she stopped. "Who said he was murdered?"

A chill rippled down my back. Maybe I'd gone too far. "I'm sorry. I just thought maybe he was. Your brother said he'd been beaten up."

She began biting the nail on her index finger.

"I wouldn't know anything about that," she said. "I don't know anything about *any* of the murders."

"What?" I said, thinking I hadn't heard her correctly.

She glanced back and forth between me and Doe. "Nothing. I…I misspoke." She abruptly pointed to the book. "That's Rose," she said, pointing to a picture of her and her sister on the front porch. Rose was sitting on the steps in shorts, her long, legs drawn out in front of her. Emily stood on the top step behind her, glowering down at her sister.

"Such a tragedy," Doe said. "It was an accident, wasn't it?"

Emily stared at the photo for a long moment and began to tap one heel against the floor in rapid succession. "She was strangled."

"Strangled? Mansfield made it sound like she drowned. He said none of you had ever had swimming lessons," I said.

She glanced up at me with a look of surprise. "Yes, I think you're right. She drowned."

My mind raced. *How could she mistake being strangled for drowning?*

"Who found her?" Doe asked.

Her eyes seemed to glaze over. "I did. And then I had to go tell my father. He was real mad."

"Mad at you?"

"Just mad. He loved Rose." She dropped her chin to stare at the photograph again. "My mother cried."

"Did you cry?" Doe asked gently.

"I don't cry." She suddenly reached out and grabbed Doe's hand. "C'mon. I want to show you something."

She pulled Doe up and led her out into the hallway. Doe shot me a panicked look, so I followed them past the big staircase.

There was a small service elevator at the end of the hallway, but she turned into an antiquated and filthy kitchen. Black and white floor tiles were crumbling and streaked with years of spilled soups and sauces. The counters were layered with crusted dishes. The old stove was covered with grease, and a fried onion smell hung in the air.

We continued through the kitchen and turned left into a sun room. The room was the size of a small bedroom. A floor-to-ceiling book case lined the far wall, while a large, paned window looked out over an overgrown backyard. But that's where the similarity to a normal room ended.

This must have been the room that Charlotte Rowe had said was set up for Judge Foster. But now, there was a crib in the corner, filled with old porcelain dolls. A rocking chair, very similar to the one we'd found in the attic sat in the opposite corner, draped with a hand-crocheted blanket. Below the window was a long bookcase, filled with children's books. And the floor was littered with dozens of toys.

When I glanced at Doe, I realized she was as horrified as I was. I actually felt it difficult to breathe.

This room looked just like the one in the barn attic.

"Do you have children, Emily?" Doe asked quietly, gazing around the room.

Emily released Doe's hand and moved to the crib, glancing around with a look of love. "No. Father wouldn't let me. He let Rose have a baby, but not me."

My stomach constricted as if someone had punched me in the gut, and I reached out to the wall for support.

Rose had had a baby? No one had ever mentioned that. I struggled to get air into my lungs and then asked, "Is that why there was a nursery in the old barn? Up in the attic?"

Emily whirled around with fear etched in her face. "You're not supposed to know about that."

I took a deep breath and tried to sound as casual as possible.

"We…uh…found a hidden room, a nursery like this one. We were doing some repairs. It's no big deal. The room's been there since the barn was built. In fact, back when there was a brothel there, they used that same room as a jail. But by the time we found it, it had an old crib and some books in it, just like this."

I happened to glance down to the bottom shelf of the bookcase and felt the blood drain from my face. Lined up in order, was what appeared to be the full collection of the Nancy Drew mysteries. We'd found the first in the series in our hidden room. Although I heard Emily still talking in the background to Doe, I was fixated on the lineup of books and mentally began ticking them off in order.

"But father won't like that you found out about that," she said behind me, her words coming fast. "No one will like it. You'll have to go now." She grabbed my shoulder, bringing me back to attention. We were ushered out of the room and back down the hallway.

"I'm sorry if we've upset you, Emily," I said. We'd stopped in the entryway. "May we still use some of your pictures?" I asked, nodding to the photo album on the coffee table.

She was biting her nails again. "No. I don't think so. You have to go now," she said, glancing up the stairs. "It's late. And I have to cook dinner for my father. I can't tell him you were here. He'll punish me if he knows you found the room."

CHAPTER TWENTY-NINE

Our visit to Emily haunted me for the rest of the evening, especially her comment that she didn't know anything about *any* of the murders. *How many had there been?*

But it was Emily herself who made me most uncomfortable. We already knew that she wasn't sane. But her behavior made the fact that she was caring for an elderly man seem dangerous. I decided to call Mansfield the next day.

"It's not that I think she will harm your father," I told him the next morning. "It's just that...well, I don't know when you were there last, but she can barely take care of that big house, let alone an invalid in his nineties. Don't you worry about him?"

"I appreciate your concern, Mrs. Applegate," he said. "My sister might suffer from a mental disorder, but she can function just fine. I think she'd tell me if there were any problems."

His response made me think that he just didn't want to get involved. I had to get his attention.

"She also said some crazy stuff, Mr. Foster."

"I'm not sure what you mean."

I paused, contemplating how much I should say. After all, I could be implicating either this man's sister, or even his father in a murder.

"She hinted that there had been multiple murders when you lived on the island. And I should tell you that someone else told me that your mother thought your sister, Rose, had been murdered."

"No. That was an accident. She drowned."

"But you suggested it might have been suicide."

"I just meant that maybe she was so despondent about Chris' death that she wasn't careful down by the lake. That's all."

"But Emily seemed to think she had been strangled. Then, she took us to a nursery set up in the back of the house, as if she's caring for a baby. And she mentioned that Rose had had a baby. Did you know about that?"

"What? No. This is all crazy. My parents would have told me." He sighed, and I heard him tapping, as if he were tapping his pen on the desk again. "But thank you, Mrs. Applegate. I see what you mean. Things *have* gotten worse. Perhaps Emily has stopped taking her medication again. She did that once before."

"I just don't want anything to happen to either of them," I said.

"No, of course not. I appreciate your concern. I'll check into it right away. Thank you for calling…really."

I felt better after hanging up. Rather than standing on the sidelines, I'd taken action, and hopefully both Emily and Judge Foster would be taken care of as a result. I spent the rest of the day feeling as if a weight had been lifted.

÷

Doe had invited us all over for dinner at her expansive home at the top of the island. Overlooking I-90 and across the water to Seattle, her home was a one-level, brick construction that looked like it was right out of a small hamlet in England, complete with ivy-covered windows, small green spaces accented with flowers, and flagstone paths.

Doe had made chicken enchiladas and rice, so we all pitched in to set the table and serve up the food.

As we worked, Blair asked, "So, how did it go with Emily yesterday?" In response, Doe and I shared a glance. Blair noticed and said, "What?"

"Well, let's just say I've never met anyone weirder," Doe said.

I saw Blair flinch and quickly added, "She was much worse today, Blair."

"What happened?" she asked.

"Where to begin?" Doe said, sitting down.

I hadn't told either Rudy or Doe about Blair's bi-polar brother and how he died. She hadn't asked me not to, but I felt it was up to her to reveal it in her own way and in her own time. As we took our seats and began to pass platters and bowls around, I tried to explain what had happened that day without hyperbole.

"She seemed much more agitated today," I began. "And while we were talking about the death of her sister's boyfriend, I asked if he might have been murdered. She got very upset with that and then implied that there was more than one murder back then." Both Rudy and Blair stopped what they were doing and stared at me. "And then she gave a different version of the story about how Rose died."

"What do you mean?" Rudy asked.

"First, she said that Rose was strangled," I replied. "But when we mentioned that her brother had said she had drowned, she suddenly agreed with that version."

"That could be a natural discrepancy," Rudy said. "Didn't you say that he was off at boarding school when it happened and that Rose was found in the shallows of the lake? Maybe something got caught around her throat."

"Yes, but guess who found Rose's body?" Doe asked.

"Emily," Blair replied.

"Bingo," Doe said, pointing her fork at her. "And then there was the creepy fact that she couldn't take her eyes off me."

"Because you look so much like her mother," Blair said.

"Yes," Doe said, toying with her rice. "It made me really uncomfortable."

"But nothing topped it off like the duplicate nursery she has set up in the back of the house," I said. "She's turned the sunroom into a nursery just like the one in the attic," I replied. "Down to the shawl draped over the back of the rocker."

"Wow. Did she say why?" Blair asked.

"No. But I asked her if she'd had any children, and she said no. That her father wouldn't allow it," Doe replied.

Blair almost choked on a sip of wine. "What does that mean? He wouldn't allow it."

"Who knows? But her father sounds like a total control freak. He adored Rose. Ignored Mansfield. And I don't know what he felt for Emily," I said. "But it was clear that he hit her."

"As in *beat* her?" Rudy asked.

"Possibly. But we haven't told you the most shocking part of it," Doe said. "Rose had a baby."

The room went still. Only the overhead fan moved silently above us. Finally, Rudy spoke up. "So, the nursery in the attic might have been set up for Rose's baby? Why?"

"No idea," I said. "But she admitted that the nursery was theirs. In fact, she said her father wouldn't like it that we'd found it."

"So, what do we think?" Blair asked. "Rose had a baby and they locked it up?"

"It still could have been Emily they locked up," I said. "Maybe they tried that before they put her in the hospital. She had a bunch of porcelain dolls lined up in the crib she had in this fake nursery. And Mansfield made a big deal out of telling us that Emily pretended her dolls were real."

"So you're thinking they locked Emily up because they couldn't handle her," Blair said.

I shrugged. "Someone spent long periods of time up there. Whether that's where the remains of the baby we found was kept or not, I don't know. The two things could be unrelated."

"But Ruthie Crenshaw had a baby out of wedlock, too," Doe said. "The baby we found could have belonged to either one of them."

"No," Blair said. "Remember, I talked to Ruthie Crenshaw. She gave her baby up for adoption."

"I guess it's looking more and more like the baby in the diaper bag may have belonged to Rose," Rudy said quietly.

"So do we think that Rose had a Down's Syndrome baby, and Emily killed it and then they locked her up?" Doe said.

Blair reached for the rice as she said, "That makes more sense."

I sat back and sighed. "I don't know. I have a hard time believing that she would kill a baby. She seems more enthralled with them. But, there is something else I noticed just before she told us to leave."

"What's that?" Rudy asked.

"She had the full collection of the old Nancy Drew books."

Rudy's eyes lit up. "Wasn't there a Nancy Drew book up in the attic room?"

"Yes. *The Case of the Missing Clock*," I said. "I know that collection really well. I've sold a couple complete sets. And guess which book was missing from her collection?"

"Oh, God," Blair said. "*The Case of the Missing Clock.* So there you have it. It was Emily who was stuck up there. Maybe with Rose's baby. How incredibly sad."

It seemed like most of us had lost our appetites and were just playing with our food by this time. There was a long silence.

"The candlestick," I finally said.

Everyone stopped and looked at me.

"What?" Rudy asked.

"The candlestick. I think the baby was struck with the candlestick."

"I don't get it," Doe said.

"Don't you remember? There were two candles in the room when we found it, but only one candlestick. Plus…" I glanced at Blair. "We haven't told you what happened Thursday night in the attic."

Blair and I told them about the strange visitor roaming the attic with the candle.

"Now *I* have the chills," Doe said, pushing her plate away.

"I think Lollie, or someone, is trying to tell us something," I said. "To get us to pay attention to the candlestick."

"Because you think that's what killed the baby," Blair said.

I nodded, and Doe said, "What's going on? All we were going to do was some basic research on the inn and write up a nice little history book. So far, we've uncovered the possible murders of a prostitute, a teenage boy and the daughter of a prominent judge. Not to mention the death of a baby, a possible case of sex slavery, new ghosts in the barn, and a crazy woman who absolutely gives me the willies."

Doe got up and went to the refrigerator. She stopped with her hand on the door for a moment as if to compose herself, and then finally opened it and pulled out a pitcher of ice water to bring back to the table.

"Maybe we should just stop," I said. "We certainly don't need to do this book. It won't make any real difference to the inn."

I looked around the table. The faces of my beautiful, sweet friends were all drawn and haggard looking. My eyes drifted over to Blair. We hadn't mentioned the scheduled break-in to Frank Miller's office. Blair barely shook her head, as if to say 'no.' She didn't want to say anything.

Rudy took a deep breath. "Look," she began. "Once again, I vote we continue. At least now we have a pretty good idea what the hidden room was used for. We don't have all the answers for the baby we found, but Julia can tell David what we've pieced together and let the police handle it. Meanwhile, we can still fill in pieces about the history of the inn. Personally, I'd like to verify what that woman told you about the Formosas."

We all glanced over to Doe, who had a resigned look on her face. Her dark eyes shifted from Blair, to Rudy, and then to me. "Okay," she said with a sigh. "That sounds safe enough."

In a perfect world, she would've been right.

CHAPTER THIRTY

It was just after midnight. Bill Haley and the Comets began to play "Rock Around the Clock," pulling me from a deep sleep. At first I thought it was part of a dream. But as the song continued, I shook myself awake and reached out to grab my cell phone off the bedside table and flick it on.

"Mom?" I mumbled.

"Julia! I smell smoke!"

"What?" I said, rubbing my eyes. "What do you mean you smell smoke? How can you smell anything from where you are?"

"I don't know. I just smell smoke, and somehow it's connected to you. Is something on fire?"

My mother had been a heavy smoker when she was alive and even died from emphysema. So I often associated her with the smell of cigarette smoke. But I didn't think she was talking about that.

I sat up against the headboard, making Mickey and Minnie shift under the throw I kept on the bed.

"Mom, I don't think anything is on fire." And then I heard sirens. "Um…wait a minute."

I got out of bed and threw on my robe. Carrying the phone, I left my apartment and hurried into the hallway, leaving Mickey and Minnie behind. As the sirens grew louder, I heard cries of alarm from upstairs. Doors opened and guests began pouring down the stairs.

"There's a fire!" a woman from Gig Harbor yelled. Her face was twisted in fear, and her husband was following close on her heels.

"Where?" I called out.

"The bakery," the man replied, pointing behind him.

I forgot my mother for the moment and rushed into the breakfast room to look out the window. The entire front of the carriage house was ablaze.

"Oh, my God!"

I whirled around, slamming into a small crowd that had gathered behind me, making me fight my way through them to the front door. When I threw it open, a fire truck had just pulled down the drive. I ran out, waving them to the north side of the building. "Around the back. The bakery!"

The driver waved to me and pulled around the main building to the back of the property. Meanwhile, April appeared at my side.

"What happened?" she asked, her eyes intense with fear.

"I don't know. But let's get back there."

We ran back inside and out the patio door. The guests were huddled on the back deck watching flames lick up the front of the bakery. As we watched in horror, fire caught the old boards of the carriage barn with a whoosh, and suddenly the entire side of the building was engulfed in flames.

As burning embers sparkled like fireflies in the early morning darkness, I reached out and grabbed April's hand. "Oh, April, I'm so sorry."

I turned to look at my dearest friend, and my heart nearly broke at the tears in her eyes.

÷

Three hours later we were seated on the deck wrapped in robes and jackets. I had called David. He sat forward in his chair, resting his elbows on his knees, watching the firemen work. Next to him were Angela and Detective Abrams. Lucy, Angela's big harlequin Great Dane was lying next to her chair, with Mickey and Minnie cuddled up next to her. There was no friendly banter. We just watched and waited.

By now the fire was out, and not only had the firemen extinguished the flames, they had protected the inn. Smoke continued to billow from the broken windows of the bakery, and firemen wandered through the debris, evaluating hotspots. April had left the group and was in the main kitchen making an early breakfast for the guests, unable to watch anymore as her prized bakery was destroyed.

"I can't believe this," I said despondently.

"It's an old building, Mom," Angela said. "I mean, most of it is over a hundred years old. A single match could have set it off. Thank goodness no one was over there at the time."

"The question is how?" Sean said.

He stood next to Angela's chair, his fingers buried in his pockets. I hadn't seen him since we'd saved Dana Finkle's life back in February. I'd almost forgotten what a commanding presence he had.

"The bigger question is why?" David added.

I jerked around to look at the two of them. "You think this was deliberate?"

They merely shared a look and shrugged. "Buildings don't normally just catch on fire. Something has to start the fire," Sean replied. "Either it was an accident, or someone set it. Do you know whether any of the appliances were left on?"

"I don't know. But I doubt it. April is rather obsessive about that sort of thing," I said.

"Have you seen anyone hanging around here lately? Anyone that shouldn't be here?" David asked.

I hesitated, thinking of the candle-wielding ghost. Sean picked up on it. "What?"

Would I have to tell them?

"Mom, what is it?" Angela asked.

I let out an exasperated sigh. "We saw someone in the attic over the bakery the other night, walking back and forth with a candle."

"A candle?!" Sean said. "What happened?"

"They went to check it out themselves," David replied for me. "Isn't that right, Julia? Instead of calling us," he said, emphasizing the last part.

"Um…yes," I replied. "But we checked the doors first and no one had broken in. So we figured it was…" I stopped and sighed. "We'd heard a story. One of the families that lived here years ago had seen someone walking back and forth up there with a candle. But when they went to check, no one was there."

"And you thought it was one of your ghosts," David said.

We were interrupted by the sight of our Mercer Island Fire chief, Chief Paul Rampart. He crossed the drive and climbed the steps to the deck. His face was covered in soot, and his solemn expression made my stomach clench.

"Can I offer you some coffee?" I asked him, standing up.

"No, thanks." He lowered himself onto a bench, allowing me to sit back down. He took a big sigh before beginning. "The fire is pretty much out, and the good news is that it didn't destroy the entire building. Just the front third," he said. "Some of the furniture stored in the back wasn't destroyed, neither were some of the appliances in the bakery, although everything was damaged by smoke and water. But you might be able to save a few things. Talk to your insurance folks." He sighed again and then glanced down at the clipboard in his hands. "The bad news is that it's likely a case of arson."

"What?" I said with a gasp.

David sat up straighter. "What did you find?"

"Probable use of an accelerant," he replied. "Looks like gasoline." He turned to gesture to the front of the building. "All along the base of the bakery."

I felt lightheaded. "Why…why would someone burn down our bakery?"

He shook his head. "I don't know. That's what these guys are for," he said, nodding to Sean and David. "But here's what else I know. From the looks of the doors, whoever it was tried to break in, but you have steel doors, which stopped them."

"Why wouldn't they have just broken a window?" Angela asked.

The chief turned toward the smoldering building again. "Most of the windows face the back of the inn here. Perhaps they were afraid they'd be seen. After all, many of the guest rooms look out on the front of the bakery. The only other window is on the side of the building, and it's pretty high up. Perhaps they couldn't get to it."

"What else do you know?" David asked.

The chief turned back. "Whoever did this was an amateur. They used the accelerant only on the front of the building, which is the newest part of the construction. So you have pressure treated wood, glass, brick and some steel. That slowed the progress of the fire. If they'd used the accelerant anywhere else, this old building would have gone up like a tinder box. That, and the fact it was still early on a nice summer evening. People stayed out on the lake late, so someone called it in right away."

I sighed and dropped my head. David put a hand on my back. "You okay, Julia?"

I nodded. "I just want to know why."

The chief stood up. "We're going to do a walk-through. You guys want to join me?" he asked the detectives.

"Yeah, thanks, Paul," David said. He stood up. "I'll stop in before I leave," he said to me.

"I have to get to the office, Mom," Angela said. "Will you be okay?"

"Yes, yes. You go ahead," I said, giving her a hug. "Thanks for coming, honey. I have to go tell April about the…about the…" I stopped, as a sob started to close my throat. I swallowed. "I have to talk to April."

Angela reached out and stroked my cheek. "It'll be okay, Mom. You can rebuild. I can help. We'll all help," she said, glancing at Detective Abrams.

David leaned down and kissed my cheek, and then the two men followed the chief across the drive, while I went inside. I met April in the kitchen, where she was just filling a large aluminum pan with scrambled eggs.

"The guests have gone back to bed," she said. She finished emptying out the big fry pan and put it in the sink. "So we can just heat this up later." She turned to me, her face tired and drawn. "I know you have something to tell me, but I don't think I want to hear it."

I grabbed a half empty carton of eggs and the carton of milk and put them back into the big refrigerator. "You're going to have to hear it sooner or later."

She grabbed a hand towel and wiped off the counter. Then she wiped her hands on a clean towel and joined me at the table. "Okay, let me have it."

I watched her for a moment and then reached out and grabbed her hand. "The fire wasn't an accident. It was arson. Someone did it on purpose."

She stared at me. When a tear appeared, I squeezed her hand.

"I'm so sorry, April. The chief said some of the appliances weren't affected, though, and I'm sure the insurance will replace everything else. We'll start over. And we will find out who did this."

"Don't you know, Julia?"

"What do you mean?"

Her body slumped. "C'mon, Julia. Don't you think it's a little coincidental that as soon as you start asking around about that stupid secret room we found in the attic, the entire building goes up in flames?"

She was right. The thought *had* crossed my mind. I just didn't want to believe it.

"So you think this is my fault?" I said in a quiet voice.

April sighed and put her other hand over mine. "No. That's not what I meant. I don't blame you. But I think it's connected. I didn't want to say anything earlier, but when I went to bed last night I had trouble getting to sleep. Something kept playing through my mind." She got up to get a glass of orange juice. "Want some?"

I nodded. "Thanks. But hold on." I got up and grabbed plates. "Let's get something to eat. I'm starving."

I served up eggs and sausage for both of us and came back to the table. She joined me with two glasses of orange juice.

She smiled. "Thanks."

"Okay, continue," I prompted her. "Why couldn't you get to sleep?"

She swallowed a bite before answering. "I kept hearing that babbling sound I heard the first day I went up to the attic with you. It kind of drove me nuts. If I got up and walked around, it would stop. And then as soon as I lay down, it would start up again. And then I heard the words, '*watch out*.'"

"What did that mean?"

"I don't know. The words came in between the babbling," she said. "I heard those words several times. But I had no idea what they meant. That's why I didn't call you."

"And now you think it was a warning."

"Yes. And I didn't pay attention," she said, staring at her plate.

"What could you have done, April? You couldn't have known that what you heard wasn't from forty years ago. You had no way of knowing it was in the present."

"Yes, but what good is this talent I have if I don't know how to use it? If I'd known how to interpret that message last night, I might have saved the bakery."

"Or gotten yourself killed." That stopped her. She just stared at me a moment and then got up to make herself some tea. "You know I'm right," I said, as I watched her fill a mug with water.

She was standing next to the microwave. "Yes. But now what?"

"Now, we get David back. He and Sean are going through the building with the fire chief right now. Since the fire was arson, it's a crime the police will have to investigate immediately. And if the arson is connected to the baby we found, or the hidden room, or anything else we've dug up, they'll finally have to pay attention. We'll have reinforcements."

"Do you think it could've been Emily Foster? You said she was distraught when she realized you'd found the hidden room."

"I don't know. It's hard to imagine her coming all the way down from Camano Island, especially when she knows we'd already found the room. I mean, what would be the point? To be honest, it could just as easily have been Frank Miller. There is something that man doesn't want us to find."

My mind flashed to the box we were planning to steal and what we might find in it. Could whatever was in that box be a motive for Miller to try and warn us off by starting a fire?

"And you think whatever he's trying to hide was in the bakery?"

"No. But maybe burning the barn down is just a way to get us to back off. I think he's capable of doing just about anything in order to scare someone away or get what he wants. And he worked here once, remember? He knows the property."

She took the mug of hot water out of the microwave and dropped in a tea bag. "All I know is, finding that room has turned our lives upside down."

I looked at her. "And you wish we'd never found it."

"Don't you?"

I had to think about that. The truth was that by now I thrived on solving these mysteries. But I realized the toll it was taking on my friends.

"I think fate had a hand in this," I said. "We didn't have a choice in finding the room, and now we don't have a choice in solving the mysteries it held."

CHAPTER THIRTY-ONE

The sun was just coming up over the Cascade Mountains by the time David and Sean left us to return to the police station. They promised to begin an investigation right away. A couple of firemen were left behind to watch for flare-ups in the smoldering remains of the barn.

I called José and Crystal to ask them to come in early so that April and I could spend the next few hours making calls to cancel bakery orders, talk to our accountant and the insurance company, and research demolition companies. Neighbors stopped by to see if everyone was okay, including Ben, Goldie and Caroline from across the street. I noticed, sadly, that Caroline had left Amelia behind. Perhaps she'd changed her mind about feeling glad that Amelia had a friend in Chloe. I was disappointed, but I couldn't blame her. After all, you can't really ask a dead girl to come over for a play date or even to join you at a birthday party. And the realization made me feel sorry for both Amelia and Chloe.

By late that afternoon, José was allowed into the back of the warehouse where he was able to access our inventory sheets from the file cabinet. He began identifying pieces of furniture and collectibles that might be salvageable versus those that would have to be trashed. Crystal watched the front desk, while I met with the insurance agent. After he left, I went to join José in the barn.

I stopped in the driveway and stared at the remains, which looked like something out of a disaster movie. Much of the front façade had been left standing, though badly burned. But the front third of the roof had fallen in, taking the floor of the attic with it. That left a gaping hole between the front façade and the back two-thirds of the building, which was left mostly untouched. It was heartbreaking, and I had to take a deep breath to prevent a sob escaping my throat.

Gritting my teeth, I forged ahead and met José in the back of the warehouse. He and I were evaluating a 17th century writing desk covered in ashes when my phone rang. It was Jake Dooley.

"I heard about your fire," he said. "It was on the news. What happened?"

"It looks like arson," I replied. I explained the sequence of events.

"But no one was hurt," he said.

"No." I turned to look at the debris around me. "But it was a close call."

"God, I'm so sorry, Mrs. Applegate. It might have been my fault."

I came to attention at that and moved outside for some privacy. "What do you mean?"

"I had a close call of my own last night," he said. "I ran into Frank Miller."

"Inside the bar?"

"No. It was just before I went inside. I was getting gas next door. He pulled in next to me."

David had returned and was coming across the drive. He glanced my way, and I gave him a brief wave. "What happened?" I asked, turning away from David.

"He went ballistic on me. He thought I was spying on him."

"Well, actually, you *were* spying on him."

He chuckled. "I know, but he didn't know that. I had a disguise in the car; I just didn't have it on yet. But T\that guy has a serious temper. He actually pushed me up against my car and threatened me."

"What do you mean threatened you?"

"He poked his finger into my chest and said 'if you and those old women don't back off, I might have to do something I might regret.'"

"Oh, dear," I said, dropping onto a nearby bench. A light breeze off the lake stirred up the smell of smoke from the remains of the fire, making me glance in that direction again. "Do you think he might have been responsible for our fire?"

"I don't know," he replied. "But I wouldn't put it past him. And the timing seems about right."

David's voice drifted across the drive from where he was talking to one of his officers. They had come back to interview each of us to determine if the incident with the candle had anything to do with the fire. He also had talked with our closest neighbors to ask if they had seen any strangers in the area over the last few days. Now, he was going to walk the property looking for clues. Right now they were taking pictures of what was left of the barn.

"So, what do you want to do about tomorrow night?" I asked.

"I think we go for it. I heard the bartender talking when I was in the bar last night. Miller was supposed to be leaving town when I saw him. He'll be gone for the next couple of days."

"That's convenient," I said.

"Oh, you mean because then he can't be blamed for the fire," Jake said.

"Right. Except Blair and I know for a fact that he gets others to do his dirty work for him. Are you going back there tonight?"

"Absolutely. I think I've got their routine down, but there are a couple of things I want to check. I'll give you a call tomorrow."

Jake signed off, and I sat for a moment in contemplation. I agreed that Miller was capable of having set the fire, or at least of having someone else set the fire. In fact, it seemed more likely that he did it than anyone else I could think of. But thinking I knew who did something that was so despicable wasn't as comforting as I might have thought, especially since I didn't think I could prove it. Breaking into his office in order to steal the jewelry box was beginning to take second place to my desire now to find something that would prove he had orchestrated the fire. Maybe we could kill two birds with one stone.

The day progressed into evening, and before I knew it, the day was over. I retired to my apartment exhausted. April had offered to bring in pizza, but I was almost too tired to eat and declined.

After a breakfast bar and a glass of milk, I finally slipped into bed. I feared I wouldn't sleep. Even though my body had trouble functioning, my brain wouldn't stop replaying images of the candle-walker, Emily Foster, Frank Miller, and even how I pictured Lollie Gates and the baby. So much had happened in such a short time, and I had no doubt the fire was somehow connected. And sure enough, I slept little, waking the next morning tired and mentally depressed.

I had a meager breakfast and got ready for another busy day. The insurance adjuster would be out to do a thorough walk-through, and the owner of a demolition crew was coming to give us an estimate. I helped with the guests' breakfast and then offered to hold down the fort while April went shopping to replace supplies lost in the fire. She would use the inn's main kitchen for everything, including baking some of her signature items for retail.

Even though it was Sunday, the insurance adjuster arrived at 10:00 a.m., along with Mr. Mulford, my bookkeeper. Together, we reviewed records and took a look at what remained of the bakery and the warehouse. Both David and Chief Rampart were back, walking through the building once more, looking for clues.

Sometime after lunch a giant dumpster was delivered. We'd also hired a couple of José's friends to come and help. They began separating things damaged by fire and smoke from those that could be saved, while José updated the inventory and the claims adjuster looked on. And even though our commercial ovens were still intact, they were blackened with soot and had some melted wires, and so were deemed a total loss.

As we rummaged through the building, something caught my eye. It was a glint of metal among the charred remains of the attic up near the front wall.

"What's that?" I said to José, pointing toward the glint.

He handed me his clipboard and climbed carefully through the debris, reaching over to pull up the candlestick from the attic. "Just this," he said, holding it up so that I could see. He glanced around the area and then said, "Uh…hold on." He shuffled through the debris toward the north wall, reached down and pulled something else out of the rubble. "And this. There's two of them."

A jolt traveled from my head to my toes. In his left hand was the missing candlestick. And the moment I realized it, a refreshing summer breeze blew through what was left of the barn, swirling up ashes and raising the hairs on the back of my neck.

Since David was there, I called him over and explained my theory about the two candlesticks. He took them both in his hands.

"Any way to tell which one is which?"

"I doubt it," I replied. "Although this one," I said, gesturing to the one in his right hand, "was found over there," I said, gesturing to the north wall.

"Does that make a difference?"

"I think so. The one in your left hand was found up by the front of the building. In other words, right below the attic. So I think that's the one we already had. The one in your right hand was found closer to where the diaper bag was found. It's a weak theory, I know."

"Not really," he said, glancing around. "So this one might have been hidden up in the rafters, just like the diaper bag?" he said, gesturing with the one in his right hand. He looked thoughtful for a moment as he studied that one. He turned it over and brought it up close to his face to peer closely at the bottom. Then he blew ashes off of it. "It looks like there could be blood on this one," he said. "It's covered in ash, but the lab can probably separate the two."

I leaned in to take a look and saw a splash of something dark across the bottom edge of the candlestick and stuck in the crevices. "So I was right. The baby might have been killed with the candlestick."

I can't say I was exhilarated by the revelation; none of this excited me. But I did feel a sense of satisfaction knowing that perhaps we'd actually found the murder weapon.

"I'll give it to forensics," he said. "And then maybe you and I need to sit down and go over everything you've learned about that secret room. And I mean everything," he emphasized.

My mind flashed to the potential trip to the Hardliner Pub later that night to steal the jewelry box. "Let me get through today, please," I said. "Can we meet tomorrow?"

"I need to know what you know," he said impatiently. "Whoever torched your barn is probably connected to the work you're doing on your book."

"I know. I know," I said. "Just give me until tomorrow morning," I pleaded. "I'm just overwhelmed right now."

I didn't have to manufacture the beginnings of tears, since I'd been on the verge of tears most of the day. He recognized my distress and sighed. "Okay, first thing in the morning."

I recovered my composure, and we resumed our work. Over the course of the rest of the day, we checked in two more guests and had a large container delivered to store the antiques that were still viable. I spent most of the afternoon running through the inventory with José and meeting with the demolition company, who said they would begin first thing Monday morning. At dinner time, April came to find me.

"You need to eat. Come into the kitchen. And call the boys," she said, meaning José and his friends. "I put out sandwiches on the counter."

I told José to take a break and eat and then followed April inside. I washed my hands and plopped into one of the kitchen chairs, rotating my neck to release tension. She already had a chicken salad sandwich and chips set out for me.

"Thank you," I said. "I'm exhausted. I think we can save the sinks and counters from the bakery. We'll store them in with the antiques for now."

"You don't have to do that," she said, coming over to the table.

"But we can rebuild, April. It won't be easy, but we can do it. I promise."

She smiled sadly and took a deep sigh. "Maybe we shouldn't, Julia. Maybe we should just stick to baking things we can sell right here in the inn. The bakery didn't really bring in that much extra money anyway."

"But you loved the bakery," I stressed.

"I did. But I can use the main kitchen here for everything we need to run the inn, and then I'd be more available to help out around here," she said. "We're booked solid again for another six months. And Crystal said we had two calls today with requests for weddings." She paused with her hand wrapped around half a sandwich. After a second, she said, "Maybe what we ought to build is a reception hall." She paused again, watching me – apparently to gauge my reaction.

"So, drop the bakery?"

"Yeah. If we had a reception hall, we could host bigger events, maybe bring in more money. If we wanted, we could include a kitchen, but more for the caterers. What do you think?"

I took a moment to consider the idea. "Actually, I think it's a great idea! A reception hall right out there on the water would be beautiful. But where would we store the antiques?"

"I've thought of that," she said between bites. "We could expand the garage. We only park the van in there anyway, so we could use half of it for the van and gardening tools and build on another section for the antiques."

"That could work," I agreed.

She seemed to be energized by my reaction and leaned in to me. "I was thinking that we could design the hall as a complement to the inn, you know, Victorian in style, with big picture windows so that guests had a full view of the lake."

"You know, if we had a separate reception hall when we held a special event, we wouldn't be interrupting guests who are staying here at the inn. They could be completely separate."

"Right. We'd probably have to add some parking," she said. "Maybe take out a few trees."

"And add lighting and electrical wiring for bands," I said. "What an exciting idea. But are you sure, April? That bakery was your dream."

"I did love it. But it was a ton of work, and I always felt like I wasn't pulling my weight at the inn. This way, I'd still get to do my baking and cooking for the guests. But now we'd have the opportunity to do some party planning, too. I think this would be a very popular location."

Her broad smile lifted my spirits, and we spent the rest of our dinner together brainstorming and penciling out some design ideas. By the time we were done, we were ready to talk to an architect, and the tragedy of losing the barn seemed diminished.

CHAPTER THIRTY-TWO

Jake and Blair arrived at eight o'clock that night to make the final decision on whether to go to the Hardliner Pub to grab the jewelry box. I had wrestled with this question all day, and my brain felt like a smudge pot. With the lack of sleep and all the stressors competing for my attention, I almost couldn't cope.

I didn't want to go.

"I can't do it," I told my cohorts. Blair's face fell, but I went on. "Blair, any way you look at it, it's breaking the law. Not only could we get caught and go to jail, we're dealing with Frank Miller, who wouldn't think twice about hurting us. I still wouldn't put it past him to have been the one who started the fire. Jake, you need to tell her what you told me about Miller."

We were spread out around my small dining table in my apartment. Jake recounted his story about Miller threatening him. Blair slumped back against her chair.

"Okay, I get it," she said. "But I thought we could figure out a way to do it without breaking any laws or anyone knowing it was us."

I heaved a sigh. "Maybe we could. But I don't want to have to explain whatever we did to David. This relationship is important to me." Blair twisted her mouth into a frown. I shifted my gaze to Jake. "You okay with that?"

He shrugged. "Sure. But I'm not going to give up just yet. There may be another way to get it."

"How?" Blair asked, sitting up.

Jake waved away her enthusiasm. "Hang tight. I have to check out a couple of things. Then I'll let you know."

We chatted for a few more minutes, but when they finally left, I felt a great sense of relief. So much so, I decided to go to bed early. A character in one of the many mysteries I'd read once said, *"Who needs sleep when you're solving murders?"* Well, that was all well and good in a book, but I hadn't slept for a couple of nights, and I needed some rest.

I took a sleep aid and fell into a heavy slumber, and yet still woke groggy the next day. I dragged myself out of bed and began my daily routine, feeling like the walking dead. I slumped into the kitchen to help April. She noticed the lack of a spring to my step.

"What's wrong with you?" she asked, looking up from the breakfast burritos she was making.

"Uh…I'm just really tired. What with the fire and everything else that's going on," I looked at my friend and noticed the circles under her eyes. "How are you feeling?"

She shook her head. "Not much better. All last night, a tape kept running through my head about all the things we have to do now just to clean up the mess and straighten things out after the fire. At least we're not expecting any check-ins today, are we?"

"No." I yawned, covering my mouth with my hand. "But I have to call David. He wants the low-down on what we've learned so far in our research for the book to see if any of it is connected to the fire. Doe will probably have to work, but I'll see if Blair and Rudy can come over."

April was rolling up eggs, sausage, black beans and cheese in a tortilla. "Well, I hope the police find whoever it was that set fire to the bakery and put him…or her…in jail," she said, putting the last burrito in the chafing dish.

"Amen to that," I said. The front door jingled, catching my attention. "I'll get that."

I pushed through the kitchen door and rounded the corner to the reception area. Aria Stottlemeyer stood at the front desk with her hand poised on the reception desk bell.

"Good morning, Aria," I greeted her. "What can I do for you?"

I hoped nothing, but when I saw a paperback book in her hands, I remembered her grandfather's memoir.

"I thought I'd drop this off on my way to work," she said. "Sorry I didn't bring it over sooner, but I've been down with a pretty bad cold."

I experienced a momentary twinge of guilt at having had snarky thoughts about her in the past. But then I remembered the time Aria had said, "You look like you've put on a little weight, Julia," right in front of six people waiting in line at the post office, and my guilt evaporated.

"Thanks so much, Aria. I'm sure this will help. I'll get it back to you."

"No problem," she said, raising that pointy chin. She sniffed the air. "I guess I'm not stuffed up anymore. I can smell your dogs."

And with that, she gave me a satisfied smile and left.

Really!

I climbed onto the stool behind the reception desk to check out the memoir. It had been written by Otis Stottlemeyer, Aria's grandfather. Aria had never married and so had the same last name.

The book was divided into decades, so I wasn't sure what chapters would cover stories about his father, Jacob.

After twenty minutes of scanning pages, I finally saw a mention of the Mercer Island Ferry. I zeroed in and read about how Jacob Stottlemeyer had run the ferry five days a week. Otis reported that when he was a kid, his father told elaborate stories about the comings and goings of good guys and bad guys on the ferry. But there was one incontrovertible truth; Jacob Stottlemeyer was on Gramley Miller's payroll and was the one who most likely had informed him about George Bourbonaise.

÷

Jake called just before lunch and asked if Blair and I could meet him downtown. Since David was tied up with something until late that afternoon, I agreed to meet Jake at a small deli downtown. I called Blair to see if she could join us, and by 12:30 the three of us were neatly tucked away in a booth, each with our sandwich of choice in front of us.

"What's up?" I asked Jake.

Jake had placed a shopping bag on the seat next to him and looked like he'd just won the lottery.

"I have news," he said.

"What's in the bag, goose?" Blair said, mimicking an old Granny Goose potato chip commercial.

A toothy grin slid across his face. "Just this," he said, reaching into the bag.

He pulled out something wrapped in tissue paper. As we waited in anticipation, he took off the wrapping to reveal the jewelry box. We both inhaled in surprise.

"Where did you get it?" I exclaimed.

"Ah...ve have our vays," he said with a fake German accent. He reached into his pocket and pulled out a photo. "I didn't tell you about this before, but..." He turned the photo so we could see the image.

It was a picture of a woman who looked very much like the woman in the photo with Miller, but this time she was in a lip lock with someone else.

I started to laugh. "Oh, my God, Jake. Where did you get that?"

"Is that Miller's wife!?" Blair asked.

Again, he grinned. "Miller was supposed to leave town the night he assaulted me at the gas station. I heard the bartender and one of the waitresses talking about it later when I was in the bar. He was going to be gone three days. Night before night, after the bar closed, I was parked at the end of the parking lot, waiting to see what time the cleaning guys came. Remember, I was casing the place. Anyway, these two showed up and slipped in the back door," he said, indicating the photo again. "I had my camera with me with a telephoto lens and clicked this picture when they came out."

"Amazing," Blair said, smiling with appreciation. "Don't tell me you blackmailed her?"

He rocked his head from side to side. "Well...kind of. I showed up on her doorstep this morning and showed her the picture. She almost fainted and tried to grab it from me. Instead, I invited myself in and did the deal."

"What do you mean?" Blair asked.

"I told her I wanted to buy the jewelry box. I described it, but I wasn't even sure she'd know what I was talking about."

"But she did," Blair said.

"Yeah. Get this...Miller brought it home and gave it to her as a present a couple of days ago."

"Probably the day we stopped by and saw it on his shelf," I said.

He nodded. "No doubt. Anyway, I told her that he'd stolen it from someone I knew, and I was there to get it back. But...I offered to pay her for it."

"Why'd you do that?" Blair asked skeptically.

"Because you convinced me to get it legitimately, and I figured money would talk louder with her than anything. So I gave her $250 and had her sign a receipt." He was nearly laughing, he was so giddy.

"But what about the photo you took of her?" I asked.

"I gave her the one I had and then pulled a photo card out of my pocket and stomped on it."

"But..." I said, confused.

He burst out with a chuckle. "I stomped on a brand new photo card. I still have the other one, just in case."

"Well, c'mon," Blair said with excitement. "Let's find out what's in the box."

Jake's expression fell. "I already looked in it, and there's nothing we can use."

Blair lifted the lid to the box, releasing the stale odor of age. Inside was nothing but a collection of old bottle caps.

"You've got to be kidding," she said, using her fingers to sort through the metal caps. "He keeps bottle caps in this beautiful jewelry box?"

"Wait," I said, holding up a hand. "Let me check something."

I grabbed the box. It was large, maybe a foot and a half long by ten inches wide and six to seven inches deep. The top was ornately inlaid with different colors of mother of pearl in the shapes of roses and stems. I turned the box over and dumped the caps out and studied the bottom. There were four brass shell-shaped feet at the corners.

"Don't you remember how Miller said his grandfather knew how to hide things?" I said. "He had the secret compartment at the bottom of a traveling chest and the trap door under the floor of the brothel." I fingered a small brass crank in the center of the bottom. "It's a music box," I said.

"But there could be a secret compartment, right?" Jake said excitedly.

"Yes," I said. "A lot of old boxes have them. Now I just have to find it." I pushed and prodded the four feet at the corners, turning the box in my hands as I did so. Nothing happened. I placed it back on the desk with the lid up and studied it for a moment. "I've seen a lot of furniture with secret compartments. There's usually a spring or a lever of some kind." I pressed the lever that would trigger the music. Nothing. I searched the inside of the box, but there was nothing to press. I turned it over and twisted the music crank. Nothing. Finally, I pressed my finger sideways against the crank mechanism and the bottom of the box popped open.

"Whoohoo!" Jake yelled.

Inside, there were two tattered old journals - a red one and a gold one. There were also some loose papers, a stack of yellowed envelopes, a ring of ancient keys, and some jewelry.

"These seem like things old Gramley Miller might have saved, except the jewelry," Blair said.

"Yeah, I wonder who it all belongs to." I picked up a delicate gold necklace with evenly spaced pearls and a gold cross pendant. "This one is quite unique, and it would have been a spendy item back in the day." As I fingered the chain, a warm rush of energy flowed up my arm.

Meanwhile, Blair picked up one of the journals. "This must be what Miller's sister was talking about," she said, flipping pages in a small faded red notebook. "Look here."

I pulled my attention away from the necklace. "What is it?"

Blair was pointing to what looked like a ledger page. "He's recorded a name at the top of each page. This one is Betsy Cannon. He's listed her age as nineteen. She was from Alberta, Canada. Then it looks like he recorded money she'd earned."

I grimaced in distaste. "God, how callous."

Blair shrugged. "Well, whether you like it or not, he was a businessman. It looks like he also noted when he spent money on them."

"You mean like for clothes and stuff?" Jake asked.

Blair was studying the book, skimming various pages. I suspected she was filing away all the information in the book for later reference.

"Yeah. Clothes, personal items," she said, turning pages. "Oh, wait a minute." She glanced at me, and I could see her blanch. She turned the book around. "Here's the page for Lollie Gates. But notice the big red mark half way down the page."

Lollie Gates' page listed her as nineteen years old, from Vancouver, Canada. But the page was only half filled out. As Blair said, in the column where Gramley Miller had totaled how much each girl was making for him, Lollie's ended abruptly with a red slash mark across the page. There was nothing after it.

"Probably when she died," I said sadly.

A feather light breeze fluttered past my ear, making me spin around.

"What?" Blair asked.

My eyes darted around the room, looking for the source as my heart thumped. "I don't know. I just felt…"

Jake had picked up the other book. "This one looks like people who worked for him," he said, skimming pages. "Here's someone he paid to haul trash." He flipped a page. "Um…here's someone who delivered the liquor. And here are two bartenders." He flipped more pages and then stopped. "Uh, oh. Here's someone named LaRue. The last date on Lollie Gates' page was August 23, right?" he asked Blair. She nodded, and he said, "Look at this." He pointed to a date half-way down the page.

"Whoa," I said.

The entry was dated August 24th in the same year and read, "Gates - $200."

"Remember what Rudy said? The old guy she talked to in Canada said Jack LaRue was paid $200 to bury Lollie," I said, astonished. "But why would Miller record it?"

"Like I said, he was a businessman," Blair said. "And he didn't say what the entry meant. He could always say that he just paid LaRue to transport Lollie back to Canada. Look, there's another entry for $200 next to the name Bourbonaise."

"Damn!" I exclaimed. "So he must've killed Bourbonaise, too."

"I wonder if there's any proof that Lollie never actually left the island," Jake said.

My water glass suddenly slid to the end of the table and flipped off onto the floor.

Jake's eyes flew open, and he jumped halfway out of his seat. "What?"

Blair and I sat there, staring down at the glass that had rolled a few feet away on the floor.

"I take it that means yes," Blair said, as a waitress hurried over to clean up the mess.

As she left to get a towel, I replied, "Um…yeah."

Jake was watching us, his face expressing full-blown shock as he sat slowly back down.

"What was that?" he asked. "No one was anywhere near that glass, and yet it...it just flew off the table."

Blair and I shared a cautious look. "The inn is haunted," I said matter-of-factly. "And sometimes ghosts kind of follow me around. That was either Elizabeth St. Claire, her daughter, Chloe, or it might have been Lollie."

"I vote Lollie," Blair said with a shrug. "So, what do we do now?"

"Wait a minute...seriously?" Jake said. "That was a ghost?"

My initial surprise had dissipated, as it always did, so I said, "Most likely. I'll loan you the book, *The Most Haunted Hotels in the Northwest*. We're in it. And I've felt Lollie's presence several times recently." I glanced down at the necklace laced through my fingers. "I'm with Blair. I think that was her, and she was telling us she's still on the property." The necklace grew warm in my hands again.

"Damn," Jake said. "I need to hang out with you guys more often."

"We're just a couple of old broads," Blair said with a smile.

"Who believe in ghosts and hunt down murderers. I'll take you any day over some of my lame friends."

"Wait, look at this," Blair said, pulling a stack of old black and white photos out of one of the yellowed envelopes.

"Look at the backs," I said, noticing that there was writing on the back of each photo as she shuffled through them.

Blair turned them over one by one. "They're pictures of the girls," she said. "Oh, my...here's Lollie!" She stopped to study the photo. "She was beautiful."

She handed over the photo of a young girl with long, curly, raven black hair. The girl leaned against the wall with her bare feet crossed at the ankles, wearing only a full slip that came to mid-thigh. Bruises showed on one arm, and her lips were pressed together in an awkward, forced smile. My heart ached. But the biggest surprise was the necklace around her neck. It was the same one I now held in my hand.

"Look at this," I said. "She's wearing this necklace."

They both leaned in to study the photograph.

"The bastard killed her and then stole her necklace," Jake said.

"Yes, so what do we do next?" I said.

Jake shrugged. "I talked to Mary Haley this morning. She said we can hold onto everything inside the box for now. But she'd like the box back, so I'm going to drive up to Leavenworth this afternoon to return it to her."

I closed the secret compartment and handed the box back to Jake. "I think that's a good idea. Drive carefully," I said, thinking I'd grown fond of young Jake Dooley.

He grinned. "Don't worry about me. My granddad says I drive like a little old lady." He stopped and looked at us, his facial expression frozen. "Oh, sorry, I didn't mean…"

I burst out with a laugh. "Oh, don't worry. We're not offended."

Blair just leaned back and smiled. "Maybe I should drive you up there so you'll get back before bedtime."

I chuckled. Leavenworth was a good two-hour drive each way. "More like before dinner."

CHAPTER THIRTY-THREE

Three hours later, Blair and Doe and I were sitting in my living room with David and Sean, ready to talk about everything we'd learned during our research and how it might be connected to the fire. Doe had cancelled a meeting in order to be with us, but Rudy was playing golf and so would be late.

The mood was glum.

"Okay," Sean said. "Time to fill us in."

"It's hard to know where to begin," I said. I had my laptop on the ottoman in front of me and had pulled up my notes. "There's just so much."

"Let's break it down," Doe said. "There are two murders for sure that have popped up as we've been researching the inn. The baby you already know about, and then there's the death of a prostitute named Lollie Gates."

"Don't forget potential murders," I reminded her. "The death of Rose Foster and her boyfriend, Chris Stephens, are both suspicious."

"And then there's what Emily Foster said," Blair added. "She said that *none* of the murders have been solved."

"Then there's Frank Miller, who stole the Kettle sisters' diamond necklace," I said.

"Yes, and the disappearance of the detective from Canada," Doe quickly added.

Sean put up a hand. "Stop! Are you serious? This all came out while you were researching the history of this place?" His chiseled features were crimped with skepticism.

"Yes," I replied. "So get ready to take notes. It's complicated."

David already had a pad of paper out, and Sean pulled a small notepad from his pocket. "Okay, where do you want to start?"

"Let's start with Emily Foster," Doe said.

"What about Emily Foster?" Sean asked. "I was told that Judge Wendell Foster once lived here. How is she related to him?"

"She's his extremely strange and nutty daughter," Doe said

I glanced at Blair, but she just sat back and folded her hands in her lap.

"She's mentally ill," I said. "She was once hospitalized, but has been living up on Camano Island, taking care of her ailing father for the past ten years or so."

"So I take it she's the potential suspect for the fire and not her father," Sean said.

"Yeah," I said. "We've been to see her twice. We also met with her brother once – Mansfield."

The handsome detective's eyes lit up. "Judge Mansfield Foster?"

"Do you know him?" I asked.

"I've run across him a few times. He's a mean son-of-a-bitch."

"That's what we've heard. Blair and I went to meet with him. He wasn't nasty to us, but…"

"He's a misogynist pig," Blair interjected.

Both men chuckled. "Okay, thanks," Sean said. "Go on. Why do you think Emily Foster might have been the one to start the fire?"

"Her sister Rose had a baby when the family lived here and died shortly after that. She was only sixteen. Her death was reported as an accidental drowning, but we were told by someone who knew Rose's mother that her mother thought it might have been murder." I paused a moment, building up the courage to say what had to come next. "And we think the baby Mr. Piper found in the attic was hers."

"Rose's?" David said.

"Yes."

The men were quiet for a moment. Then David asked, "What makes you think that?"

I took a deep breath. This was where I had to have faith that David cared enough for me that he wouldn't write me off as a kook.

"Because we believe that Rose's baby was a Down's Syndrome baby, and that's why it was locked up in the attic. From what we've learned about Judge Foster, he probably would have seen a baby like that as an abomination. And we think that perhaps Emily was locked up there with her."

"We haven't heard anything back from the ME yet. How do you know the baby was female and a Down's baby?"

There was a long silence.

"Because Chloe and Elizabeth told us," I finally said. "Elizabeth told us her name was Marigold, and Chloe told the little girl across the street about her…her…"

"I get it," David said. He sat back against the sofa with a frown. "Messages from the beyond. Not exactly something we can include in our notes."

"But we can ask for a rush from the ME," Sean said. "And maybe that will corroborate what you say."

I smiled at him. "Thank you."

"Do you think Emily killed the baby?" David asked.

"Yes," Doe said. "She got very nervous when she found out that Julia had found the hidden room, and she's the one who let it slip that Rose had even had a baby. And that got us kicked out in a hurry. She kept saying that her father would punish her if he knew we'd found the room. She became unhinged at that point."

"But why burn down the barn?" Sean asked.

"We never told her that we'd already found the diaper bag with the baby inside, so she might have been trying to burn up the evidence," Doe speculated.

The detective nodded. "We'll have to take a run out there and talk to her."

"Good luck with that," Doe murmured.

"What else?" David asked.

"Well, then there's the whole thing with Frank Miller," I said with some trepidation.

David turned and gave me a curious look. "What whole thing with Frank Miller?"

"It starts all the way back when this was a brothel," Blair said. "And a prostitute named Lollie Gates was kept here."

Both men looked at her with clenched brows.

"A prostitute?" Sean asked.

"Yes, we found out about her because we decided to research the entire history of the property, not just the inn," I said. "And the property goes all the way back to the turn of the last century. That's actually when the barn was built. There was a hotel here then."

"Which burned down in 1920," Rudy said from where she stood in the hallway. She was still dressed in her Bermuda shorts, magenta shirt and golf cap. "And a guy named Gramley Miller bought the property and built a brothel during Prohibition. He moved his family here." She came into the room, dropped her purse on the floor and sat on the piano bench. "But when he started abducting young women from Canada to force them to work in the brothel, his wife took their daughter and left him. She moved to Leavenworth, where their granddaughter still lives."

"The granddaughter's name is Mary Haley and her brother is Frank Miller," I said. "He owns a bar down in Puyallup." I shut up at that point. I didn't want to recount the confrontation with Gold Tooth and his buddy in the bar.

"How do you know this Gramley Miller was abducting women from Canada?" David asked Rudy.

"I drove to Canada and interviewed Lollie Gates' grandniece," she said. "The story about how Lollie had been lured away from her home had been passed down in the family. Along with how her parents had hired a private detective named George Bourbonaise to find her. He found her right here at the brothel."

"Here," I said, producing the letter from Lollie's mother. "April found this in the drawer of an old chest up in our attic. It's from Lollie's mother."

Sean took the letter and scanned it quickly, handing it over to David. "So the parents knew she was here and were going to rescue her. What happened?"

The three of us shared sad looks. I was the one to speak up.

"We also have her diary, in which she talked about being pregnant. She might have been murdered because of her pregnancy, but more likely because Gramley Miller found out about Bourbonaise snooping around."

"What makes you think she was murdered?" David asked.

"Again, my trip to Canada," Rudy replied. "I met an old guy up there who used to hang out at a bar in the area where a man named Jack LaRue had come from. LaRue was Gramley Miller's employee at the brothel. As the story goes, after the brothel burned down,

LaRue returned to Canada and told people that Miller had killed Lollie and then forced him to bury her…somewhere on this property."

"Jeez, this is better than a soap opera," David said.

"But there's more," I said. "Miller knew about Bourbonaise coming to find Lollie because of the man who used to run the ferry back then. He was paid to let Miller know when police were coming over to bust him or anything else that might threaten his business."

"So the ferryman let Miller know about Bourbonaise," David said.

"Yes. Bourbonaise asked him about Lollie when he took the ferry to the island. The story is included in the great-grandson's diary." I had Aria's memoir sitting right next to me and handed it to Detective Abrams.

"The memoir also says that Aria's great-grandfather heard voices from the bottom of a trunk that Gramley Miller used to travel back and forth with," Blair said.

David looked up. "What does that mean?"

"Frank Miller told us that's how his grandfather moved his *product*," I said with distaste.

"So Frank Miller might be the guy who torched your barn?" Sean asked.

"Maybe," I replied. I couldn't help but glance again at Blair. "Blair and I went to see him last week. We told him we were writing a book about the history of the property and wondered if he had any stories about the brothel passed down through the family. And that's when he mentioned that someone else had been out to talk to him about the same thing."

"It was Jake Dooley," Rudy said. "His granddad is my old editor. I'd talked to him about our project, and Jake found out about an article a reporter had written a couple of decades ago about the brothel, but never published. Jake decided to see if he could corroborate the story. So he also went to see Miller down in Puyallup."

"Miller didn't like talking about his grandfather much," I said. "To us…or to Jake. He kicked us out when he saw me looking at a picture of him and his wife." I didn't mention the jewelry box.

"Why?" David asked.

"We didn't know it at the time, but we found out later that his wife was wearing a very expensive diamond necklace in that picture that had once belonged to Pearl and Pettie Kettle. They lived *here* in the early 80s. Turns out that Frank Miller worked for the Kettle sisters back then. They found him riffling through their drawers one day and fired him."

"And he disappeared with the necklace you saw in the photo," David guessed.

"Yes," I replied.

Sean ran his fingers through his hair as he glanced at his notes. "That's an amazing amount of information. And a lot of grandfathers, grandsons, and I don't know what else." He looked up at us with a smile "I should put you guys on the payroll."

CHAPTER THIRTY-FOUR

We finished recounting our stories and everyone left. I told Crystal I would be off the grid for a while in order to take a nap. I returned to my apartment and dropped onto my bed fully clothed and fell into a deep sleep. I awoke two hours later feeling slightly refreshed. It was almost six o'clock.

I checked in with April, who said the afternoon had been uneventful. After washing my face to freshen up, I fed the dogs and made myself a light dinner. I was cleaning up the dishes when my phone jingled. It was Rudy.

"I just got a call from Rush, Jake's grandfather," she said. "Jake is missing."

"Missing? But he only drove to Leavenworth."

"That's just it. He never made it. They found his car in a ditch up on Highway 97, but Jake wasn't in it."

I dropped into a chair. "Oh, my God. Miller."

"Frank Miller? You think Miller did something to him?"

"I don't know, but he did threaten Jake the other night."

There was a long pause. Rudy sighed on the other end of the phone. "This is my fault," she mumbled.

"No, it's not. Jake's the one who made the decision to pick up the story. And I guess we shouldn't jump to conclusions. Maybe he just had car trouble and went to find help. Still, I wish he'd never gone to see Miller."

"I think I'll call Rush and let him know about Miller, just in case," she said. "And then I've got to get going. Blair will be here in a minute. We're going down to Torero's for dinner. Want to join us?"

"No," I said, rubbing my eyes. "I just had some soup, but thanks. And Rudy, they'll find him. Jake will be okay."

"I hope you're right. I'll let you know if I hear anything."

After we hung up, I sat for a moment feeling emotionally drained. My mind wandered back to lunch when Jake had been so proud of his ability to secure the jewelry box for Mary Haley. Now he was missing. First the fire, and now this. They say the death of famous people comes in threes. I wondered if that extended to tragic circumstances. If so, what else was in store for us?

÷

I was watching TV at nine o'clock that evening when my phone pinged. It was a text from Doe that read, *"Heard from Emily Foster. On my way home. Meet me there. Ten minutes. Important."*

I wondered why Emily would contact Doe directly, but then called April to let her know I was leaving. I put on tennis shoes and a light jacket over my peasant blouse. Five minutes later, I was in my car, heading to the top of the island.

The night was crisp and cool, and I passed a few people still out walking. The small bluff that Doe lived on was divided into three adjoining lots. As I pulled into the main driveway, I noticed lights on in the house to the right. But the big home to the left was dark, even though the tail end of a sports car was evident in the driveway.

I parked in the large circular area in front of Doe's entrance. After turning off the engine, I glanced through the trees toward the twinkling lights of Seattle and sat for a moment, thinking about Jake and wondering where he was. More importantly, I wondered if he was okay. I had grown tired of all of this. I wanted my life back.

Doe's front porch light was on, and her big Mercedes was parked in the side driveway in front of the garage. I got out and walked up to the front door. Doe wasn't a big TV watcher, but she typically had some kind of music playing, and I could hear Vivaldi playing in the background.

I rang the bell and waited. Nothing. I rang again. Nothing.

She must be in the kitchen, I thought.

I circled around the front planters and moved down the driveway to the side door. As I stepped up onto the brick landing, I glanced through the kitchen window. The blinds were drawn, so I could only catch a glimpse of the countertops. The light was on, but it didn't seem as if anyone was moving about. I reached out to knock, but the door swung ajar.

I grabbed the door handle and stuck my head in. "Doe?"

There was no response, so I stepped into the large kitchen and glanced into the great room. No one was there. A cutting board sitting on the counter was covered with sliced vegetables, and the bottom of a fry pan on the stove had a sauce in it. I stuck my finger in it. *Whiskey sauce.*

"Doe!" I called out again. "It's me!"

The sound of a door closing down the hall brought me to attention. *She was in the bedroom.*

I moved through the kitchen and crossed into the darkened hallway toward the master bedroom. My adrenalin had kicked in, but I passed the first two bedrooms and a guest bathroom when "Rock Around the Clock" interrupted me. I stopped and reached into my pocket and grabbed my phone.

As my thumb reached out to click on the phone, a hand appeared over my shoulder and a strong arm encircled my waist, pulling me in tight. The hand pressed a cloth firmly against my nose. I tried jerking away as the familiar smell of chloroform flooded my nasal passages. Been there, done that. Didn't want to do it again.

I reached up with both hands, dropping my phone, and clawed at the hand that held the chloroform-soaked cloth, while trying to twist away. All I saw was a black sleeve and a gold ring before the drug began to take over. A few seconds passed, and then I slumped into unconsciousness.

÷

I came to smacking my tongue against my lips because of a sour taste in my mouth. That, plus the feeling that I'd swallowed a large lump of sculpting clay, made me feel nauseated.

Eventually, my eyes fluttered open, but my head swam. I glanced around at a dimly lit room. A four-poster bed sat to my right, flanked by dark wood side tables and Victorian lamps. I took a deep breath, but a pungent smell of decay made me gag, and I closed my eyes to steady myself again.

"Slap her," a voice ordered.

"What? No," another voice replied, as my eyelids began to droop.

I heard movement and then felt the sharp sting of a slap on my cheek.

My eyes popped open.

Someone moved away from me to the far wall. I tried to focus on the figure and lifted my chin to find the blurry image of a man standing in the doorway.

"Hello, Mrs. Applegate."

My eyes adjusted, and a chill ran the length of my spine.

"Mansfield," I said with a slur.

Mansfield Foster was dressed impeccably in a black long-sleeved polo shirt and black slacks. His eyes were as dark as two cesspools, and yet a strange glint reflected off them. The soullessness of his gaze made me fight to catch a breath.

"Where am I?" I managed to say. My mouth was dry and my throat burned. I tried to move my hands, but they were tied behind me. "What's going on?"

"You're on Camano Island. You've created a problem," he replied casually.

"And so you abducted me?" I said weakly. "You're a District Court judge."

"Yes, but I'm afraid something had to be done about the two of you."

"Not mother!" a female voice screeched.

I turned all the way to my left. Emily Foster stood next to an old-fashioned, high-backed wheelchair; the kind with cane backing. When I realized who was in it, I gasped.

Doe!

My dear friend was propped up in the chair, her head lolling to one side. A needle stuck out of her left arm, secured with tape. A tube ran from the needle to a bag of clear liquid that hung from a metal rod in the back.

"What are you doing?" I turned to Mansfield for an answer.

He shrugged. "My sister made me promise that she could have your friend."

"What do you mean *have* my friend?"

His eyes shifted toward his sister, and he nodded. Emily stepped to one side. Behind her was another old wheelchair, facing the window.

Her father!

"Judge Foster!" I blurted.

"He's not going to help you," Mansfield said. "But I suppose it's time you two met. Emily, if you would do the honors." Emily took hold of the wheelchair and began to turn it around. As she did, Mansfield said, "Mrs. Applegate, let me introduce you to Judge Wendell Foster."

When the chair was turned to me, I sucked in a deep breath and felt bile rise to my throat.

Judge Wendell Foster was dead.

Had been for years.

All that was left was a mummified corpse wearing a brocade smoking jacket and gray slacks. Soft slippers covered the bones of his feet. His bony mouth hung open, showing a set of yellowed teeth, and empty eye sockets stared back at me.

I began to hyperventilate and leaned forward, trying to catch my breath.

"It's okay, Julia. Don't you see?" Emily said with encouragement. "Now I'll be able to take care of mother and father. Just like before. We'll be a family again."

"What?!" My head shot up, and I stared at her, horrified. "What do you mean?"

She pointed innocently to Doe. "She looks just like Mother, don't you think? I'll take care of her. I promise."

My head spun in the direction of her brother, making me dizzy. "You can't do this. This is crazy."

"The heart wants what the heart wants," he said with a Cheshire Cat grin. "But now we have to move on." He stepped forward and used a pen knife to reach around and cut my ties, releasing my hands. "Stand up," he ordered. He stepped back, while I got unsteadily to my feet. "We're going to the basement." He reached behind him and produced a small pistol from his waistband and gestured towards Doe. "You'll push the wheelchair. Emily, you go first and open the elevator."

Emily hesitated, but then stepped past me and hurried from the room.

Mansfield used the gun to point again at Doe. "Don't try anything funny. Now, let's get going. I have one more stop to make tonight."

"You won't get away with this," I said, moving behind Doe's chair.

"Oh, you'd be surprised at what I get away with," he said confidently.

"I'm the Governor's ex-wife."

I didn't like to play the governor card, but if I was ever going to use it, now would be a good time.

He merely laughed. "I can't think of anything I'd enjoy more than sticking it to your sanctimonious husband."

"Ex-husband."

"Whatever. Let's go."

He followed me as I pushed the chair forward with faltering steps. We moved out of the room and across the landing. The chair creaked as the big wheels rolled along a dirty carpet runner.

We passed a bathroom and a second bedroom before stopping at the back of the house. My mind raced as the adrenalin began to lift the chloroform fog. I scrambled to think of some way out of this. Even if I got away, I would have to leave Doe behind. So what were my options? Doe would be no help. I had no weapon, and we were alone on an isolated piece of property more than an hour from home.

As I made a left turn into a dimly lit hallway, something shifted inside my blouse. Keeping my hands on the wheelchair, I used my elbow to locate whatever it was and press against it. The peasant blouse I had on was belted at the waist. From what I could tell, something flat and hard was caught in my blouse down by my belt.

My cell phone!

I'd had my phone in my hand when someone, probably Mansfield, had knocked me out with the chloroform. I got a chill, thinking I might have a means of communication with the outside world.

And then I panicked, thinking my mother might call at any time. She always seemed to know when I was in trouble. That would alert Mansfield, and he'd certainly take the phone from me. I silently reached out to my mother, pleading with her NOT to call.

I turned the corner and saw Emily waiting expectantly at the end of the corridor. I continued slowly forward as real panic began to build in my chest. Doe and I were trapped in the movie *Psycho* with no way out.

I stopped halfway to Emily.

I couldn't do this. Getting into that elevator meant certain death.

"Why are you stopping?" Mansfield growled from behind me.

I felt the barrel of the gun dig into my lower back.

"Mansfield, please. We're just writing a book. This is crazy. Let us go. We won't say anything."

My fingers toyed with the clear tubing that ran up to the drip bag above Doe's head as I spoke.

"Move!" he commanded. "Or I'll shoot you right here."

A sob caught in my throat, but I took a step forward, crimping the tube in half as I moved. I glanced down, and before I could change my mind, I pushed the crimped end through one of the holes in the cane backing of the chair. I didn't know if it would work, but maybe, just maybe it would cut off the drug supply to Doe.

When I reached Emily, I whispered, "Please, Emily, don't do this."

A tear glistened in her eye, but she turned her head away.

Rebuffed, I wheeled the chair around and backed it into the small, ancient elevator, feeling as jittery as if I'd drunk a gallon of coffee.

"Wait here," Mansfield said to his sister. "I'll be right back."

"Why do you have to take Doe?" she said in a pleading voice.

"I won't hurt her," he said, reaching out to stroke Emily's cheek. She flinched away. "I just want to make sure they're both safe underground until I get back."

He stepped in with us and pressed the button to close the old accordion-style door. An immediate sense of claustrophobia took hold of me when the door latched shut.

The elevator began to descend with a lurch. Neither one of us spoke. At this point, I didn't know what to say. My heart raced, and I felt a trickle of sweat on my neck.

The trip to the basement was short. The elevator bumped to a stop, and my stomach turned over. I took another deep breath when the door slid open, but was overwhelmed this time with a strange, antiseptic odor. Mansfield stepped out first and then gestured with the gun to force me forward.

"Move!" he ordered again.

I pushed the chair over the elevator rails and into a short hallway. Mansfield stepped in behind me. The hallway opened into a large basement room. My gaze roamed the walls, looking for another door or window. There was none. The only way out was the elevator.

"Get over there," Mansfield said, pushing me toward an old, beat-up metal chair.

I left the wheelchair and stumbled forward.

"Sit down," he said.

I did what he told me. He produced zip ties and quickly secured my wrists to the back of the chair, and then he zip-tied my ankles together. I felt a tear slip down my cheek as I remembered other dangerous situations I'd gotten out of.

Would this one be the end?

"Now, there's one more loose end I have to take care of. Then I'll be back," Mansfield said.

"What?" I mumbled.

He giggled. "Your hot little friend."

"Blair?" I said, looking up.

Once again, a cold sweat washed over me.

He smiled seductively. "She knows too much. I'm going to bring her back here. You'll have a happy little reunion, and then I'll take care of everything all at once." He spoke quickly and the fingers on his left hand played a nervous rhythm on his leg. "Although I may have a little fun with her first." His eyes strayed to the far side of the room, but I dropped my head and allowed a sob to escape my throat. He just laughed. "Don't bother trying to get away. The only way out of here is the elevator, and I'll be turning it off once I get back upstairs. And Emily won't be any help, either. I've cut her medication so she's in la-la land. So just sit tight."

A minute later, he was gone.

The moment the whir of the elevator's motor retreated, I struggled against the zip ties, pulling my hands this way and that. I tried to get my ankles loose, although I had no idea how that would help. In the end, all I succeeded in doing was digging the rigid plastic edges of the zip-ties into my skin until my ankles began to bleed.

I tried hopping my chair over towards Doe. But instead of moving very far, I mostly just rattled my brain. I stopped struggling, breathing heavily. I considered tipping my chair over, but decided there was no point. It was a metal chair. It wouldn't break.

What could I do?

Real panic began to rise again in my chest, and I glanced around the room, looking for anything that might help release me from my bondage. I studied a bookcase against the wall. I peered into the shadows, past boxes and old furniture. There was nothing.

After a good ten or fifteen minutes of futile effort, I gave up and began to cry. And cry. And cry. A couple of times, I called out to Doe, but she didn't respond, so I cried some more. I had almost worn myself out when a voice interrupted me.

"Julia, why are you crying?" Emily said.

My head shot up. I hadn't heard the elevator return. She was standing just inside the room, holding the gun by her side. It wasn't pointed at me.

I tried to suck up some snot. "I'm crying, Emily, because your brother is going to kill us."

"I know," she said simply, stepping closer.

"Emily, I'm surprised you'd want to hurt us." I was hoping to play on her sympathies.

"Oh, I don't, Julia. But I have to do what Mansfield wants. If I don't, he…he…"

"He hurts you, doesn't he?"

She dropped her head in shame. "I have to do what he says. I'm sorry, Julia. I thought he was going to have you play the game, like he's done before."

"What do you mean?" I asked.

"Usually, he gives the women a chance to get away. They never do, but at least he gives them a chance."

Once more, my stomach clenched. "What do you mean? What…women?"

Emily seemed like a little girl, completely unaware of the magnitude of the situation. She chewed on a cuticle and swayed back and forth. Then I remembered what Mansfield had said about cutting her medication.

"Oh, there's been a bunch of them," she said. "He picks them out. They always look like Rose. He loved Rose, you know. He didn't mean to kill her. He was very sorry about that, but she rejected him. I think he kind of liked it, though. Killing her, I mean. He used to kill birds and squirrels all the time around the house. That's why I didn't like to play with him. That and…"

She stopped and turned her head to the side as if listening to someone. I kept quiet, mainly because I felt like screaming. I took a deep breath to quell the tornado inside my head.

"What happens with these other women?" I finally asked, bringing her attention back to me.

"I help bring them here. I'm the decoy; that's my part in the game. Sometimes I just catch them in conversation, and then he drugs them. But the last girl was at a restaurant with a friend. After the friend left, Mansfield had me get her to drive me to Kirkland. I told her my car had died. She never suspected anything. She was really nice."

Oh my God, I thought. She was talking about Melody Reamer, the girl who had floated up on the shores of Mercer Island.

"And then he plays with them," she said, finishing her thought.

"He plays with them?"

Her eyes drifted over to the counter against the far wall. I followed her gaze this time, noticing the glint of metal. The counter was littered with small tools of some kind, and I swallowed a ball of spit.

Oh my God!

"He never plays fair, though." she said sadly. "Even when we were kids. There are rules to the games, but he always changes the rules so that only he wins."

"But, Emily, these girls were innocent. How could you help? Why didn't you ever call the police?"

She looked over at me, her eyes round with fear. "You don't understand. He...he..." She stopped speaking and began to hyperventilate. Finally, she pulled up the sleeve of her left arm. Her skin was covered in bruises and scars from old cuts.

"Oh my God."

She sucked up a gulp of air and stared at me. "I have to play the game, don't you see?" she said, tears rolling down her cheeks. "Actually, he's a monster," she whispered. "Worse than my father ever was."

A cold chill rolled over me. This poor woman had endured more than just her own mental illness. The men in her life had taken advantage of it and put her through hell.

She had begun to bite her nails again, and I noticed that her cuticles were now bleeding. A drop of blood fell to the floor, only to blend in with what looked like several other blotches of dried blood.

I took a deep breath. I had to say something. I had to get her to help us. Somewhere in that distorted brain of hers was a decent person.

"Mansfield cheats, doesn't he? But you don't, do you? You play fair."

Her eyes brightened. "Yes. I always play fair."

"I know you do. So maybe you could play fair with us tonight."

She blinked several times. "No. Mansfield will...will...no, I can't."

"But Emily, he's not here. He must trust you. He left you in charge, didn't he?"

She smiled weakly. "Yes. He did, didn't he? You know, I had a riddle all worked out for you, Julia," she said proudly. "I was sure you could figure it out, because it had to do with the *Wizard of Oz*."

My breath was irregular, and I thought I heard a buzzing in my ears. I glanced at Doe. Her eyes were half open now and she seemed to be trying to focus her gaze on me.

"What...what were the clues?" I asked, trying to keep Emily talking.

"I was going to give you *two* clues from the *Wizard of Oz*. If it's really your favorite movie, then you would know the answers."

"Tell me the clues, Emily. I'll play fair, I promise."

She perked up. "You're smart, Julia. You might just get away." She whirled around to a shelf behind her and grabbed something. It was a giant toy hour-glass, just like the kind from the movie. I hadn't noticed it in the shadows.

"I've had this since I was a little girl," she said, putting it on a rickety table. "It's not a real one, like in the movie. This one takes a little less than an hour to run out."

My head was reeling. She wanted us to reenact the *Wizard of Oz* scene, when Dorothy is imprisoned by the Wicked Witch of the West. And I was going to play the part of Dorothy. Under normal circumstances, I'd have been thrilled. But now...

"So you'll have about fifty-five minutes," she said with apology.

"To do what?" I asked weakly.

"Get away, silly. I'll be watching." She gestured to the corner of the ceiling. A camera was focused right on the center of the room. "But I won't interrupt you until the hour glass has run out. That's the deal. But then, I'm afraid I'll have to come back," she said. She awkwardly pushed a strand of hair behind her ear, smearing a streak of blood along her cheek in the process.

"Okay," I agreed. I'd do anything. "What are the clues?"

Real joy lit up her face. "Well the first one is…how did the Tin Man help the Wizard escape?"

"What?" I snapped. "That doesn't even make sense."

She giggled like a little girl. "Yes, it does. Just think, Julia. You'll get it."

"What's the second clue?" I said with some impatience.

"You can escape the same way the Wicked Witch of the West arrived to meet Dorothy. There you go." She grabbed the hourglass to flip it over. "I'm counting on you, Julia."

"Wait! Emily, I'm still tied up. I can't go anywhere even if I guess the clues. That isn't fair, is it?"

She paused a moment. Clearly, cutting me loose posed a risk. But logic won the day.

"No, that wouldn't be fair."

She reached into her pocket and pulled out a small knife. Why she had a knife in her pocket gave me the creeps, but I was hardly in a position to worry about it at that point. With practiced ease, she cut my ties and then stood back. "I doubt you'll be able to take your friend with you," she said pointing to Doe. "The drug lasts a long time in their systems."

"But your brother said the elevator is the only way out of here."

She smiled indulgently. "I've already told you, Julia. My brother lies. He lies all the time. There's one other way, but you'll need to find it. That's the game," she said with a creepy smile. "You asked if we used to play games in the barn, and we did. I just never won." Her smile faded, and she dropped her chin.

I glanced around the room. There were four walls. No doors.

"How the heck am I supposed to find the second way out?"

"Think of the clues, Julia. The clues." She gave me a nod and then held up the hour-glass.

"Emily, wait! I have to know one thing. Did you kill Marigold?"

Her facial muscles froze, and her eyes filled with tears. "Yes. But it was an accident. Really, it was."

"What do you mean an accident?"

Her shoulders drooped. "I was taking care of her, and she started to cry. I couldn't get her to stop. So I carried her around the room. But I knocked over the candle, and it set the rug on fire. When I tried to put out the fire, I stumbled over the candlestick and dropped her." She sucked up a sob and wiped her nose. "Her head landed on the candlestick base." Her eyes pleaded with me. "My father hated her because she was different. He wouldn't even look at her. But I loved Marigold, Julia. She was the sweetest baby. I would have never hurt her on purpose. You have to believe me."

Her pain was palpable. "I do. I do believe you, Emily. But why did you hide her? Why didn't you just tell your parents what happened?"

"You didn't know my father. I was scared," she said. "My father always said I was an imbecile. He beat me when I couldn't do something just the way he wanted. So I lied. I told my parents that someone must have come into the attic and taken her when I was in the house using the restroom. But they didn't believe me, and my father sent me away a short time later."

"I'm sorry, Emily."

She wiped her nose. "I hope you get away, Julia." Then she flipped over the hour-glass. "I have to go. Mansfield will be back soon. I'll have to turn off the elevator again, so you'll have to solve the clues to get out of here. Good luck." She turned and disappeared down the hallway toward the elevator. A moment later, I heard the whir of the engine again, and she was gone.

I turned to Doe, whose eyes were still only half open. "Doe! You need to wake up." I ran over and pulled the syringe out of her arm. I shook her. "Doe, wake up."

"I'm awake," she mumbled. "Sort of." She glanced around. "Where are we?"

"We've been abducted. We're at Emily Foster's."

"What?"

My gaze swept the room, taking in stacks of boxes, broken furniture, an old exercise bike, and a bunch of PVC pipe stacked in the corner. The floor was covered in broken, stained linoleum tiles. There was a drain in the middle of the floor, with an old hospital gurney above it. The gurney gave me pause, but I had to ignore it.

I looked past the gurney to the far wall, where a set of floor-to-ceiling shelves stood. The shelves were filled with a variety of jars containing different kinds of liquids. Next to the shelf unit was a chipped sink and the countertop where the tools were laid out.

"How do we get out of here?" Doe mumbled.

"I don't know."

We were too isolated to have heard when Mansfield actually left the property. Unless he knew right where Blair would be, he'd have to find her. If he drove as fast as Blair, I figured the shortest time he'd be gone was a little over two hours. And by my estimate, a good 45 minutes had already elapsed. I had to hurry.

But first things first.

I found a small scalpel on the counter and ran to Doe. "Doe, I have to cut you loose."

She nodded. "Okay, but why am I so groggy?"

"You've been drugged."

"Drugged? Why?"

"Never mind about that now. We have to get out of here."

"I don't understand," Doe said. She was still slurring her words.

"Emily and Mansfield Foster abducted you," I told her, while I began to saw through her constraints. "They're going to kill us."

Her eyes opened wide. "Kill us? Whatever for?"

"Because Emily admitted too much to us the other day, and I made the mistake of calling and telling Mansfield about it. Now, he's gone after Blair. When he gets back, he plans to kill all of us. So you have to stay awake."

"It's so hard," she said, closing her eyes again.

"No!" I slapped her.

"Ow!" she said, her eyes popping open.

I tugged at the zip ties binding her wrists and finished slicing through the first one. I got halfway through the second one and then said, "Here." I handed her the scalpel. "Can you finish?"

"Um...yes, I think so," she mumbled.

"Okay, but don't get up," I said. "You're too woozy. And cut away from yourself," I said, guiding her hand. "Be careful. I have to figure out how to get us out of here."

While she fumbled with the small knife, I turned to the rest of the room.

Okay, what the heck were Emily's stupid clues? I thought. *Something about the Tin Man and how the Wicked Witch of the West arrived to meet Dorothy.*

What had Emily meant? I plopped into a nearby rocker a moment and dropped my head into my hands to think.

In the movie, the Wicked Witch of the West arrives in Munchkin Land in a burst of crimson smoke.

I glanced up and around the room. Were there gas canisters in here? What did Emily mean by that clue? The Wicked Witch normally traveled by her magic broom. But there were no brooms or canisters of smoke that I could see. In fact, there was just a bunch of junk in the room.

Damn! What else?

I got up and began pacing around the center of the room. Doe was beginning to come around. Her eyes were open, but she was staring stupidly at me.

"Get out of the zip ties," I ordered her.

She glanced down and went back to work, while I continued to pace. As I paced, I kicked an old bucket in frustration, and then it hit me.

The Wicked Witch actually arrives on the *movie set* of Munchkin Land through a trap door in the floor. It's pretty obvious if you're watching closely. Crimson smoke emerges in the outline of a trap door for a brief second when she emerges. Early special effects.

I stopped and studied the floor, mentally dividing it into quadrants. As I moved around the center of the room, I looked for an area where the space between tiles might appear darker or wider than everywhere else.

Nothing.

Then I moved the area rug and noticed some inconsistencies in the flooring.

That made me think of something I'd seen in a TV show, and I ran for the shelf unit to grab an old bottle of some kind of cleaning solution. I unscrewed the top and began to pour it over the tiles. When I hit the tiles that had been under the rug, the liquid drained through a crack in the floor.

Bingo!

I put the bottle down and studied the floor. If this was a trap door, there was no hand pull, no way to lift it.

I ran back to the shelf unit and found a long, flat piece of metal that had probably been part of an appliance or a bed. I dropped to my knees and was able to slip the rod in between the tiles. But when I tried to angle it so that I could lift the floor area, it bent and nothing moved. I put more pressure on it, and the bar snapped.

Damn!

I was breathing hard now and chanced a glance toward the hourglass. More than a third of it was gone. My heart fluttered in panic. There had to be a way to lift this thing.

I stopped and put my hands to my head. I had to think.

What was the second clue? Something about the Tin Man. *How could the Tin Man help the Wizard escape?*

I sat back on my heels. Tin Man. Wizard. *What had Emily meant?*

The Wizard didn't escape anything in the movie. He chose to fly off in his balloon and was going to take Dorothy with him.

I closed my eyes and imagined the scene from the movie.

Dorothy and the Wizard are in the basket of the balloon. Dorothy is holding Toto. Toto sees a woman's cat and wriggles out of Dorothy's arms. Dorothy quickly climbs out of the basket and runs after the dog, while the Wizard is saying goodbye to people. And then the basket starts to lift and float away.

Wait! No.

The Tin Man is standing *outside* of the basket, holding onto one of the ropes tethering the balloon. But…while everyone is focused on Dorothy, the Tin Man actually unwinds the rope from the pole, *releasing* the balloon.

That's right!

Clearly, the moviemakers counted on people being distracted by watching Dorothy and the Wizard. But I had noticed it. And so had Emily.

I climbed to my feet and looked around the room. What could Emily have been referring to here?

Just then, a hand grasped my arm.

"Julia, where are we?" Doe mumbled.

She was free of the zip ties and finally coming around.

"Oh, Doe," I said, leaning over. "We're in the basement at Emily Foster's home. We have to get out of here."

"Okay," she nodded and started to get up.

"No. Not yet," I said, holding her down. "Wait until I tell you."

"Okay," she said again.

I moved through the room, pushing boxes aside, looking under things, opening cupboard doors and peering into corners. I reached the shelf unit again and turned to study the room from that perspective. I started at the left wall and slowly rotated my gaze to the right.

And then I saw it.

In the far corner was a rope looped through a pulley. The rope dropped to the floor.

I ran towards it, moving boxes and pulling furniture out of the way. Once there, I stood back and studied it for a moment.

There was a hole in the floor where the rope dropped out of sight. The pulley above my head was securely anchored into the ceiling. I reached up and grasped one loop of the rope and pulled.

Nothing.

I reached over and grasped the other loop of rope and pulled.

The rope moved.

Bingo!

I pulled harder until I heard a scraping noise. I glanced over and saw the square of flooring begin to move. As I pulled hand over hand, the secret trap door began to rise.

Doe's eyes grew wide. "Where does that lead?" she said weakly.

"I have no idea." I pulled until the trap door was all the way up, and then I secured the rope on a hook on the wall. I scrambled back over to look through the trap door. A set of wooden stairs led down into a dark, dank, musty hole.

"We need a flashlight," I said.

Once again, I searched through everything in the basement. I was just about to give up and then remembered my phone. I reached into my blouse, brought it out and turned it on. The battery was low, but it worked. I looked at the hour-glass again. We had less than fifteen minutes to go.

"Okay, Doe," I said to my friend. "It's time to get out of here."

CHAPTER THIRTY-FIVE

Adrenalin coursed through my veins as I stood in that basement and stared into the abyss. I'd solved the clues and believed Emily when she said she would play fair. We had a chance and could be free in a few minutes. But first we had to find our way out of a deep and dark underground tunnel.

Doe had revived enough to get herself out of the chair, but she was wobbly on her feet.

"I'll go first," I said to her. "But you'll have to get onto the stairs yourself. If you have trouble, hopefully, I can help you from below. You okay with that?"

She nodded. But she reached out and pulled the wheelchair over for support.

"Okay," I said, feeling jittery. I shifted my gaze to the camera in the corner. I contemplated saying something to Emily, who I knew was watching, but decided against it. I turned my back to the hole and reached backwards with my left foot.

My foot met the top rung. Carefully, I backed down the stairs. My foot slipped at one point, making me grab the railing for support. So I called up to Doe. "Be careful. The stairs are slippery." I pulled out my phone and shone the light below me. I was halfway to a dirt floor. "Okay, Doe. C'mon down."

She appeared at the opening and glanced down to where I hung onto the stairs below her. She teetered a bit, and I held my breath. I aimed the light as best I could up the stairs.

"Thanks," she murmured.

She turned around and crouched down. She reached back with one foot and felt for the top step. She drew back her other foot and dropped it to the second step. I continued down the stairs, as she walked herself backwards. I reached the bottom and stepped off onto a hard-packed dirt floor.

My instinct was to look around to see where we were, but I had to keep an eye on Doe. She was making slow progress. We had to hurry, but as I watched her descend, it occurred to me that even in this dangerous and insanely creepy situation, her clothes looked perfect. I wondered how long that would last as she wavered off the last step and onto the ground. She leaned against the staircase, breathless.

"Good job," I said.

I used the light from the phone to get our bearings. We were in an underground dirt tunnel that was supported every fifteen feet or so with timber posts. Above us was another pulley wheel, where the rope connected to a lever that operated the trap door.

Clever.

But if I calculated correctly, we had less than an hour to make it out of the tunnel and off the Foster property before Mansfield came back. And he'd come back with a vengeance. We had to get moving.

But first, I tried to make a call.

"Damn! We're too deep underground," I said when it wouldn't go through. "I should have tried it in the basement. C'mon, we have to go. Can you walk?"

Doe let go of the staircase. "I think so."

I grabbed her hand and looped my arm through her elbow. "I'll hold you up."

We started forward, but our progress was slower than I wanted. We had to be careful to avoid rocks and holes in the dirt floor where moisture had seeped into little puddles.

When a rat squealed and scuttled out from under my foot, I screamed and stopped to take a deep breath. I inhaled, and the cloying smell of swamp water and mold almost shut off my airway.

"God," I whined. "This is awful."

"Keep going," Doe urged me. "We have to keep going."

"You're right."

We began again, a little more briskly. But twenty or thirty feet ahead I tripped and went down onto one knee. Doe fell sideways against the tunnel wall. I gasped for a breath and heaved myself back to my feet. I was about to reach for Doe when my phone began to play my mother's anthem.

"Mom," I almost cried. "We need help. Doe and I have been abducted. We were being held in a basement and have escaped into a tunnel. There's a madman on his way back here to kill us. We have to get out of the tunnel before he gets back, or we'll die a horrible death. Can you alert the authorities?"

"No. You know I can't. I'm only connected to you."

I had to think quickly. "Mom, there's an elevator in the house above us. It connects to the basement where we were being held. Can you short out the motor?"

"Uh…I'm not sure. Listen, you get out of that tunnel and let me work on the elevator. But Julia…"

The phone went dead, throwing us into darkness. I shook the phone in my hand and blindly clicked the buttons, but the battery was gone. I cried out in frustration.

"Darn it! We're on our own," I said through gritted teeth.

"She can't do anything?"

"She's only ever helped with mobile devices or things that run on electricity. I'm not sure what she could do down here," I said in the dark. "Hopefully, she can at least disable the elevator." I knew the doubt had seeped into my voice. "Let's keep going."

"I can't see a thing," Doe said fearfully.

"Take my hand," I said, reaching out.

We played a form of blind man's patty cake in the dark as we fumbled to find each other's hands and clasp onto each other.

"Okay, we're going to have to be more careful," I warned, grabbing Doe's hand and forearm.

We took a few steps forward and stumbled over something, almost tumbling to the ground.

Doe groaned. "God, I nearly twisted my ankle."

She was breathing heavily now, probably partly from fear and partly from exertion.

"Okay, listen. Let's slide our feet forward. But as we do, I'm going to count one-two as we take each step. We push forward a step, plant one foot firmly on the ground and then move forward again."

"That will take us forever," she said with a moan.

"Better than killing ourselves in the process. So, here we go. First step…slide forward one."

We each pushed forward a step.

"Okay? Two."

We took another step.

"One," I repeated. "Now, two."

We continued in that slow and aggravating way for a good twenty minutes, until I screamed when something grazed my head. I stopped abruptly, my heart beating wildly.

"It's just a tree root," Doe said.

"How do you know? It could be a spider web," I said. "Either way, I *hate* it. I hate all of this!"

I stopped when a sob caught in my throat. I flinched when Doe reached out in the darkness and placed her hand on my shoulder.

"It's okay, Julia. We'll get out of this. How long has it been?" she asked.

"You mean since Mansfield left? I don't know. God I hope he can't find Blair."

"She can take care of herself," she said, her voice betraying the lack of confidence she felt.

"How are you feeling?" I asked her.

"A little better. I need fresh air though. Are you up to continuing?"

"Yeah. At least Emily hasn't come after us. But let's get out of here. This tunnel has to end somewhere."

I was just about to start out again when something began to glow in front of us. I heard an intake of breath from Doe.

"What the heck?" she murmured.

The glow expanded into the hazy outline of what appeared to be a woman.

"Who is it?" Doe asked in alarm.

"I have no idea."

We clasped our hands more tightly together. I felt something brush my elbow, and I wheeled around.

A second glow had appeared just behind me.

"Doe, look!"

The luminous image of a woman, a young woman, stood behind me and to my left. I glanced back and forth between the two of them. Each of the women had long hair and both appeared to be naked. I inhaled, feeling slightly dizzy.

"Oh my God! Doe, I think these are women Mansfield has killed."

As soon as I said it, the one in front of us nodded once. Behind her, a third image appeared. And then a fourth, further down the tunnel.

"They're lighting the tunnel for us," Doe said with excitement. "C'mon, Julia, let's go!"

"Thank you," I called out to them. "Thank you! Thank you!"

I dropped the phone into my pocket, and we moved forward, quickly now, aided by the soft illumination from the ghosts. We walked for what seemed like forever, following the twists and turns of the tunnel. Tree roots had indeed invaded the walls and ceiling in places, hanging down to brush our heads, but now we could just push them aside.

As we progressed, the ghostly images would fade in place and then appear further ahead. There were five in total, each similar and yet different.

The tunnel grew increasingly cold and damp, raising goosebumps on my arms. We passed some discarded lumber and empty cans along one wall. Finally, the tunnel ended at a metal door. A heavy padlock made me panic. I rushed forward and shook it, but it didn't budge.

"No!" I screamed, banging my fists against the door. I turned to the closest ghost. "I don't suppose you can magically open locked doors."

She stared at me, her dark eyes expressionless.

"I wish I had my gun," Doe said in a breathy voice.

"Dang, me too." I looked around my feet. "Wait." I found a large, flat rock. "Maybe this will work."

I moved up to the lock and smashed it with the rock. The rock splintered, cutting my fingers, but the lock stayed. I found another rock and did the same thing. Again, no luck.

Wiping blood off on my jeans, I returned up the tunnel to where I'd seen a short two-by-four and brought it back. Holding it with both hands, I lined myself up with the door and came down on the lock with an overhead blow.

The lock broke.

I exhaled with relief and then quickly removed it.

"C'mon, Doe. Time to go home."

CHAPTER THIRTY-SIX

I pulled open the door, allowing a fresh breeze to flood the tunnel and fill my lungs with the bracing salt air.

We stumbled through the door into a gulley that rose about ten feet on each side, lit only by the full moon. I turned, but the ghosts had faded back into the tunnel.

"They're gone," Doe murmured.

"I guess they did their job. Or maybe they can't go beyond the tunnel."

"I need to sit down, Julia," Doe said.

She lowered herself onto a boulder with a heavy sigh.

I glanced around us. I had no idea where we were, or even if we had gotten clear of the Foster property. And if we hadn't, we were still prisoners.

"We need to get out of here, Doe. It's been over two hours and Mansfield could be on his way back by now, with or without Blair."

"I know," she said. "Just give me a minute."

I wanted to leave, to run, but recognized that Doe was in a weakened state. "Okay, a short break. Tell me how they got you. I mean, back at your house?"

Doe took a deep breath. "Emily showed up with one of her photo albums and just waltzed in," she said. "I was so shocked, I didn't say anything. She asked for a glass of water. When I came back, I had my phone out to call you. But she was standing by the coffee table and had the photo album open, with a picture in her hand that she wanted me to see. I leaned over to look, and someone, probably Mansfield, came up behind me and stabbed me in the neck with a syringe."

"Oh my God. I'm so sorry, Doe. They got me with chloroform."

I was pacing back and forth in front of her, anxious to go. Doe finally pushed off from the rock. "Okay, let's get out of here. But which way?"

I turned toward the sound of the surf. "The moon rises in the east and sets in the west, right?"

"Yes," she replied.

"Well, I'm pretty sure there's a big home north of the Foster property, so let's head that way."

"I'm afraid that won't work," a male voice stopped us.

We both jerked our heads up to the top of the rise on our left. Mansfield stood outlined in the moonlight, holding the gun again and a small flashlight. My heart sank.

"You're back," I murmured in defeat.

"Yes, and it looks like I made it just in time. I wouldn't want you to start the party without me."

The buzzing began in my ear again. "What about Blair?" I asked.

He paused before replying. "It seems she was more resourceful than I anticipated. But I'll attend to her later."

Inwardly, I cheered for Blair. At least she was safe for now. Not so for us. As I contemplated our situation, Mansfield came down from the hill.

"Now, let's just march right back up that tunnel to the basement again," he said, gesturing with the gun.

"Why not just shoot us here?" I asked, feeling I had nothing to lose.

"Too messy. I like things where I can control them."

"It's all about control with you, isn't it?" I snapped.

"Quit stalling, Mrs. Applegate. Let's go."

As we turned toward the tunnel again, I got a glimpse of Doe's face as a ray of moonlight cut across the gulley. Her beautiful features were etched with a sadness that cut me to the core.

We were going to die.

We took two steps toward the tunnel, when the door slammed shut with a hollow echo.

"What the hell?" Mansfield shouted.

Keeping the gun pointed in our direction, he rushed forward and pulled on the door. It didn't budge.

"Emily!" he cried. "Open the door!"

There was no sound except the surf crashing somewhere behind us. When a glow appeared around the edges of the steel door however, I said to him, "I don't think it's Emily."

"Yes, it is," he growled. He slammed his fist on the door, kicked it, and shouted again. "Open the door, you crazy bitch!"

Mansfield had almost forgotten about us. We both inched backwards. I had no idea how we could get away, but I began to look for something to use as a weapon.

And then he reached out and grabbed the metal bar handle on the door and shook it trying to pull the door open. The door handle began to glow red, and a second later, he screeched and let go. He backed up with his hand outstretched, palm up.

"God damn it!" he shouted, shaking his hand in pain.

Doe and I just stared in shock. It was the ghosts. They wouldn't let him back in the tunnel. My heart nearly sang. But could they help us any further?

As if he heard my thoughts, he spun in our direction. "That won't help you. Let's go! Back to the house."

He gestured for us to climb the hill. We did as he said and scrambled up the small rise, holding onto each other as we went.

Doe whispered to me when we reached the top. "Maybe if we both go after him."

"No," I whispered back. "Too risky. Just do as he says."

"Here, take this," he said.

I turned and he threw the small flashlight at me.

I barely caught it before we were herded onto a small path that wound in and out of the trees. Tendrils of ivy and other creeping vines crawled up tree trunks and along the ground, threatening to trip us. Although he kept urging us forward at a faster pace, I went slow – partly to stay safe on the trail and partly to stall for time.

We trudged along like criminals on our way to our own executions, which we kind of were. It took us a good ten minutes to make it to a clearing where we could see the lights from the house in the distance.

I stopped mid-stride and doubled-over, a wrenching pain clenching my stomach. I couldn't go back there.

"Keep going," Mansfield ordered from behind.

But I didn't budge. I just couldn't.

"C'mon, you old biddy. Move, or I'll shoot you right here!"

"No," I replied.

Better that, I thought. *Better to be shot than tortured.* The smell of pine and sagebrush, which would have normally enthralled me, made me think this wasn't a bad place to die.

But then Doe reached out and placed a hand on my arm. "C'mon, Julia. Don't give up yet. Not yet."

I took a deep breath, swallowed hard and straightened up to keep going. But the going was tough; the terrain was uneven and rocky. Twice, Doe stumbled and fell. And when we entered the trees again, several branches slapped me in the face. As we descended a small incline, I slipped and slid to the bottom.

"Are you okay?" Doe called out.

"Yes," I said. I was breathing hard and my hip hurt. In the distance, I could hear a car approaching on the road somewhere nearby. The thought that someone who could help was so close made my heart flutter. If we could only get a message to someone on the outside. But as the sound diminished, I hefted myself back onto my feet with a feeling of deep sadness.

"Hurry up," Mansfield growled.

"Would you rather carry me?" I snapped. He didn't answer, so I turned to Doe. "Be careful, Doe. It's steep."

Doe reached out and grabbed branches as she descended the hill, taking small steps. At the last minute, her foot slid out from under her and she fell, too, awkwardly rolling the rest of the way down.

"Ow!" she cried out, rubbing her ankle when she came to a stop. "Oh, damn. This happens in every bad chase movie ever made."

I crouched next to her. "Did you twist it?"

"Yes," she said, wincing with pain.

"Great," Mansfield said. "Get the old cow back on her feet. My patience is running out."

"Why should we hurry? You're just going to kill us anyway?" I snarled back.

"Yeah, and if you don't, I'll shoot you here and let the animals take care of you."

"No you won't. Not the pristine Mansfield Foster. Like you said, too messy. And when they found us, every finger would point at you." He kept quiet at that, so I took a breath and looked around me. "Hold on." Before he could stop me, I grabbed a sturdy branch off the path and ripped off some of the smaller branches. I handed the improvised walking stick to Doe.

She took it and I helped her up so she could lean on it. With a nod, she said, "Seems like a lot of work just to get snuffed out by this guy."

"No kidding," I murmured, with my head turned away from him. "But I for one don't intend on going quietly. No matter what, hang onto this. It's the only weapon we have."

Our pace slowed considerably, and I cringed every time Doe took a step and emitted a small moan or cry of pain. But as the path curved to the right, it finally leveled out.

A few minutes later, we emerged from the trees into the front drive next to Mansfield's Mercedes coupe.

"Okay, back inside," he said.

The sound of a high-powered engine caught my attention, and I turned to glance through the trees to my right. Headlights flashed through breaks in the branches about a half mile away.

"That's a Porsche," I said under my breath to Doe, thinking of Blair.

"No it's not, Julia," she whispered. "No one's coming for us. We're on our own."

As the car roared past the property, a tear slid down my cheek.

With a feeling of profound defeat, we stepped up to the front door and I pushed it open, only to be re-assaulted by the sour smells trapped inside. We shuffled back into that house of horrors, but it was quiet. I wondered where Emily was.

We crossed into the foyer and stopped just to the side of the staircase. Doe reached out and grasped the bannister for support.

"What now?" I asked, turning to our captor.

"Now we start all over again," he said. "I've already turned the elevator back on. We'll take a little trip downstairs again, but this time you won't be leaving. Not in one piece, anyway."

"Why can't we let them go, Mansfield?" a voice said quietly. "They won fair and square."

It was Emily. She was on the staircase above us, twisting a lock of hair around her index finger. While I knew she probably still had the knife in the pocket of her jumper, she no longer had the gun. Mansfield had that.

"Shut up! If you hadn't let them go, we'd be done with this."

I glanced in Emily's direction. The side of her face sported a fresh red welt.

"You beat up your own sister. What a man," I said.

"Shut up!" He swung the gun and clipped me in the forehead, knocking me up against the wall. "You'll see in a minute just what kind of man I am."

I hung on the wall, my hand to my brow. The dampness under my fingers told me I was bleeding. "How do you intend to get away with all of this?" I said through gritted teeth. "Blair will go directly to the police."

He laughed. "She never saw me. I had on a ski mask."

I turned to look at him. In the light, I realized he had his own bruise above his left eye and a bite wound on his forearm, just north of his expensive watch.

Despite our situation, I smiled. "Looks like she did a number on you."

"Yeah, well, I'll take care of that bitch soon enough. Now, let's all head back to the elevator."

"Wait," I said. "How did you know where we were?"

He smirked. "Technology. Go ahead, open those doors behind you."

I turned to find a pair of closet doors that led to a space under the staircase. I pulled them open and was surprised to find a couple of computers and four monitors, all lit up and clicking away. The monitor screens were focused on various places on the property, including the backyard, the front driveway, and the tunnel.

"You see? Even if you'd gotten away, all paths circle back to the house, so it was only a matter of time," he said.

I glanced back at the monitor, feeling so tired. *We'd never really had a chance.*

While I stared mutely at the screen, a breeze rustled the bushes closest to the house. Something blue flashed past the monitor, making me suck in a quick gulp of air. I quickly closed the doors again, my heart racing.

"You're a monster, you know that?" I said loudly, turning toward him.

"Save it. Let's go."

He pointed down the hallway to the back of the house. I stared that way, feeling unable to move. I had to stall.

"Emily said you killed Rose. Is that true?"

He shot a hateful glance toward his sister above us. "It doesn't matter," he growled. "Now, move! Or I'll put a bullet in your friend's head." He pointed the gun at Doe, who was leaning against the stairs.

"No, not mother!" Emily screamed.

"Don't shoot," I shouted, holding my hand up. "We'll go."

I helped Doe stand up again, and we turned and began to shuffle in the opposite direction. I glanced up at Emily, hoping against hope that this time she would defy her brother.

She turned away again, toward the open door behind us. This time however, her eyes grew wide, just as her brother demanded, "Hurry up!"

But another voice responded. "They're not going anywhere!"

I whipped around to find Blair standing right behind Mansfield with a gun of her own pointed at his back. Rudy was by her side with a tire iron in her hands.

Full blown tears sprouted this time, and my hand flew to my mouth. "Oh, my God!"

Mansfield remained facing me, his face expressionless. He was thinking. Processing his situation.

The sound of sirens made him move.

In one fluid motion, he spun around with his gun hand outstretched, ready to shoot. But his wrist connected with Blair's. Her arm flew up, and her gun went off. The bullet went wide.

She was thrown off balance and fell sideways. I let go of Doe, grabbed the branch from her and slammed it into the back of Mansfield's knees; his legs buckled, and he nearly collapsed. That gave Rudy time to jump forward and swing the tire iron down on his gun hand, making him cry out.

As his gun skidded across the floor, he back-handed Rudy, spinning her away. Blair stumbled to her feet, while I scrambled for Mansfield's gun.

But by the time I had the gun in hand, he had fled out the open front door as sirens and flashing lights filled the front yard.

"Are you guys okay?" Blair rushed forward to throw her arms around me.

Rudy picked herself up and went to Doe, who was leaning weakly against the wall.

"Yes," I said, "but how in the world…"

"Never mind. We're here. We're *all* here."

The sound of barking dogs made me turn. "What's that?"

"I told David to bring a police dog," Blair said, running for the open front door. "I was afraid we'd be looking for you out in that forest."

"Stop! Police!" a deep voice shouted outside.

Blair and I made it to the front porch just as Mansfield spun away from his car and took off running into the trees, with Mickey and Minnie in hot pursuit. I watched the little dogs streak past his car thinking, *Really? David brought the Dachshunds?*

Two squad cars blocked Mansfield's BMW, and David had just emerged from his big SUV.

"Go!" he yelled to two officers, pointing after Mansfield.

The officers drew their guns and gave chase into the woods, while David turned toward me. In a few strides, he was beside me, grabbing me into a bear hug. "God, Julia! Are you okay?"

"Yes, yes," I said, as he squeezed me. I pushed myself away from him. "But…you brought the Dachshunds?"

"I was at the Inn, looking for you when Blair called. So I just grabbed them. No time to get a police dog." He shrugged. "I thought they might help."

A smile slid across my face. "Okay, but now go get that bastard. And save my dogs."

"Is he armed?"

"No, I have his gun," I replied, holding it up.

"Okay, hang onto it and lock yourself in."

He gave me a quick kiss and then jumped off the steps, ordered one of the officers to stay with us and followed the other officers into the dense foliage. The dogs were still barking, but the sound had diminished. I looked in their direction, hoping they'd come back safe and sound.

"Julia!" Rudy called from behind me. "We need an ambulance. It's Emily."

We hurried back inside and found Emily where she'd fallen on the stairs. Blood was spattered on the wall behind her.

"Oh my God. She's been shot."

Rudy already had her cell phone out, while I rushed up to Emily. She lay like a broken doll on the stairs, a large splotch of blood darkening her abdomen.

"Help is on the way," I said, grabbing her hand.

She gave me a wan smile. "I'm glad you're okay, Julia," she said with a weak voice. "You won the game fair and square. Just like Dorothy. You and your friends."

I tried to shush her. "Don't talk. They're going to get you to a hospital."

"I'm sorry I had to be the Wicked Witch, Julia."

"No, Emily," I said, patting her arm. "If anything, you were Glinda. You helped us escape."

"But, remember? I don't like Glinda," she said. She tried to chuckle, but winced instead. And then her muscles spasmed, and she moaned.

"Take it easy. Just breathe."

"Glinda did help, though, didn't she?" Emily said weakly.

"Yes, she did. She was a good soul. Just like you, Emily."

"I'm glad," she said. "I never wanted to be bad."

CHAPTER THIRTY-SEVEN

We stayed with Emily until the ambulance arrived. When they had her safely loaded on a gurney into the back, we encouraged them to take Doe as well. Not only because of her sprained ankle, but because of the drugs that had been poured into her system.

Rudy rode with them, while Blair and I stayed behind to wait for David. We did as he said and locked ourselves in the house and sat on a bench up against the staircase. I had a wet cloth to my forehead, while a young police officer stood guard outside.

"What happened, Blair?" I asked, reaching out and grabbing her hand. "We were so worried about you the whole time Mansfield was gone."

"He tried to get me, Julia." She shook her head, and I could see tears in her eyes. "Rudy and I had dinner downtown and then went for drinks. I was taking Rudy back home when I got a text from Doe asking me to come to her house."

"He had her phone. That's how he got me, too," I said. "Did he know you were with Rudy?"

"No. Since I was driving, Rudy took my phone and texted back and just said, '*Okay, heading up to your place now.*'"

"So he thought you were alone?"

She shrugged. "I guess. When we got to Doe's, Rudy got a call from Rush Dooley about Jake. So I went into the house alone."

There was a familiar noise at the front door. The dogs were scratching to get in. I ran to the door and opened it. They scrambled inside and began to jump around my feet, tails wagging and tongues lolling. They were happy and excited by their adventure. It had all been a game to them. Wish I could have thought so, too. But I crouched down to pet them, anyway.

"Good police dogs," I said, giving them each a hug. I glanced out into the surrounding trees. "I wonder what's taking so long out there." I sighed and closed the door. I returned to the bench, allowing the dogs to jump into my lap. "Go ahead, Blair. Finish your story," I said, hoping to override my fears that David was out in that underbrush with a mad man. "What happened when you got inside Doe's house?"

"Mansfield came at me from behind. He tried to put a rag filled with chloroform on my face, but I bit him."

I chuckled and shook my head. "God, I wish I'd thought of that."

"Well, I had an advantage. I had on my heels."

My eyes opened in surprise, and I glanced at her feet. They were encased in tennis shoes.

"As we struggled in the hallway, I lifted my leg and stomped on his foot so hard, the heel broke off." She started to laugh. "He screamed like a baby and let go of me. I whirled around and punched him in the face, just as Rudy came up behind him and sucker-punched him in the kidneys."

I clapped my hands. "Oh, God, I wish I'd seen that."

Blair smiled. "And then he took off."

"But how did you know it was Mansfield? He told me he wore a ski mask."

"He did. But I recognized that expensive Italian cologne he wore the day we were in his office. Remember? Plus…I noticed his car when we drove in."

"What? He parked where you could see it?"

"He parked in the driveway next door. I glanced that way as we pulled in and noticed the car. But at the time, I only thought it belonged to the neighbors. When he roared away, though, then I knew."

I glanced off in the direction of the trees again. "Damn! I saw a car in the neighbors' driveway, too, but didn't think anything of it. So you followed him," I said, still distracted by what I imagined was going on in the woods.

"Not right away. We didn't know where he was going. We looked around the house for you guys and found Doe's phone. He must have dropped it. Then we found the texts he'd sent to us…and to you." She gave me a grim look.

"And yet neither one of us was there."

"But your car was. And then we found a picture on the floor in the living room under the coffee table. It was of Emily and Mansfield when they were young, up here on Camano Island. Well, that's when we figured he'd taken you to the compound. So, I called David to let him know and found Doe's gun in that big satchel she carries around."

"David would have called the Stanwood Police. I wonder why they didn't get here sooner."

Blair got up and opened the front door where the young Stanwood Police officer stood. "Officer, do you know why you guys didn't get here any earlier?"

He had his thumbs looped through his thick belt. "Somebody threw a firebomb into the Rockaway Bar & Grill. Everybody on duty responded."

"Shit, I wonder if that was Mansfield," Blair said, looking back to me.

The sound of voices brought us both to the front porch. David emerged from the darkness. His shirt was dirty and he looked tired as he trudged over to us.

"What happened?" I asked, squeezing Blair's hand.

His expression was tense. Whatever had happened hadn't been good.

He made it up onto the porch before he replied. "The dogs chased him to the tunnel, but he closed them off with the metal door. We followed him in, but…"

He paused.

"What? What happened?" I asked.

"He was dead when we got into the basement. It looks like he used a syringe to inject something into a vein in his neck. Frankly, I think it was an air bubble, because I didn't see anything in the syringe. Anyway, he died almost instantly."

"I wonder why he didn't just take the elevator back up here," I said, realizing that Blair and I might have still been in danger. "And I thought the tunnel was blocked," I said, not wanting to mention the ghosts.

"No, it was open. But, that's not the weird part," David said, running his fingers through his hair. "He was lying by a counter, but we checked the basement, just to be sure no one else was there, and we found the elevator. I think he tried to use it. But it looked like when he pushed the button to call it back, the wires fused. There were black smoke marks running up the wall, and you could still smell the burnt wires in the air. So I guess he was stuck." He noticed my quick grin. "What?"

I tried to erase the sly smile on my face. "Oh, nothing. I'm just glad he got caught in his own torture chamber."

Thanks, Mom, I thought to myself. *As always, your timing was perfect.*

CHAPTER THIRTY-EIGHT

It's true that adversity can make you stronger. It may be why I felt a new sense of empowerment over the next few days as a result of our near-death experience. Though each of us was in our sixties and probably written off by the millennial generation, we'd shown strength, ingenuity and courage and saved our own lives. I had no desire to repeat the experience, but I felt a greater sense of confidence that at least I could navigate my way through a dangerous situation with a clear head when I had to.

Doe recovered quickly, and a few days later, the four of us decided to make a trip to British Columbia, where we met with Lollie Gates' grandniece, Luanne, to report what we knew and to return Lollie's diary. It was an emotional moment for all of us, but also one that felt good.

I tried to return the delicate gold necklace we'd found in Miller's jewelry box, but she wouldn't hear of it. She said Lollie would have wanted us to have it, and so I decided to mount it in a shadow box along with Marigold's small pewter necklace, to be hung in a place of honor in the new reception hall.

Caroline stopped by after we returned to borrow the book on haunted hotels. She said she thought her husband might be ready for a conversation. Hallelujah!

By the end of the week, we were all gathered on the back deck, sharing margaritas and April's tasty raspberry bars. April and I had invited everyone over to discuss our plans for the new reception hall.

In the background, the demolition crew was busy removing the final barn debris. They had left a stack of lumber from the old barn we planned to use for the floor of the new reception hall as a way to maintain the legacy of all that had happened. But it was strange to look out and see right across the lake. I sighed, feeling a wave of sadness roll over me. Not only was the charming old barn gone, but I thought I was going to actually miss Lollie.

We had just pulled out our sketches when David and Sean appeared with Angela. The dogs barreled over to them, barking and wagging tails. Angela bent down to pet them, while the two detectives stood awkwardly behind her.

"Are we interrupting?" David asked.

"No, come and sit down," I said. "We were just going to go over our plans for the reception hall. You must have news."

The two men pulled chairs over and sat down while Angela came to give me a hug.

"Let me guess," Blair said. "You're here to tell us that Mansfield Foster was the serial killer everyone's been looking for."

Sean sat forward, his feet separated and his elbows resting on his knees. "Yes. Obviously, some things you already know."

"Emily said something to me about Mansfield being in love with his sister, Rose," I said. "He had quite a temper, and apparently when she rejected him, he killed her. Emily said she thought that he liked it. So he went looking for women that reminded him of Rose."

"Well, we found the garrote he used on all the women he killed, at least the ones we've found. It was in that basement," David said. "But here's a news flash – Rose wasn't his sister. Not by blood, anyway. She was adopted. She was the daughter of a distant cousin of Judge Foster's. He and his wife agreed to take her in when her parents were killed in a car accident."

"Wow, did Mansfield and Emily know?" Doe asked.

"Yes," David said. "Emily told us when we interviewed her in the hospital."

"That's why there wasn't much of a family resemblance," I said.

"And now Emily is in a mental institution again," Rudy said

"She's being processed now," Sean said. "She'll be transferred within the next day or so. It was Mansfield who got her out of the inpatient mental facility after her mother died. She hadn't displayed any dangerous tendencies, and the doctors felt if she stayed on her medication, she would do fine. Mansfield wanted her to take care of their father, and he wanted an accomplice. He knew how to manipulate her. Besides, it appears he cut her medication when it suited him. We found various bottles of meds in his home."

I saw Blair flinch at that. "What a monster," she mumbled.

"Well, they'll never hurt anyone again," David said.

"But Mansfield murdered for what? Ten years?" Rudy said.

David shrugged. "Looks like it. Emily remembered seven women. We've found five," he said. "And most likely he was killing before he recruited his sister. But with him gone, we'll never know for sure."

I felt sick to my stomach, thinking of the five female ghosts in the tunnel. "She didn't want to help him, you know? He tortured her."

David took a deep breath. "We know. He used the threat of violence to force her to befriend the women. Sometimes she feigned car trouble. Other times, she would strike up a friendly conversation about something and walk out into the parking lot with them, where he would drug them. But you're right, the doctor says Emily shows evidence of long-term abuse. Broken fingers. Burn marks."

"Will you ever be able to identify all the women you've found?" Rudy asked.

"We've already ID'd four. Emily might be able to help with the last one."

"What about Judge Foster?" Blair asked. "Did they kill him, too?"

"No. The ME says he died of natural causes. But then Emily mummified him. She wasn't stupid, whatever you think of her. She worked in the library, remember. She read up on how to do it, and I think Mansfield might have helped. He wanted to keep her dependent on him. We think that's one of the things they used the basement for – the mummification," Sean reported.

"And probably why the house smelled so bad," Blair murmured with a sneer.

"Mansfield also used the basement for the women he abducted," I added with a shudder.

Sean shifted his gaze to me. "We found jewelry and personal belongings to a number of the women down there, plus blood and fibers. The crime scene guys were there for a long time."

"So, who burned our barn down?" April asked.

274

She'd been very quiet, and I glanced over at her. Although the reception hall had been her idea and everyone applauded it, I knew there was a part of her that mourned the loss of her bakery.

"Emily," Detective Abrams said. "She had never told Mansfield about the accident with the baby. From what she says, her father wouldn't allow the baby in the house. So while he looked for an institution that would take her, Emily's mother, Rose and Emily all took turns taking care of her out in the barn. Emily most of all. She loved Marigold and was distraught when the baby died. She knew it was her fault and was deathly afraid of what her father would do. So she lied and made up a story about the baby being abducted. She was only thirteen after all. I'm sure they didn't believe her, and that's probably why she was shipped off to a mental institution so soon afterwards."

"That's really sad when you think of it," Doe said.

I glanced at her and recognized a softening of her attitude toward the woman who had nearly gotten her killed.

"Anyway, Emily panicked when she realized that she'd told you about the room and the fact that Rose had had a baby. She thought you might put the pieces together, so she hoped to burn the building down so that you wouldn't find the diaper bag and the candlestick she'd hidden up in the rafters. She was especially afraid of what Mansfield would do if he found out."

"Little did she know that we'd already found the diaper bag," I said. "So did Mansfield kill Rose's boyfriend?"

Sean turned to me. "We don't know. But Emily thinks he did. Her father sent him off to boarding school right after that. He was home for a break when he killed Rose."

"So will Emily be locked up for good now?" Rudy asked.

"Most likely," David replied. "She has a lawyer. Even though she helped her brother abduct all those women, he physically and mentally abused her and did threaten to kill her in a horrible way if she didn't do what he wanted. Anyway, there's really no way to prove what happened to the baby all those years ago. My guess is that it really was an accident."

"I think she's better off," Blair said quietly.

"What about Jake?" Doe asked.

"Oh, he's out of intensive care," Rudy spoke up. "I was going to tell you. I stopped by on my way here."

When Jake had had his accident off Highway 97, he had exited the car with a head wound and wandered off into the woods. It had taken a high mountain rescue team to find him and get him to a hospital.

"What did he have to say?" I asked.

"He was run off the road by some big guy in a small red pickup."

I inhaled and glanced at Blair. "Didn't Frank Miller's goon own that small red pickup outside the Hardliner Pub the day we were there?"

"Sure did," she agreed. "My money is on Frank Miller for that one."

Sean stood up and pulled out his cell phone. He stepped into the breakfast room to make a call.

"Excuse me, Mrs. Applegate?" a voice said.

We all looked up to find the demolition crew chief standing at the bottom of the steps. I got up and walked over.

"Yes, what is it?"

"We found something I thought you should see," he said.

"Oh, God, not again."

I turned to the group on the deck, and suddenly everyone was in motion.

We followed the crew chief out to the slip of land the barn had once stood on. They were just finishing loading charred pieces of lumber into a dumpster. We followed him to the end of the property, to an area that would have been directly behind the barn, perhaps even right up against it. When the skip loader used its big scoop to pick up piles of lumber, it had dug down into the earth a foot or two.

"Here," the crew chief said, pointing to the hole.

We formed a half circle and gazed into it.

Buried deep within the hole was a jumble of old bones.

"Oh, my God, Lollie," I murmured.

The moment I said her name, a flock of birds lifted from the trees above us and a voice whispered past my ear, forcing a chill to snake its way down my spine.

CHAPTER THIRTY-NINE

The four of us settled back into our normal routines, which brought us to the final night of the art class. We'd missed the third class due to our command performance on Camano Island, and I, for one, was eager to spend a night lost in creating something positive. Unfortunately, the moment I stepped into the room, I was approached by Milton Snyder.

"Are you going to finish your book?" he asked churlishly. "After all that has happened?"

"Yes, but we're taking a break for a while."

"What is it with you women, anyway?" he asked, the corners of his mouth pulled into a frown. "What's wrong with staying home and doing what normal women do? Isn't there enough laundry at the inn?"

Snyder was a good six inches taller, so it wasn't hard for him to look down on me, even without his antiquated belief system. But his sanctimonious expression and mocking tone pushed me over the edge. And then there was that new found sense of confidence I had.

"Oh, there's plenty of laundry, cooking, and cleaning, Milt. May I call you *Milt*?" I said with a snap. His eyes flared. "But since there are men like you out in the world constantly gumming things up and creating bigger problems than local authorities can deal with, we occasionally feel the need to lend a helping hand. And speaking of hands…" I said, glancing over towards Mabel. I used my index finger to entice him to come in closer to me. "If I ever see thumbprints on Mabel's wrists again, I'll call the police and have them throw your ass in jail, naked or otherwise. Are we clear? I have a close working relationship with the police, as I'm sure you know."

His mouth opened and closed twice in quick succession, but he didn't utter a sound. Instead, he slunk away to the other side of the room.

"Jeez, Julia," Rudy said from behind me. "You've become a verbal ninja."

I turned to find Doe and Rudy putting their belongings down on the table. Doe was watching Milton as he approached Mabel.

"I wonder if your threat will do any good," she said.

"I have an idea on how we can keep a close eye on her," I responded. "Why don't we invite her to join our book club?"

They both gave me skeptical looks.

"Wouldn't that bring Milton into our universe more than we want?" Doe asked.

"Maybe," I replied. "On the other hand, he might just leave her alone if he knows we're on the lookout."

Rudy shrugged. "Okay by me. I'd love to find out if Mabel has ever had a thought of her own, anyway."

"Speaking of women who have minds of their own," I said looking around. "Where's Blair?"

"She said she had to be late, but she'll be here soon," Doe said.

Tap. Tap. Tap.

Welping was ready to start. Tonight, there was a curtain drawn between stanchions at the front of the room. I suspected he had a surprise in store, so we all sat down.

"Tonight, we're going to try our hand at sculpting," he said with a smile. "So cut off an eight inch chunk of clay and get out your tools."

We donned our aprons and did as we were told. Once again, Snyder merely sat with his arms crossed, stubborn as a mule, shooting nasty looks at the teacher.

"Okay," Welping said, once everyone was ready. "I'm pleased to say that we have a volunteer tonight who will serve as a model. This will be a little more difficult. So far we've worked with animals, flowers, and utensils. Tonight I give you, Venus!"

With that, he pulled a cord and dropped the curtain.

The room erupted in gasps.

Every mouth dropped open, including mine.

Snyder jumped from his chair, his eyes nearly bulging from his head.

Sitting demurely on a stool was Blair, wearing nothing more than a Mona Lisa smile and a purple scarf — an elongated purple scarf — drawn over one naked breast and draped down in between her long, shapely legs.

The rest of her was bare.

"Oh, my," one older woman murmured.

While everyone stared in shock, Snyder was apoplectic. His face had turned red, and I thought I saw spittle at the side of his mouth.

Blair saw it too. She merely raised a slender shoulder and gave him a single, seductive wink.

Count to three.

The room broke out in a thunderous, standing ovation.

Damn, she was good!

THE END

Author's Notes

In my mid-twenties, I spent three years of my life working at and then running a psychiatric board and care facility. It was really just a run-down, old motel that had been turned into a halfway house that the owner used as a tax-write off.

Five of us took care of 52 adult schizophrenics; we gave them daily medication, fed them, and provided counseling. A licensed psychiatrist visited the facility once a week to meet with clients to largely adjust their medication. It was some of the most difficult, and yet rewarding work I've ever done.

I realized that these were mothers, fathers, teachers, secretaries, and students who had had their lives turned upside down by their illness. They wanted nothing more than to be "normal" like the rest of us – to work, to play, to be with family. But they were trapped in the revolving door of their illness and the mental health system.

Mental illness is a systemic problem in our country. The National Alliance on Mental Illness has estimated that 61 million people suffer from some form of mental illness in any given year. The cost to the country in lost earnings is over $193 billion a year.

We all know that mental illness is one of the leading causes of homelessness. And as so many news broadcasts have shown us, mental illness has now stepped front and center as the cause of a number of mass shootings.

Politicians keep saying that we need to have a national conversation about mental illness. Well, yes, we do. But more than that, we need to do something about it. Too many people are relying on the services and support they need to reintegrate into society as productive citizens. Unfortunately, we keep letting them down.

Thank you so very much for reading *A History of Murder*. If you enjoyed this book, I would strongly encourage you to go back to Amazon.com and leave an honest review. We "indie" authors survive on reviews and word-of-mouth advertising. This will help position the book so that more people might also enjoy it. Thank you!

About the Author

Ms. Bohart holds a master's degree in theater, has published in Woman's World, and has a story in *Dead on Demand*, an anthology of ghost stories that remained on the Library Journals best seller list for six months. As a thirty-year nonprofit professional, she has spent a lifetime writing brochures, newsletters, business letters, website copy, and more. She did a short stint writing for *Patch.com*, teaches writing through the Continuing Education Program at Green River Community College, and writes a monthly column for the *Renton Reporter*. *A History of Murder* is her sixth full-length novel and the third in the Old Maids of Mercer Island mysteries. You can check out her other books, including the Detective Giorgio Salvatori mysteries, on Amazon.com. She is hard at work on the fourth book in this series. *All Roads Lead To Murder* will take Julia and the girls on a road trip and should be out summer 2017.

If you would like more information, please visit Ms. Bohart's website at: www.bohartink.com, where you can let the author know you'd like to be added to her email list to be notified of upcoming publications or events. You may also join her author page on Facebook.

Follow Ms. Bohart

Website: www.bohartink.com
Twitter: @lbohart
Facebook: Facebook @ L.Bohart/author

Made in the USA
San Bernardino, CA
18 August 2016